I.V.OPHELIA

THE ARACHNID

ALSO BY I.V. OPHELIA

The Poisoner

THE ARACHNID

I.V. OPHELIA

**SIMON &
SCHUSTER**

London · New York · Amsterdam/Antwerp · Sydney/Melbourne · Toronto · New Delhi

First published in Great Britain by Simon & Schuster UK Ltd, 2026

Copyright © I.V. Ophelia, 2026

The right of I.V. Ophelia to be identified as author of this work has been
asserted in accordance with the Copyright, Designs and Patents Act, 1988.

1 3 5 7 9 10 8 6 4 2

Simon & Schuster UK Ltd, 1st Floor
222 Gray's Inn Road, London WC1X 8HB

Simon & Schuster Australia, Sydney
Simon & Schuster India, New Delhi

www.simonandschuster.co.uk
www.simonandschuster.com.au
www.simonandschuster.co.in

The authorised representative in the EEA is Simon & Schuster Netherlands BV,
Herculesplein 96, 3584 AA Utrecht, Netherlands. info@simonandschuster.nl

Simon & Schuster strongly believes in freedom of expression and stands against
censorship in all its forms. For more information, visit BooksBelong.com

A CIP catalogue record for this book is available from the British Library

Paperback ISBN: 978-1-3985-6214-1
eAudio ISBN: 978-1-3985-6215-8

This book is a work of fiction. Names, characters, places and incidents are either
a product of the author's imagination or are used fictitiously. Any resemblance
to actual people living or dead, events or locales is entirely coincidental.

Printed and Bound in the UK using 100% Renewable Electricity
at CPI Group (UK) Ltd

MIX
Paper | Supporting
responsible forestry
FSC® C013604

To terrible friends and messy lovers—
let us be selfish together.

Kinks

PRIMARY KINKS INCLUDE:
Dub/non-con, vampires, primal, a variation of knotting, risk-aware consent kink, chasing, biting, hair pulling, blood play, forked/split tongues, light creature features, brat/brat tamer, spitting, predicament, mutual stalking, impact play, degradation/praise, sadism, gunplay, floor licking, choking/breath play, temperature play, and edging.

My dearest reader, if you are ever unsure of a kink or what it entails, please research the name to make sure you are going into this with informed consent.

Otherwise, enjoy.

Content Warning

THIS IS A GOTHIC romance and will include explicit sexual scenes. The book will also have elements of horror and mystery, which means there may be descriptions of violence and blood. Following some horror elements, deaths of humans are described in detail, along with the emotions following, such as discussions of grief, pain, and depression. These characters may take part in consuming substances or misusing firearms that may not be appropriate and should not be repeated. Do not repeat any foraging depicted in this book, as Vipera can eat poison berries; you cannot. This book contains a farm animal death and descriptions of hunting. Some scenes include BDSM concepts, which in reality would be performed by experienced partners who have had extensive talks about trust, consent, and boundaries. Nothing in this book shall serve as a tutorial. As always, depiction is not endorsement.

Prologue

BEHIND MY EYES WAS a red-hot moon.

The vessels pulsed steadily until they slowed, and the blood ran black.

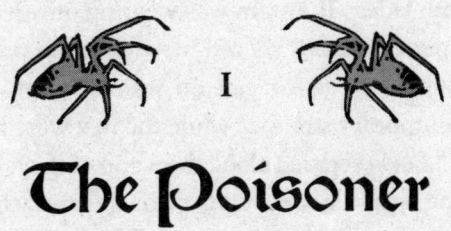

The Poisoner

Present Day
Buffalo, New York, America

CONDENSATION DRIPPED AS MY finger swiped a line along the cool glass, outlining the chapel steeple across the square.

Fresh snow settled like confectioners' powder over the streets, muting the colors of the town smothered beneath it. Carriages dragged their tracks through the virgin coating, staining them a sodden color before it churned into an inevitable slush.

A new cylinder slipped onto the phonograph, the music player crackling to life on the small table in front of the window. A steady waltz was a pleasant tune for a bitter day. The scratching of the needle lured my mind back inside the room.

Over my shoulder, a wide-eyed man stared back.

He reminded me of a bat pup, sweaty and disoriented, but instead of his mother's teat, an old rag plugged his agape mouth.

He hung upside down, his ankles bound to a meat hook and hands tied and dangling above a bucket like a stag prepared to be bled.

My fingers wrapped around the hilt of the butcher's knife, placed neatly on the table, caressing the walnut handle as I inspected both sides. The stain was wearing off where my hand had held it many times. It served me well when preparing hog and lamb, so it would do just fine on a simple man.

It was a temporary stand-in while the rest were being sharpened. The dull blade scraped along the wood of the table as I lifted it tenderly, the weight comfortably balanced in my hand.

My guest squirmed. A whine or two made it past the fabric filling his mouth. His eyes darted at anything but me.

"*Shh, shh,*" I soothed, crouching in front of him.

The vocal strain of a tired cry, praying someone could hear him. He threw his head over one shoulder, then the other toward the open door.

Leaning forward beside his face, my cheek nearly touched his as I looked in the same direction.

"Crying for ghosts, are we?" I whispered before sloping my head to the side.

His eyes flared wildly. A noise, pleading, muffled words I would never hear through his gag.

I dragged a finger over the side of his face, feeling every weather of the skin down to the slightest prick of unshaven scruff.

His eyes were bloodshot, a web of black blood vessels like I had just flicked a piece of untempered glass.

"This will only take a moment," I assured.

It may have been cruel to stall, letting his heart palpitate like that. There was no good reason for letting the panic ferment like a fruity mead. My issue was that I simply couldn't help myself. Teasing was part of the fun, and I was in a *phenomenal* mood today. My bedside manners had improved quite a bit in the last year, all things considered.

The cleaver blade dragged across his throat, tearing through the trachea. The cut might have been cleaner if I had something sharper to work with, which was my mistake, waiting so long to tend to my saws.

There was no yelp, no cry, no more pleas—only a gurgle before the sight faded into oblivion. The obsidian fluid drained into the bucket in a steady slick.

How interesting that a man could be reduced to one and a half liters of blood.

While my original goals were more in line with extermination, I realized sustainability is more important than anything. These things were pests, of course, but it was disrespectful to waste the remains of any living thing. Vipera were more useful alive than dead.

"Do you have venom?" the timid girl spoke from the door. "I'm leaving for my shift."

"On the table." I watched the bucket fill sluggishly, creeping up to the half line.

"Could we keep them alive a little longer next time? Gather more fluids from them in one go?"

"That means someone has to be here and watch them. I'm too busy."

"I don't mind staying and helping one of these nights."

"You have night shifts at the hospital."

"I can take a night off!"

"*Edith*." I narrowed my eyes at her. "That is all I have for now. Make do."

Edith's throat lurched, as if my words were stones. Her nursing uniform was already starched and cleaned, her personal addition of a white head scarf hiding most of her head and neck. A few curls of blond peeked out from under her covering, framing her freckled face.

Phoebe and I had met Edith in the apothecary, the new one, all those years ago.

She was looking for common medicines for her charitable home visits for the elderly. Only after bonding did we find that she was a young Vipera, about fifty years old. Of course, in Vipera fashion, she did not look over twenty-five. With her unassuming demeanor, she could pass for younger. Little did we know, she would be the first of many.

"I'm sorry." I approached, cupping her face with both my hands as if to convince her not to cry. "I will get more. We can ask the girls to help. I will bring glassware home so you can bring the samples to work tomorrow. Deal?"

"Deal." She allowed herself a skittish smile, my promise thawing some tension.

I patted her cheek and let her go.

When I turned back, the man was nearly the color of chalk. I placed my index and middle finger on his neck. His arteries were still. My chore for the day was officially finished.

I transferred the blood into an amber glass jug and into the ice box in the corner. The best way to store it was away from light and in cooler temperatures, safe and sound, until it was ready to be used.

One thing I have learned about Vipera is that their blood is dead, that is why it is black. The chemicals, however, are very much alive and fermenting. It was similar to how stepping on a dead bee would still envenomate you through its sting. Safety when handling such toxins was crucial.

THE SKY DULLED ALMOST as fast as a corpse on ice, the day's postmortem leeching what little warmth was left as it settled into night. Most were safe and sound at home by now, kissing their wives and children and eating a hearty meal fresh from the stove to fight off the dreary night ahead.

I climbed on my mount, my extra weight not generating so much as a flick of an ear. With a mammoth like him, I wasn't sure there was anything that could bother him. If a landmine went off beside him, he would let out a yawn. My blue roan steed was the most reliable man I knew. His name was *Horse*.

I know what some may think—how lazy must I be for naming a horse after itself? The truth is, I had trouble picking a name. I could not decide on the absolute perfect one. It became a joke for me to just refer to him as *Horse*; then it stuck, and he began to respond to it. A simple thing like him never minded.

Adjusting the reins, I clicked my tongue and encouraged him forward. His form heeled forward and started on the path home.

The dirt road was long, and soon the sight of the charming city turned into trees with an occasional home along the trail.

Our own humble abode was elevated on a slight hill before it turned a corner into the dark wooded road.

The farmhouse was a concept Phoebe and I wanted to try. Inexpensive and in dire need of repairs, it was nonetheless a convenient thirty-minute ride outside Buffalo. It was a comfortable property nestled into the temperate landscape. A field spanned behind the house, surrounded by maples, firs, and oaks.

It was the perfect grounds for burying bodies for natural decomposition, a respectable end to disrespectful men.

The field bloomed with wildflowers in spring, and the grass stayed long until the frost weighed it down before winter. When autumn came around, the trees turned the brightest oranges and reds, like the world set afire when the air began to bite; a reminder to keep warm thoughts.

The front porch steps creaked, most notably the third, since I had neglected to replace the warped wood. The house was white— or rather, it was *supposed* to be white. Chipped paint faded and peppered the facade. Charcoal trim turned to an ashy slate around the shutters and porch railing.

But even with its run-down exterior, the stirring silhouettes in the windows made me forget I was nitpicking the aesthetics of a place I called home.

Phoebe and I had bought two properties when we arrived in Buffalo: the farmhouse and the apothecary. Our only trouble was with the law. Only married women could buy property in New York.

Phoebe had to forge marriage papers. She took my last name. Admittedly, we were unsure if they would verify the records. Turned out to be a nonissue, as Phoebe brought a large amount of cash from London. We made up an imaginary brother. I suggested the name *Alin Lis* for her imaginary husband, who worked overseas. As far as strangers knew, I was her sister-in-law.

I gripped the brass doorknob, pushing twice to get it unstuck. When I entered, the scent of cooked rabbit, potatoes, and fresh bread embraced me like a lover after a long trip at sea.

It was home, every time, no matter what horrors awaited me in the world.

The hall stretched past the living room and a narrow stairway to the second floor. At the end of the hallway was the kitchen. A fire burned leisurely in the living room fireplace, with women scattered about and settled into their spots for the evening.

I shed my scarf and coat upon entry, piling them on whichever hooks I managed to find among many other coats. Immediately, I was drawn down to the kitchen, dodging a few women as they left it.

"Smells like heaven." I inhaled deeply, sousing in the scents.

"It's the same as the past three nights." Phoebe wiped her forehead with a sleeve, her face physically flushed from the heat of the stove. The very sight was the highlight of my day, particularly on long ones.

"My remark remains," I laughed.

I sat on the other side of the counter, watching as Phoebe kneaded dough for one last batch of bread before supper. Cooking was the perfect hobby for a detail-oriented mind like hers.

We had a particular routine. Every night we had feeding time. Our ratio of Vipera to Hosts was almost even, although I took on an extra feeding, typically. The Vipera would cook dinner for the Hosts, a new rotation of girls every night, then the Hosts would feed the Vipera.

Phoebe was the only person who could make friends wherever she went, no matter the circumstances. She was personable, agreeable, and pretty. Within the past two years, she had gathered over a dozen Vipera and Hosts to live with us.

The sleeping situation was less than perfect, as we only had four rooms, some containing several beds. We shared everything at this point. We even pooled money to save for things like food, medicine, and other necessities when we could not make them ourselves.

We were a commune. A Nest, if you will.

Our Nest was not complicated. We had three rules.

Autonomy, sustainability, utilitarianism.

A large padding of our income came from draining Vipera men of their fluids for pharmaceuticals, which covered our costs comfortably. The gifts that keep on giving.

This was the birth of our Nest. We were bonded by the cause of creating a better world, since the men were not the best at improving anything. If we were to live the lives we sought, we must be the first to start the motion. Aside from those who lived with us, we were able to gather nearly two thousand women to join our union, designed specifically for Hosts navigating the new landscape.

"Was the shop busy?" I asked Phoebe.

"Decently. Sickness thrives in wintertime, after all." She put in the last batch of bread as the stew was finishing. She spooned some in a bowl for me and then rang the dinner bell.

She slid the bowl across the counter with a wooden spoon, and I stopped it with my palm. She sat beside me as women began to crowd the kitchen area in a neat queue.

"How were the extractions?"

"Typical. I need to ask John to make another hook. It's terribly inefficient doing one at a time," I said before taking a spoonful of stew in my mouth.

Phoebe had a habit of staring at me while I ate. I don't know if she did so because she was living vicariously or because she liked watching someone appreciate something she made.

I cleaned my own dishes and cutlery in the sink upon finishing. It helped that everyone just cleaned up after themselves to keep the chore load to a minimum. There were much more important tasks than cleaning dishes.

A tanned, dark-haired woman came to grab a second serving. "Rebecca?"

She reluctantly looked away from the stew.

"There is a body in the lab. If you have time tomorrow, would you mind bringing him to the woods?"

"Of course. Buried whole or scattered?" she asked as she made herself another bowl.

"Scattered, preferably, I'm sure there is an animal out there that'll pick up the pieces."

"I will see to it tomorrow night." She nodded, retreating to the living room.

When I turned to Phoebe, I saw that little glint in her eyes.

It was *her* feeding time now.

The first Sunday of the month was Phoebe's designated feeding time. Most Vipera typically fed once a month on a Host, or every week on anyone with standard blood.

"Do you want to feed down here or upstairs?"

"*Our* room." She grabbed my hand and pulled me from the kitchen.

Vipera slept every three days on average, so the girls rotate sleep schedules. Phoebe was the odd one out; we shared the bed every night. I didn't mind. If it were any other person, I might. She'd grown attached, and she wasn't keen on letting me out of her sight.

Our room was no more grand than the rest. A single bed, laid in a scratchy linen with worn patches from too many washes, a shared dresser, and a writing desk. Dried herbs and wildflowers from this past summer were as dull and gray as the deteriorating sun-bleached wallpaper.

We sat side by side on the bed, settling before we started.

I popped the buttons out of their loops down my blouse, peeling one side of the collar away from my neck.

"Are you cold? Do you want a blanket?" Phoebe fussed, fidgeting with her hands.

I lifted my gaze. "It won't take long. I will sit by the fire if I get stiff."

She shifted in place, a vivid blush rising to her cheeks. This happened every month. I was the one who suggested this arrangement. Despite her palpable jealousy when I let others feed on me, she always became bashful when it was her turn.

She placed a timid hand on the other side of my neck as she leaned in. I could feel her breathing against my skin, hesitating again.

"Go on." I placed my hand at the back of her head, anticipating the bite.

Shallow, shaky breaths escaped past her lips, finally pressing those fine needles past my flesh. She took a sharp breath as if the sensation was new. Then came the tingle of reluctant sucking, the blood beginning to flow.

I flinched but kept a firm hand at the back of her head to ensure she wasn't scared away by the reflex. It often took Phoebe a few bites to properly latch. She was overly worried about my feelings and would only bite down halfway. She forgot that the only relief I would get is if she bit down *firmly*, with both sets of fangs.

The pain was minimal due to her teeth's lack of size, but her venom potency was overpowering.

When her second set of accessory fangs settled beneath my skin, the all-too-familiar wave of ease melted my agitation, invading the muscles and mind as it brought me somewhere warmer, somewhere peaceful. The feeling of her teeth in me dissipated as I closed my eyes. A soft humming of clicks escaped her, like a cricket almost. The fabric of my blouse was balled in her delicate fists.

After, she laved at the wound, her saliva clotting it shut to stop the bleeding, her face was almost as red as the blood on her lips.

Her tongue ran over her teeth to wipe away the remaining stain.

"See? Not worth a fit." I lifted the corner of her lip with my thumb. The fangs were small, but they were fitting for her. The two sets of teeth were minuscule in comparison to some older Vipera.

"What?"

"They're cute."

"My teeth?"

"Yes."

I did not think it was possible for her to become more red.

"How are the toothaches?" I pressed gently on the gums above those deadly little needles, her split tongue curling in discomfort.

"Better, though I'm running out of cannabis. About a dram left." She pulled away from my hand.

"I can get more. I'll ask Edith."

Her expression soured upon the mention. She looked like I drank the last of her favorite tea without permission. I had a feeling her dislike of Edith had something to do with her being my second feeding partner. We had more Vipera than Hosts, I did not know what she would have me do otherwise.

No realistic family ever gets along completely, anyway.

II
The fixer

Two Years Earlier
The Nest, United Kingdom

THAT WAS THE LAST time I played with my food. I should have killed her while she was caught between my jaws.

The flesh of my face scorched like I rested my head on a live woodfire. I could still smell the skin burning. When I touched it, the skin had become textured from the peeling, the burn spreading like a dry-season fire. Even with my mouth closed, I could feel my canine tooth left exposed as the skin tightened. My left eye would not stop filling with blood; it was coming out in tears. The poison was eating through my skin, my nerves. At least now it was slowing.

All I could do was hold a cold cloth to my face and hope I began to heal soon.

I was lucky Alina was inexperienced at her craft, just tinging the surface. Otherwise, I would have lost the left side of my face, down to the bone.

"Settle everyone!" The elder Vipera chittered at the end of the banquet table, holding up a glass that chimed with a pure sound as the delicate knife tapped against it. One thing about the true-born Vipera was that they didn't let interruptions dampen their masquerade as nobility.

Silas was outside of the room, leaning against the edge of the staircase just past the archway. Any normal Vipera would have been decapitated for such a childish transgression as before. Since his father was the Sire, the Nest had collectively chosen to let him decide what to do about his estranged son. His arrival wouldn't be long now.

Two red lines stroked boldly along his cheek where my fangs dragged during the fight, a less impressive mark than the one left on me. He was already healing in the few hours the mark had been present. Mine, however, still burned.

Nevertheless, I was seated at a table with food.

He was not.

I tipped a blood-filled glass at him before my attention went back to the arrangement before us.

Prime porterhouse, well marbled and a perfect char. Cooked with only olive oil and salt, as God intended for a cut of that quality.

Ossobuco, with the bone standing proud in the spread. Rosemary, parsley, bay leaf, orange zest, and saffron, all tied together by the warmth of a dry white wine reduction, paired with fresh ground black pepper.

Lastly, my favorite, the offal. Deviled kidneys and sautéed tongue cooked in fat and browned to perfection in a Dutch oven.

There were certain advantages to living in a Nest, especially one as affluent as this one. My favorite part being the meals made from recipes tailored exactly to a Vipera's taste, or else it would all be such a waste. I would say I missed the other side of a tongue's palette, but I truly couldn't remember. The only nostalgic hint would be found in a Host's blood. Though meat, liquor, and the occasional sour or burnt item would do.

"Let us raise a glass for Elanor," the man said with a solemn drawl, eyes falling over the feast. "She retired last week at thirty-five. A fruitful twelve years of service. Luckily for us, she makes a wonderful wine, as well as a meal."

There was a soft chatter of approval and solemn nodding heads as if they weren't giddy the week before they retired her.

I raised my glass along with everyone else and took one last look at Silas.

A few of the staff stood in the corners behind and beside him to make sure there wouldn't be any other disruptions, blocking him from participation.

Except, instead of the pout I expected, he had the most wicked and conniving smile I could imagine. He tipped his head at me, amused at my own expression of confusion.

Silas reclined casually against the banister and reached into his pocket, pulling forth a silver cigarette case. He met eyes with me again, as if to ask, *"Are you paying attention?"*

When he reached in, it was not a cigarette pinched between his fingers.

It was one long, empty glass vial.

Quickly, I plunged my hand inside my suit jacket pocket. All four vials I confiscated from his sister were *gone*. Had he swiped them during our brawl? How many had he used? Where were they now?

The crashing of glass and the sound of gurgling discomfort, not dissimilar to drowning, jolted my attention.

The Vipera to both sides of me flailed, one hitting me with their elbow and the other clawing at my arm. When I looked at the woman across from me, her eyes overflowed with blood, the tears more harrowing than a saint's statue, choking on the poisoned blood and coughing in my face.

I stumbled out of my chair as the bodies around me in the overcrowded room crashed into me, into each other, grasping at what they could in their desperate need to breathe. Though breathing wasn't going to be an option based on how their skin was flaking away the more they clawed at it.

The Vipera who had dedicated a toast was now slumped on the table, the blood wine mixing with his own as it seeped from the hole burned in his throat.

Some died quickly, some struggled for a protracted period as the poison ravaged their organs.

The death of a Nest and the mark of a new predator, in the matter of a minute.

III

The Poisoner

*T*HE DARKNESS CALLED ME *in the form of clicking.*
My body is bare in a never-ending landscape.
Snap snap.

Something like the snapping of jaws, an eager hound, sounded around me in short spurts. A snap to my left, more snapping to my right, then a nip at my heel. I stumbled forward, but nothing was behind me. A nip at my calf, then behind. I jolted forward, walking away from whatever it might be, just to feel it again, more forceful this time, at my heels and at the back of my shoulder. I spun around to see a dark figure looming, dripping the same blood that stretched across the dark expanse.

A hand reached out and I ran as fast as my legs could carry me, with the wild rush of hope for freedom, only to be yanked so forcefully my chest landed on the ground. I couldn't breathe, and the feeling of teeth clamping down on my neck robbed me of any hope.

DESPITE THE TERROR, THE draining feeling was replaced by a slow resurfacing of consciousness. The wet stains on the ceiling came into view in all their brown and gray glory. There were about thirty seconds of peace, a sense of relief returning before the throbbing set in.

I peeled my back from the floor, drenched in a cold sweat that made my nightgown cling and leave indentations on my skin.

The sun crept across the floor and up the wall, awakening the dust that fluttered to life as I rose to my feet.

The subtle crack of the steps on my descent to the ground floor were no interruption to the lively scene. The hum of chatter and the soft crackle of the fire tickled my ears before I caught the scent of freshly cooked porridge, coffee, and biscuits.

In the living room is where we mostly gathered, cozied up to the fireplace. Phoebe was chatting as she plucked berries from a bowl, popping them in her mouth and washing them down with unsweetened tea.

Adeline and Rebecca sat across from her on the opposite sofa, listening intently to whatever tale Phoebe was embellishing.

Adeline was picking at a pastry aimlessly as Rebecca's arm draped across the back of the couch behind her, fiddling mindlessly with the lace of Adeline's tea gown sleeve.

Sometimes I found myself jealous of their companionship. The way Rebecca looked only at Adeline as they conversed. Rebecca's harsh brown eyes softened at the sight of her, a lingering of sorts. Not of hunger, but in a way where Adeline's words were hypnotic, making Rebecca unable or unwilling to focus on much else.

Mary claimed the corner, lost in focus as she embroidered pink silk fabric. The quality of the silk meant we must have done well with our endeavors recently. I admired her work ethic. It took dedication and discipline to work on your rest days.

Cordelia was next to Phoebe, nose buried in a book, though she would give an inattentive nod when Phoebe said something exceptionally agreeable or funny.

My stomach lurched, a rolling rumble reminding me of my more human needs.

"Alina!" A squeak came from the living room, followed by the soft clatter of a teacup.

I hadn't even taken a few steps toward the kitchen before she was out of her seat and by my side.

"You're . . . wet." Phoebe's smile pressed into a thin line as she gingerly held my arm. "Let me bring you breakfast."

"Bad dream," I mumbled, suddenly all too aware of the perspiration. "I can serve myself."

"I'll do it!" She pulled me along to the kitchen. The small oven hadn't cooled down yet, acting as a second furnace to battle the chilly environment beyond the walls. "How did you sleep? I didn't want to wake you since you *rarely* sleep in."

"Like any other night." I leaned against the table, a sullen slouch to my shoulders.

Phoebe paused mid-pour with the spoon, squinting at me. "Should I have . . . ?"

"No, no . . ."

"You smell anxious."

"Stop doing that."

"I'm not doing anything!" she huffed, sliding the bowl of porridge to me across the table.

The bowl hit my hand, warm to the touch. "Stop trying to scent me. I just had a nightmare, is all."

"Fine! I was just trying to be helpful." She plopped down on the stool and stared between me and the bowl. An awkward silence loomed between us, and by how she picked at her nails, another question was inevitable. "What was your dream about?"

I glared at her in warning, taking a bite of my food.

"I'm just curious!"

"You are nosy."

"Yes, I am so horrible for my extraordinary empathy." She tossed her hands up before crossing them.

"Dogs" is all I said.

Her frown twisted into a sneer of defeat, biting her cheek. After another silence, "Was it a small dog or a large—"

"Phoebe!" I laughed, gesturing as if I were about to throw my spoon at her.

The banter was promptly interrupted by the chiming of the doorbell.

I wiped my mouth with my sleeve, then my hands on my skirt. Hastily tucking my hair back into something manageable, I rushed to the door.

Peeping through the viewfinder of the door, I squinted at the early-morning visitor. There was a man, dark-haired with creeping grays around the forelock. His tired expression shifted when I opened the door, a slight smile and a softening of the eyes settling.

"You're early." I opened the door wider, beckoning him inside.

"I said early; I'm here early," he grunted as he picked up his box of tools before stepping through the entryway.

"Is that John?" Phoebe shouted from the kitchen.

There was a chorus of greetings from the living room upon hearing the name.

"You can borrow him after!" I gestured for him to follow me to the second floor.

In the middle of the hallway, I reached for the rope for the attic door. A ladder unfolded as I pulled the cord. The creak of the old, dry wood invited us to the darkness above.

The attic was shallow, and I had to lean down whenever I was up there. I could only stand with poor posture under the gable and that was it. The space was stuffy and humble, with a simple chair and a circular window facing the front of the house. A few clothing lines strung like a web with our laundry sulking in the torrid air.

Tap. Tap. Tap.

"Here." I pointed at a spot on the ceiling, a deep stain above an overflowing bucket. "Can you patch it?"

John tilted his head, touching the wet wood. "You need to replace the roof."

"Well, how long does that take? We can go up there now."

"It's covered in snow and ice; we will likely have to wait until it melts."

"Then what do we do about the leak?"

"Get a bigger bucket."

My head fell back, and I let out a groan.

"It's just a small leak," he laughed. "Just be grateful it held up this long. It's not like you bought this place in pristine condition."

"I know, just another thing for me to do that can't be done yet." I rubbed the back of my neck, tapping the bucket with my slipper.

"Patience is a virtue." His tone was full of humor. "But not often paired well with tenacity."

"I am patient!" I rolled my eyes. "It just never feels like I am able to rest until everything is perfect."

"Then you may wander a lifetime unsatisfied." He patted my shoulder, squeezing reassuringly. "I'll fix it in early spring. Should be able to replace the entirety of it if we get a week of nice weather."

"You should show me how." I squinted at the stain.

"It's not safe; just let me do it."

"No safer for you than for me."

"I suppose," he chuckled. "Someday you may not need me at all if I teach you all my tricks at once."

"Oh stop it, don't say it like that." I turned into him and hugged, squeezing around his torso and resting my head on his shoulder. "We will always need you, Pops, even if we have to make up things for you to fix."

"Well, I would sure hope you would. To keep my mind young, right?" His arms wrapped around my shoulders. "Don't get all soft on me, Crow."

A wave of relief washed over me. Like the weight and pressure of a hug was enough to make my coal of a mood into a diamond. He never broke our hugs until I did first. He was not a replacement for my father, but some days I wished he had been.

IV
The Fixer

Two Years Earlier
The Nest, United Kingdom

T HERE WAS NOT A single tile that hadn't been smeared with black blood. The bodies were piled together, some unrecognizable in their state of carnage. The only thing worse than the sight was the smell, like horsehair as a fire starter.

Dumb luck was the only reason I wasn't among them. I hadn't had even a drop of the wine, but it was hard to be grateful when there was a decorative sword pinning you to the wall.

When the sounds of sizzling flesh and screaming calmed, the rooms were still. It was rare I was surrounded by this many bodies for them to be completely silent. The only discernible movements were the fleeting shadows of birds outside, interrupting the morning light flooding the space. Reflections of the windows rippled in the wet blood coating the floor, the last drops freeing themselves from the corpses.

The slapping of finely made shoes against the wet floor stopped in the archway.

"Ah, right where I left you," Silas spoke, brushing his hair neatly into place with his bloodied hands as he tucked a handful of dazzling heirlooms inside his pocket. Thousands of collective years of Vipera lives, only to end due to a tantrum.

He failed to acknowledge me with any sense of urgency. He approached a slumped body in a chair, digging through the pockets and finding a small gold folding knife and a roll of bills. His lack of a response prompted my brow to twitch, though I was unsure if that was from annoyance or the poison eating away at my nerves.

"*Now* you choose to defend her honor?" I taunted. "Were the social repercussions suddenly of low importance to you once you realized she no longer needed you?"

"There are no social repercussions if there is no one left to pass judgment," he said calmly, staring at the collection of miscellaneous photographs on the wall, tainted with small droplets of blood across the glass.

"He'll kill you for this."

He followed the wall until he stood beside me. "I am his only son. He won't," he replied.

Then he grasped my face, tilting it to either side before settling his gaze on the burnt side. "Having trouble healing, are we?"

He flicked the knife open, pointing it right above my eye.

All I managed was a thick swallow.

He rested the blade above my brow, digging into the tender burning flesh and dragging it down past my eye, then following through to the chin.

"The mark of Cain," he hummed. "Welcome to the club, kin killer."

I hissed, the skin searing with heat as it was cut. I attempted to bite him, just for him to step back. The blade in my shoulder prevented me from tearing the brat to shreds. The skin pulled taut as I sneered, "What are you talking about?"

"You did this, *remember*? Remember how you helped me slaughter several generations of this Nest? You and I tore through like honey badgers." He patted my cheek, causing me to flinch. "Your head is on the same spike as mine."

The lie registered slowly like mud settling in brackish water, slowly, heavily. "You are letting me live?"

"On borrowed time, as long as we establish something." He turned away, sitting down in one of the chairs. The fabric absorbed the blood, soaking his finely tailored clothes.

I waited for him to continue, but he dug through the inner pocket of his jacket, finally finding his cigarettes and lighter.

"Why not just kill me?" Every shift of my body made the blade cut deeper. I was standing on my toes just to keep it from cutting more. "Or are you too much of a coward to do that as well?"

Silas let out a cruel laugh, amused. "No, Luka. You are not mine to kill. That will be up to her."

"Is that it?" I scoffed. "You think that delivering her revenge for her will make her forgive you?"

He let the cigarette hang loosely in his mouth as he flicked the wheel of his lighter a handful of times, struggling to spark.

He was just torturing me now.

"See this? I want you to really look around." He gestured with the cigarette, jerking his head toward the pile of bodies, looking to either side to admire it for himself. "You are the only survivor of this mess aside from myself. No one will believe you didn't have something to do with this. Every Nest in the world will know that you took up arms against one of the most powerful Nests that exists. I'm sure you are very aware of how far its influence reaches."

The look in his pale eyes went somewhere far away as he surveyed his surroundings, finally flicking back to mine. "Do you understand?"

I nodded.

"If you try to run somewhere else," he continued, "they won't trust you. They won't hire you. Wherever your name goes, mine will follow at your heel. I telephoned already, taking responsibility—*you and I*."

"Why?"

"Because you are going to help me."

"You are delusional."

"Perhaps." He smirked. "Besides, you will find yourself in a better position if you help me."

"With—?"

"Finding my poisoner."

I could only muster enough energy to laugh, spitting some leftover blood from my burning mouth.

"Nests should not be this *weak*," he began. "Why was it so easy to reduce them to simple piles of blood and bone? Sitting ducks neatly gathered for slaughter. All in the name of civility. A tradition like that will kill us off faster than any witch hunt."

"What do you mean?"

"If we only allow those with at least *some* talent, skill, or otherwise . . . imagine what we could do if we gathered the strongest of us, regardless of class, age, or pedigree." He stood, taking a drag as he approached. I could smell a metallic tinge mixing with the tobacco.

"Your own Nest? No one will let you live long enough to finish it."

"Not here," he said with a crazed spark in his eye. I could see him envisioning his grand prophecy, high on an idea. "But I've heard good things about New York."

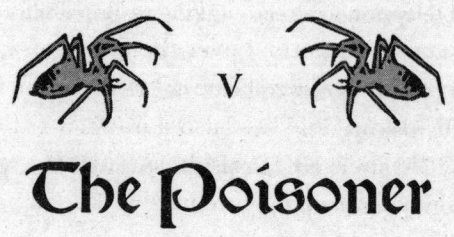

The Poisoner

"YOUR MARKINGS ARE SO unique. I once shot a piebald fawn up north. If you ever find yourself in the city, I can show you the bust. I had it articulated." The man grinned, puffing a fat cigar.

"How sweet of you to think of your prize when you see me." I smoothed my fingers over his lapel. "What other things have you collected? I am so curious to know. You must be a very skilled hunter."

I couldn't bring myself to listen. I feared I would gag.

His mouth was moving, but I could not make out a single word. I was eyeing the gold of his cuffs as his thick hand clutched his cigar. His teeth were jagged and crooked, but his fangs were the same. Somehow, even with the gift of looking youthful, this man got the short end of the stick genetically, years added from how poorly he took care of himself. He was old, older than he put on. I could tell by the fangs. They were thick and long, and there were compliments sprinkled throughout his speech that did not read as compliments *anymore,* at least not in the current year. A typical hog.

Clammy hands smoothed over the fabric of my dress, too thin of a barrier for my liking. The dress was red—it always got their appetite going. Blue was also a popular color, but more eye-catching than palatable. This dress had a low, square neckline and stayed close to my figure until it draped past the slope of my hips. Then it dragged down into a subtle train. The shine of the fabric reflected an expensive sheen, even in light as dim as a candle. I forgot what well-made fabric felt like until nights like these, as we had left most of our material belongings behind when we moved here.

One of the girls in our nest, Cordelia, was a dressmaker, though. She had fitted me with this one for hunting purposes.

There were about three known establishments in Buffalo. They were like something between Nests and Dens, which was ideal if you did not have any family connections, as many had come here for a new life. The downside was that they were creating classes of their own, and there weren't many places to go for the civilized corrupted or Vipera without wealth.

These new American Nest-Den hybrids were like exclusive clubs, so we called them Guilds. They blended well, as there were many clubs in this city for a variety of things, and it was all the rage. Explorers Clubs, unionized organizations, and other things to pass the time. The Guilds had dress codes, and some required entrance payment or monthly dues for Vipera. They were not especially picky with Hosts, but they did favor the finer-looking women. Payment went directly from the patron to the Host, so the Guild made their money from entry fees and substances.

My hunting ground was the Northern Guild, the least sophisticated of the three that were up and coming in the area. The girls and I were allowed to come free of charge, but surely these buffoons paid a handsome price just to get in through the door.

I wish I could say it was difficult, luring these creatures to their death, but it was easier than doing so to a regular man. These animals lunged at the sight of a plunging neckline and a pretty face. Simple creatures, simple vices.

This particular patron had been poking his nose around my Nest for some time. He often stalked outside the apothecary, the hospital, or our house. A detective. My fears had come true, but if dealt with swiftly, he wouldn't get far with his investigation.

"Maybe—" I cut his blundering short, "you should show me your collection, rather than tell me?"

"We're not supposed to—"

"What? Are you on the job?" I stared at the beads of sweat pearling at his temples.

He swallowed thickly and answered with a nervous laugh.

"Do you always listen to what *other* men tell you to do?"

He shifted in his seat, puffing his chest at the insinuation that he listened to anyone but himself.

Like I said, easy.

He stood, his sweaty hands fumbling with the buttons of his jacket before extending one out to me.

I smiled, possibly too wide, as I could feel my lips pull taut. We were almost done; this one would be the last for tonight.

"Let us use the other door." I led him in the opposite direction, to the side entrance.

"We will have to go out front for the carriage—" he said as we stepped into the alleyway.

"No need; why don't we wait here?" I held him closer by his coat collar.

The apples of his cheeks grew red; his eyes were glassy. I wouldn't be surprised if when I opened him up, there was a surplus of fat around his heart and liver from overconsuming more than his fill of humans, even by Vipera standards.

Clang!

A metal rod clashed with the back of his head. He collapsed like a piece of cinder.

"What took you so long?"

"I went to the other alley first!" Edith clutched a crowbar. She was dressed in fitted men's clothes, black from head to toe, even her head covering. We had a strict uniform for when we hunted, the dark clothing hiding us better in the night and obscuring our features.

"Is Horse out front?" I wiped my palms on the dress.

"Yes, at the end of the alleyway."

IT WAS QUITE A chore getting him up the stairs to the lab. It was more of a workout than usual, so Rebecca and Adeline rushed downstairs to help. When we all made it to the second floor, we rested before we had to process the four naked men slumped against the walls, bound with their arms behind them and their ankles together.

I changed out of my dress and into our uniform—fitted men's trousers with a shirt. Everything was tucked neatly. The pants were tucked into boots, the shirt was tucked into the trousers, and my hair was in a neat pleat held back by a wool scarf. All black, of course. There was no use wearing any other color if you planned on making a mess.

"Did they give you much trouble?" I asked as I reentered the room.

"No trouble, they actually walked themselves up the stairs," Rebecca laughed.

"So gullible. We told them they could have us both at once; it worked all three times." Adeline shook her head.

"What are we doing with them tonight?" Phoebe asked, tapping her foot impatiently as she glanced between us and the unconscious Vipera.

"Tonight is venom; others will come later if any of you get tired." I grabbed a wooden wedge block and my axe, placing them on the center table. "You are free to leave now, Phoebe, if you are going to get squeamish."

"I-I'm not!" She crossed her arms. "I'll be perfectly fine spectating."

"If you say so." I picked up my satchel, pouring the contents onto the table. There were a few glass bottles that rolled across the table, as well as a roll of gauze, needles, miscellaneous blades, and then a spare tourniquet.

Along the walls were containers organized by trinket. A stiff hat case of Vipera teeth, as they made great buttons, beads, and clasps when carved. A trunk of spectacles, to be resold or used for scraps. A chest of flasks, keys, belt buckles, yet to be melted down or separated by metal for John.

"Do we start extracting now?" Rebecca inspected the bottles.

"No, we must do one thing first. I've tweaked the procedure." I picked up the wooden wedge block and the axe. "Rebecca, come here," I instructed.

Rebecca was a butcher's daughter, and her arms were strong. She had almost the equivalent of a farmer's strength from the years she spent helping her father, which was useful for our hunting nights.

Tonight, I was trying something new in the name of efficiency.

"Hold his head back, by his hair, at the top preferably, so your hands are not in the way." I turned my attention to the first man in line.

Rebecca lifted the first man's head, his mouth drooping lazily as he was unconscious.

"Right there," I praised, taking the wedge-shaped block and placing it in his mouth, making him open his jaw wider to hold it. He started to wake up, his eyes darting wildly around. "Keep his head still." I backed up slightly.

I flipped the axe in my hands, the blunt side facing forward.

He let out a squeal, looking up at Rebecca pleadingly.

"Don't look at her," I demanded. "Look at me."

With one swing, the blunt end of my axe smacked the wide end of the block, wedging the man's mouth open and detaching his jaw with a *crack*.

He drooled as he screamed, sobbing when we removed the block.

On to the next one.

Crack!

The next one.

Crack!

Then we stood before our detective. His head wobbled in a daze, seemingly unaware of the suffering of his peers. His own snoring woke him, finally.

"Good morning," I purred, crouching down in front of him, my axe balanced across my knees. "How pleasant of you to join us."

"What . . . is this?" He groaned, feeling the pain from Edith's blow to the back of his head, no doubt.

"Retribution." I was unable to hide my grin as I watched him come to consciousness.

"You . . . You're the . . . he warned us about you," he gasped in pain.

I raised my brow at him, my smile falling before glancing at Rebecca.

She only lifted a shoulder, just as unsure of his words as I was.

"And what, pray tell, are they warning you about?"

"A black widow . . ." he breathed, his concussion making it hard for him to keep his eyes on me or his head lifted. "A poisoner."

I grabbed his jaw, nails digging into his cheeks when I yanked it up.

"Speak clearly," I demanded.

"Your experiments . . ." He panted like he was overheating. "Your victims are strictly Vipera."

"Subjects," I corrected.

"I told you we shouldn't have dumped the bodies in the river last week," Phoebe hissed from behind me. "Burning is the only way."

"Christ, I didn't think a few would hurt, they can't *all* go on the property. The coyotes don't eat them fast enough. The crematorium isn't that accessible yet." I shoved his face to the side and stood.

Rebecca gripped his hair and held the block up to his mouth.

"Wait! Wait please . . ." he begged.

I drew a patient breath and leaned on the handle of the axe. "What is it now?"

"Killing me will get you caught." He must have benefited from a hit of adrenaline for one last cryptic message. "He will find me, then he will find you."

"Then I best make sure you are never found." I jerked my head in his direction in a gesture for Rebecca to continue.

She placed the block in his mouth, making his jaw open wide enough where he couldn't spit it out, only bite down.

Crack!

The wail that came from the detective was sharp and distinct, like the yowl of a cat.

I tossed the axe back on the table and began prepping the bottles.

"Was that necessary?" Phoebe hid her face from the others as she lowered her voice.

The three men before our detective were passed out from the pain, but very much alive. My catch was sobbing, his slacked jaw shaking with every heave of his chest.

"It was taking too long; this is already going to take us all night." I snatched a bottle from Adeline as she handed it out. "Edith said she needed more."

"Is this not too many for one night? It seems that someone has already noticed if rumors are spreading. Do I need to remind you what happened the last time you rose to infamy?"

"Stop talking," I snapped. "I know what I'm doing."

Phoebe and I fastened the gauze tightly over the opening of the bottles, securing it with twine.

The first three men were the ones taken by Rebecca, Adeline, and Edith. Phoebe stood beside me to observe, on standby in case any of them got too rowdy.

I took my own catch. With a dental tool in hand, I pulled both fangs by placing the long metal rod straight across the roof of his mouth and sliding it forward. Each fang had a turn biting through the cloth, the amber liquid spraying into the vial before steadying to a light drip. I pushed up every so often, like I was milking a cow, though the liquid from this animal was, without question, more valuable.

After an hour, Rebecca, Edith, and Adeline switched with another set of volunteers, working through the same process and repeating throughout the long night.

"WE GOT AT LEAST five liters."

"I can't believe we got so much! We should do something like that every few weeks. I can cover most of my patients that way."

Edith watched me slip the bottles into the saddlebag, patting the horse's hind once it was securely latched.

"We will see; it was a long night. Use it sparingly." My eyelids were heavy as the light illuminated her from behind. "I would have brought them myself. I'm sorry I took up your work recess."

"It's no trouble. The apothecary isn't far from the hospital. I don't mind." She smiled. "I do have to get going, though."

"Of course, of course." I shooed her with a lazy gesture. "Go."

Edith nudged the horse with her heel, the heavy thuds of the draft's hooves crushing the ice beneath as she turned around, returning down the road toward the hospital.

"Do you really think a stunt like that so often is a good idea? Is that not too much labor?" A haughty question came from the doorway of the shop.

I let out a deep, aggravated huff as I turned on my heel, my shoulder knocking against Phoebe as I reentered the apothecary.

The shop was fashioned similar to the old one, with dark wood cabinetry and more drawers than I could count, though it was warmer. It smelled different, less old. The construction was relatively new, but it did have nicer drawers that lined the back wall behind the counter, extending up a third of the way before they became enclosed glass cabinets. My tinctures were so beautiful displayed like that, though we did have some shelves and displays by the window. The tinctures in the display were not real, as I didn't want to put any real product in the sun for that long. We just filled the bottle with colored water to attract the eyes.

Behind the counter, I took the sixth bottle of venom that was sitting on a stool and slid it into a drawer for later.

"What was that?" Phoebe asked from behind me.

"Booze," I answered.

"*Alina*."

"Leave me be, Phoebe."

She did not speak to me, but her eyes said everything she had to. She pitied me and was ashamed at the same time. She was not one to judge; she was not the one who was made to suffer.

It had taken months for the scathing of my throat to heal from biting Luka. While I was grateful I did not die, I did not feel any different from a corpse, aside from one of us no longer feeling pain. While my wounds had healed, my mind still replayed that night. I have dreams of my two creatures coming for me, plunging their fingers into my gut, and ripping out all my pieces until I was but a shell.

Warm fingers touched my neck, and my skin nearly jumped from my bones.

"Alina," Phoebe whispered to me, her other hand resting on top of my hands that were gripping the edge of the countertop. A cold sweat left my skin clammy. "What is it?"

"Nothing." I let go of the counter and pushed past her.

"Is it what he said? The man? I didn't mean to frighten you when I brought up—"

"Yes, I know, you are harmless of any damages. You just speak your mind. *I know*," I sneered.

She didn't argue. Not that I would have heard if she did. My boots were already thumping against the stairs, retreating back to the lab.

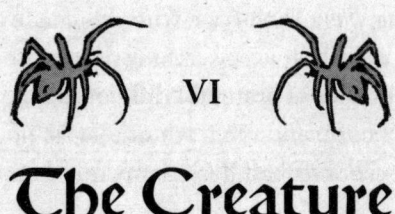

VI

The Creature

NO MATTER THE RICHES, the gold, the luxury, it was as fulfilling as purchasing premade taxidermy—no hunt, no meat, devoid of a soul, a cast with no substance, purely for display. No matter what story you made up for the conquest, it would never make it true. It was as empty a gesture as spitting out food before swallowing, all the taste but none of the calories.

For once in my long, formidable life, I had become insatiable. Not one second of ease was bestowed upon me in two years, the most unsatisfying season of my life. I wanted to take my skin off like a suit and wash it, scrub the bones until I was clean once more. It was all so useless.

The most ironic part about this whole ordeal was that I had accomplished more in the past two years than I had in the past millennia. I was never this motivated to create something that extended past my own comfort. I told myself this undertaking of founding my own Nest would be rewarding, but I did not feel rewarded. Something was always missing.

New York City, New York. A place of dreams, they said. It was impressive, I will say that about it. Every handful of steps could land you on the corner of opportunity. My opportunity was nestled comfortably in oil and steel, which allowed me to purchase the place I now call my Nest, but it was not home. It could not be home, *yet.*

It would be a bit ridiculous to call this a townhome, considering the estate occupied half an entire block on Fifth Avenue. The limewashed brick and white stone made for an impressive display for those passing by, and I had just as impressive a view of the park. It was rather fun to have such a large green space in the middle of such an industrial hellscape.

As I stared at it now, I could see bodies of water glistening in the distance from my window. The sun was hot as it was magnified through the glass, though it still struggled to brighten the dark office.

The entire room was detailed with a rich, dark maple. It extended to designs along the ceiling and the walls, even lining the doorframes and windows. There were hints of crimson scattered around the room, from the rugs to some details on the upholstery.

Along the walls were a few paintings. I chose autumn hunting scenes to complement the rest of the room. On the only other wall without windows was my bookshelf, though it was much smaller than the collection I had in London. I had brought nothing to this new and mysterious land; I could always buy more things.

I ashed my cigarette above the crystal glass before proceeding to suck the last bit of life from the paper.

"I knew you would be sulking in here," a Russian accent chimed at my door.

"What did I say about entering my study uninvited?"

"Whatever it was, I wasn't listening," he laughed. The other side of the desk creaked—presumably, from him sitting on it. It was wise to keep the desk between us. "Be thankful I come bearing good news."

Luka was not quite second hand, but for safety reasons, he was close enough to be one. The cost of keeping an eye on him was his proximity to me. A *barely* tolerable nightmare. I kept him busy with a recruitment position, which was more of a glorified secretary at best.

We have spent the last two years pitching to individuals in his network who were skilled enough in their trades, but with no bloodline to reap the benefits of an old Nest. The response so far has been positive, as unattached Vipera have no loyalty to anything but their own survival. We curated our Nest to only the best, brightest, and deadliest. We had nearly five hundred recruits, twenty of whom lived on the estate on the lower floors.

We had only one issue: none of them were Hosts. The competition unionized them, boycotting just our Nest. Not everyone was ready for something new, I suppose. *Normal* people were fine for some dining occasions; it was something to chew on. But in this day and age, Hosts are expected at any respected establishment. They were just convenient, refined. A Nest can get much done if they only have to feed on a Host once a month rather than normal bodies weekly. We were in the age of convenience, so modern Vipera expected nothing less. It was already a hard bargain recruiting to a brand-new Nest, never mind food insecurity added to the list of concerns. Class pride is a finicky thing. Not everyone was partial to the wealthy or swells, despite my money being older than any of them five times over.

"The world must be ending if you are the one to blow the trumpet."

"So theatrical." Luka leaned forward, slapping a piece of paper on the desk and plucking a fountain pen from the holder, circling and underlining a line of text. Before he spoke, he looked up, as if to take in my reaction. "I found Alina."

His voice in my ear became a mere buzz. My heart rose in my throat with every beat before I swallowed it back down. "*What?*"

"I found—"

I hurled the glass ashtray at him.

He ducked forward, and it shattered against the floor behind him. "This is good news—"

I reached across the desk, grabbing him by the jaw.

His nostrils flared, but he knew better than to do anything else to display his displeasure.

My fingers dug into his scarred skin.

He had never healed from that night, the skin remaining darker where he had been burned. The scar and discoloration went from his brow to his chin, cutting through his eye and lip. A gift from her and I. A reminder. A *warning*. The parts of it that cut through his lip exposed his canines slightly due to the taut scarring. While I would have called this permanent maiming punishment, it would never be enough.

"I told you that you are forbidden from looking. I wish to not hear her name on your filthy tongue. *Ever.*" I looked in each of his eyes, searching for a reason to crush his head on the ornate mahogany between us.

He grabbed my wrist, squeezing it to remind me he could break it if he had to. "She's not going to come back—"

"She needs time."

"It's been two years, Silas."

"She will come back; she knows where to find me. I left her letters—"

"*She's not coming back,*" he repeated slowly, sternly.

I let him go with a sneer, sitting down behind the desk, the leather of my chair warm from the glow of the window.

"I didn't have to seek her out." Luka rubbed his jaw and slid the paper forward. "This came from your father's account."

I snatched the paper from him and held it close. "How did you get this?"

"Anonymous source."

There was a date, an invoice from Fethermans & Company. Against the ache in my throat, I followed the dotted line across the page to an account number and the billed items.

To be shipped to Buffalo, NY............... *1 Bolt of Aniline*
dyed silk (Pink).

"No."

"Yes," Luka countered, sinking into the guest chair across from me. "She wasn't waiting; she fled across the globe with your sister to escape you."

"It wasn't me she was escaping."

"What is it you said to me those years ago?" He tapped his chin. "*Where your name goes, mine will follow?*"

"This is a coincidence."

"No, it is your sister's inability to live without the luxuries she was raised with, and thus use of your father's account to comfort herself. I had a detective sent not too long ago, just to make sure it was truly them. I received confirmation a day ago."

"You must have a death wish getting anywhere near this."

"No, I am pulling the wool from your eyes and ending this arrangement."

"Oh really?" I scoffed. "How so?"

"Let us make a wager."

"I don't gamble."

"If you want to see her again, alive, you *absolutely* will. Because it won't be long until Levi—"

"*Don't,*" I warned, squeezing my eyes shut, grounding myself in the pain of a clenched fist.

"I am willing to put my neck in the guillotine to show you how delusional your plan is," he continued. "Hear my bet and place yours."

"Fine," I let out a slow breath before opening my eyes. "What are your terms?"

"We go to her, in Buffalo"—I opened my mouth to speak, but he held a hand up—"we will bet on the outcome, and I guarantee both options end in her living."

I closed my mouth and leaned back, crossing my arms and nodding for him to continue.

"If we seek her out, and she accepts you with open arms, I will be killed, and you both will be on your merry way. Just as you planned in the event of her return."

"Or?"

"*Or,*" Luka continued, "this elaborate revenge plan blows back in your face, and I get a stake in your company."

"Excuse me?"

"You heard me." Luka leaned forward. "I think she will hate you more than you know, especially keeping me alive. You've passed the point of no return. Whether you kill me or let her do it, she will still hate you for what you are to your core, aside from being a *man.*"

"Aside from that insinuation being *ridiculous,*" I laughed, "why would you want to tie yourself to my company? Are you afraid you'll miss me if I cut you loose?"

"No matter how we resolve this, no one is willing to accept me as part of their Nest or hire me for the next century because of that sick stunt you pulled. I'm tired of hunting in the streets, and you don't even have Hosts in this place."

"This is really the thing you're asking for?"

"If I'll bet my life, I want something good on the other end of the scale."

"Fine," I mumbled, "but only because I know you'll lose."

"Deal." His mouth curled into a grin, and he extended his hand across the desk.

"Deal." I grasped it and shook.

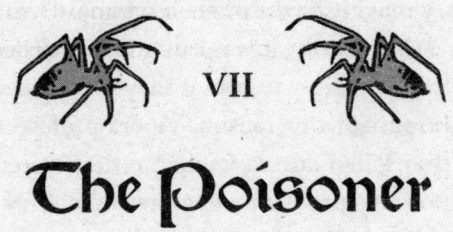

VII

The Poisoner

"ANOTHER ONE?" I POKED the pale corpse with my boot. "This is the third one this month."

"Unfortunately." Rebecca adjusted her grip on the hilt of the hatchet.

The body still twitched, but it was undoubtedly dead. Its head was three meters away from where it was supposed to be attached to the torso, leaving a trail of black sludge in the snow from where it rolled.

The body was pale and skinny, even for a grown man. The feral corrupted had a very particular look, like their own body was eating away at them, their nerves fired up like they were made of gunpowder. Even with the head detached, his dried and curled lips twitched as the skin tightened around his skull.

Recently, we have had a problem with the corrupted. It was not until we settled here that we could see the full extent of how invasive a newly turned corrupted could be without accessible Dens to feed within. They were like animals looking to scavenge for anything they could. If a corrupted consumed blood every day in a Den, they could possibly be functioning members of society.

That is what the other Vipera claimed, at least. They say if a corrupted doesn't eat, the lack of sustenance starts to eat away at their brain, wreaking havoc on their organs, driving them into a rabid state. Which is why it was rare that a well-fed corrupted lived past thirty—possibly to fifty if they took exceptional care of their condition. For this reason, Vipera preferred to behead the humans they killed during feeding if they weren't Hosts, as Hosts don't have this problem when they turn; they have all the right parts hidden deep within their bodies.

The hysteria is too much, and a low profile is paramount in their world.

The increase in incidents unnerved me. Especially with a house full of Hosts.

"Don't mention this to anyone yet," I muttered. "I will dig around. I don't know which Guild these are coming from, but I will figure it out."

"Are you sure you want to hide something like this?" Phoebe looked up at me as she crouched next to the body. "I can understand if it were just one every few months like before, but they're becoming too frequent."

"It could just be the same group; maybe this was the last of them." I stepped over the body to get another look.

The two exchanged glances without a spoken word. I know they don't like keeping things from the Nest, but it would hurt us more if we were too high-strung or lost our heads.

Rebecca frowned as she hoisted the hatchet over her shoulder, shifting on her heels as she waited for me to give instructions.

While everyone loved to tell me what they thought, they never had an actionable plan. It was of the utmost importance that we were able to think several steps ahead of an incident.

"Drag him to the river. This one isn't ours, so no harm in sending him off the property." I pushed the corpse's languid shoulder with my shoe to see if it would move again.

Rebecca nodded, but the tension in her jaw told me we were not in agreement on the next steps.

Phoebe adjusted the strap of the shotgun over her shoulder, letting out a puff of frozen breath as thoughts knit at her taut brow.

"I'll check with Henry today, see if the morgue was busier than usual." I pressed the back of my neck in an attempt to release the knot in my shoulder.

"Have you told him yet?" Phoebe's eyes snapped in my direction.

"Told him what?"

"About the corrupted, the Vipera. Has he not wondered what all these things are?"

"He wouldn't believe me even if I told him." I shrugged. "Henry is the practical type, too analytical for his own good."

"That sounds familiar," Rebecca snorted.

A small smile tugged at the corner of my mouth before it disappeared again when I looked toward the head of our specimen.

In the near distance, the head sat upright, staring blankly in our direction. The jaw was slouched, tipping the head to the right as the empty eyes stared through us.

One thing I could never understand is how something could go from feeling the entire spectrum of human behavior, only to be stripped of it entirely. The worst thing I could imagine, next to death, would be becoming the thing you hated the most. Often people fantasize about losing themselves, to not have to take control of their lives. But I could imagine no pain worse than the emptiness that must come from becoming a shell of your former self.

THE FLAT ABOVE THE shop was not strictly for deconstructing subjects. Most of my time in my lab was used for many other miscellaneous tasks, such as distilling venom, concentrating poison, or just making tallow candles.

Today, I was to process the blood I had extracted a few nights ago. The process was simpler than making an extract out of plants, though I did that as well. It was safer to use Vipera blood as poison since it was untraceable, and it did not take much to kill a human with it. When I diluted it, it turned almost a violet color when the black was dispersed. The other half of the volume was kept for research.

The blood was marketed as a pest control, for which purpose it worked remarkably well, though many had been known to use it for nasty things such as unfavorable husbands and other such men.

While it was rewarding to give relief to those in terrible situations, I was delighted with my new branch of study.

From the Vipera saliva, blood, and venom, I was able to offset more pain than just ridding the world of the creatures of man. The saliva was strictly a healing agent, but we had not yet found the best way to extract it in the quantity that we needed. Venom was our best painkiller, but it was riskier to use and had more side effects, and yet it was slightly easier to collect than spit.

Blood was plentiful. It was the only easy part of the process.

During my research, I found that if the solution was composed of less than five milliliters of venom, it would not turn the subject if they happened to die. While the risks of turning were heavy, the remedies had worked on most pains from arthritis, womanly aches, and even harsher injuries, rendering something as severe as an amputation into a light throb. As much as I hated the gimmicks of peddlers, this was truly a miracle elixir.

Unfortunately for myself, my time with this chemical inside and outside my body was forming a tolerance. I had begun concentrating it further for my own personal uses, but I would advise against such things if I were to prescribe to another. While I understood this was a problem, it was one for another time. It was the only thing that relieved me of my existential existence on this earth, in this town, in this very shop.

I did not understand the feelings myself most days, as I had no reason to be in such a depressed state. I had a family now, friends, and love that could thaw even the coldest of hearts. So why did mine feel like a stone forgotten under a late-winter's sleet?

"Are you ready?" a voice called from downstairs. *Phoebe.*

"Finishing now!" I shouted, tucking the used needles into the drawer in the workbench. I cuffed my sleeves down my arm before taking a long, deep breath to collect myself.

Outside the shop, Edith and Phoebe sat next to one another in the front of the wagon as they waited.

The weight of the wagon shifted as I stepped up into the back, taking a seat behind them.

Some things never changed. There were certain traditions that were held most sacred. For Phoebe and me, it was our morning strolls. Only recently did she allow guests on our little prome-nades. Edith was usually in attendance, but that was only because it was important to include her. She was a flighty thing, not the best at making friends, which I could relate to with a heavy heart.

The park we frequented was a quiet one. There were many trails for walking. Benches were scattered along the water for viewing pleasure, or if you preferred to walk, there were stone bridges to look over the water and feed the ducklings in spring.

There were more limited activity options in winter, as there were no ducks, no color, no flowers to enjoy. I wanted to like winter, but it was all too sad for me. Despite my morbid attire, I enjoyed the color and sounds of nature. There were no plants to steal cuttings from and no birds to sing to me when morning came around. I still had my crows, who were darlings when it came to cleaning up messes.

Phoebe needed these walks more than I did. It was some attempt to maintain whatever remained of normalcy from our past. Many days, I could see that she missed her life from before. The days when there was a reason to keep up appearances and take advantage of the finer things in life. She somehow still found a way to keep up her fashionable tastes, even on a budget. Today she wore a wool skirt and matching overcoat. It was dyed a deep magenta with white rabbit trim. She had a matching fur hand muff, as well.

Edith wore a green walking suit with a matching cape. The fur trim was a natural brown around her sleeves and neck. She did not wear a head covering today, but she usually chose to wear her golden curls up with a hat that matched the trim of her coat.

Two sets of green eyes stared at me as if waiting for me to respond.

"Did you ask me something?" I took a drag of my cigarette from the long, thin holder.

"I asked if we could plan a white elephant swap for Christmas. It would really mean a lot to the girls," Phoebe said.

"I don't see why not." I shrugged.

"You seemed lost in thought before," Edith said from my right side.

"I think many things, at many times. I thought that was what walks were for."

"You spend more time in your head than you do with the living." Phoebe hooked on to my left arm.

I held the cigarette holder to my lips again, breathing deep before letting it all go again. The weather made me want to sleep rather than walk. Though with how warm I was getting under my dress, I think I could manage to sleep in a snowdrift.

"When are you going to tell the others about our pest problem?" Phoebe raised a fine brow.

"After the holidays," I answered.

"Do you mean the *corrupted*?" Edith chimed in, glaring past me at Phoebe. "They are no more pests than you or I. It is not their fault."

Here we go again.

"Well, we do not rip through people so recklessly." Phoebe's brow twitched. "We are sophisticated. They are just turned."

"I was turned."

"But you are civil and sensible. You were also a Host."

"What does being a Host have to do with it? You are just a purist."

"They are not meant to be turned; mellifluous are different. It is cruel to turn typical men and cut their lives short."

"They are like children; you can mold them and show them the way, show them how to live in the little time they have left."

"Children who could tear through us as easily as warmed bread fresh from the oven."

"*Enough*, both of you." I narrowed my eyes on Phoebe.

"Are you taking her side?" Phoebe gasped.

"I am not taking anyone's side. I would like to avoid politics on our walks." I had burned through the cigarette, it was more unashed dust than it was paper.

"I told you I don't like it when you speak of them that way. You are disgusted by the wrong thing. They don't have anyone to show them how to control it," Edith continued.

"Maybe you should show them on your own since you are so adamant about charity cases."

"*No*," I interrupted, "I can barely feed the two of you, we don't have any more room without taking on new people, and we barely have rooms for those we have already. No more of this."

The two of them glared at each other, but thankfully did not speak another word on the subject.

"I'm thinking of goose for Christmas," I broke the silence. "We can splurge for a few large ones, also some fruit and wine."

"I love that idea," Edith hummed. "Could we spare some money for another cylinder for the phonograph? I would love to get one with Christmas carols on it! For the ambiance of course."

"That is fine." I glanced at Phoebe, who was still quiet. She was lost in thought. "Phoebe?"

"Hmm?" She blinked up at me.

"What were you thinking for presents?"

"Well, I was thinking we all get a small allowance and pick names from a hat so we can all get each other something or make it ourselves. It would be fun, I thought, but it might be silly." She blushed. There was something bothering her; she always second-guessed herself when she had something else on her mind.

"I think it would be a lovely idea. That way no one is left out." I nudged her. "You are the expert of these things. I do not know how to organize parties aside from deciding what cups go with what liquor."

Edith laughed at my remark, and I earned a small smirk from Phoebe. That was enough for me.

"How about we go window shopping? We have walked the whole length of the park at this point. Come," I said, as we turned onto the footbridge, the street opening up to us as we exited the park.

The streets were rousing with people going about their business or leisure. We walked to our favorite street to gaze at all the displays in the windows.

Phoebe always lingered around this one fur shop that she liked, though we promised we would not cling to anything too material. It did not stop me from asking the furrier how many rabbits I would have to shoot in order to get a full coat. The answer to that was about thirty for a full set of anything.

We told ourselves we would be sustainable and refrain from buying anything frivolous. Any sound mind would find it suspicious if we accrued too many expensive things.

As I watched Phoebe scan the windows, Edith tugged on my sleeve.

I glanced down at her. Those deep green eyes peered up at me nervously. Edith had a hard time asking for anything; she was not one for confrontation most days, but she was able to speak up if she was passionate enough about a subject.

"I do not mean to be a bother, but could we head home soon? I would like to feed before my shift if it is possible," she bit her lip, her gaze briefly darting to Phoebe.

"Ah, yes. I forgot. After this block, we can head back," I assured her.

She smiled and nodded at me, holding my arm and resting her head against my shoulder as we walked. She was a gentle soul, a golden heart. Unlike myself, Edith was one of those people who would give even a rabid bear a second chance.

VIII

The Creature

THE STEAM ENGINE HISSED, the metal whining and creaking as it settled like the industrial beast that it was. I could practically taste the coal in the air, the carbon burning the roof of my mouth.

Out of all things, smoke should be the least irritating, but for some reason, the steam engines were overpowering. Maybe it was the buildup of whatever else they burned in their furnaces to make these mammoths go forward. At least cigars and cigarettes attempted to hide some of that tar with cocoa and cedar.

The platform bustled with passengers, passing us left and right as they filtered into the doors of the station to relieve themselves of the frigidity between platforms.

"You do not pay me to be your footman." Luka placed our suitcases down beside us with little care.

"I could pay you enough to be anything I wanted, greedy thing. Are you too weak to carry another bag?" I glanced at him.

"Do not be unpleasant; it is too early." Luka adjusted his fur-lined jacket. "Are we ready for the hotel?"

"There should be a coach in front of the station. Should not be too much longer to travel."

"Will you look for her tonight?"

"No. It can wait for tomorrow." I was hesitant to give him any more details than that. While he knew not to touch her and there was seemingly no ill-will toward her for the marks she had left on him, I couldn't help but be cautious.

"I still have not received word from Detective Moore. His assistants gave us the address, but I have yet to hear more about his findings from the horse's mouth himself."

"How odd. Relay to his assistant where we are staying in case he decides to crawl from whatever tavern he's inevitably holed up in."

I checked my timepiece.

If I could distract him for just a couple of hours, I could make headway on finding her and settle this wager of ours.

UPON OUR ARRIVAL AT the hotel, bellhops trotted around and took our things before much notice could be granted. We were given our room keys—two keys for two *separate* rooms. I needed space from my irritating travel partner.

I preferred the company of the bar rather than my room, as an empty room was not good for a brewing mind. My mood was becoming more unstable the more visions of *her* seeped deep into the cracks of my skull.

The bar was decently populated for a weekday and full of interesting company. The light from the bar illuminated the bottles and counter, fading anything in my peripheral vision into darkness.

The tender opened his mouth to ask me to pick my poison, but I was already pointing to the top shelf.

"Bourbon. Any of them." I propped an elbow on the countertop to rest my head in my hand.

"Are you celebrating?" a timid voice asked.

I followed the sound to a petite woman. She had curly blond hair that was gathered neatly in some elaborate knot. Her eyes were a deep green that reminded me of a summer forest. Pretty, no doubt, but I was in no mood for *that* kind of company.

"Yes, celebrating," I muttered as a drink was poured before me and the bottle placed neatly beside.

"Is it too forward to ask the occasion?" She took a seat next to me.

"I am not buying."

"And I am not selling." She frowned. "Just a curious patron."

"Aren't there a handful of idioms about the danger of being nosy?"

She lifted a dainty shoulder. "I wouldn't imagine your reasons would put me in any danger."

The corner of my lip flicked up at the remark, "Well, if you insist on knowing, I am celebrating . . . a lost lover of sorts."

"Oh." Her face twisted in concern. "Has she passed?"

"No," I took a sip, "but she is surely a danger to be celebrated."

"You say that fondly," she pointed out.

"That is because I am fond of many vices, her included." I reached past the bar for another glass, pouring her a drink as well.

The woman's shoulders slumped, relaxing as I spoke. She was curious, derailed from whatever her original motive was for joining me.

"Do you do this often?"

"Do what?"

"Prowl around establishments for men." I poured more bourbon for myself.

"Oh . . . well it is not often. I am not usually here—I am usually taking night shifts." She played with her own cup nervously.

"Night shifts?"

"The hospital," she sighed.

Amateur.

I leaned close, taking a deep breath by her neck. A strong perfume may have masked her scent—a sweet, metallic one, like brass. "Is a bar the best place to hunt for food?"

Her face paled, and her shoulders visibly tensed as the question registered "I-I'm sorry, I didn't realize—"

"You smell like blood and bleach," I told her, a gentle clicking coming from my throat as I glanced down at her, "but do not fret, I'll forgive you, if you tell me one thing—are you with a Nest?"

"I-I don't exactly belong to a Nest," she stuttered, too embarrassed to look at me.

"Tell me about it." I twisted a piece of her hair that had fallen out of place.

"It is a female-only home; it isn't quite a Nest. There are some in town, but I do not belong to any of them."

"How interesting. Are you here with your housemates, then?"

"No, but they are expecting me home soon." She glanced behind her. "I must go."

"If you must." I shrugged. "I would take more care in who you hunt next time."

She nodded quickly, mumbling a form of apology paired with a wild blush on her face. She slipped away as soon as she could.

Her panicked expression was the perfect treat to end the night. I would be seeing her again, no doubt.

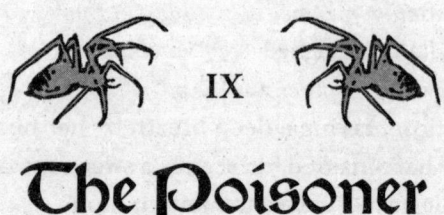

IX

The Poisoner

*T*HE CHILL OF THE snow stung the bottoms of my feet, no matter how numb the cold made them. Each step was like walking over tiny shards, but standing wouldn't be much better. Small crunches sounded from under my heel. My feet were pale, a bit red at the tips, a sure sign of poor circulation under the weather. Despite the pain, the snow under me and around me looked so soft. Undisturbed and peaceful.

Looking back at the farmhouse, it seemed to me like the last ember in the ash. Windows alight, soft muffled sounds of life within. It was a warm feeling, knowing that even if I wasn't missed, I was somehow responsible for creating a place for people to belong. A labor of love.

Even so, domesticity as it was did not bring me the comfort I had hoped for; something was missing.

Within the dark wood, the powdered path between the old, proud pines, an endless shadow loomed just beyond reach. They say you are born with the fear of the dark, of the unknown. I say we are born with an insatiable curiosity, and that hunger alone is enough to ward people from dark places.

Some see it as self-harm to leap into unforeseen circumstances right as the dust settles. The danger of insatiability, yet the dark is filled with wonder, practically teeming in the void. It called for me, I hungered for a taste.

Every step was no different from the last, the pain ensued, and the void always at arm's length.

The physical limits of my body screamed and begged me to stop the more I pushed. The ache of my joints, the prick of the pads of my feet, the numbness that followed. Yet, the void still called louder, not unlike the groan of some large ship, something so calm yet unable to be ignored.

Even when I tried running, my bones must have turned to lead with the gravity of it all, the equal and opposite pull to protect me from myself. A constant trudge upstream of brackish water.

The pain grew, an unforgettable memory bled into my throat like tasting a long-lost flavor of adrenaline. An unmistakable dread came over me, and when I looked down, the snow had changed. Blood dripped, staining the ground. Blood seeped through my nightgown, the drip turning to a dribble, and my blood spilled over the expanse of rice. Millions of grains cut into the sole of my feet. Every step was more painful than the last, and there was nowhere to go but over.

"*ALINA.*"

Something wet in my hands, dripping down my forearm.

I blinked, my vision coming to me slowly like the steam clearing from glass.

Phoebe stood in the archway of the kitchen, hugging the frame. Her face was stern, alert despite the soft way she called my name.

The tiles of the floor were cold on my feet, but not as cold as the snow dripping down my ankle until it made a puddle where I stood.

The house was gray at such an hour. The chairs were neatly tucked under the table, the table spotless, not even crumbs for mice. No pots and pans on the stove and the sink vacant of any dishes or cups. One would find it hard to believe that anyone lived here, never mind over a dozen, with no evidence to suggest otherwise.

I glanced back at my hand, wild belladonna berries dripping from my palm in clots, escaping between my fingers.

Soft, pale hands took mine, then placed my hands over her shoulders. Phoebe wrapped her arms around my torso and squeezed me tight, not caring that the berries stained dark across the back of her nightgown collar.

There was no use for words, because not even I could come up with what to say.

THE SNOW CAST A stiff shell of ice over the ground, gracing the morning with a seasonal mystique. Rebecca and I used the morning to forage for things needed or wanted. Past the tree line surrounding our field was a forest with much to give. Despite the season, there were many delights hidden among the foliage. I used to refuse to partake, as I had my reservations about eating wild plants. That was until Rebecca showed us the safest things to forage and worked from there.

It was a harsh transition moving to a place surrounded by nature while not being too far off from civilization. I became more comfortable as the months went on. Rebecca and I bonded over our wilderness finds. She was quite handy, that one.

There were old tracks in the snow, *mine*. Last night's footprints in a stiff trail. I kicked the fresh cold powder to fill them in, erasing last night's wanderings.

"What is on your list for today?" Rebecca nudged my side as we stepped through the unbeaten path.

"Staghorn, sumac, and rosehips," I answered, staring down at the places I was stepping to avoid the roots.

"Phoebe's favorite." She smirked. "I have juniper and pine. I thought it would be nice for seasonings and tea."

"That is only because you like how Adeline tastes after," I teased, nudging her back.

"Is that so unfair? She doesn't mind. She loves pine tea!"

"I would rather one of you made use of the juniper and learned to make gin."

"We have nothing but time." Rebecca stopped to rustle through a small shrub, plucking small waxy berries from in between the brush.

I helped her gather, rolling the pale berries between my fingers before putting them in her bag.

"How are you and Adeline?"

"What about us?" She frowned, her attempt at hiding her blush was poor.

"Don't get flustered! It isn't unusual for feeding partners to get so close," I laughed. "I figured it was a matter of time, and the two of you have been paired the longest out of the rest of them!"

"It is purely beneficial. An efficient pair doesn't need to be changed," she said matter-of-factly, a small smile tugging at her lips.

I saw a lot of myself in her. Stern, purposeful, concise. There was nothing she did without a plan or purpose in place. Neither of us were very good at empathizing, which led to our walks in the woods to escape the chatter. Sometimes we would just silently walk, perfectly content with a presence without the noise.

She was one of those Vipera that had been in the Americas for a while, only two hundred years old. She often spoke about her culture, the one that was here before settlement taught by her mother. She had a particular interest in my work and had helped me plenty with native flora.

Her parents currently owned a butchery in town where she worked during the day and often brought us meat.

On our way to the house, I spotted the raised spears of stag-horn along the tree line. The reddish-purple berries tasted of bitter lemon, tangy to the senses. They were perfect for the tastes of Vipera.

The house looked perfectly quaint from afar, like a painting you may see on the wall of a nice estate. It was almost as pale as the snow surrounding, bleaching the landscape in an innately pure blanket of frost. The only movement in the frozen wonderland was the sluggish rise of smoke from the chimneys. Occasionally, you could smell whatever was cooking if the wind direction allowed in between nips at your nose.

Upon entering the house, I could smell cider brewing passively in the fireplace. We left our boots and outerwear in the mudroom next to the tools and small wood splits.

Adeline and Mary were sitting on the couch, chatting amongst themselves as they kept a steady eye on the flames. They were identical with brown hair, milky skin, and dark blue eyes. Despite the two of them being twins, Mary always looked colder. Her brow was always drawn tight, and a smile was rare to grace her features. To her credit, Mary was the critical one.

"Did you find any?" Adeline squeaked as she shot up from her seat, planting herself in front of Rebecca once she entered.

"Of course, I can put the kettle on for some tea. No need to move from the fireplace," Rebecca chuckled, looking down at the bubbly brunette.

Watching Adeline and Rebecca interact was as confusing as watching a cat and dog meet for the first time. Adeline's high energy and ironclad optimism would make even the most experienced pessimists hopeful. Rebecca did not smile often unless she was alone or with Adeline.

I was to blame for pairing the two, as I always believed one needed an opposite. I took pride in my girls; they were my family. It was even more important during the winter months, when bitter memories liked to surface. They kept me going, all of them. It may be that I just liked having a purpose, people to take care of.

"YOUR EYES ARE RED."

"Tell me that I am hideous once more, dear friend." I pressed my palms into my eye sockets, chasing the relief of the pressure.

The market was busy, as people were beginning to put out Christmas decor and taking delivery orders for Christmas geese. While it was a seasonal delight, the scent of pine and cinnamon was overwhelming the market today. I much preferred to wait for the fresh shipments of citrus.

"We need to talk." Phoebe's voice lowered.

"About what?"

"You know."

"No, I don't." I pulled my hands away from my face, blurry vision clearing the image of the haughty redhead. "There is nothing to speak of."

"Ah, yes, because your behavior is so very normal." She looped her arm in mine as we walked along the market for fear she might lose me in the packed walkway. "What if you walk somewhere dangerous? Freeze in your sleep? Lose a toe to frostbite if you walk on a particularly nippy evening?"

I shook my head, distracted by the food and the overwhelming number of conversations around me. A tingling sensation tickled my wrist, then up my arm. I scratched at my sleeve just for the itch to crawl up my spine, then raise the hairs at the back of my neck. A sharp noise from the racket flew in and out of my audio purview, teasing me like a low-flying gnat. Even the smells were too strong, each step inviting new scents, both pleasant and unpleasant.

Further into the market was fresh produce, then meat. Fresh-caught haddock and salmon, fully butchered and ready to be taken home in the oily brown paper. Suddenly, I did not mind the pine scent to the fishy odor. The market was my least favorite activity. I begged not to attend.

"The stress isn't good for you—"

"The only one stressing me is you," I snapped at her.

She squeezed my arm, her nails digging into my bicep, "You will wear yourself down to the bone, and I will not be the one to clean up the scraps."

"Oh?" I raised a brow at her. "Be honest, dear friend, haven't you always been the first to pick at scraps? You're always in for a long haul."

A sneer pulled at her pink lips before it transformed into a less-than-sincere smile, the look in her eyes sharp as they narrowed on the new movement.

"Did you see the wreaths on the north side?" Adeline asked excitedly, pulling her pearl white gloves tighter over her wrist.

"You know how I feel about decor," I mumbled, plucking a cigarette from my purse.

"We know how you feel about extraneous spending," Rebecca said, a small grin playing on her lips as she squeezed one of my shoulders. "We can make them. I know we have a few good fir trees on the property."

"Give Alina a break; you know she's not one for crafts." Adeline pinched Rebecca's arm.

"Oh! We could add some ribbon if we ask Cordelia for any scraps," Phoebe offered.

"Did either of you purchase any food for this week?" I interrupted, sucking on my cigarette.

"Not yet—" Addie adjusted her bonnet impatiently.

"Isn't that more important than decorations?" I mumbled, having to relight a match for another puff.

"It's stew this week. I just need a few more herbs; the rest comes from my father's shop. We just got in some cuts of pork."

"Pork." Phoebe wrinkled her nose.

"You won't be eating the pork; why are you complaining?" Rebecca raised a brow.

"I don't like the aftertaste in the blood," Phoebe grumbled.

A soft-spoken mutter piqued from behind me, barely audible among the market chaos and the redhead in my ear.

Phoebe, Rebecca, and Adeline averted their eyes in unison, huddling the group closer together like startled geese.

"We can't possibly be expected to hear you when you speak like a mouse, dear," Phoebe said, withholding a smirk as best she could when Rebecca snorted, turning to hide the laughter.

I craned my neck over my shoulder.

Edith stood, admittedly a bit embarrassed, as she clutched a basket. "I didn't mean to interrupt."

Snickering ensued beside me, and my head snapped in the direction of the girls, who pressed their lips and bit their cheeks as if they weren't chittering to each other. Phoebe was unable to hide a subtle clicking.

"I'll go—"

"No. Edith, walk with me." I held my hand out, grasping at the air between us to urge her along.

I managed a glare in Phoebe's direction before Edith caught up with my stride; one of mine was two of hers.

"I really can go somewhere else if you were in the middle—"

"They were on my nerves." I sucked on the last bit of burning paper before flicking it into the snow.

"Speaking of . . ." Edith began, rummaging through her basket before pulling out a small jar.

"What is that?"

"Christmastime gift." Edith smiled, a blush glowing in the apples of her cheeks.

I held the small jar up. Small, dried flowers with a dusting of warm pollen powdering the inside of the jar. "Cannabis?"

"I-I heard you weren't sleeping." Edith glowed with excitement. "And before you say it! I didn't spend any!"

"We already steal too much from the hospital."

My words made her nearly physically stumble. "But we give a lot to the hospital too." Her voice became shaky with uncertainty. "I just thought—"

Edith bit the inside of her cheek, unable to say what she needed.

I pulled Edith in, my arms wrapping around her shoulders. I squeezed her frail body gently. "Thank you; I will use some tonight," I said before she could throw herself into an anxious rant. Just the words *thank you* seemed to calm the flighty thing. She was well-meaning, even if it was an invasion of my privacy.

"Did I do something wrong?" she muttered into my cloak.

"No, no. Everyone is just anxious. Holidays and all." I glanced down at her. "How are you doing?"

"Can't find the will to sleep either. I may join you if you light any of that." She looked up suddenly. "I have an idea for an experiment, if you'll entertain it."

"An experiment?" I raised a brow. "I told you we can't afford to do anything too skewed from what we norm—"

"It won't demand any more personnel, just myself! I can do it! The great thing about its design is that it doesn't require any materials, per se—"

"Alina!" Phoebe shouted from across the market.

The group was gathering by the entrance, prepared to depart.

"Another time, Edith," I mumbled, waving her along as we approached to leave.

Even from afar, the palpable flare of fire in Phoebe's face made her annoyance all too obvious. She wasn't good at hiding her feelings, and it was obvious from the beginning how she felt about Edith. Though she never acted out toward anyone else. Petulant, at best. But it was a problem best solved back at home.

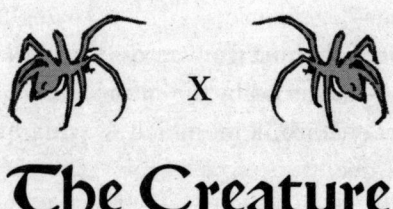

X

The Creature

WHETHER OR NOT I wanted to kill her was a question that had been on my mind.

While my heart raced at the thought of finding her again, of holding her in my arms, opposing ideas tainted my thoughts. Thoughts of squeezing her hard within that embrace, hard enough to break her ribs in my grasp. I wanted to crush her bones under my grip. To squeeze her until her heart popped from the pressure and she bled freely into my arms. I have known betrayal, but none as deep as my pariah's, *Alina*.

When I found myself pining for her, I wondered about the moments we shared. Had they meant anything to her aside from simple carnal pleasures? I was sure she wondered the same, though I thought we'd had an unspoken bond that assured her of those pestering anxieties. I did not think she meant it when she said she never wanted to see me again. She couldn't have.

Surely she would come find me once she escaped, once it was safe, I assumed.

But there she was, completely at ease, in no rush to find me, better off than she'd been before.

Of course, I did not expect her to leap into my arms and profess her ever-burning love for me, but I did not expect her to abandon me altogether either. It filled me with indescribable anger that would allow me to burn the world if someone just gave me enough petrol and a matchbook.

The incessant shaking in my hands would not cease. It was an annoying tick I had adopted whenever she haunted me. I was unsure if it was caused by unrest, hunger, or rage. Surely it was all three, considering I was staring at *her*. The only one who could evoke such a visceral reaction.

There was a seating area by the waterfront. Small, circular tables with equally delicate chairs lined the dock. On warmer days, it was likely a perfect place for tea or lunch. But only one would sit in this Siberian weather to watch something as mundane as frozen water.

Alina sat facing the river, her back to me as I watched from afar. She was studying something off in the distance, faded off somewhere deep in that mind of hers. I could tell because her cigarette had collected ash that had yet to fall, and the cherry had burned out in her neglect.

Her midnight hair was tied in tight braided knots to contain it in a reasonable manner. Her coat was not nearly thick enough for the current weather. Just a humble attire made of black wool. How typical. Always mourning something.

She was alluring in the most wistful ways. Radiant, even.

I wanted to shout at her, make her look at me so I could see those merciless eyes again. The only thing colder than today's bitter wind would be her gaze. I had forgotten how much I missed it. How much I wanted to see those eyes again, even if they were not looking at me in kind.

All my boiling rage had settled into a steady rolling simmer.

She turned her head to her cigarette, tapping the ash before lighting it again. Her cheeks were more defined, as was her elegant neck. Her eyes did not look as tired as I remembered. If anything, she looked like she spent less time scowling.

Oh, to be the reason for those wicked expressions once more.

My limbs carried me before my mind could wrestle with me. I approached.

My hand moved out to her, not knowing if it would strangle her or caress her when it reached her fair flesh. I wanted to tangle my fingers in that endless cascade of hair once more, to bend her to my will.

To make her scream for me, or at me, as long as it was only for *me*.

I could almost smell her.

Feel her.

Taste her.

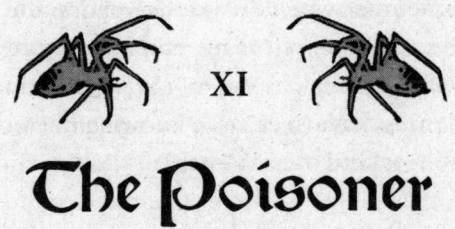

XI

The Poisoner

A CHILL RACED UP MY spine, the hairs on my neck vibrating as they stood erect at the sensation. I shivered and leaned forward to flick the roach from my cigarette holder into the water.

I had been here long enough. The frost would start to nip at my face if I daydreamed any longer. I patted the white flakes from my garments as I rose from my seat, turning to head down the pathway. The walk was pleasant, just not as much as it would be if all the trees were not dead and everything was not turned to many hues of black and white.

A loud clicking made me freeze in my path. It trilled again, and I spotted a woodpecker up in the tree along the walkway.

I tilted my head at the creature. "Look at you, proof that I haven't gone colorblind." I smiled at the bird, and his head tilted at me as I spoke to him. He was probably wondering what this large creature was doing talking to him. He was a beautiful specimen, sporting bright crimson feathers at the crest of his head. "I will leave you be, do not worry, fellow," I mumbled and continued on my way.

A familiar scent graced my walk. Maybe someone's cigarette from far off, but the winter air played tricks on your senses like a mirage. Sometimes when I used the venom, the colors were brighter or the smells were stronger. This morning's dose had been a larger one than normal, as the morbs were hitting me harder this winter. It must have been resurfacing some nostalgic scents for me today, how kind of my senses.

I WENT TO THE hospital to see Edith. I wanted to see how she was faring. Today she worked two shifts, so I brought her something.

The building was made of a light brick color. It was quite bleak and intimidating. I was wary of hospitals, though at ease knowing Edith was caring for people inside. They had finished an expansion not too long ago. It was all very exciting, as an expanded hospital meant more resources, hopefully. I stamped the snow off my boots on the rug past the front door.

The front desk area had a nurse working away.

"Looking for Edith?" the nurse piped without a second glance.

"How did you guess?" I grinned. "Just dropping something off."

"Second floor." She smiled in return.

The upstairs had tall ceilings and a long hallway lined with doors. For each large room, there were two entrances and maybe three windows. The number of patients per room would vary, but typically, there were many beds with curtains in between.

Upon entering the room, I could see the beds were full. Many patients did not look well, but they did not look in pain. That would be thanks to me and the effort of my girls.

I smiled at the thought. It was one thing to know what the drug did, but another to see it work.

"Alina!" Edith chimed as she extended a curtain. She wore all white, a skirt and blouse with a high neck, paired with a bandana to hold her hair back. She also wore a smock with a few stains at arm's length, most likely from wiping her hands on it.

"I brought you something to hold your stomach over," I whispered, reaching into my basket and handing her a bottle of freshly drawn blood from this morning.

"Bless you." She smiled.

"How is your supply?"

"I am a few liters into what you gave me last time."

"Already?"

"It is winter. People do not fare well in the cold."

"Right." I sighed. "Let me know when you run out."

"I will." She nodded.

"I will see you at home, then," I said before stepping back into the hall.

The day had made me feel uneasy. Even with venom, it had been particularly long. A migraine was percolating, causing dark spots to bloom in my vision.

I would return home and sleep until supper, just in case.

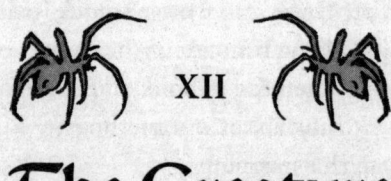

XII

The Creature

"SO?" LUKA LOOKED AT me expectantly.

"What?"

"Did you find her?"

"I don't know what you mean."

"You left your room yesterday."

"I went to the bar."

"You left the hotel."

"Am I *your* prisoner now? Tracking my every move?" I scoffed. "I stepped outside for some air."

"Are you afraid?"

"Why would I be afraid?" I took a long sip of my bourbon.

The action alone made Luka raise a brow, those auburn eyes boring holes in the side of my face. I wanted to poke them out so they would stop staring at me.

We sat across from each other in the hotel lounge within the bar area. The chairs were comfortable, despite not being able to sit still. It was no Explorers Club, but the space was fine for taking a drink or two.

"What's the plan?"

"No plan. Not one involving you," I muttered.

"Do you not trust me?"

"Of course not. You kidnapped her, *tortured* her. I think she would be wise to kill you if she saw you."

"Ah yes, I forgot about that," he remarked, then slowly smirked. "That's a lie. I still think about it sometimes."

"*Watch yourself,*" I snapped.

"There's been a telegram."

"From whom?"

Luka took a long sip of liquor, as if he had not heard my question.

"Luka," I snapped my fingers in his face. "What telegram?"

"From London."

"I said *who,* not *where,*" I seethed.

"Your father."

I returned the rim of my whiskey glass to my lips, finishing it off before staring at the refractions of the crystal, letting the liquor bite before swallowing.

"We have to prepare a reply," Luka said, though he didn't seem any more enthusiastic than I was, "even if it is just to delay."

"We will not entertain him."

"I don't think we have a choice. We must respond, or he may resort to less diplomatic approaches. We have no Hosts, and the Nest is getting anxious."

"They should be."

"Silas," he warned, "you've been running for too long. No matter how justified your actions, there are consequences." He raked his fingers through the brown waves of his hair, and I swore there was a tremor. "I'm surprised he has taken so long to initiate any sort of correspondence."

I waved a dismissive hand. "Do what you must to delay him. He will only entertain a goose chase for so long. Hopefully, we are back by then."

He stared at me for a beat too long, displaying something like hesitation. "I'll send something back to the Nest," Luka finally said.

Right past Luka, I spotted the little blond sprite from the other night. "Excuse me." I abandoned my seat, eager to escape the conversation in more ways than one.

If anyone would know more about the politics of the area, this one would.

She pressed her palms against the edge of the bar, glancing at the mirror behind the bottles.

I stalked forward, appearing behind her in the reflection. "Were you hoping to see me again, or is this a typical hunting ground for you?"

Her eyes widened, and she spun around.

"Don't look so surprised; at least try to look like you expected a threat." I rolled my eyes, sliding my empty glass to the bartender as I took a seat.

"Why not leave me alone? You already know why I frequent here from our last talk." She hesitantly sat next to me.

"Relax, I am not here to cause any sort of heartache for you." I laughed. "But I did have some questions."

"What about?"

"Just helping out a lost tourist."

"Well, I will try to help where I can."

"Where does a stranger get a bite to eat?"

"You'd be looking for a Guild," she laughed.

"And that is . . . ?"

"There is not much to tell. They run like Dens with a member list. Some are more exclusive than others, but all are welcome with the right fee."

"How much do *you* pay, then?"

"I do not pay, and neither do Hosts," she started. "I don't know how it works where you're from, but here the Hosts are unionized. My Nest was the one to start it."

"If your Hosts are within your own Nest, why would they go to another?"

"Hosts don't have to pay to enter a Guild; they are paid to be there," she explained.

"Where is your Nest?"

She shook her head. "I cannot tell you that."

"May I know your name, then? We are friends, are we not?"

The blonde appeared to internally debate whether it was a good idea to tell me. It was undoubtedly a terrible decision to tell me anything, but she seemed naive enough.

"Edith," she said after a while.

"Edith," I repeated, tilting my head at her. "What about the Dam of your Nest?"

Edith shifted in her seat at the mention. It did not take an academic to see that she was not allowed to talk to strangers about her. What a sweet little thing.

"You do not have to tell me; I was just curious. You speak of her highly." I shrugged, nonchalantly swishing the liquid in my cup.

"She is a force," Edith said softly. "Sometimes I am afraid to say her name. I fear she will appear if I do."

"I am sure you are safe. She must be very busy." I kept my questions light, but I was restraining myself from prying.

"Alina is her name," she practically whispered.

"*Alina*," I couldn't help but purr as it slipped off my tongue. "A beautiful name."

"It is fitting for her." She smiled shyly.

"Is she waiting for you now?"

"She is expecting me to be at work." Her smile faded. A guilty furrow of the brow gave her away. She reminded me of my sister, so very expressive. Her face could not lie.

"I see. So you are not allowed to be here?"

"It's not like that! She just gets anxious when we hunt on our own. I am conducting my own research. I feel I need to do it myself sometimes."

"Fair, there is no use denying your nature."

"She's different. She thinks we can do some good in the world." Edith smoothed down her skirt. "It gives us some hope that we aren't some sort of plague or curse on mankind."

"Mankind," I scoffed. "I'm pretty sure we were here first."

"Doesn't mean we have to make people suffer for it," she said softly. "I'm sure you would think the same if there was a chance you might harm the ones you love."

My lip twitched in a sneer, but I dampened it.

We sat silently for a while, finishing our drinks before she eventually slipped away. It seemed like fate, meeting Alina's pet here. It sounded like she ran her dogs on short leads. Destiny was in our favor today. It was a matter of time before she would be by my side once more.

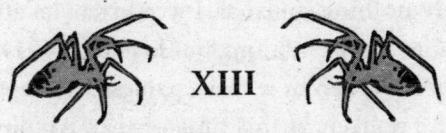

XIII

The Poisoner

"**W**HAT DO YOU THINK could have caused it?"

"Oh, I don't know," I trailed off.

The answer is Vipera blood.

"You will make a terrible undertaker," Henry scoffed. "Have a guess."

"Poison?"

"That is a lazy answer."

"But it *is* a possibility."

"Obviously. But then it turns into a matter of whether the poisoning was accidental or malicious, something much harder to prove."

"Allergy, then."

"That's just another type of poisoning, Miss Lis. What *caused* the poisoning?"

I lifted a shoulder, biting my lip.

"You are a lousy thinker today."

"I'm tired."

"No more than our John Doe," he quipped, returning our attention to the subject. "There seems to have been an allergic reaction.

There is swelling in the throat and some internal bleeding, but no chemical that reads to me as suspicious. The contents of his stomach were nothing unusual. I would say he ate something that didn't quite agree with him, but his body says he did that in addition to being bitten by a snake. Unless he keeps critters like that handy, it's unlikely at this time of year. An illness that just looks like an allergy, or something imported. I am starting to suspect some type of fever." Henry pinched the corpse's cheeks to look down its throat.

Henry was a bright young man. He was under the guise that I was preparing to become an undertaker, which wasn't entirely untrue. He just didn't know it was so I could study the Vipera and their effects on humans without suspicion. Here, I could dig through the corpses in peace.

"How peculiar. What else?" I loomed over his shoulder to peek.

"Asphyxiation, as far as I can tell. Possibly an allergy to an insect due to some traits of the blood, but it is winter." He removed his hands from the cadaver before turning to look at me.

The coroner's son was short, or just shorter than me. His sandy blond head rose to my shoulder. I am sure he was looking to take over after his father, with how passionate he was for the trade.

"How odd," I commented. "Any other outliers recently?"

"That depends on what your definition of outlier is." He shrugged and wiped his hands on a used rag. "Though, I did get a corpse that was thought to have rabies before passing."

"How can you tell?"

"You can't. But the description is similar to other cases. Could be the same virus or affliction. It's the best answer we have, for now," Henry explained, his chestnut-colored eyes lit up as he spoke about the intricacies of cadavers.

He was passionate about his work; I would always respect that. Undertakers were the caretakers of the dead. We trusted them to tell our truths, and to make sure we were truly at rest when we finally slipped into the final wooden walls that we would call home. It was an amicable profession, one of the few sacred things left that transcended tradition and religion. It was simple admiration of life and respect for the dead. Precisely why I chose to begin apprenticing.

"Leaving so soon?" I asked as he gathered his coat.

"It's not like my clients pay any mind." He tipped his head toward the cadavers.

"Unless you get a walk-in."

"Now *that* would be a reason to leave even earlier." He shook his head before popping on his flat cap, holding the door for me as he waited to lock up.

THE RIDE HOME WAS always a bit slow. I was tired from work, but there was more to do at home. The household could not upkeep itself. Just because I founded this little home of ours, does not mean I would slack off on work. If I had energy to give, I was a strong believer in giving it. The girls worked so hard, it would be disrespectful not to work harder as the person who managed it all.

The first thing I did when I got home was continue to the back of the house, gathering some wood pieces from our neat and bountiful pile. The fire would be dying down from lunchtime, and it would be about time to feed it.

I put on an apron—not that any ash or soot would show on my gloomy attire. The fire would crackle and fill the house with the scent of smoked hickory. I made sure to put on hardwood so that it would last a bit longer. I used the heat to boil a kettle, pouring myself some tea before I started on the chores for the afternoon.

Most of the girls did some form of work throughout the day. Some worked at the hospital with Edith, while others brought their own trades.

Rebecca worked at her parents' butchery. Mary was a seamstress; Cordelia was a furrier and dressmaker; and Adeline was a baker. Whatever we needed, it could be provided by the women of our Nest, be they Vipera or Host. We took care of each other, which was a nice change from fending for ourselves. We were all bound by the mission of making the most out of ourselves and giving to the world the best that we could.

I started by making a midday meal while the fire was still alive. I used the heat to prepare some leftover bread so we could make sandwiches. I ate one myself so that I did not need to stop until supper for a break. I was behaving well by staying away from liquor until after dusk, but I suppose that urge was suppressed by the multitude of cigarettes throughout the day on top of my other homemade injections.

"Rebecca," I called to the dark-haired woman in the living room, "can you spare us three geese for Christmas from your father's shop? I can give you money in advance."

"Yes! Let me know when you would like them, and I can take the order." She smiled as she sat down to eat her spread with her peers.

"Cordelia!" I caught her as she came down the stairs. I met her at the railing. "I have some pelts—do you have an estimate for me? I would like to have them worked for Christmas for Phoebe. I'm thinking mittens."

"I don't mind doing it for you without a cost. I already feed on your dime," she laughed.

"Ah, just give me a number, and I will make it work," I said as I passed her.

The next chore was to groom the horses and turn them out. I enjoyed the task, even though it smelled unpleasant in the barn, and I always found myself coated in dust from all the brushing. I did love my steed, my handsome Horse, and his pretty mare, Duchess.

Their bodies were full muscle and tall, and even with my height, I had to reach for some spots when grooming. Noble animals, they were. Doing whatever we told them without question. In return, we fed them and gave them shelter. Though sometimes I found myself napping with them in their stalls when they would lay down in the hay. They were so warm and charmingly absent-minded; it was hard to resist snuggling such a beast.

I turned them out to the small paddock after grooming. The two horses loved to watch and run along the fence when other carriages would pass along the road. Phoebe's and my horses were inseparable, always grazing next to each other. Sometimes Duchess would nip at Horse if he was not paying enough attention to her. It was humorous watching their innocent interactions.

As I leaned against the paddock fence, a presence settled beside me.

"They aren't making any trouble, are they?" Phoebe crossed her arms over the wooden rail.

"Not much, though they are enjoying the snow now that their fur has grown out. I don't recognize my own horse; it seems he always turns a new color with his overgrown coat," I laughed.

We watched the trees rustle behind the paddock and our beasts running along the powdery expanse.

"How is the progress with the Guild on the east side?" she asked. "I know you had plans to go in a few days. *Spaulding Club,* was it?"

"Yes, we had received the official invite. I don't know who is coming with me. I haven't posted it to our board yet."

"Just . . . be careful," she stressed. "You know how I feel about these club types. Feels unnatural."

"Everything here is unnatural. It is a new world, a new order. Give it a chance, I heard they have good reserves."

"Take some Vipera with you, please." She sighed, her breath frozen in the air as she watched the horses. The snowfall made her look even more vibrant. Her hair was like fire against the white landscape.

"I will take Edith." I glanced at her. "She's been wanting to come out for more hunts lately. I'm glad she is getting less squeamish. We will be all right. At this rate, we may be able to afford a new rooming situation."

"That would be nice." Phoebe rested her chin on her arms. "And what of you? Will we share a flat? A home? Or will you be bored of living with me?"

"I could never be bored of you." I wrapped my arm around her shoulder. "We are best friends, sisters. We stick together *always*."

"Yes, sisters," she whispered, looking down at the frosted tallgrass that was frozen in place along the wooden fence.

"Morbs?" I asked her, as she had done to me many times before.

"Morbs." She rested her head on my shoulder. I could feel she was in some sort of state; it did not take any extra human senses to see it. I hoped I could make it better. I blamed the dreary weather most of all.

AS THE NIGHT GREW cooler, the house only became warmer. The girls filed home, one by one. We gathered for our nightly routine, keeping mostly to the living room next to the kitchen. Tonight's meal was pork and potato stew.

Most of the night was spent socializing, though I did not mind this type of chatter. We discussed our days, town gossip, or other happenings. I mainly listened instead of participating.

There were two parallel couches facing each other in front of the fire. Several girls sat on the couches, and many sat on the rug on the floor to share the small table. I was brushing Adeline's hair as she sat on the floor between my legs, with other girls performing similar tasks as we got ready for our nighttime routine.

This situation was all new to me a few years ago. I had never had a meaningful relationship with women outside of Phoebe. I did not have a mother to look up to, and most of my professional career was among men who did not think I belonged. For so long, I thought female friendships were mostly useless, but that may have been the influence of the lack of women in my life. I suppose that is what happens when you are raised by a callous single father who was clueless to social expectations.

It was nice to take care of people, and for them to care back. There was an unspoken love and commitment to each other that was more powerful than any bond I could imagine.

One thing did not change—the need to protect them from the world.

It was hard to believe that someone like me deserved the love they had all shown me these past few years.

As my gaze passed over the faces of chattering peers, my eyes landed on Phoebe, who had been staring. When our gazes met, she glanced away. Even in the dim light, I could see the blush on her cheeks. It brought a smile to my face.

I could not imagine a more perfect moment. Surrounded by those whom I loved and who loved me fiercely back. No matter the season, my girls would be by my side. There was no need to feel alone, ever.

XIV

The Creature

EVEN IN THE EARLIEST hours of the morning, that blond-haired sprite was still in the bar of the hotel. At this point, I knew when the nymph's supposed night shift started and ended. It was from nine o'clock at night to two in the morning, typically, leaving time for her to travel home and back, of course. It was silly to hide something as primal as hunting for food from her Nest, though I supposed I did not fully understand the dynamics at play.

"If you keep showing up, I may start to think you're looking forward to seeing me." I slid onto the barstool next to her.

"Sometimes it is easier to talk to a foreigner than a local." She shrugged.

"Here for another round on me? Or will you actually be hunting this time?" I asked her, the tender already pouring my usual request.

"You ask an awful lot of questions."

"Well, I am a visitor, after all! It is important to know the places you visit. I wouldn't want to insult anyone." I smiled sarcastically.

"You may be wiser than I thought, then," she replied disdainfully. "You should be more subtle with the interest of my Nest. You are becoming quite suspicious."

"I am curious."

"But how do I know that you pursue in good faith?" Her brows knit together.

A smirk crawled across my face. "Perhaps I pursue in better faith than you expect."

"Possibly." She shrugged, pausing to sip on my glass. "Though I suspect it is not unrelated to your lover, or whoever you were celebrating before."

"What if it is?"

"Then, maybe I am inclined to help, if you answer some questions."

"I'm as open as the Bible," I smirked. "I swear it."

What a sweet sense of trust she held in strangers. It was odd, but I supposed she may not have had any reason to mistrust. Alina was talented in that way, sheltering those closest to her. I would not hurt dear Edith, but she was perfect for purging information. The best part was that I did not even have to torture her.

"You are looking for her," Edith stated.

"Who?"

"Your lover."

"What makes you say that?"

"You are interested in the Nest. I suppose you were celebrating finding her when I first met you."

"I suspect many things, though it is possible she is under your roof."

"What makes you so sure she wants to be found?"

"She doesn't."

"Then why chase her?"

"Because I made a mistake. I want to fix it."

"What makes you so sure she will forgive you?" She raised a fine brow.

"She will. I know she will."

"Silas, we have another correspondence—" Luka stumbled next to me at the bar on my opposite side. He froze as soon as he saw Edith. "Am I interrupting?"

"No, actually. Edith was about to tell us about her Nest." I smiled, looking back toward her.

She stared at Luka quite intensely. If I didn't know better, she appeared quite bashful. She reminded me of how my sister would blush when she was embarrassed. The small, reserved creature did not seem to like the extra company.

"Oh?" Luka walked over and sat on her other side. "Maybe I came at the right time."

"I am not going to share anything with your friend here." Edith glared.

"Why not? Is he not to your taste?" I teased. "Is it the scars? He does look a bit less like a sissy with them."

"Rich coming from a blond man," Luka laughed. "Recessive at best."

"Thank you for the commentary." I rolled my eyes, just for them to land on Edith again. "He is employed by me, and he is only here to help, despite his attitude."

She shifted in place before glancing between us. "Well, what would you like to know?"

"The Dam of the Nest. The one you were so afraid to mention." I reclined back in my seat. "I'd love to hear more. I've never heard of a woman being the sole head of a Nest."

"Alina." She withheld the last name from us, even though I only needed a first.

"Tell me about her," I urged her.

Luka shot a glance at me before looking at Edith.

"She isn't like other heads; she is a Host," she explained. "She takes care of us like her own. She even lets us feed off her if there is no one available to take on the chore."

"Who does she feed?" The tension was building in my jaw, but it rippled through my body like electricity buzzing at my nerves.

"Myself and another girl, sometimes patrons," she answered. "Alina and the other girl both founded the Nest."

"How many are in your Nest?" Luka asked.

Edith left his question unanswered.

"Fine," he grumbled, slouching against the countertop.

"How did you *lose* your lover?" she pressed, watching me carefully in anticipation for more clarity on my intentions.

"I tried to leave messages, but they, apparently, were not delivered."

"How do I know you're not estranged?"

"I suppose you have no way of really knowing."

"Does she want to be found?"

I straightened my posture, adjusting the buttons of my jacket. The words bothered me, but I couldn't find an argument against them.

"Why would anyone allow a Host to be in charge of their livelihood?" I scoffed. "Humans don't hold any real power. What are you afraid of? Why must you hide your nature and cower at the mention of your Dam's name?"

"That is where you are wrong." Edith's voice became stern in warning. "I have seen her relieve men of their limbs in as many ways as you can think of, always creating new ways to drain them."

"Drain them?"

"Our blood, venom, even saliva . . . She turns them into miracle cures or a quick death."

Luka and I exchanged glances.

"Where is your next hunt?" I resurfaced from my thoughts before I could drift too far.

"Tomorrow. A Nest we have never been to before. They call it *Spaulding.*"

"You seem comfortable telling me about it. Why?"

"Because it took months for us to gain their trust enough to let us attend. I doubt they would permit you. She had been negotiating with the Sire since he was not very keen on following any conduct rules in order to get Hosts in attendance."

I nodded as if her answers were enough. I stood leisurely, and she mirrored the movement. "I think that brings our little meeting to an end for now."

"You haven't told me who it is you're looking for."

"Maybe the next time we meet, I will have found her." I grinned. The most harrowing part was the way she seemed enamored with Alina's infamy. It seemed this time she was respected for what she did. It was important to find out how many were under her influence if we were to take over her Nest—though I was hoping to convince her, violently if needed. It was clear she had more to lose this time around. I would only expect an extreme reaction in response to any threat.

"Silas." Luka gave me a warning look as he followed me. "I know what you're thinking—"

"No, you don't."

"We will be outnumbered."

"No, Luka. These are sensible people. We only need to put a blade to one's throat, and Alina will fold; they all will. We could have an army of Hosts with one threat. She would not risk her delicate little flower garden."

"How do you know they will be daisies and not thistles?"

"Alina is the only thistle."

"How do you know Edith will not tell her about your questions?"

"Because Edith is not supposed to be here in the first place. You should have seen the way she checked over her shoulder like my dear shadow would be summoned by the simple utterance of her name." I smirked. "Oh, this is going to be such fun for us."

I MISSED OUR TIME together, even the stolen moments when she did not know I was there.

Alina did not come to her apothecary until seven o'clock. The building was a dusty red brick with some windows above the shop, indicating a residence of sorts. I was curious to see if her setup was more or less the same as the old one. She was sentimental for those types of details, a creature of habit, so I could expect there to be a torture chamber attached.

The only new thing was that she arrived later than expected. She used to wake at dawn, but now that she lived with my sister, they did not need to wake so early to see each other.

They arrived together that morning. It was quite amusing seeing my sister dressed like a common genteel. Despite the cheaper fabric and more practical working design, she still managed to make it *pink*.

Alina disappeared deep within the shop while Phoebe set up in the front. The glow of the shop contrasted against the sooty atmosphere. My favorite part about winter was how dark it was in the mornings. It made the surroundings more cozy, making people appreciate any light they had. The magic of the yuletide season.

The room above glowed faintly. I could see the shadow slipping about. Her shadow settled at a working desk in front of the window that was out of my view, but I could tell she was keeping herself busy.

It was no secret she was still studying Vipera, but I wondered how successful she had been in her endeavors. Her inexperienced poisoning attempt had maimed Luka already; it was valid to wonder if she had gotten any better at her craft.

I did not have to stand outside for long. Alina bid Phoebe farewell before leaving the shop after about three hours of work in her makeshift lab. She carried a basket as she left, though she did not take the horse.

I followed as she strode through the streets. Not too far was the general hospital. This must be when she visited the young Edith. I allowed a few minutes to pass before following her inside. The nurse at the front was busying herself with something.

"Hello." I approached the desk. "My wife forgot something. Could you tell me which way she went? She just came in."

"Upstairs to the left!" The nurse smiled, though she was perplexed.

"Bless you." I smirked and began making my way up the stairs.

Down the hall, I could only see openings to rooms, but I could hear her clear as day. Her voice was melodic but stern. It was rich like a perfume oil, intoxicating and easy to lose yourself in.

I leaned against the wall, just enough to hear her.

"You are using the dosage I recommended, correct?" Alina spoke.

"Yes, of course!" Edith said.

"All right." She took a deep breath. "Apologies, I'm paranoid about the corrupted. I wanted to make sure it was not us causing them."

What is this?

"I promise, it's not on my end, at least. It is hard to know where they are coming from."

"I'm worried about them getting too close to the Nest." Alina drew another breath before letting out a nervous laugh. "Is it so much to ask for an easy holiday season?"

"There is no such thing," Edith teased, "but it will be fine. I trust you and Phoebe will make it memorable like you always do."

"There are so many mouths to feed."

"We have made quite a bit since then. Selling the garments from our hunts, our collective dues to the Nest, money from the shop—what is there to worry about?"

"I suppose it is just general anxiety."

"Alina." Edith paused. "You are doing perfectly fine. They trust you, and they know you work hard for them. That is why we love you."

Alina did not reply, but she sighed. There was a long pause. I suppose they were hugging.

"I have to drop off my tools," Alina mentioned.

"I will see you at home then. Wait up for me for dinner?"

"Of course, I will wait for you."

I nearly forgot that I was not supposed to be there, disappearing down the hall at the cue of her footsteps.

I made it outside the hospital and turned around the corner of the building. Not long after, my shadow appeared. She was an intimidating figure now that I could see her better in the light. Her black wool dress and short cape around her shoulders made her look like she was there to collect the coins from the eyes of the deceased. How fitting that she hung around a hospital. I would not mind her being the last face I saw before passing on.

The rest of her day seemed to be her own time, as I doubt she went to the mortuary for errands. I wished I could go in to see what she was up to, but unfortunately, there were no windows to the brick building except at the entrance. All I could see was her slender figure disappearing into the depths of the establishment.

The last stop before she headed home was the blacksmith, where she dropped a bag off. I wanted to see so badly what tools she had that needed sharpening on such a regular basis that she had a blacksmith in her pocket, but I was sure I would find out soon enough on my own.

As if she wasn't interesting enough two years ago, she had seemingly formed weirder habits. The mortuary and blacksmith were new. She had a few more friends than I expected. How had she gathered so many in her Nest that she was worried about feeding them all at once?

My stalking for the day came to an end when I followed her home. I stopped on the road where the tree line ended and the field surrounding her home began. It was quaint and a bit dirty. I don't know how Phoebe was faring in these conditions.

There couldn't be many in the small place aside from her, Phoebe, and Edith. This would not be as hard as I anticipated if this was all she had.

XV

The Creature

 HE AMERICANS WERE CREATIVE. Feeding parlors disguised in the open as a gilded club. Where exclusion, secrecy, and scandal were expected—the perfect place to hide a Den in plain sight. Though this was nicer than any Den I'd ever seen.

The scenery was as impressive as any club in the city. The walls were covered in painted scenes of hunts and landscapes. There were many rooms to get lost in, with a bar poised in the corner. Guests filtered in and out of the rooms like blood in a heart chamber, the life of the party. It was less conservative than what I was used to, but I would not complain about that. It had the prose of a Nest with the energy of a Den. It was actually quite refreshing to have something so new, to witness it in the flesh.

At the head of the main room was a monstrous mantel, taller than any person. I would imagine they must need to use ladders to decorate it. Above it was a large mirror that reflected the shimmer of the chandelier that hung proudly from the crown molding of the ceiling. Not one corner of the room was left plain, and I would assume the same was true for the rest of the rooms.

Amid all the chatter, all the bustling, all the fine silhouettes flut-tering about like birds impressing their attentions upon each other, nothing could compare to my dearest shadow among the flames.

Alina's elegant fingers swept along the face of a girl, our little sprite, Edith. Her lean arms were bare aside from gloves since her dress did not possess sleeves. The neckline dipped enough to reveal the slight curvature of breasts, held gently by the pressure of her corset. Her form was more stunning than I remembered. She had lost the sickly look she always had in the years she had hidden from me. Her shoulders and neck were more defined, and her skin held a healthy pallor instead of the ghostly shade I remembered so well. A vibrant blush adorned her cheeks and décolletage, though that could be from alcohol. Which was an odd observation considering she was not holding any glassware.

The movement of her lips made my teeth itch with every word uttered out of earshot. I wanted to devour them, bite right through. They were as soft as the expression she held.

Her eyes were so bright, so relaxed. Even in their coldness, they were capable of warmth when no one was looking, like a ghost that did not wish to be seen by the living, disappearing when they were just about to be perceived.

I could make myself known, but I wanted to savor her before she was relieved of her peace. I could only restrain myself for the length of one more drink.

Her fingers slipped over Edith's cheek again, and she gestured off somewhere that I could not see.

When Alina was left on her own, the sweet tenderness evap-orated like steam. Her expression was not displeased, nor angry, nor holding remotely any discernible emotion. She was stoic, focused, but not unlike behavior witnessed prior.

I remembered that her fixative behavior could make her quite disordered and clumsy, even careless at times.

This was not that type of fixation.

That coldness hardened her eyes like a permafrost. She was a predator through and through. Her blood might be red, but it was black at heart.

That dangerous look in her eye narrowed in on what she wanted, and she stalked toward it. Despite the hunger in her gaze, she moved with the grace of something otherworldly. I would not blame anyone who might be lured by her energy alone. It was dark, tempting, lethal. Everything about her made me want to drop to my knees and repent for the things that came to my mind. All the terrible, awful things I wanted to do to her.

A heat lit at my core when I realized she was *hunting*.

She approached another man, sliding him a cool smirk as her fingers found her way to his lapel, complimenting an emerald green handkerchief poking from the breast pocket.

Careful.

He blinked a few too many times, trying to convince himself that a mirage like her would be interested in a plain thing like him.

She will eat you alive.

Her demeanor reminded me of the movements of certain felines. Slow and calculated because she did not have to be quick to catch these fools. She only needed to be still, and they would fall to their knees before her. I would wager that they would knot their own nooses voluntarily if she said, *"Pretty please."*

I had to remind myself to breathe, so easy it was to forget such an insignificant thing in her presence.

While she could not have become more beautiful, she became more *terrifying*.

Alina smoothed her hand over the fabric of his jacket, whispering sweet nothings in his ear. I half expected her to bite it off.

The man lowered his face into her neck, flirtatiously dragging his exposed fangs over her skin, teasing the flesh with a pale pink line.

Her sultry smirk never reached her eyes. There was an unmistakable voraciousness, a narrowing-in on her next victim.

She was in the middle of making the poor boy blush when her lips stopped moving, and her eyes dazzled as she took in the gilded finery. I watched them slowly track across the sea of people. Her gaze cut across the room like a blade across a stone, sharpened by the time it landed on me, and suddenly there was no one but her and me.

Electricity shot through my spine and made my fangs twitch, like I was setting sights on something to be caught. Nature was taking over, and all I could think of was to *pounce*.

The tingling of blood filling my eyes made the colors alight, vibrancy bleeding throughout the scene, and replacing the colorblind binary.

In the moments we held each other's gazes, her expression twisted. I could see scenes flash before her eyes, those of every horror I put her through resurfacing, breaking through the ice like a hot pickaxe.

I don't know what was worse, the desire to see her run, or the fact that she was approaching, not helping to dampen the urges.

She was so polite in departing the conversation with the man she was toying with, moving through the crowd like she belonged, uprisen and proud. With every step she took toward me, the more my heart beat, faster and faster until I feared I would lose control.

She was close enough now to smell, to hear. Her eyes locked with mine. Everything around us was a blur, the blood flow to my vision making her vibrant as ever.

She stepped before me, her perfume overwhelming my senses. Black cherries and bitter almonds. I could get lost in it.

She placed a gloved hand on my shoulder, dragging it across my chest as she circled.

I followed her with my eyes, my hand reaching her waist as she returned to the front. I stepped, and we circled like an ouroboros, wondering when the tail ends.

She replaced her hand on my shoulder.

I took her forearm, extended it as my lips trailed over her wrist, then down her arm, until the coolness of her skin presented itself as the cloth of the opera glove ran out, and her chest pressed against mine.

The chill of her skin was almost unbearable, prickling at my nerves, sizzling like cold water over cast iron.

The flushed skin around her neck and her cheeks made the pulsing grow louder in my ears, in my chest. She began to pull her arm away, and I let my grip on her arm slip the silken opera glove off as she did so.

She was breathing rapidly; no matter how calmly she presented herself, the heaving of her breasts and her heart gave her away.

She leaned one way; I pulled her the other. A natural push and pull that turned chaos into a fluid, impetuous capriole. Her nails clawed at my clothes, desperate to pierce the skin beneath, a subtle violence that filled the heart with a gleeful fever, the very energy that made us move each other, forever locked in a deadly waltz.

Her nails retreated from my shoulders, but I held her closer before she could slip completely from me. Then, a sharp twinge in my side.

Upon looking down, I saw those beautiful, delicate fingers curled around the hilt of a small blade, buried intimately just beneath the surface of my skin.

"*Creature.*" Her voice was different, warm and stern, calm and deadly.

I relaxed into the knife, plunging it deeper. Like the pain itself was reassurance that it was all real, she didn't take her eyes off me.

I shook my head at her. "And here I thought you liked to watch while you prod and dissect, you vicious thing."

"I'm afraid that if I do, it may turn out to be some sort of dream," she said.

"Well." I pulled her closer by her waist, her skin tingling against mine from the flash of excitement. "Is it all that you hoped for?" I whispered in her ear.

She leaned close, angling the blade sharply upward, enough to make my lip twitch into a sneer before collecting myself. "Not as good as it would be if you were dead."

Just the sound of her voice made me hold on to her tighter, a subtle clicking chitter rising in my throat and reverberating down to my chest. "There it is. I've looked forward to hearing the venom in your voice once more."

A crease in her brow as she restrained herself from what she really wanted to say.

"Could you find it in you to put aside your anger?" I grazed my bottom lip against her ear as I spoke. Close enough to bite, but I refrained.

"I want nothing to do with you."

"That's a lie, I know you missed this."

"I am happy without you."

"Liar."

"I do not need you; men are plentiful."

"I am no man."

"*Creatures* are just as plentiful." She smirked.

"Have you found the company of many creatures, then?" I raised a scrutinous brow, studying her, undressing her in my mind already.

"It is none of your business who I have."

"Foolish of you to think such a thing, but I will forgive you."

"*You* are the one who should be seeking forgiveness."

"Should I? Will you make me?"

"You know I could."

"Then do it." My voice dropped lower as I hovered my lips over hers.

Alina was different. I would not call it maturity, but more like a fermentation of whatever she had been before. Her audacity was fascinating. Though she had never been truly afraid to begin with.

"No," she breathed, "I want nothing from you, not even remorse. I can have any man I want in this room, this city, and all the populations surrounding. *I don't need you.*"

"I do not care how many men have been inside you," I spoke through a clenched jaw, tangling my fingers in her hair low at the back of her head and forcing it back. "It only matters that your body knows who it truly belongs to."

"Using me like you always do?" she bit out.

I couldn't help but laugh. "Using? No, I am *reminding* you."

"Was there something worth remembering?"

"So stubborn." I tilted my head at her, but I admit I was salivating at the thought of putting her in her place.

I tightened my grip on her hair, and her hands flew to my chest to keep whatever distance she could.

Her pulse beat against my lips when they met her neck. Self-control was something I practiced often, but she made me forget every practice of such.

My other hand smoothed down her waist, then her lower back, holding her hips close to mine. Her scent was intoxicating enough to put me in a trance, fingers lingering along the seams of the dress she was wrapped in.

A thrum of satisfaction sounded deep in my chest, and I kissed down her neck before kissing lower down her chest as I dipped her backward.

"Tell me you don't want it," I breathed, looking up at her from between her breasts. Those cold eyes peered wide at me through her lashes.

"I despise you."

"That's not what I asked." I smirked, fingers digging into her hip.

"Your gestures mean nothing."

"That's not what I heard when you used to scream my name."

"Do you remember the *last* time I screamed at you, by chance?"

"How could I forget a single indignity that manifests on those soft lips?"

"*Undignified* certainly is an appropriate description."

"I would use the same description for yourself." I dragged my tongue between her breasts and back up to her neck.

"Alina?" A sheepish voice spoke.

Alina stiffened against me like a board, her eyes tracking over to the voice. If I didn't know better, I would say she was mortified.

"Oh," I practically purred. "Hello, *Edith*."

Alina's shoulders shrank with tension.

"Don't be rude," I scolded, jolting her by her hair and forcing her face to turn to Edith. "Is that how you treat your Nest? Not even a *hello*?"

"Edith, please . . . you have to go," Alina begged.

Edith's eyes were wide and unable to take themselves off the situation before her, frozen in horror.

"You look like you've seen a ghost." I managed an innocent, mocking tone, glancing at Alina. "I am getting déjà vu from the first time you laid eyes on me, *my love*," I teased.

"Alina—" Edith cupped her hands over her mouth and nose, like she was about to apologize.

I pressed my cheek against Alina's as I regarded Edith. "I should be thanking you for making this happen, Edith. I couldn't have found her without you!" I laughed. How delicious it all was.

"What . . . are you saying?" Alina growled.

"Do you want to tell her?"

Edith looked like she was about to crumple into tears. I could see the wetness forming in her eyes and a trembling lip. She escaped the question physically, disappearing back through the crowd. People were beginning to stare at the scene unfolding.

"She is quite cute, chatty as well," I whispered, gently nipping at her cheek before she began to struggle. "Ah-ah! I am not finished with you."

"Let me go," she gasped, shoving against my chest.

"Never again." I took in a deep breath, holding her tightly. "Though, in the spirit of old times, I will give you one more night of peace."

And despite the tension, I let her go.

She stumbled back, wasting no time slipping away from me, disappearing through the crowds of mingling bodies.

I grasped the knife in my side, yanking it out with one swift pull, the black blood dribbling onto the marble tiles. I shook my head, wiping both sides of the blade on my jacket.

Until next time, my dearest shadow.

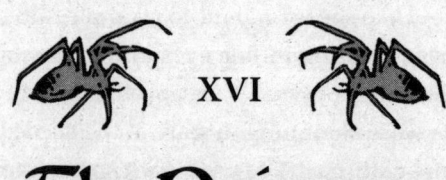

XVI

The Poisoner

WHILE NORMALLY OUR NIGHTTIME rituals were my favorite, tonight, I could not bring myself to enjoy any of them.

Even pleasant aspects of my day were stained with overarching guilt that slowly tightened around my organs until I could not bring myself to eat, to breathe, to think. The journey home was like a march off a cliff, colored by the dread of having to pretend all was well. The time meant for winding down would become a performance once again.

The entire household was in the living room. Most of us huddled by the fire and helped each other get ready for bed. I mindlessly brushed through Phoebe's hair as she sat next to me on the couch. My lip had taken abuse throughout the day from chewing it, itching to find any loose vials of venom once everyone was asleep.

While in the past my creature would not bother me with others around, it seemed he had outgrown that reservation based on last night's events. Uneasy was the only way I could describe how the evolution of his habits made me.

I thought my words were enough to sever those ties years ago, but I was clearly wrong. He was obsessed. If he truly thought he had any ownership over me, of course he would come looking. I should have been more careful.

My only wish was for the mistakes of my past to avoid the Nest. Knowing what he was capable of, especially when I ignored him, made the discomfort weigh inside me like steam in a kettle.

I did not tell anyone what happened, not even Phoebe. Edith did not come home.

Maybe it was out of shame that I kept it from them, though I planned to tell them at a more suitable time. Though it was never a good time for bad news, I would rather bear it alone. Just until I could get the situation under control.

The images from the other night haunted my subconscious. In some ways, it was like a mere dream. The all too familiar feeling of trepidation when my body was in his grip, the bruises that formed when his fingers dug into my skin, the sensation of—

None of that. Banish it from your mind.

"Alina?"

Phoebe was looking at me, as if she had asked me something already.

"What?" I mumbled. "I must have drifted; what did you say?"

"You are quiet. Are you well? You look paler than usual."

"Yes, I am well. Thrown off by the poor hunting."

"You are sure?"

"Positive."

"Could you grab an extra blanket from upstairs for me?"

"Of course." I nodded, shifting off the couch.

The middle few stairs made a sharp squeak as I put my weight on them during my trudge up the stairs. The light leached from the atmosphere the farther I ventured into the house, the rooms retaining a blue hue from the cool atmosphere outside.

The room Phoebe and I shared was no more gloomy than the others. I sat alone on the bed and gathered the folded blanket on my lap. There were little balls of lint forming from the many uses. I remembered when Adeline made it for us after she was given a loom. It was such a small gesture, but something about a handmade gift made me feel such hominess.

The powder outside the window fluttered and stuck to the glass, a rustling sound scratching as the wind picked up.

The room was a special kind of peaceful. A type of bliss reserved only for the somber.

I laid on the bed and stared at the ceiling.

No cracks, only a small wet stain.

My heart was heavy, like it beat slowly and hard. It was like when I breathed, I sank deeper into a slow-sinking mud. The same feeling I gleefully ignored when I took my morning dosage and went through with my day. There was no time to feel such things when so many depended on me to have my head on straight. I could only close my eyes and hope to let go.

As my mind danced between my dreams and the room around me, the sound of a summer cicada itched at my consciousness.

I opened my eyes; the room was empty.

Then, again, but with footsteps.

I turned my head to look at my bedroom door. The darkness produced the shape of a railing, the doors across the hall, a small hallway table with withered flowers forgotten in a vase. The glow of the downstairs light creeping, just barely presenting at the top of the stairs.

Footsteps at the end of the hallway, and a stronger chittering like the clicking was just warming up.

My heart leapt as fast as I stood. My fists gripped the sheets of the bed, as if to steady me. Should I run? The stairs were there. But how far were they from that point? They could be right outside the door, just out of sight.

I stood, walking heel to toe to prevent much distress to the creaky wood.

Once at the doorframe, I savored my last breath and stepped out into the dark. In my peripheral vision, I saw the light from downstairs, but also a new shadow in my home.

At the end of the hallway was a window, blocked by a lean frame and the flash of eyes.

All I could hear was the rush of blood in my ears before the sound of a click, a flame producing, and the cherrying of a cigarette. The silhouette leaned against the window, head tilted back to release a steady trail of smoke.

What will you do?

I was still, knowing that any movement might provoke him. He could kill me right here, and I suspect I wouldn't be found until everyone turned in for bed, if he was kind enough to leave the body for them.

His hand snapped out, and an object flashed.

I caught it in the air with only a distracted glance. He was still there as my hand stayed raised, something sharp poking my palm. No movement from the shadow, just the brightening and dimming of an ember. My hand lowered slowly; it was a handkerchief.

Carefully, without peeling my eyes from him just yet, I opened the silken emerald folds to expose one long, porcelain fang placed in the middle.

I had seen this before; the owner of both fang and fabric. I stepped back, faltering on the first step.

Suddenly, a hand choked me with my own shirt collar. I grasped at his wrist—out of fear or preservation, I did not know which.

Only then did I see Silas's face.

That alone was enough to light my rage.

A scream from the ground floor and the clamoring of chaos sent me over. I dug my nails into his wrist and flung my weight backward, the two of us tumbling down and smacking against the wall before the last couple of steps.

He landed flat on his back, and I straddled his waist, my knuckle digging into his face twice before he bit down on my wrist.

I flung myself back, shrieking as his teeth dug into the skin, dragging a slash in my wrist as I pulled away. He lunged at me, but before he could grab anything more than my skirt, he slumped forward into my lap after a blow from behind.

Phoebe held the butt of her rifle up; a bit of black blood smeared on it from his head.

We caught our breaths, choking back every exhausted breath.

WE USED THE SNOW from outside to ice our wounds. No one was seriously hurt. I bore the worst of it. I wrapped my arm, the slash no longer bleeding, but the skin slightly raised.

Some of the girls huddled upstairs. Mary was helping to ice any bruises. Phoebe was downstairs dealing with the situation as best she could.

Clamoring ensued from downstairs, then escalated into shouting.

Rebecca knocked on the doorframe of my room, everyone—including myself—looking to her. She jolted her head in the direction of the stairs, holding out the axe hilt first.

I took a deep breath, rubbing my arm before standing. I took the axe from her and descended.

I couldn't hear much of the commotion through the sudden rise in heart rhythm drumming in my ears. More shouting, then a crashing of metal.

Within the living room, my long-overdue nightmare.

The girls crowded, shifting anxiously

"Let me through." I pushed a shoulder, then another, before the wall of the crowd opened up.

My two lives had finally collided, in all the worst ways.

Silas looked like a landmine had gone off beside him in expression alone, never mind the battering from the marks on his face. It was when I stepped into the room that his horrified expression dampened, as if he thought I would not see through his shock.

How embarrassing. For him, that is.

I finally looked beside him.

My heart slowed, and a chill ran through me faster than my blood drained, pooling into my legs to save me from the shock.

Kneeling beside Silas, just as battered, was *Luka Novikov.*

My eyes tracked Phoebe, who was standing in front of them. She held the barrel of a sawed-off shotgun a meter from Silas's face.

"Guests?" I approached slowly, cautiously. The girls who were not actively pointing weapons at them stepped back, giving us space to work.

Phoebe never took her eyes off Silas when she asked me, "Are you sure you want to be here?"

"Why wouldn't I?"

"You don't have to if you feel—"

"I *feel* like this is something I should be here for."

She stepped back after a moment's beat.

I leered at the two *dogs* before me. Rebecca had a Winchester to the back of their heads.

"The position suits you." I crooked my head at Silas.

"Only for you," he smirked.

I ignored his comment for the moment, stepping to the side to look down at Luka. I used the blunt end of my axe to lift his chin.

I reached out to run my nail over the scar on his face.

"*Careful*," Luka warned, those dark eyes unwavering. "I would hate to remind you that I bite."

"Likewise." I grinned, lifting his chin higher. "I always wondered what became of you. I assumed by the smell of burning flesh that you would have perished. I never expected it would leave such lovely branding if you survived."

Luka's expression only became more playful as I spoke, and he leaned into my touch. "If we're speaking of trauma—"

A crisp crack sounded when the back of my hand met Luka's face.

Luka flinched but simply glared at Silas.

"How sweet. When did the two of you become fellows?" I teased, stepping back to get a good look at them both.

"Long story," Silas said.

"Must be some tale. I'd be interested to know how leading my captor to me was considered a good idea in your mind."

"Well, if you hadn't run off, you would have seen the lovely gesture." Silas grinned.

"A lovely gesture would have been to have finished the job." I rolled the axe in my palm. "But you're not really one to see anything through, I suppose."

"I guess we are both terrible at our jobs."

"Do you want to test that theory? A taste test of something new?"

"Not after what it did to the Nest." Silas spoke slowly, as if he hoped the words would hook into me. "I thought you'd appreciate them gone after that whole ordeal."

"Gone? What do you mean?" Phoebe spoke from behind me.

"Ah, my sister has decided to speak to me! Hello, Phoebe, how have you been?" he teased her. "I heard you were married! Who is the lucky *man*?"

"Silas," she warned, "what do you mean by *gone*?"

"Exactly how it sounds. I searched high and low for you two doves, though the bodies really did end up getting in the way."

I could see thoughts blooming in real time before Phoebe grew pale.

"What are you saying?" I pressed.

"There is no more London Nest." Silas shrugged.

I glanced at Luka, but he didn't even look in our direction. The weight of the situation was beginning to dawn on me. It was bad if Luka had nothing to say.

"Rebecca," I spoke, looking toward the dark-haired woman, but I did not need to ask for her to understand what I wanted her to get.

"Usually when one grants such a favor, you say *thank you*." Silas frowned.

Rebecca returned with an amber glass bottle.

For once, neither of the men spoke.

There was a needle as long as the glass inside. I drew it out slowly and watched as it glistened in the fire's light. The floor creaked as I approached our captives.

"Here is what will happen now," I began.

Silas's eyes were focused on the needle in confusion, but Luka knew exactly what it was.

"The both of you are going to end your little excursion early. You will take the next train out of Buffalo back to whatever ring of hell you crawled from, and you will not return." I spoke slowly to make sure the words were soaking through their heads. "Alternatively, if you do decide to return, I will make you subjects. I will tie you in knots, and you will live out your life in the lab. You will only exist for me to drain you of almost every fluid you can produce, only kept alive enough to not expire." I stepped in front of Luka again, "If you are lucky, I will kill you. But it will not maim you, it will grant you a slow and painful death. You remember the sensation well, I suspect, right, *Luka*?"

There was such malice in his glare I could practically taste it.

I hovered the needle above his scar, then slowly lingered to the other side of his face, only a hair's distance from touching his unscarred skin. His jaw twitched from my insinuation, and it brought the most joyous smile to my face.

"We have an understanding then?" I stood straight once more. "Send them on their way."

As I turned to exit the living room, someone spoke.

"I have a proposal," Silas blurted. "A modest one."

The sigh from my lungs was no doubt audible. It was harder than it looked, keeping my temper. Reluctantly, I turned back to face the room. I gestured for him to continue before returning my hand to the hilt of the axe.

"You are having a problem with corrupted, right? They are venturing closer to your Nest," he stated.

My shoulders stiffened as other curious eyes peered at me after hearing his declaration.

I lifted my chin stubbornly. "There is no problem."

"You are vulnerable." He stood. Luka shot him a warning glare, sharper than any of the weapons pointed at them, making him hold his hands up in an attempt to be innocuous. "If you cannot handle corrupted, how will you handle organized, sane Vipera?"

"We are handling it fine on our own."

"I heard you have a union of sorts, for the Hosts." He took a step forward. "It is quite admirable, adorable that you think that will last longer as the population of this city grows."

"It works perfectly fine."

"What happens when they are sick of your rules? They will drag each one of you out of this house and lock you in a glorified cage. And you, Alina? Oh, they will have the most fun with you, especially if you anger them more than you already do."

"They respect me."

"They *despise* you," he hissed. "You are getting in the way, and they will not hesitate to take you out when they tire."

Whispers bounced around the room between the girls, and some even lowered their weapons, too distracted by the newly implanted fear.

"That will not happen." I glanced from the crowd to him.

"Maybe." Silas shrugged. "What do I know? I've only over-thrown one Nest. I guess I am an amateur when it comes to these messy politics. Maybe I know nothing at all," he trilled innocently.

"Why are you here?" I glared.

He slowly stepped toward me, both of us aware of the many eyes watching our exchange. Two predators, neck and neck.

"I want you to join me."

"No."

"You have not heard the terms."

"I do not need to hear them to know that it will not be fair."

"Hear them anyway; then you can decide on your own. We will give you a week." Silas and I were toe to toe. His eyes flickered with a sadistic glint, looking to light me like dry wool.

The air in the room was thin, dry. The situation manifested itself in a way I could feel.

"Tell me plainly, what do you want?" I lowered my voice, uncomfortable with so many eyes on us, waiting on every word we exchanged.

"My Nest is the most powerful in New York City. An estate that covers an entire city block," he explained, side-eyeing the crowd to gauge reactions. Subdued mumbles traded around the room. Satisfied with the chatter, his eyes rested back on me.

"You want us to be part of it." It was a labor to keep my emotions linear, at least in appearance. I wouldn't let him have the satisfaction of watching me sweat over it.

"Yes. We have some of the most talented Vipera in the new world. Our Nest is not bound by class, family connections, or bloodline. Unfortunately, with that, we also do not have Hosts, as they are limited in the city."

"There is more, though," I stated.

"Your girls would not just live comfortably, they would live in luxury."

More mutters from the peanut gallery, though they seemed to believe his deceptive words. There was no way that he was offering this without an *ask*.

"What is the catch?"

"They would be protected far better than any reserves or palace," he continued.

"What are you not telling me?"

"The estate is five and a half stories, the park can be seen from the windows facing north and west—"

"What do you want from me?" My voice was strained.

"—the finest clothes, imported food, allowances, anything."

"*Silas.*"

"Marry me."

Everyone watched in silence. I could hear every crack of embers in the fireplace and every loose floorboard creak. Whispers, loud in the stillness.

"No." I managed the first word on my mind.

"I do not need an answer immediately. Think on it, for the sake of your establishment."

"I would be your prisoner."

"Whether you are my pet or my prisoner is up to you."

"Leave."

"Alina—"

"I said *leave!*" I screamed, the axe whistling faintly as I swung it through the air.

Silas leaned back with his hands clasped behind his back, a victorious grin crawling across his face at the inflection. He took a step back.

"One week," he warned, his eyes darkening. "You have one week to decide."

"Leave before I *decide* which way I want to *disembowel* you," I sneered.

He let out a low whistle in faux surprise. "Sharp as ever," he chuckled, gesturing for Luka to get up. "I would advise that you save your energy."

I shoved past the girls, storming from the room before I could hear him say anything else. I would explode from rage if he spoke another word. How bold he was to try and bend my will. I might have considered the deal if he had not added that insulting term. It was clear from the beginning that he only meant to possess. This was nothing but a game to him.

Nothing had changed.

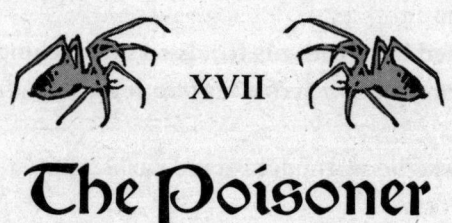

XVII

The Poisoner

THE SHOP BELL RANG as I gathered some bottles into my basket for home delivery.

"We are closed this morning; come back at midday," I called out.

"Alina?" Edith spoke ever so softly.

I glanced up at her, my eyes narrowed. She shifted in the doorway, looking like she might cry.

"What is it?"

"I wanted to explain, to apologize."

"I have very few rules, Edith. Could you not manage to follow just *one*?" I pulled on my coat before hooking my arm through the basket handle.

"I know, I know!" she whimpered, rushing to the counter as if eager to convince me.

"What did you tell him?"

"Nothing! A little about the union, the landscape—but I *never* told him where the Nest was!" She followed at my heel as we approached the door.

"What did *he* tell *you*?"

"He said he was looking for a woman—I would not have spoken with him if I knew it was you they were looking for." Her eyes were welling up with tears. "I felt so terrible for him. He said he was looking for his lost love and I . . . I . . ."

"I understand." I stopped at the doorway.

Her brows shot up in relief. "You do?"

"Yes, he is rather manipulative and violent; I do not blame you for believing his lies." I pulled on my gloves and took a quick glance outside. "But—" I paused and turned to her, "this is why I have a rule about not talking to men about the Nest. It's easy to be fooled by those who promise good intentions. You cannot trust words alone."

"It won't happen again." She was pitiful, so weak as she pleaded with me. I could barely stand to look at her.

"I know; I trust you learned." I placed my hand on her shoulder to reassure her. "We must solve this problem first. Do not let them on the grounds."

"Yes, I heard about last night."

The muscle in my jaw twitched from the tension. "Oh, did you now?"

"Will you take his deal?"

"No."

She averted her gaze quickly to the floor.

"Go rest. You have a long shift tonight," I told her, my hand falling from her face before leaving the shop. "Maybe pick up extra hours, just in case."

Girls like her irritated me at times, but I must remember that not every woman is as strong or as experienced in the dealings of men. She would learn once she outgrew that Christian hope that everyone was good at their core. It was paramount that she realize that not everyone was there for her benefit.

Midday errands were my favorite. They were the most relaxing, even though it was becoming increasingly difficult to enjoy the simple things. It was like trying to eat an apple that kept turning to ash in my mouth.

My mind was still reeling from the night before. I wished so badly that it was a dream. The girls were tiptoeing around me, unsure of what they witnessed. His words had frightened them successfully.

He was ruining *everything*.

In my mindless state, my shoulder collided with someone in the walkway, and I dropped my basket.

"Oh, apologies—" I muttered as we crouched down to gather the small bottles from the snow. My hand came in contact with a hand clad in black leather.

Speak of the devil.

"Watch where you are going," I growled.

"Good morning, my lethal flower. What happened to pleasant greetings?" Silas laughed.

"That is reserved for decent people, not animals." I immediately turned back on my path along the walkway.

"What have you saved for an animal like me then?" He hooked his arm with mine. "Hopefully something involving less clothing?"

"Get off me."

"Have you thought about my deal?" His arm tightened around mine.

"Absolutely not. I wouldn't entertain such a joke."

"What happened to the art of bartering?" He frowned.

"It's called strong-arming."

"Well, a barter usually starts with an *offer*, then you *counter-*offer, then I counter—"

"You don't have to explain bartering to me."

"Oh, I wasn't sure, since you haven't countered yet."

"All right." I stopped in my path to face him. "New terms. No marriage, you adopt the rules of my Nest, and you fund everything."

"Marriage is back on the table, and I will accept all of the latter."

"Do not insult me."

"It should be flattering, as you are quite unpleasant. You're lucky I find it endearing."

"I am happy being a spinster, thank you very much."

"What are the rules of your Nest?" he asked as we continued along the path into the heart of town.

"Autonomy, sustainability, utilitarianism," I droned.

"I would like to know a bit more about your little terms before I add them to our barter."

"You are a smart man, Mr. Forbes. I know you understand those words quite well," I started. "All that matters is the Nest's well-being."

"The community?"

"Yes, like making distasteful men disappear."

"Ah, still on that same old grift?"

"It has changed."

"How so?"

"Turns out I can squeeze a small amount of good out of things like you. Medicine and poison."

"I would love to dig inside that mind of yours someday." Silas gave me a look that might be something like amusement. "I can accept those additions. But my initial term stays intact."

"Well, I have a week to say no."

"Which means you have a week to decide whether you prefer diamonds, rubies, or emeralds."

"Whichever strains your wallet more," I murmured. "The answer is still no, even if you brought me a jewel the size of my head."

We stopped by the butcher's. It was my turn to pick up fresh ingredients for dinner, as we had run out of meat. We still had more than enough potatoes and jarred items for a stew.

"Alina!" The stout man from behind the counter called, though he eyed Silas as if he were surprised at the company. I did not blame him; usually, my errands were my only alone time. Unfortunately for me, today I had company. "What will it be? The usual?"

"Yes, eight pounds," I replied.

The butcher acknowledged my request with a simple nod, though he was already reaching for the cuts I usually chose. My usual was always an economic cut of beef so that we could make three days' worth of leftovers for the girls.

"Why do you get such cheap cuts?" Silas furrowed his brows.

"How else do you feed a large group?"

"Hopefully with something higher quality. Has the poison business been slow?" He teased me.

"Hush," I muttered as the butcher returned with the neatly wrapped cuts in a brown paper secured with twine.

"I have not kept up with the current market for pharmaceuticals; has it been treating you well since arriving?" Silas asked as I finished paying and receiving my change.

"Booming, actually. For my shop, at least," I said as we departed.

"Is there such a demand for your miracle elixirs?"

"Of course."

"Is that your only income?"

"None of your business."

"Do you collect dues from those in the house? Are there others outside of the house?"

"Yes, all Hosts of the town are part of our union. Don't go getting any ideas, I've already warned them about you."

"How does that work? Are they really desperate enough to pay loose Hosts?"

"They have to respect our autonomy, as the Host chooses who feeds. The Host gets paid for each feeding. There must be no damage to our bodies, they have to provide food for Hosts, and lastly, they must have a doctor on site," I explained.

"Seems like a lot of regulation."

"It is no longer a free-for-all. We are adding civility and decency."

"And do you get paid to be the madam?" He smirked.

"No, I do not take any commission."

"Does this mean you've taken other feeding partners?"

"Occasionally," I answered, adding, "You ask too many questions."

"I am simply protecting my investment."

My stride was interrupted when he dragged me off the pavement into the alley between shops. His chest pressed against mine as my back met the hard brick wall. The heat emanating from him would make me believe he was hiding hot coals under his coat.

"I am not property," I scolded.

"That is not what I said."

"You might as well have."

"You are just as bitter as I remember, like grapefruit." He cupped my face in his gloved hand, our noses a mere inch from each other.

"You are stubborn, like a coffin nail." I shifted in his grasp, turning my face from him to look toward the walkway. People passed the alley, unaware of us in the shadows.

"So macabre this early in the day?" He tugged my face toward him again.

The light from the alleyway entrance barely crept through, making it especially cold with the snowdrift padding the ground. It was difficult to look at him. So many memories of these eyes were tainted.

His pupils constricted when I did not speak. Many words could have been traded between us that were surely thought, but none dared manifest into even the slightest utterance.

We were still for several moments, all of which felt stolen. The only evidence that we were alive was the frozen vapors, indicating that we were breathing.

He lowered his lips to mine. They were as warm as I remembered, possibly hotter now that we were in the cold. His hand slipped to my lower back to hold me. His thumb smoothed along my cheek. Between the wall and him, I think I had a better chance of falling through the brick. He did not seem keen on letting me go.

His lips braced against mine, deeper, like he was finally feasting after a famine.

"Stop," I breathed.

"I cannot bring myself to." He trailed kisses from the corner of my mouth to my ear, nipping at the skin where my neck met my jawline.

"I haven't forgiven you yet." My hand reached up to grasp a fistful of his hair to pull him away, but it was an effort in vain.

"*Yet*," he repeated, slowly running his hot, wet tongue across my neck.

"You cannot just make what you did better by being temporarily pleasant."

"You think I am pleasant?" He gasped; I could feel his breath fan across my neck. He placed a knee between my legs, moving it to the side while lifting my leg.

"You are anything but." I squirmed.

"Such flattery makes me want to be generous." He hiked up my dress and took off his glove.

"What are you—" He shoved the glove into my mouth, enclosing it by clamping his hand over it.

I gripped his wrist, attempting to pull his hand from my mouth, my protests muffled.

"Hush, now." He grinned. "Bite down on it if you have to. You don't want passersby to hear, do you?"

My eyes widened as his hand disappeared under the wool of my skirt. My leg was lifted as he hooked it around the outside of his thigh.

Two of his fingers stroked between my legs, spreading and teasing the wetness that formed.

I flinched at his touch. His hand was the only thing keeping the chill out from under my skirt, aside from the two layers of wool stockings.

His mouth was on my neck, sucking as he cupped my pussy in his hand. One, then two fingers pushed inside.

A muffled, pathetic squeak rose from my throat. My eyes darted, hoping our position was enough to shield me from any possible wandering eyes.

"Behaving so well for me, aren't you?" he purred in my ear, his fingers sliding in and out. While his demeanor was cool, he was absolutely savoring any reaction he could get out of me.

I clenched my eyes shut as the heat rose to my face, denying him the pleasure of seeing any emotions.

His fingers curled inside me, smoothing along the front of my vaginal wall before pressing against it in a gentle pulse.

I groaned and tightened my grip on his wrist, as well as my *other* grip on his fingers. My abdomen tensed, resisting against his movements as my nerves made me shake.

"You feel so good wrapped around my fingers like that," he whispered. "It brings back fond memories."

My head slumped back against the wall, looking up at him as he loomed over me, moving his fingers faster inside me.

I whined, sinking against the wall as my only supporting leg was becoming tired.

"Endure it." He spoke low, slowly inserting a third finger.

To my embarrassment, I moaned under his hand. My body adjusted embarrassingly fast, accepting more of him without consulting the brain before the womb.

I shook my head, tossing it under his grip. My hands flew to his chest, shoving.

He pinched my cheeks between his fingers, pulling me back.

"No, I want to see you when you let go." His wicked expression made that knot tighter. The heat kept rising, threatening to allow me to feel pleasure from a wicked, vile thing like him.

With the pace he was going, it was not long before I practically melted into his hand. My knee finally buckled, and I slid down slightly against the wall. I would be on the gravel if he weren't holding me up.

My eyes squeezed shut instantly before opening again, looking up at his blond figure. The overcast had cleared, and the sun illuminated him like some prophetic figure, but I knew the devil came with many beautiful faces by now.

As I was grappling with my nerves, he removed his hand and took the glove from my mouth.

I coughed at the lingering taste of leather, inhaling for air.

His eyes fixated on my lips, his proximity stifling, suffocating more than the glove. Every breath barely escaped my lips before brushing on his. He leaned close, the brick wall behind me pressing hard on my back.

"There it is." His lips were so close to mine, I could feel every word he whispered against my skin. "That face you make. Do you make it when you play with yourself?"

I bit down on his lip till it bled, but it did not stop him from hooking his fingers sharply inside me.

My throat began to burn, tightening.

"I will ask you one more time, a chance for peace. Answer carefully; it will mean your life." His lips were just above mine. "Give yourself to me."

"You are not asking." My throat strained, a slight whistle from the constriction. "And you will continue to make demands of me until I find a way to put an end to you and all those like you, you foul beast."

Silas sighed and trailed his thumb over my lip, smearing his blood over it like a ceremonial balm.

I coughed, unable to keep my eyes from watering, burning. The dry air made it harder to fight the asphyxiation. He just stood there, watching out of morbid curiosity, some cruel experiment.

"You could have had it all with just two simple words to grace your lips." He gave a coy smile as I began to breathe heavily. "It would be so easy. All you'd have to say is—" His shadow overcame me as he leaned over, his cheek against mine, his mouth by my ear. "*I'm yours.*"

I managed a laugh that sounded more like a cough, a gag. "Not even . . . in death . . . would I utter those words." My breath was raspy, tears clouding my vision and warming my cheeks as they began to numb.

He trailed his lips from my ear to my cheek, tasting the tears before they hovered above my own. I leaned up, the antidote just out of reach, but he leaned away. I was going in and out, his eyes blurring and focusing in my vision.

"*Please . . .* " I mouthed but couldn't speak anymore.

He cupped his hand over my mouth and kissed the back of his hand.

My body slumped, the stars in my eyes clouded, and all I could see was light and shadows. Even with a limp body, there were still arms grasped possessively around me.

All I could do was breathe out, and then the feeling of his lips on mine, faint like a daydream.

"*Can you taste it, Alina? Your life dangling on the tip of my tongue?*" His words were almost a hiss, yet the tone was begging to possess.

It was clear to me then that Silas had learned nothing in my absence. He was one of those men I would say was not dissimilar to a hound, in need of clear boundaries. Luckily, I knew how to deal with animals. How else do you set boundaries other than with threats?

If he was so set on using force, then I would not shy away from doing the same.

XVIII

The Creature

JUST THAT SINGLE INTERACTION was enough to fuel me, rekindle the excitement of what I came for in the first place.

The way her lungs struggled in the cage of her corset, her skin radiating that palpable heat, the delicious scent of her *panic*. Who knew what I needed was just a bit of fun?

Everything was so *good*. I couldn't really describe it better than *euphoria*.

As I lay in bed the next morning, the sheets were softer, the floral scent of the room was stronger . . . I even dreamed in full color that night.

The only thing I regretted from the night was the fact that I did not taste her. The bartender made for poor-quality fare, a bit flat for my tastes. A familiar lurch in my stomach festered now that she was back in my life. It had taken the better half of a year to be able to hold down blood that was not hers. I craved it like opium straight from the pipe. I could feel the need settling in again, though hopefully this time I would not need to feed on anyone else for long.

As I rolled over, something hard poked against my cheek. I mumbled under my breath, but I soon forgot my irritation when

I picked up the hard piece. As I held it between my fingers, my heart stumbled strangely.

A tooth.

A *fang*, to be specific.

There was a tinge of inky blood at the root, insinuating it was fresh from someone's mouth.

My tongue ran across the roof of my mouth to check if it were mine, but it was not.

I sat up, unable to pull my attention from the tooth before I noticed the glass cup on the nightstand contained *more* teeth. I would have thought it was a vision, borne of being hungover from some type of nightmare.

I went to put the tooth in the glass with the rest of them but then felt a granular rustling on top of my sheets.

This has to be a joke.

Scattered across my bed were hundreds, possibly thousands, of teeth. They clicked and clattered against each other like beads as I rustled.

I kicked the sheets off, scattering them over the floor.

The adrenaline made my room spin in the best of ways, like a carousel bent on overstimulating a bairn. I pulled on my shirt and kicked one leg at a time through my trousers. I barely remembered to tuck my shirt in before my shoes were already on my feet.

I made my way to the front desk, adjusting my pace to contain my excitement.

"You. Who did you let into my room this morning?" I demanded once I reached the reception, the fang hidden away in my balled-up fist.

"Room number?" The man behind the desk peered at me over the rim of his thin glasses.

"One seventy-three."

The carefully groomed man glanced down at the logbook, licking his thumb before turning the page, "Ah . . . that would be Mrs. Forbes, sir."

"Mrs. Forbes," I repeated slowly.

Cheeky play, Alina.

My heart could burst just thinking about her being in my room, watching me. I wonder if she had brought a knife or held it to my skin in my sleep. Could she have saved some of her sweet poison for me? I am sure the urge to cut my throat was unbearable for her. Instead, she decided to leave me a gift. She had never done such a thing for me. I say it was *about time* she returned the favor.

"Did she give you the message?" The man interrupted my thoughts.

"Pardon?"

"She said she had a message for you," he repeated.

"Ah, yes, it was received loud and clear." I couldn't help a grin.

XIX

The Fixer

I T WAS A CLEVER disguise for something like her—a humble shop maiden. There was no discernible reason to suspect she might be the mad hatchet-woman that she was.

I watched from across the street as the shop sign flipped to "Closed" and Alina swept the dried dirt tracked in by the day's patrons. She even wore an adorable smock apron to truly sell the image. Feasibly, she would be better off like that. Is this why Silas could somehow see her being subservient? I couldn't help but laugh at the thought.

My cigarette became half an inch shorter with a single breath. The snow dusted the shoulders of my coat; I hadn't moved in an hour. Alina wasn't very observant of her surroundings, so I could probably go another hour in the same spot without her noticing. It was a miracle she was still alive, truly.

The sun took its time rising this morning, the outside dark and stale, my wait only accompanied by the streetlights and the single lamp flickering from inside the shop.

As Alina wiped down the counter, she paused.

You can feel me, can't you?

Her actions slowed, as if she was trying to confirm who she was seeing in her periphery.

Would you rather it be him or me?

Alina stopped cleaning the counter, turning her head to look out at the darkness beyond her haven. At first her eyes were distant, desperate to adjust to the outside. Finally, they settled on me.

The pulsing of my jugular was hot and fast, as was everywhere else. The slight tingle of blood filled my eyes, and inevitably, a dribble of blood escaped my blind side.

One quick gesture and her face went dark, so did the shop as the light went out.

A heavy sigh manifested itself in a cloud in the cold air, and I crossed the frozen street.

With one heavy kick, the front door slapped open, the small bolt lock clattering to the floor along with its screws.

Empty.

Slap!

The door behind the counter closed, and skittering steps sounded behind the wall.

In the stairwell, a movement at the top of the stairs came as that door closed, too.

Stupid girl.

I skipped steps until I was flinging the door open.

Something shimmered in the dimness, coming for my face directly upon my entrance.

A needle glimmered, just inches away from my nose as I leaned back. A soft brush of air indicated how close it was. Just not close enough.

My boot buried in her abdomen as the needle passed, her body dragging across the floor until her back smacked against the opposite wall.

"You would have had better chances running. It seemed to work well the last time," I chuckled, brushing off my hands and stepping into the room.

It was grimy. Unorganized tools, the scent of dried blood and bodily fluids. It reminded me of the basement kitchen at the London Nest.

Footsteps.

She was up again, hoisting her arms above her head to stab me with that needle as if it were a sacrificial blade. She brought it down, and I caught her wrists, squeezing.

Her eyes locked with mine, evincing so much *rage*. A delicious, savory delicacy.

I gave her a pitiful smile, her arm shaking as she continued to hold the pressure, the long upholstery needle dangling above my chest. "Do you think this one will work as poorly as the last one? Poison is a girlish weapon for a reason."

Her lips curled into a menacing dare. "How about we test that theory?"

"Well, I am still your *lab partner* after all." I leaned a little closer, hovering it over my heart, "How about here? Directly into the blood and everywhere else."

"Let go of my hand, and I can make that a reality."

"Another time," I cocked my head, crushing her wrist in my grip. There was a notable pop and the dull chime of the needle hitting the floor.

Alina muffled a cry and yanked her wrist away, holding it tenderly.

"Not so easy to control when someone doesn't want to follow your silly rules, is it?" I clasped my hands behind my back, walking over to her cluttered workbench, "I'm impressed. Don't get me wrong. I would never expect anyone to listen to you, but here you are with an army of dolls."

She leaned against the opposite wall, grasping the hilt of a shovel, but she didn't engage just yet.

You're getting smarter; good girl.

"With your intimate experience with my poison, one would expect you to have a little more faith, possibly a bit more caution," she said through clenched teeth, her heart racing. I could hear it.

"It is the only thing you've done worth remembering. It sure left an impression. I'm thankful to have gotten the faulty batch." I ran my finger over the table, rubbing the grime between my fingers before slouching into the chair.

"Maybe so—but that is why people trust me. I can protect them. They will be safe from the likes of *you*."

"*Safe*." I laughed, shaking my head. "It would only take one fully mature male Vipera to reduce you all to ribbons."

"Many assumptions. I thought you were a man of proof," she scoffed.

"Women are not dangerous enough to respect, to keep people in line."

"And why is that?" She laughed, approaching the middle of the room with the shovel head dragging behind her on the floor. "This is why you are left maimed. Your weakness is your"—she paused—"*blind eye*."

I snapped my head toward her. "Choose your next words wisely, Alina."

That earned a smirk from her.

"A woman will always come above you because you believe they cannot be violent and cruel. You will die at the hands of a woman, and you won't know until it is too late."

"You can drink to it in your dreams, *Dorogusha*, because it is a fantasy."

"You bear my mark upon your face and still believe the lie you tell yourself after all this time?" Her brows furrowed, her smile coy with pure disbelief.

"It is well earned, but ultimately a sign of your failure."

She swung the shovel, and it smacked against my palm as I caught it.

I stood quickly, stomping forward before pinning her to the wall with the handle across her chest, pressing down on her.

I lowered my face, just above hers. A few black drops of blood from my eye landed on her forehead, then her cheek. "I'm not here to hurt you. Not today."

She laughed, straining against the pressure I was putting on her physically.

I refrained from any response.

"I can't imagine anything worse for you; under the control of a man you hate." Her tone was cutting, spiteful. "I suppose it's about time you wore the collar."

XX

The Poisoner

THE WOODED AREA SURROUNDING the farmhouse was dense, almost obscuring the house from where I stood. I did not intend to hunt today, but I needed time away from everyone, to get lost for a while. If I were lucky, maybe an unlucky creature would cross my path, and I would have something to butcher.

The sleet crunched under my boot as I stepped over the logs and twigs along the path. The sun was rising and adorning the icy branches of the forest. Despite the cold, the sun was pleasant on my face as I passed between trees. My heavy attire helped some with insulation. I wore pants and a jacket that I had taken from a test subject a while back. I wish I knew the craftsman, but there were no tags.

The rifle was heavy, the strap weighing on my shoulder.

As I approached a downward hill, I spotted the most regal sight.

In between the thickness of the forest trees was a buck. He was well-muscled and steam rose from his body, as if he had been running. His antlers stretched high to the heavens, three points.

He was perfect. Majestic in ways that I wish I could leave be, but we could use some extra meat for dry reserves.

I knelt down and lifted my rifle steadily, careful not to make a sound or even breathe, for that matter.

Ba-dum, ba-dum, ba-dum.

I watched him in line with my barrel, waiting for just the right pause between each thump of my heart within my chest. One spell of stillness.

He lifted his head quickly, his ears flicking to turn toward whatever sound he thought he heard. Steam burst from his flared nostrils like an angry engine, standing as still as the trees.

Snap!

The illusion of stillness was broken when he leaped, the ground beneath me vibrating with diminishing frequency as he ran farther away.

I lowered the rifle, swiveling my head to my surroundings. Everything was still, even the birds pausing their cheerful trill.

Snap!

Another sound over my shoulder. But when I checked, nothing except the path from whence I came.

Slowly, I rose from my knees, keeping a cautious grip on my gun.

The sun had disappeared, the overcast clouds rolling in and covering the forest in a blanket of shade that somehow made it colder than it already was.

A low, rattled clicking bounced through the wooded area. One would assume that it was a woodpecker, but I knew better.

Raising the gun, I continued forward. I avoided stepping on any sticks, only stepping in patches of snow in the middle of a small clearing between the trees. I watched my surroundings through the sightline of my barrel.

For an instant, everything was still again.

A stream piddled as the ice melted around it. The white landscape was a stark contrast to the dark, wet bark of the trees. Little sounds here and there made me jump, but I was listening for those insufferable clicks.

Snap!

I whipped around and squeezed the trigger. The gun jolted against my shoulder, a pang of pain as I did so. The shot echoed through the trees, dissipating into the tense air around me. Unfortunately, my bullet would have met a tree, as there was nothing there.

I lowered the gun slightly, looking closely at the scene before me.

"You missed."

I swung the barrel around, just in time for a gloved hand to grab it at the end.

"Not so fast." Silas smirked. "What is a pretty thing like you doing out here all alone?"

"I still have bullets."

He yanked the gun from my hands and held it, positioning it at his shoulder and pointing it at me, those unfeeling eyes peering at me from his aim. "Now you don't. What now?"

"Don't point that thing at me unless you are committed to pulling that trigger." I glanced at the blackened inside of the barrel before meeting his eyes again.

"Feisty," he laughed, lowering the gun slightly as he looked me over. "It might be wise to dull that tongue when there is a rifle in your face."

"Spare your threats for someone who fears you." I clenched my fist. "Now give it back; you already scared off my meal."

"Is that why you are trembling? Because you are *not* afraid?"

"Buck fever."

He smirked at me, something flashing behind those eyes. A spark. Nothing good could come of it. "If it truly is buck fever, take off your coat."

"That's not—"

"Do it, *Alina*." He cocked the hammer, a wild flare to his gaze at the sound.

Whatever witty response I had dried up and caught in my throat, making it hard to swallow. There was only sincerity in his expression.

I did not break eye contact as I popped the buttons one by one, shedding the coat from my shoulders and exposing the blouse underneath.

He touched the tip of the gun to my neck, my pulse pushing against the cold metal with every throb. He dragged it over my throat, making the cold trail down before resting it between my breasts. He tugged the gun to tear open a button on the shirt.

"I don't think you need this either." He jabbed the gun at my sternum, pushing down on the next button. "Are you scared?"

"No, but *you* should be." I glared. "You will be lucky to sleep even half an hour without worrying about the ways I could get rid of you."

"You misunderstand my tastes if you think I wouldn't look forward to such an encounter." He stepped back a few paces, moving behind me. "Now get rid of those horrid clothes. It is insulting that you would wear something so cheap."

"And if I refuse?"

"I could take them off *for* you if you prefer," he whispered in my ear from behind.

I only responded by reluctantly undoing the rest of the buttons on my shirt, then beginning to take off my pants. When the pants pooled at my ankles, I kicked the boots and garments away. I was left in two layers of wool stockings. It was too cold to be without anything.

Silas kicked the back of my legs to force me to my knees.

"What is the point of this?" I seethed, the stockings soaking with freezing snow.

"Does there have to be a point? I'm just making sure you didn't get soft in my absence," he teased, sitting down on a fallen log with the rifle across his lap in front of me.

My knees were becoming numb from touching the cold, wet ground. No matter how hard I tried to keep from shaking, I couldn't stop the ice from chilling me down to the marrow.

His eyes were full of blood, enjoying this entirely too much.

"*Alina*," he called sweetly, pointing to the ground before him as he sat with his legs poised wide.

I lifted my knee.

"Ah-ah!" he scolded, shaking his head.

"What is it?"

His smirk grew wider.

I frowned, lowering my knee down to the frozen ground.

There was no need for wool clothes to keep out the weather; my rage burned within me like a furnace.

Slowly, I placed my hands on the ground, stiffly crawling to him. It was only a few paces, but it took forever to reach him. I stopped in front of him, sitting down on my knees and staring at the snow under my palms. My fingers were pale, losing blood flow as well as the color in my limbs. The frost almost burned on contact.

The barrel was placed under my chin, tilting it up to him. A crazed smile twisted his handsome features as he became infatuated with the display before him. My gut twisted at the thought of our position. The way he looked at me in this state. It made me feel in a way that would be shameful to admit.

"You are so captivating when you are angry," he taunted.

"You are a cruel man."

"Then tell me to stop."

I contemplated his words, looking for any sense of a trap. I glanced at the tip of the barrel that touched my cheek before returning my gaze to him.

"Will you still find me pretty if I lose a limb to frostbite?"

"You will have to find other ways to keep warm," he smirked. "Have you tried touching yourself? It may help."

"Will *you* keep me warm?" I lifted my hand to the barrel, caressing it as I dragged my tongue along the cool metal.

He froze in place, but he was intrigued, from the look in his eyes. He followed my tongue along the gun. I think I even saw him swallow.

I leaned up between his legs, placing my hands on his thighs. "You vile things run hotter than humans; you will suffice." I lifted myself up so we could almost be face-to-face. "Don't you want to touch me, Silas?"

For once he was quiet. I wasn't sure if it was due to shock or because he was angry that I wasn't playing his insufferable game the way he wanted me to.

"Tell me." I clasped him by the jaw, digging my nails into his cheek as I held his face. "Do you think I will not kill you? Is that why you taunt me?"

"I would think that you would have done so already if you wanted to." He traced over my hip with his finger.

"What has convinced you that I still won't?"

"Because I am still breathing." His lips hovered close to mine.

"Give me your coat," I whispered to him.

"You haven't earned that yet."

"I am so . . . *so* cold." I shivered, allowing my free hand to palm over the evident bulge under his trousers. He looked down, but my hand holding his face squeezed and tugged his face up. "Look at me."

He stared at me through his lashes. I could see his breathing pick up at my demands. It could have been the cold, but I swore a rosy tint graced his stern features.

"You're a good boy, aren't you?" I smirked. "Now keep those hands on your knees unless I tell you otherwise."

To my surprise, he obeyed.

I slipped my hand under the fabric of his pants, his hot skin making the tips of my fingers burn as the blood flowed back to them. He was already erect, the only thing keeping him restrained was his trousers.

I let go of his face so I could pop the buttons of his jacket loose. "Put it on me," I instructed.

He slipped the coat the rest of the way off. It was a long, dark coat, and it was lined with some type of fur. When he draped it over my shoulders, his hands lingered by my neck.

"Now put those hands back on your knees; you aren't allowed to touch," I whispered, nipping softly at his neck as I stroked his cock. He was getting wet already from the little stimulation I was allowing him. My other hand smoothed over his chest, then his waistband. A hard object was tucked away from reach.

He turned his head to look at what I was touching but I bit his lip, letting out a playful moan. "What did I say about staying still?"

He couldn't take his eyes off my lips.

I kissed him, locking our lips as I stroked his length, eliciting a whimper from him. The sound alone made me smirk. The coat against my skin was reminiscent of his body heat.

He kissed me back, but the tension in his shoulders made it clear how badly he wanted to touch.

Not today, Creature.

I seized the hard object tucked into his waistband, a hunter's knife. The blade sank through his band and into his thigh.

He bared his fangs at me, distracted by the piece of metal pinning his limbs together. He tried to get up, but the blade twisted in his leg.

I retreated, pulling his coat closer over my shoulders.

I ran, taking off for the clearing by the house. My heart was beating so fast, I could hear it in my ears, feel it through my limbs. I hadn't had a kick of adrenaline like that in some time, and I had even gotten a new coat as a result. The branches of shrubs and leafless saplings whipped at my legs and arms as the tree line came in sight. Closer and closer, until I could almost throw myself into the wide-open clearing.

Just as I could touch freedom, it was ripped from me.

Silas scruffed me by the collar of the coat, like I was a misbehaving pet.

Throwing me to the ground wasn't enough to keep me still. He placed his shoe on my pelvis to keep me down. He held the bloodied knife, inspecting it carefully. "Look what you've done now." His tone was one of disappointment.

"You *beast!*" I screamed at him, grabbing a handful of snow and hurling it at him.

He lazily dropped the knife in the snow.

My hand snapped to grab it, only for it to be just out of reach.

He put more pressure down as I reached, the track of his shoe rubbing against all the sensitive places. "Keep going," he taunted, "your limbs would sooner freeze than break free from me."

"If it means you won't have me, so be it," I huffed, gathering the coat closed over my chest, panting from a sudden wave of exhaustion.

"Is that so?" He removed his shoe, bending his knee down in the snow in front of me.

I took advantage of the change in position to lunge for the knife, and he yanked me back by my legs, but it was too late; the knife was pointed directly at him.

"Oh? I was going to suggest a safe word, but I suppose this works, too," he laughed, amused at the knife gleaming at him. "You won't use it."

"Try me."

He crawled closer, both of us covered in dustings of snow. His leather-clad hand reached forward, and I placed the tip of the knife against his neck. Even then, he didn't stop, but he was extremely aware of its position.

His finger skimmed against my chest, the cold, smooth leather brushing across my nipple. They were cold, and his touches made me painfully aware of how stiff they'd become. It was beginning to hurt, the chill hard to ignore.

My posture straightened, but I did not remove my weapon.

"Are you cold?" he taunted, leaning into the knife, but I found myself holding it just above his skin, not letting it plunge inside him.

I refused to answer.

He was over me now, the proximity reminding me that while he was the coldest man I knew, he was a warm body. He took my hesitance to impale him as his answer and leaned down. He cupped my breasts, squeezing gently before his breath tickled the skin, teasing the warmth that it didn't have. He glanced up at me, and I clenched my eyes shut.

Lips against my skin, sucking gently on the skin of my breast. Then, his lips trailed to my nipple, teasing it gently with his bottom lip, waiting for my reactions. Only when my breathing calmed did he lave his hot tongue over the taut bud.

The audible gasp that came from me made him laugh, his hands gripping me tighter as he pressed his hips between my legs.

My eyes flashed open as I slashed his cheek with the knife, the thin line slowly turning black.

"Hear me, creature, don't displease me now," I warned.

"If only you'd let me pleasure you."

"You have only *displeasured* me," I spat.

He caught me, hoisting me up before slamming my back into the thick bark of a tree.

My arms flew over his shoulders for stability, but I held the knife securely to the back of his neck.

He pressed his hips against me, holding my legs around his hips.

"You are not a good liar, Alina," he purred in my ear. "If you hate it so much, tell me to stop," he dared, his grip tight.

"You disgust me."

He smirked, his face lingering in my neck, as if that was some sort of positive answer. "I think you like it," he whispered.

"I do not." I pressed the knife harder against his skin.

"At least your body is honest." He kissed my skin, I wasn't sure if the heat was from the cold environment or because I was sensitive.

I couldn't see his face, but I could feel everything. I didn't have to see his expression to know what he was waiting for. I stole a second for myself, tipping my head back against the tree. The coat was draped off my shoulders, the bark scraping my shoulders as I made up my mind.

Slowly, with my legs around his waist, I shifted against the bulge of his trousers. Even with this sort of positive encouragement, I still had the knife secure.

"You've always had a nice scent to you," he said, slowly grinding against me. It sounded like he suppressed a groan, like he was holding something back. "But I can't help but want to smother you with my own."

"That's what dogs do, I suppose." I turned my head to him, and he finally met my eyes before grinding against me.

The bark scraped my back, the warmth deep in my core involuntarily pulsing.

"S—"

His hand clamped over my mouth.

"Not another word from you," he breathed, resting his hips

between my thighs. I had to squeeze my legs around him, pressing the knife flush against the nape of his neck.

Even with his threatening words, I could feel the hair standing on the back of his neck like hackles, well aware of the blade threatening to scalp him with one wrong move. His grip was firm, his breathing light, fluttering as if he didn't have time to take a proper inhale. He ground against me at a painfully slow pace. It was either to savor or to torture me; I would never know with a man like him.

A soft sound against his palm, the roughness on my back preventing me from enjoying the friction of his clothing too much. My free hand pressed flat on his chest. As I began to shiver, his chest pressed closer to mine. Every breath, every sound, I could hear it all.

Silas's lips brushed against my numb ear, his breath tickling as the blood rushed to the warmth. Then it lingered by my neck, a kiss as soft as a flake of snow.

Heat flared inside. At this rate, I might not need external sources of warmth. His coat slipped down my shoulders, and he took advantage by placing love bites where he could.

Before, his words were, no doubt, violent. His actions were aggressive, but never deadly. Even now, even when he pretended to hate me, and I him, he was so gentle when he finally caught me.

He took his hand away from my mouth, holding my waist firmly as he ground against me, my hips knocking into the wood of the tree. Then he began to pull at his belt.

"Silas, stop." The words were barely a breath.

"Do you say that because you want me to stop"—he lingered by my ear—"or because you don't want to admit how this makes you feel."

"I . . ." I shook my head, the knife trembling in my hand. "I want to stop."

To my surprise, his body was still. We were still. He pulled away just enough to look at me, but his eyes didn't lift to mine until a beat later, like there was something he didn't want me to see.

"*Please*," I whispered. "Can we . . . can we stop?" I dropped the knife, and it landed in the snow behind us. I revealed my palm to him to bear proof of my disarmament. It wasn't until I saw his expression change that I realized my face was hot. And wet. "I want to stop," I rephrased.

He dropped me, withdrawing completely.

My back scraped down the bark as I landed in the snow at his feet. He rolled his shoulders, as if it was some annoyance being a terror to me. With an air of nonchalance, he dressed. Buttoned his trousers closed and tucked his shirt in.

He checked his trouser pockets, patting several of them before looking down at me and holding his hand out.

I brought my hand up to his, and he swatted it away.

I stared in confusion before he cocked his brow, pointing. "Cigarettes."

I reached inside the coat pocket, pulling out his silver cigarette holder before it was snatched out of my hands, and then I was staring at his backside.

"Keep the coat; I can buy another," he jeered over his shoulder as he retreated down the path, leaving me under the fir tree, humiliated, used.

Bastard.

XXI

The Fixer

GIVING ME THE TASK to stalk the Catholic must have been a lark coming from Silas, but I went anyway because where there is a hospital, there will be blood—among other fluids.

Every task, even as a joke, is the perfect opportunity to play a part. I had decided it was time to play doctor once more. It is not like I would be fraudulently impersonating a doctor; I had re-done my medical training of all kinds every fifty years or so, or when something new was discovered.

I borrowed a morning suit and frock coat from the hordes that Alina's Nest kept, though the hospital was small enough that they may have been excited to receive any new doctors at all, no matter how nicely they dressed.

"Excuse me?" I asked a passing nurse.

She stumbled when she saw me, though I could not gauge if it was from shock or from being flustered due to the cloth mask covering her mouth. I assumed my scar was a bit jarring.

"Y-yes?" she asked, her furrowed brows indicating she was confused at the unfamiliar doctor.

"Could you point me to phlebotomy?" I attempted my friendliest smile.

"That would be down the hall and to the left."

"And what about osteology?"

"All offices are on the first floor. Are you looking for any doctor in particular?"

"It's my first day—I'm shadowing a nurse. She gave me instructions, but I've forgotten exactly where I'm supposed to be. Her name is . . . Eden?"

"Oh, Edith! Yes, she should be just upstairs. Come, follow me," she chirped as she nearly fluttered from the desk.

THE HOSPITAL WAS AN older building, but it was updated regularly. The nurse babbled about the new wing and then littered her tour with complaints about small annoyances over the structure or the inventory.

My home village did not even have a hospital; the only things we had readily accessible were liquor, potatoes, and wheat. I had seen hospitals that were basically run out of abandoned buildings. This place seemed like a luxury if you were to find yourself falling ill.

The second floor was no different from the first, though there were extra rooms and beds up here due to the offices being on the first floor. Nurses fluttered about from room to room, carrying bowls, towels, and other tools as they rushed about. Among the chaos, they still managed to throw a glance our way every now and then.

As I entered the room, one nurse in particular stood out. The uniform was a mousy-colored, long-sleeved dress with a white smock and hat. While others wore a standard uniform with their hair tucked into a neat bun, Edith wore a hair scarf as a modest addition.

Edith was tending to some poor clammy soul with a yellow tint to his flesh. When she looked up, she grew nearly as pale as her patient, and she quickly pretended that she had not seen me.

Leaving the side of the nurse escorting me, I stopped across the bed from Edith.

"Are you not going to greet the new doctor?"

She startled, a wild, angry blush across her cheeks when she saw me. "You are not a *real* doctor."

"I most certainly am."

"Liar."

"I promise you that I've done more amputations than years you have been alive."

"That does not make you a doctor."

"The hundred collective years of schooling or apprenticing would say otherwise."

"Fine," she grumbled, wringing out the wet towel she was wiping the man with over a bowl. "Are you here to help or for fun?"

"Could I say both?"

"Did Silas tell you to keep an eye on me?"

"Yes, but I am genuinely curious to know what you girls do with the Vipera fluid—"

"Keep your voice down," she snapped, glancing over her shoulder at the other nurses in the corner of the room, one of whom was tending to an old woman who had bedsores from her immobility.

"*Vipera fluid*," I repeated in a whisper, teasingly looking over my shoulder to mimic her.

"Don't be so childish," she scolded.

"Isn't using venom a bit risky?" I watched her gather her care items on the rolling cart. "Since there are so many deaths, would you not start having a corrupted every day?"

"The venom does not turn them if we keep it under a certain amount. Just enough to take their pain away."

"I see . . . and this is Alina's discovery?"

"Yes."

"How many did you kill in order to get that number?"

"Enough. That is how many."

"That is the first I have heard of it. What else?"

"What do you mean?"

"What else do you use it for?" I asked as she wheeled the cart out of the room, and I followed by her side.

"The venom is for pain. We use the saliva on wounds for healing and numbing," she explained, keeping her voice quiet as we passed a group of nurses.

"What about the blood?"

"Poison. Works perfectly on mice and men."

"Interesting philosophy." I glanced at the tools on her cart. "What do you think is causing the increased number of corrupted disturbances?"

She lifted her shoulder before letting it slump again.

"Not one inkling as to the cause?"

"Probably one of the Guilds. There is barely an organized structure in this city; I am sure someone is being careless."

"I see." I trailed off. "So why are you here? How did you come to meet Phoebe and Alina?"

"I'm not supposed to be talking to you."

"Were you a nurse before you turned?"

She shook her head, but did not offer any elaboration.

We arrived at the inventory room, and she started to unload the trinkets, towels, and bowl from the cart.

"So what is the reason for"—I gestured to my own head to indicate her scarf—"that?"

"I was in service to my church."

"Oh." I grimaced. "So you're a virgin."

"T-that is none of your business." Her face became red faster than a cherry on a cigarette.

"No need to get flustered; you're safe," I proclaimed. "I have a strict rule against virgins."

"Too much information." She dumped the murky water bowl in the sink, a bit aggressively.

"It's an ethical issue." I shrugged, leaning against the edge of the sink as she worked. "You might as well be an adolescent. I can't stand it."

"Could you refrain from talking about your promiscuities?" She flashed a sarcastic smile before she returned to scrubbing the bowl and refilling it with clear water.

"Impossible, I'm afraid." I shrugged. "What else is there to talk about at work?"

"The *patients*, possibly?"

"I would never talk about a patient's promiscuities."

"You are insufferable!" she snapped, hoisting the bowl onto the cart and grabbing clean washcloths from a shelf.

"I try my very best."

She was irritated, though she had been uneasy even before she noticed me in the patient room.

"Is there something aside from me bothering you?" I tilted my head at her as she hastily wiped her hands on her apron.

"What is it to you?" She shot me a look of suspicion.

"Well, I am an excellent listener, among other *wonderful* qualities." I shrugged nonchalantly. "Besides, if we are to be part of the same Nest soon, it might be nice to have a friend."

"A . . . friend."

"Do you not have friends, Edith?" A pitying smile played on my lips. "How sad."

"I-I do have friends!"

"Aside from Alina, your *master*."

"She is not a master; don't be obtuse. I have *friends*."

"Well, now you have one more." I held out my hand to her. "My name is Luka, friend for hire."

"You want me to pay you?" Her expression turned grim. "Are you going to ask me for any disgusting favors?"

"Did you not hear me before? No virgins." I scrunched my nose at her in disgust. "It was a jest. I am a mercenary, a Fixer of sorts."

"Oh." Her shoulders slumped, and she stared at my extended hand. She fought with it in her head for a minute before she grasped my hand, "Edith . . . um . . . healer for hire."

"There you go." I patted her on the top of her scarf-covered head. "Good job, Catholic, you've made a friend."

She smiled sheepishly at me, any reservations melting like butter. A crumb of praise; that's all it took to win the trust of a loner.

"Now that we are friends . . ." I smoothed the scarf on her head. "Maybe you can help me with some errands after work?"

"Only if you help me on my shift." She frowned. "*And!* And if you do whatever I say until we punch out."

"Ah, I may consider it if you throw in some spinal fluid. I can even do the draw myself." I winked.

"Spinal fluid?"

"It is quite tasty, very nutritious. You should try it."

"I will stick to blood."

"More for me, I suppose."

THE EARLY MORNING WAS much softer than the darkness that came before midnight. While still void of sunlight, the sky was tinted in deep purples and blues, hopeful colors of the dawn to come. A perfectly good morning for a walk.

"—and then he put them on sticks! I didn't think the man would really do it, but by God, he did!" I laughed.

"That is not funny!" Edith punched my arm.

"Considering I said it as a joke after too much mead, it was incredibly funny." I took another drink from the bottle I found in one of the doctor's offices.

We were walking through the park nearby. The city had not woken up yet, and neither had the sky. I could still see stars.

"Look, Edith." I placed my palm on top of her head, tilting it back to make her look up. "It is a full moon."

"Oh," she breathed, staring with her eyes wide at the marvel in the sky.

The moon was bigger this witching hour, a little closer than usual.

"We must have caught it on a special night."

"Yes," she said, and cleared her throat.

When I peered over, she was already looking at me with those sad eyes of hers.

"What is it?"

"Was it a jape when you said we were friends?" I could see her lip twitch, her head shifting under my palm when she turned her head to look my way.

"No, why would I do that?"

"You make many unserious comments. I am not sure when you are sincere."

"Then let us talk about something more serious," I said as we followed the pathway by the pond. We approached a bench, and I dusted off the powder on the seat, sitting down and patting the spot next to me.

"What do you want to talk about?"

"Tell me about yourself." I took the bottle from her and drank from it. "Tell me about the nun situation . . . I assume you are not one anymore."

"I'm not a nun." She sat down and rubbed her arm nervously. "I was in service as a sister, but I did not think it was right for me to continue."

"Were you turned at your convent?"

"I didn't have a convent. I was at my church. It was the night before I was supposed to leave for service." She sighed. "I remember walking across the courtyard, on a night not unlike this. I remember the moon, a sign of hope." Her eyes lowered in reminiscence. "Then the next thing I knew, I woke up under the dirt. It took three days to dig myself out."

I watched her shift in discomfort, and it wasn't from the algid air around us. I took another drink and slid closer, wrapping an arm around her shoulder.

"If it makes you feel better, I was thrown into the bottom of a lake once. I had to break my ankle to get it out of the ball and chain."

"I appreciate the anecdote."

"Why do you still cover your head?"

"I am not comfortable enough to show my hair at all times, but I am working on it," she mumbled. "Besides, I have an unsightly scar." She looked up at me and immediately widened her eyes. "N-not that all scars are offensive! Just mine! I didn't mean you—"

"I understood; relax." I laughed. "You should be bold; you do not need to cater to others. Say what you mean."

"Right."

"Now." I leaned closer. "Are you going to tell me what is really bothering you?"

She focused on picking the pilling on her coat fabric distractingly.

"It is complicated."

"Try me."

"Alina is not happy with me," she murmured. "It feels like no matter how hard I try I always end up misstepping."

"Ah, that has nothing to do with you." I squeezed her shoulder. "Alina has a stick up her cunt. Silas's, to be specific."

Edith jumped when I cussed, as if Alina would hear from miles away.

"You need not be afraid of her; she would never dream of hurting a woman, no matter how foolish a mistake she made," I assured her. "Besides, you should assert yourself more. Don't let her bully you. She's harmless."

"Harmless is not how I would describe her." She buried her face in her hands.

"I guess it would be a paradox of sorts." I patted her back awkwardly. "Don't let other people get in the way of the greatness you want to achieve. You have your skills and morals; Alina has her own." I held out the bottle, swishing the remaining liquid at the bottom. "Do you want any more before I finish it?"

She lifted her face and grabbed the bottle, throwing her head back and taking several gulps before she emptied it.

"There we go, Catholic! See? What is more fun than public intoxication with a friend?"

"I could name many other things, though not when liquor is on my mind."

"Shall I escort you home then?" I teased, holding my hand out.

"Of course, how could I say no to such a charming bastard!"

"It seems the monk has discovered jokes."

"*Sister*. Not a monk."

"Same difference."

XXII

The Poisoner

I WAS NOT KEEN ON the idea of meeting strangers while they wore masks.

The gathering was supposed to be a masquerade. The girls had crafted their own masks. Rebecca whittled hers from wood that she would hold up with a stick. Adeline made some out of fabric that tied in the back with a ribbon, though it would only cover their eyes. My mask was not as creative. It was a simple strip of lace across my eyes paired with a mourning veil over the top. The tulle covered my entire head, the excess wrapping over my shoulder.

We often received invites to new Nests, and the first visit was for negotiations.

My evening gown was sleeveless and hung nearly off my shoulder, the neckline meeting at a wide V shape at the top of my corset. The dress clung strictly to the shape of the corset before it passed my hips, at which point it turned to fine ruffles until it hit the floor. It was a deep green color with black lace details, including silk gloves. I wore a choker around my neck with an ovular stone resting at the front. I had my hair done in a half-twist, with some falling over my shoulders beneath the veil.

The inside of the home was covered in dark wood paneling and intricately carved archways around the doors. A vibrantly pigmented Persian rug led us through the hallway and into a sitting room. The ceilings were tall, grand enough to facilitate an overly ornate chandelier and a fireplace mantel decorated with a fresh wreath. The smell of pine, dried citrus, and apple created a welcoming ambiance that could wrap me up and lull me to sleep faster than mulled cider.

The girls wore their finest tonight, though I was too nervous to inspect everyone's attire. Adeline and Mary had dressed everyone, and I trusted their judgment. Appearances were important, especially when entering new territory. On top of that, the frivolously dressed were remembered. When it came to murdering members of a Nest, no one usually suspected the dolls wrapped in silk.

On each of our fingers was a memento mori ring. Typically, these bands would hold chords of braided hair from the dearly departed, opening to reveal the contents. For us, we had a more unorthodox use.

Inside the chamber of the rings was homemade Vipera poison, fashioned with a cat-claw-like piece of brass that stuck out once you flicked open the chamber. It was a prototype in every sense of the word, my first mechanical invention, thanks to John, as we had never had cause to use it in practice. Hopefully, we never would.

The guests fit the scene, like they were specifically cast to play their parts. Caricatures of what wealth should look like. The lineations held some of the rarest fabric colors I had seen in some time, some never at all in person. Shades of purple, magenta, green, and yellow. Each lady had a signature perfume, strong notes of florals and oud, but it did little to mask the metallic scent of blood on their breath.

Everyone had a part to play on visits like these. Rebecca and Adeline paired up as the pleasant social duo, Edith watched my back, and I handled negotiations. The girls fluttered around like birds, showing their colors, begging for a bite. Male Vipera couldn't control themselves, so most were quick with their wallets. Though this Nest was owned by a Sire and Dam, it seemed the wife was the one in charge of anything of great importance. I could respect and sympathize.

Unlike the Guilds, it was not located in town, and it did not pretend to be a club. They took a traditional approach, that of an estate where Vipera and Hosts could meet. Though no matter how traditional they modeled it after, no Host would agree to being exclusive to a Nest when they could get paid to attend many. It seemed they had finally decided to accept that the Hosts would not be staying on the property.

The Dam had her arm looped in mine, immediately striking a familiar and friendly conversation upon arrival as she took me hostage on her tour and introductions. Her husband eyed us sourly from the corner, surrounded by his wolfish acquaintances and cigar smoke.

"Come, sit with me." The mistress of the house guided me to a lounging chaise scattered in a corner of furniture.

Even the fabric itself was rich and noticeably old. It was delicate, inspiring fear that sitting on the chaise would somehow rub away the small threads of gold and deep purple dye from many centuries ago. The entire room could be stored in a museum, though I suppose it wouldn't be farfetched to think wealthy Vipera didn't own those private collections too.

"Your home is very . . . warm," I said. It was not my intention to hesitate; I was having trouble with the distractions surrounding me. I had nearly stumbled on two dogs perched beside the furniture. They were long and regal, windhounds of sorts, or another ancient breed. I nearly thought they were statues at first with how still they were. Even when quiet, I preferred the seat furthest from them.

"Do you not like them?" She smiled as she petted one of their thin heads, playful in her question.

"I don't prefer them." I managed the most polite answer I could muster.

"Is that so?"

"I tire of attending to wolfish things nowadays."

"I assume you've had your fill of *other* types of dogs?"

I nodded, laughing off the attempt at a cozy jest.

"I have been looking forward to your attendance." She smiled, but it was pulled too tight. Forced. The polite facade would only last as long as her temper or her hunger; Vipera were all the same.

"I assume you are familiar with our terms from the others, Mrs.—"

"Georgiana," she corrected, "and of course. We would love to have you and your girls here regularly."

"Fifty per feeding," I said, "and if anyone within your Nest breaks the code of conduct or if you skip payment, a Host will never step foot in your Nest again."

"Straight to business, I see." Her smile fell, turning to something dispassionate, though I suspect it had been like that the whole time behind that sickly sweet facade. I was afraid that it was going to rot my teeth if she kept it up any longer.

"I wouldn't insult you or your establishment by wasting your time."

"You wouldn't have been invited if I suspected you were worth anything less."

"Then why dance around the subject?"

Georgiana patted my leg. "The art of negotiation is only refined with time. You are young, so I will not hold it against you."

"I don't understand the need for extra steps."

"Negotiating isn't purely for the goal of striking a deal, it can also be a test of when *not* to," she said smoothly, tipping her glass to her lips as she eyed something in the crowd as she spoke. "It is much like dancing with a stranger. You do the rehearsed movements first, test their pace, their skill of step."

"Perhaps when there are more options, but so far I don't see any competition."

"I will do you the kindness of telling you plainly, woman to woman"—her eyes shifted to me, and she turned her shoulders to face me more—"I am still interested, I believe in you. What you've built is beautiful, but in its infancy. It will take more than just my own investment for it to prosper. *Sell* it."

"How about a taste?" I suggested.

"While I am excited to sink my teeth into the talk of the town, I need to know you can work a crowd." She was close enough that I could see the intricate beading on the edge of her mask. "We are not like any Nest around here—we have esteemed guests who travel here to feel the comforts of home, something civilized. I know you can work an eager crowd, but what about those with taste?"

"Are you insulting my taste, Georgiana?" I tilted my head, leaning close to her ear. "You wouldn't have asked us here if you hadn't heard anything less than exceptional, especially with your hesitancy toward more progressive Host relations."

"I would love to believe you, but it isn't me who will need impressing." She slanted her head to the side. "We have some new guests aside from yourself tonight. They have not shown much interest in many so far. Get them to feed, and I can pay all of you double what you're asking. That is, if you are as good as you say you are."

"New guests?" I raised a brow.

She pinched my chin and guided my view to the figure lounging on a sofa, surrounded by cigar smoke and malice. A very familiar face. "From the city," Georgiana hummed, leaning close. "Types like that are worth the trouble."

I didn't have to see the face under the mask to recognize Silas. I knew it was him from the rage in my heart alone.

"You said you will pay double?" I turned to look at her.

"If he and others take a liking to you, then you and your girls are welcome here every week if they choose. If it means attracting more like them, I will pay whatever it takes."

Damping down any outward signs of disappointment or hesitance, I rose from my seat to move across the floor.

I smoothed out my skirt before approaching.

A passing guest's shoulder shoved mine as he passed.

My head snapped up to confront, but he was already stopped, nose to nose with me.

Luka.

"Happy hunting." His words were laced with sarcasm. He flicked his split tongue out at my lips. I flinched as I moved away. His laughter melted into the background as I approached Silas.

"Is this seat taken?" I glanced around.

"Would it make a difference if it were?" He tilted his head at me, clearly a few drinks of booze or blood in already.

I spotted Edith off in the crowd, eyeing me before looking away when I nearly caught her staring. Her smile was so bright, so confident, so well-rehearsed, I nearly believed it. It could also be how unfamiliar she looked without her head covering.

"Don't be unpleasant. People are watching," I muttered, slipping into the spot beside him. I leaned in, and he nearly flinched away when my lips met his ear. "If you were looking for a chance to make it up to me, now is the time."

"Is that even possible in the eyes of your impossible standards?" he played.

I ran a finger over the hem of my neckline. "Feed on me, *Creature.*"

"Is this a trick?"

"It is *permission*." The words nearly came out as a sour hiss.

His hand smoothed my veil from my neck before slipping his fingers beneath to grasp the partially loose hair underneath, tugging me close again.

I winced at the pressure at the base of my neck, a chill racing up and down my spine.

A playful smile danced as he studied my reaction, reveling in the upper hand. "Admit it, you missed me."

"I did not."

"Tell me you never dreamed about me." He playfully swept his bottom lip against mine, the veil our only barrier.

"I had nightmares about you."

"Because you wish me to haunt you?"

"Because you broke my heart," I whispered, my lips brushing against his as I spoke, the proximity entrapping.

He was silent for once; that is how I knew he heard me.

"Alina—"

"Stop talking." I leaned in, pulling him close, so close his breathing fanned against my neck, ragged in constraint.

He hesitated, the only proof of a sober thought. His fingers traced over the hems and folds of the dress around my waist until it reached my back. A deep breath before the fangs buried beneath my skin, the first opportunity they could.

My moan was involuntary, but it was hard not to feel the pleasure that overtook me as he fed. His cologne became stronger, my heart jumping; I'm sure he heard it, because his bite became firmer on my neck, as if to trap me.

Pictures overtook my mind suddenly like a silver screen.

The dull, gray room. Powerless in the dark, unable to sleep or else I would be teased by dreams of freedom or be subjected to another nightmare, only to have no relief when I finally awoke in the middle of another night terror. I could feel my skin heating up; I was seeing stars like a combusting reel of emulsion film.

I clung to his shirt, steadying myself.

His hand was firm on my waist, his hand on my head moved to a firm grip on my hair, as if the bite wasn't enough.

Curiously, he was not feeding anymore, just biting.

That is when I realized I hadn't let him go.

"Silas," I said shakily.

He withdrew his fangs quickly, flattening his tongue over the wound as if he anticipated it, waiting for even a whisper of his name on my lips. Just one word to stop.

He lifted the veil, just enough to expose my lips. That is when he kissed me, like he was desperate to taste the very word, hoping it would come again.

The metallic brass taste of blood and bourbon stung at the back of my throat. My eyes fluttered open, and I separated the kiss, his grip on the back of my neck keeping us in whispering distance.

"How does it feel," he whispered, blood dripping from his lips to mine, "to be caught in my grasp again?" He pulled his gaze from my mouth to my eyes. "Is it as decadent as my venom coursing through your veins?"

"All I taste is *malice*." I pushed him back, but he caught my hand before I whipped it away from him.

XXIII

The Creature

MY HEARTBEATS MATCHED EACH step she took away from me, except instead of becoming quieter, they became louder as the distance grew. Oh, what it would be to paint the walls with her. What a feast that would be.

I jerked my head back along with a mouthful of bourbon, then another. Once the second swallow was down, the Fixer was already breathing on my neck.

"Slow down," he said as he snagged my arm. "What are you doing?"

"This is stupid; why are we entertaining this foolery?" I shoved my empty glass into his hand before taking the full glass from the other.

Before he could grab me, I stepped up onto the coffee table and swiped a silver spit from a nearby appetizer tray, using it to chime the glass.

The rumbling of laughter and chatter died down like a wet ember.

"I just wanted to say that I am just so grateful for such a lovely invitation, and such wonderful hospitality from the Sire and Dam,"

I began, tipping the glass to the Dam, who politely tipped hers back. There were some laughs from the pun and confused looks relaxing among the guests. "Not to mention the handsome crowd gathered here today!"

A few whistles and raised glasses.

In the middle of the menially jovial faces was one sour grape. My darling shadow, appropriately named for her mood-dampening attire, still and focused as ever. Not even the black veil could hide the visceral disgust she held just for me. My core was alight with a fire I could not dare name.

"You know, it feels good to be welcome somewhere." I paced along the table, sipping the mouth-numbing cocktail that went to waste in my throat. "America has been a bit of a shock for me. New York is so cold; it takes forever to get to the next city, but I do agree the food is better," I joked. Another couple laughed, but I kept eye contact with Alina as I finished my drink.

"Though I'm a bit muddy on this, let me walk it through." I gestured in the air. "See, I come from a rather large Nest. Larger than life! You would not believe how many Vipera we could fit on one estate. I could greet a new person every day and maybe only see the same person a handful of times in a year. High turnover, I suppose. Dozens on the premises at once, thousands more in loyalists. Reserves enough to buy fresh human meat every night, three square meals along with some of the most beautiful Hosts you could imagine." I smirked at Alina before being handed another drink. They started to whisper among themselves.

"And now they're all dead."

It was as if I let off a shotgun. The silence was deafening. I took my time and soaked it in, reveling in the tension.

Luka stiffened beside me; I could smell the sweat beading on his forehead. I could also hear dozens of pulses elevate, the sound of blood flowing faster and faster.

"Do you wanna know why?" I laughed, and no one else joined, though I caught my composure after nearly sputtering my drink. "Because they were weak. They tricked themselves into thinking they could be like humans, civilized and poised. Which I suppose would work, if they had any sort of strength or talent. I hear America is about merits. So why are you letting humans hold you by your *taints*?"

"Here, here!" the drunken Sire whistled, raising a glass.

"What is stopping you from taking what you want?" I raised a glass back to the accompaniment of some whistles and a slowly resonating sound of favorable chatter. The noise of the room rumbled into a shuffling.

Blood-black eyes leered at the relatively few number of Hosts. The only ones squirming were Alina's pretty toys.

Luka tugged my sleeve, yanking me low. "Stop it now, you *fool*."

I pulled my sleeve away and threw my glass across the room. "Why do you let the food decide when you're hungry, brothers?" I shouted, and a couple more crashes of glass followed like the symphony of a party.

Luka's chastisements faded into the noise of it all.

Now the party is finally starting!

The phonograph skipped with the occasional screech as people bumped into it, each other, and the like. The voices became louder, jovial as the energy of the room fed on each other, catalyzing it at a rapid rate. Many rose to their feet, some caught Hosts, the jumping of glasses and scraping of chairs really gave me a hungry itch.

Alina desperately clawed through the crowd, unable to collect her birds before being snatched by the same rowdy Sire from the corner.

Bodies bumped and crowded me like a swelling tide, crashing into each other in careless chaos. I could see her just in between riots, closer and closer.

I couldn't help but get giddy. Finally, I could step in, and she would have to admit I saved her. That she needed me. That—

Alina slipped from the man's arms, her hair falling from her neat entanglement as he snatched her veil instead of her hair. Then, she dragged her knuckle across his throat, a fine line appeared, and his eyes shot open. Genuine disarmament.

It was then that I knew that the death of my Nest was no accident, no outlier, no miracle. It was destined, a matter of time. The sight before me was something I knew would be historic, a new era for our beloved prey.

Along the slice on his neck, blood came but stopped just as fast; instead, the veins turned black from the source, the skin around it slowly degraded into a leathery ash as it crept along the live skin. He fell to the floor, his body tense like he was made of wood, and the foam from his mouth was violet, diluted with Vipera blood.

She had done it.

She had perfected her poison.

The only noise present from the aftermath of the Sire. The attendants carefully made room to inspect the example that was made of a once-living man. The silence was harrowing, the loud ring of fear polluting the room like pure incense. It was thrilling, even more so knowing it could have been my neck on the end of her blade.

The Dam of the house shoved past, her talons for nails cutting through the guests in her way. Nothing would stop her from reaching the ashen remains of her lover. She tumbled to her knees, a puff of dust from the corpse making bystanders step back.

The Dam's palms trembled as they hovered above her mate's chest.

You would think a bloodbath would be next, and it certainly would be the case if there was much capacity left to feel after something so terrible. I could only describe it as shock, denial of the vision before her. Vipera were not supposed to die, not by anything less than a snap of the neck, a task requiring an inhuman amount of strength. Even I felt the air of unease, the improbability of the thing we just witnessed. A predator was born; the scales of nature had tipped. Evolved.

"Leave!" she wailed, a slender finger pointed at Alina. *"Leave!"* A horrid sob followed before she, herself, crumbled over her lover.

Georgiana hid her face, dedicated to the delicate corpse. The scent of tears pinched my senses. The amazing thing about our keen senses was how you could read minds. The body was honest, Alina used to say. She was right. The Dam's tears were of some sorrow, but the overwhelming tang of adrenaline nearly aroused my own instincts. Her shaking was not of grief, not from her cries, but because her body was fighting the overwhelming inclination that there was something in the room that was able to kill us without as much as a lifted finger.

Alina was still, amid the havoc, unmoving before lifting her gaze from the pile of a man. She looked directly at me.

The girls did not scatter, nor did they panic at such a grotesque happening.

In her eyes, I wished I saw rage. I hoped she would scream at me, shout, or spout profanities like she once did. Considering the event, I would have taken a smug look from her at the very least.

No, she simply shook her head and walked from the abode, her girls neatly filing behind her without a word needing to be said.

Something burned in my chest, and it wasn't the liquor. It could have been jealousy of their fervent loyalty, but was it from power? From fear? Both? Somedays I thought her allure was that she was beautiful and hard to catch. The revelation should have dawned on me earlier, but it was her terror. Raw yet tame. A fire I wanted—I *needed*. To possess such a thing that brings gods to their knees—or rather, turns them to dust. The ultimate flirtation with death.

I glanced at Luka, frozen, pale, and betraying a slight tremor, a once-steady man reduced by the image of what could have been all those years ago.

XXIV

The Fixer

THERE WASN'T MUCH TO say about what we saw the night before, but the gravity of it settled hard the next day. Things were different now, a shift in the air. My heartbeat was uncomfortable, all too aware of my own blood pumping through my wrists, my temple, even the twitch of my good eye.

My hand shook as I pulled the stitch through the patient's skin with forceps. I tied a few knots as I closed up the wound on the patient's forearm. "You are set to go. Keep it clean until it scabs. The stitches should fall out on their own," I instructed as I stood, glancing over at Edith.

She was occupied with a stiff patient, a sickly woman in a hospital gown and a blue scarf holding the hair away from her clammy face.

Edith was fidgeting with something, focused. Her body hunched over a little, hiding.

I approached and peered over her shoulder. "What are you doing?"

"We are low on venom. I was going to use my own." She turned around to show me the glassware with gauze stretched over the entrance. "Or would you care to donate some of your own?"

"It wouldn't be much use if I did."

"What do you mean?"

"I have low venom potency."

"How do you feed, then? Does it not hurt your Hosts?"

"Through the spine. It is just strong enough to numb someone if you inject it there. Besides, spinal fluid isn't half bad."

Edith kept me in the corner of her eye as she turned back to her patient, her nose scrunching as she processed my answer.

"Relax, Mrs. Foster. Just one pinch," Edith assured the older woman, sticking a syringe of amber substance into her arm.

The sickly woman immediately relaxed, settling into the sterile white sheets. She could not have been older than forty, with fine lines blessing her face. When her pain was taken away, she looked about ten years younger.

"You shouldn't rely on venom." I followed.

"A little more won't hurt." She placed the syringe in the sink.

"Nothing good comes from saying a thing like that." I leaned against the counter.

"She is low risk," she muttered as she washed her hands. "It is unfair to let someone suffer due to chronic ailments. It is the least I can do."

"You shouldn't distribute it so liberally," I said. "Make it last so that you can help more people."

She shrugged and refused to hear me.

I pushed away from the counter, heading toward the door.

"Where are you going?" She frowned at me. "We still have work to do."

"I'm stepping out to smoke. Would you like to grace me with your ever-sought-after company?" I teased.

She considered saying no; I could see it in her face, but she eventually decided against her better judgment and followed me.

WE FOUND A COMFORTABLE stone banister along the stairs to sit, right outside the side entrance. I plucked a cigarette from my inner breast pocket.

A few wisps of snow fell in flurries across the yard, like ghosts dancing about the ground before disappearing.

I caught Edith staring. Her eyes darted away quickly, just not quickly enough. It did not take a detective to know she wanted to say something. I could practically feel the tension emanating as she shifted, sitting on the opposite banister facing me.

"What is it now? Spit it out."

"I have told you everything about my life."

"What are you on about?"

"I don't know anything about you."

I stared at her before bringing the cigarette to my lips, letting it hang loosely as I found my lighter. "You never asked."

The wind whistled through the buildings in our silence. I breathed heavily, letting the smoke singe my throat before letting it go through my nose.

"Then let's make a deal."

I glanced over at her cautiously.

"If one of us starts talking about our past, the other has to listen. Both ways. That goes for questions; you have to answer honestly. That's what *friends* do, right?"

I lifted my gaze to the sky, as if to contemplate. It wasn't my favorite game, but it would pass the time. I nodded in reply.

"Did you have a profession before you were a fixer? Where

are you from? What about your family?" She gulped, scratching nervously at the head covering.

"I was a muse." I glanced down at the cherried end of the cigarette. Somehow, focusing on the details of the ash was soothing as the embers crept up the paper.

"A muse? Like those of the master painters?" She smiled.

"Exactly." I tapped the ash off the end of the paper. "It was the easiest way to make money."

"Are you in many paintings, then?"

"No," I laughed. "There wasn't really much painting going on."

She nodded in acceptance of the answer, but more like she was trying to encourage. "Where are you from?"

"A small, forgettable place in the Siberian wilderness."

"Where is your family now?"

"Orphaned."

"How did you turn?"

"What if I were true-born?"

"You weren't. If you were, you would have made that known obnoxiously early."

Another pause at my discretion. I drew a long sigh, the icy air soothing my lungs in between drags.

"What were you before?"

"Just a boy."

"You were turned as a child?"

"Barely an adult."

"What happened?"

"Greed."

"Tell me."

"He was enlightened, and for a time, I got to be part of such a bright strike of glory," I started, though I was undecided on how much detail to spare. "I served as a muse and a Host for him. It got me through one of the harshest winters I had ever seen. Not many of my foster siblings could say the same by the time the springtails spawned." I tossed the roach of my cigarette on the ground, stamping it out. "He was brilliant. He taught me all that I know."

"What happened after?"

"He was drunk, fed for too long." I laughed. "It is troubling how one slight mistake can result in cursing another with something worse than death."

"Luka." I didn't notice she had closed the distance until her arms wrapped around me. "I am sorry you had to go through that alone."

"It wasn't so bad."

"You should write down all your stories. It sounds like you've lived a long and interesting life."

"I would, but I don't have a pen."

"You're an artist, and you don't own a pen?"

"Not all stories deserve the decency of being written," I laughed.

"Why not?"

"Because then we must acknowledge that they were real."

"Excuses, excuses," she muttered.

Instinctively, I tensed at the feeling of her squeezing me.

"No need to get all soft," I grumbled, but I rested my arm around her shoulder. She didn't let go, even when we stood for a while. A soft brush of ease washed over me, filling me with an unfamiliar peace; just one spark of bliss.

XXV

The Creature

DEALING WITH THE MESS back in the city was cutting into my personal time.

I crumpled the small collection of messages, all from my father asking for correspondence in vain. There were too many things to do, instructions to send that wouldn't fit on telegram cards. The pressure weighed so heavily that, if I wasn't careful, I might fall to dust by the time I returned. It all went away with the help of distractions, including my favorite of all.

This was the only time I could spare to see her. Curiously, Alina did not go back to her beloved Nest after her errands; she went back to her makeshift lab late in the night.

Now, where have I seen that before?

She took her horse to the apothecary, no wagon in tow. I was sure she would make some excuse about forgetting something, but I wanted to see what she was truly up to. My shadow was most comfortable moving at night, and the company of others was not always what she needed.

Little Edith went to work early. Phoebe was busy managing the Nest in Alina's absence, and the rest of the town was cozied up in their homes. There was not a single soul to bother us when I inevitably caught her between my teeth.

The town transformed under night cover. It was a shame that not many stayed awake to enjoy it. Most ventured more toward the center, where the lights were bright and entertainment kept everyone distracted through the night. It was a time when the snow was the fluffiest, the air free of fumes, and the stars could be seen following the moon across the sky until dawn.

I watched as the singular, gloomy light appeared in the window above the shop, her shadow fluttering about as it passed the candle.

My teeth ached at the thought of her, my heart trembled at the memories of her touch. It was like my soul craved her far more than any food on earth could sustain. I wanted to have all of her, as much as she would let me, or as much as I could *take*.

When I opened the front door, it creaked eerily as I reached up to mute the bell, closing it quietly behind me. She had forgotten to lock it on her way in.

Or had *she forgotten? Was this an invitation?*

How foolish, though I suppose it would be more idiotic to assume a simple lock would keep me out.

As I ascended the stairs, I did not hear much movement in the flat above. My steps were careful as I reached the door at the top. It was intimidating, the stair corridor long and narrow, leading to that single door. It was claustrophobic, but maybe it was because I was holding my breath.

As I opened the door, I was finally able to see the lab she spent all her time in. Those same two windows I stalked from the outside were on the wall directly in front of me, a workbench off to the side, along with some cabinets.

On the other side was a blank wall, but it was obvious it was not left unused. The walls were stained brown, and soot-like smudges were left on the walls despite obvious attempts at scrubbing them.

The wood floors were unfinished, stained a color that could only be described as a logbook of victims to get that specific shade of char.

Speaking of the color of char, there was a curious image before me. My dear shadow with her knees to her chest, curled up. Her head tipped back, resting against the wall. Beside her, a bottle.

Still a drunk, I see.

Though as I approached, my cheery state was dampened when I saw her poison of choice.

On the floor next to her was an empty syringe next to the tall, corked bottle. It seemed she had progressed past simple spirits.

As I crouched in front of her, I was able to see her peaceful face. I do not think she had ever been this serene. Her eyes were moving under her lids as she dreamed, as though she were asleep.

I placed a hand on either side of her face, tipping it up straight. She drifted into one of my hands, cheek creased as she slumped into it.

"*Alina,*" I hummed, "dreaming of something?"

Her eyes opened, looking at me through her mismatched lashes before her eyes rolled back into her head.

Why wasn't she fighting?

I removed my gloves and forced her face upright. Her skin was clammy, and I didn't need a keen sense of touch to feel her shaking, clumsy like a newborn cat.

She smelled different. Not bad, just different—which was usually bad. Her typical sweet scent was dampened, watered down, exhausted. It was like a fever, depleted of the things that make her vibrant.

My giddy mood fell flat when I realized how far she was gone. It was like she left her body. This was not like her at all. The Alina

I knew would have thrown something at me by now, clawed at my eyes, *something*.

"Alina."

She moaned timidly before letting out a breath, slowly slumping to the side before I caught her, placing her back into an upright sitting position.

Her eyes opened again, but this time they stayed open. A cryptic smile played on her lips when she saw me, her fingers reaching out and touching my face. The nonabrasive gesture concerned me above all else.

I took a long look at her, this unfamiliar thing before me. Her condition made my chest tight, my grip on her tighter as if she were fading before my eyes.

"Are you awake?" I whispered.

"I'm alive?" She reached out to touch me, her cold fingers making me shiver.

"Yes, yes you are," I breathed, but I could only exhale, for she stole every breath I had.

"Come to me," she cooed, grasping at my coat weakly. Her lips came close, and I wasn't sure if she would kiss or bite; at least that part was the same.

My eyes closed when her silken lips brushed against mine. The taste of her on my tongue sent sparks through my nerves like loose gunpowder. There was very little restraining me from grabbing her and taking her there on the floor. But I knew this tenderness was not real, a mirage, a hallucination.

She clung to me, holding me there as she kissed me.

I could not stop myself from touching her, holding her face, and soaking in the attention. Her fingertips left cool trails wherever they touched. I wanted her to plunge them inside me and squeeze my burdened heart already.

"Why must you do this to yourself?" My throat strained as I forced the words out. "Who gave you this affliction?"

Her arms slithered around my shoulders, around my neck. Thin fingers traced along the back of my shoulder. She threw me a quizzical look, full of bemusement and some sense of longing in her glassy eyes. "Don't you remember?" Her lips skimmed my jawline, then fell to my neck. Her arms wrapped tighter around my shoulders. "It was you, my long-lost fixation."

It was almost heartfelt, being regarded with any intimacy from her. But it was short-lived as I watched the blue of her irises roll back into her head, her skin paling.

"Alina?" I grabbed her face.

The muscles in her jaw tensed, and her head threw back. Her entire body flexed back, a bit of blood dripping from her lips as she salivated.

As if the first time I witnessed this wasn't terrifying enough, this time was much worse.

"No! No, please." My voice caught as I held her to me. I supported her head as best I could as I lowered her to the floor. I put her on her side like I remembered Luka did once. I let go, just for a shake, to tear off my coat, tucking it quickly under her head as she shook, every muscle under the skin visible as her body seized.

"It's okay; it's fine, you're fine," I chanted, mostly for myself as I laid next to her, pulling her shaking body to my chest. I was afraid to move, afraid of her injuring herself if I let her go. My trembling hand smoothed down her wet hair, unsure how to soothe her.

Is this my fault?

Is this how it felt to be powerless? No option but to do nothing and wish for the best, wonder when it would end? I forgot to count how long she shook for. It could have been thirty seconds, or two minutes, an eternity. My body would be just as tense as hers, my hand never left her neck, monitoring the pulse.

Even when she stopped, I couldn't bring myself to move either of us, frozen in time and terror, a delicate moment that was all but stolen.

AGAINST HER SOBER WISHES, I went to her Nest.

I made her sit in the saddle in front of me. Even as I held her in my arms, it was unfamiliar. Not once had she ever been so limp, held with such ease.

As I approached the house on the hill, there were already figures hovering impatiently on the front porch, all of whom stopped to watch my steady approach.

Phoebe was the first to step into the moonlight, then a few other women I was unfamiliar with. I raised my hand, though I am sure they all would have their reservations.

As I dismounted, I gathered Alina into my arms. Two women took the horse away as Phoebe approached with purpose. When she reached me, she struck my face with the back of her hand, one of her rings cutting my cheek with an inevitable sting.

I winced and turned to look at her once more. Her chest rose and fell quickly, like she was either going to scream at me or weep.

"Hate me all you like, but I did not touch her." I shifted Alina in my arms so her head could rest comfortably on my shoulder.

"Bring her inside, first room on the second floor." Phoebe glanced over her shoulder at the girls as she chewed at the skin around her nails. "*Quickly*, please."

I did as I was told, attempting to be respectful of their domain.

As I walked up the stairs, other girls stole glances out of the corner of their eyes and whispered amongst themselves as they pretended they weren't frightened and morbidly curious.

The room Phoebe led me to was dull and cold. I did not expect luxury, though it seemed Alina was focused on living as humbly as she could. It really would not hurt her to use some color in her decor.

I set her down in the bed, peeling back the sheets before tucking her underneath. Alina did not look like she was ever disturbed, like she had been in a deep sleep this whole time. I knelt next to the bed, taking the pins out of her hair to let it down so she would not hurt herself in her slumber.

"Was she in the lab?" Phoebe spoke from the doorframe, chewing at her nails.

I nodded. "She was on the floor, just a needle and a bottle beside her." I refused to take my eyes off my dear nightmare of a woman. "Do you know what she's been taking?"

Phoebe let out a deep sigh. "Venom."

My gaze parted from Alina to look at Phoebe. "What did you say?"

She crossed her arms, scowling at me. "I said venom. Vipera venom."

"And you knew?" I rose slowly, the pressure of my anger threatening to reach the surface as it boiled over.

"Yes, but not until it was too late. I fear I enabled her," Phoebe spoke more quietly than before. "Come, let her sleep."

I nodded, stealing one last glance at Alina before I followed my sister out of the room.

When we descended, the talking stopped almost instantly by the time I made it to the bottom floor. The walk from the stairs to the front door was short, but the silence made it even longer. It was hard to tell if it was unwelcoming or just somber.

We went out to the front porch where Phoebe sat on a bench, patting the spot beside her.

I took a seat and stared out into the night. We had a view of the dirt road and the wooded area on the other side. The house was on a slight hill, so we could see the sky and the way the road wound down and disappeared into the darkness.

"I suspect she had been doing it since before she was kidnapped." Phoebe clutched her wool shawl tighter around her shoulders. "She did not get much better after we left London."

"You said you enabled her." I glared at her.

"She was in pain." Phoebe shot just as deadly a look back.

"What did you do?"

"I fed on her, and some days when she suffered, I bit her without feeding." She chewed at her lip as she fiddled with her necklace. "I stopped when it became a weekly, daily, then twice daily occurrence. I was worried for her, and I knew her physical wounds would heal. I did not anticipate she would need pain management for any mental scars."

I crossed my arms. I expected her to be angry, traumatized possibly, but I did not realize how much pain she would be in after.

"I think she has been stealing venom from the batches we collected."

"What makes you suspect that?"

"We are always missing a liter. She claims it is because the solution is concentrated and loses mass, but I know that isn't true. I count the inventory as we take it."

"How long does a liter last her?"

"I suspect until the next month when we do it all over again," she mumbled, "but it is worse than you think. She modifies it, adds things to it, concentrates it. I fear she will kill herself with it."

We sat in silence for a minute, then many. The fact that this was because of anything I had done made me want to disappear in shame, which was not something I was used to. She didn't deserve that.

"You should not have added those terms," Phoebe spoke up. "Forcing her hand is the last thing you want to do."

"Forcing her hand is my favorite thing to do." I tried to make light of the conversation.

"Silas." Her expression was grim. "You don't know what has become of her."

"What has she become, then?"

"A reaper."

"You are dramatic."

"She won't admit it, but she likes it. Killing them." Phoebe diverted her attention to her hands. "She has changed. She's erratic . . . sleepwalking . . . She disappears physically and mentally so often, she may as well be a ghost."

"I am jealous that you have such experience with her," I laughed, but I knew she was serious. I only got a taste of it when I made my proposal, but Phoebe had successfully piqued my interest regarding Alina's new habits.

"Silas." Phoebe paused, the toe of her slipper scratching at the worn wood while she sat, "What . . . what did you mean back there?"

I leaned back on the bench, crossing my arms as I looked up at the stars. "What do you mean?"

"Is there anything to go back to?" She bit her lip. "In London?"

"Nothing but father's wrath."

"We are in danger, then."

"No, Father isn't bold enough to waltz into uncharted territory." I pulled my cigarette holder from my pocket, only to find there were none left. "For now, we live in bliss," I mumbled.

"For now," she strained, her eyes landing on me, not in anger, but solemnly. When I didn't return the look, her jaw twitched, and she crossed her arms, turning back to look out into the dark. "Damn it, Silas. Kin killing is no easy stain to brush out. Out of all the ways you could have lashed out, did it have to be something so gratuitous?"

"Would you rather me leave more heads to hunt when they come for her?" I finally looked her way, her cheeks bright red, angry with the insinuation.

"Why did you come back?" she snapped. I could see her jaw tensing and relaxing, like she was working out the tension emanating from her rage.

"I came for her."

"No, the first time."

The first time?

"Seven years," she laughed, "you didn't visit me for seven years, after so many routine reunions. You just up and left, gone, not even a letter, a telegram, nothing." Her eyes were glassy, despite her blinking away the emotion, "My year without Alina was my loneliest. I hoped you would at least show up with a half-decent excuse."

"I couldn't bear it anymore." I kept my answers steady.

"Oh! Right, let me guess. Father, the Nest, the pressure." Her laugh was comical this time, steeped in sarcasm. "What? Is imagining any responsibility to your Nest—to your family—too much for you? Did you find what you were looking for out there? Your purpose? Do you really lament any sort of responsibility to anyone besides your appetite?"

"Phoebe . . ."

"No, I want to hear it! What, pray tell, called the oh-so-independent Silas Forbes back to civilization?"

"He didn't tell you, did he?" I winced. Her words were always sharp, I knew that, but something about how she spoke to me was just critical.

"Let me guess, another thing you assume I don't know."

"Your engagement. I feared it was too late."

"Pardon?" She laughed but didn't continue after I showed no humor. "I am *not* engaged."

"Well," I took a deep inhale. "That was *Father's* reason for returning home."

"He wouldn't do that."

"Why else would he request you return to the Nest so suddenly? I am not the only man in your life who was absent, dear sister."

"Don't change the subject."

"Did you think you would be different from any of the others?"

"I'm his favorite; he said so," she said, though not with the same confident edge.

"I was his favorite too," I said softly, reaching out for her hand. "We all are until he wants something new."

"That doesn't make sense; you're not married."

"That is because I was born a son, Phoebe."

"Are you really implying that Father sold our sisters for some sick game of power and estates?"

I took a deep breath, lowering my eyes.

"I don't believe you," she scoffed.

"I wasn't going to continue his sick game," I snapped. "It has left too many motherless children. Just like you."

"That is not his fault!" Her voice cracked. "My mother passed in childbirth; so did the others."

"Is that what he told you?"

"I have no reason to distrust it!"

"He killed her, Phoebe. Same as all the women before her."

"That's an absurd claim. Your mother had five daughters after you."

"My mother was bred to death."

"He wouldn't do that!"

"Your mother, and all the others after mine, were killed for having one too many daughters," I hissed.

"That's not true—"

"Phoebe!" I raised my voice at her. "One after the other, he killed them if it wasn't a son. He had an obsession with having a spare. He was driven mad from the obsession born of my mother's death."

She didn't speak, and there was a deafening silence between us. Something clicked, and it was like we were seeing eye to eye, even if it was reluctant.

"Why are you here, then?" she spoke softly.

"You already know."

"Are you here for Alina or for your Nest?"

"Both. I do it for her."

"All of it?" She raised her brow at me.

"Of course. I need her. She will realize she needs me too. Sooner with pressure."

"Why wouldn't you let her choose you, then?" She crossed her arms. "Are you afraid she won't?"

"We don't have the luxury of waiting to find out, not this time." I glared at her.

"That is your fault. *You* are the one who turned to kin killing."

"You know very well the offer is the best you will get," I droned. "What is the rule again? Utilitarianism?"

"Silas, trust me when I say you do not want it to come to that. She will hate you for it."

"Our bond was born of hate; she will come around." I stood from my seat. "Have a good evening, sister; extend my well wishes to the girls."

XXVI

The Poisoner

THE STAIRS SQUEAKED LOUDER this morning, or maybe I was hungover. In reality, I was not sure how I got home. My body ached, more so than the standard drunken recovery. It was like I had pulled an ox cart all on my own. Not only that, but I had a dreamlike mindfulness and a dry croak in my throat.

When I dragged my feet to the kitchen, Phoebe sat at the table as she spoke quietly to Rebecca and Adeline. A few other girls were present as they were cleaning their plates from breakfast. The clinking of utensils against plates chimed in my ears louder than necessary.

Phoebe caught me out of the corner of her eye as I snuck past to the living room.

"Alina! Good morning." She glanced at the other two girls before looking back at me. "Come sit, come sit."

She kicked out the chair next to her, and a smile tightened across her face. I knew that look meant I was about to be lectured.

"I spared you some porridge." Adeline gently scooted a bowl toward me.

"For the hangover." Rebecca placed a dram of bitters and scotch before me.

"If you need anything," Adeline fiddled with her apron and glanced nervously at Rebecca, "just let us know, all right? Make sure to rest."

"Right." I raised a brow at Phoebe.

"Leave us for a moment?" Phoebe asked quietly, and the girls filed into the living room.

It was a somber morning. I could hear the dying fire crackle, the dripping of melting ice creating a calming harmony between the two. The house smelled like the ghost of breakfast, as welcoming as always, although the light from the window was burning my corneas.

"If you have something to say, do it now." I took the small glass of alcohol and tossed my head back with the glass pressed against my lips.

"How was your midnight walk?"

Just like that, sobriety crashed into me like a pile of bricks. Like someone cracked a cane over my head. I choked on the liquor, too early to clearly find an explanation.

"Excuse me?" I coughed.

"Your ears work well, Alina, despite how selectively you listen." Phoebe shot me a disdainful glare. "Do you not remember?"

"No," I admitted, poking the porridge with my spoon.

"Late night at the lab?"

"Just had a few more things to tie up from the day—"

"Do not treat me like a fool, Alina." Her voice was austere, too grating for such an hour. "Silas brought you home."

I choked on my food. It was too early for such a name to be uttered.

Heat rose to the back of my head and neck. I did not know if I should be embarrassed or angry. It was worse hearing it from Phoebe.

"Well, maybe he will rescind his idiotic proposal now that the word is out that I am unwell!" I joked.

"Unfortunately for you, he is not easily dissuaded."

"Persistent like a termite."

"You must gather yourself. Don't fall apart at the seams now; the girls are worried. They need you to be strong for them. If you are not going to take his deal, make damned sure that you show them that you can hold your own." She took my hand and squeezed. "I know it is not what you want, but if it comes down to it, you have to have a good reason for declining. You have to convince the girls that they need not want for more, that you can protect them well enough on our own."

I pulled my hand from hers, shoving a spoon full of porridge into my mouth as I ignored her. It was too early for talks as silly as this.

"I do not expect them to come here tonight. Silas might be inclined to let you rest after last night, if we are hopeful."

"Emphasis on *hopeful*," I laughed.

"He did bring you home, with no foul play that I could see."

"He is only being nice because he is waiting on an answer. I am sure by the week's end, when I reject him, he will be back to his bastard self."

"Possibly," Phoebe trailed off, but not another word was spoken on the subject that day.

I SLIPPED INTO SOMETHING comfortable, a three-piece wool walking suit with a matching shawl paired with three layers of wool stockings. The day's air was purely arctic, the tears from the wind in my face threatening to freeze every time my lashes became wet from them. I took Horse into town with me and brought him into the neighbor's carriage house behind the shop due to the weather.

It was becoming hard to walk quickly when even my bones could feel the cold. The blacksmith was not too far off, and I needed to pick up my tools. My amateur carving knives were not cutting it, pun aside.

The white coating made it easier to spot even the slightest shadows, including the one that began walking in stride with me.

"You might turn blue if you keep insisting on walking in such weather," Silas commented as he caught up to me.

"I don't know what you mean." My teeth chattered as my jaw was beginning to lock up. "Besides, it would be cruel to make my horse wait outside for small errands. Walking is healthy."

"You don't have anything warmer to wear?" He pinched at my sleeve.

"Nope." I raised my chin and practically said the words to the sky in an attempt to ignore him.

"If you say so, Krampus," he teased, brushing some flakes off my fur hat.

"What brings our paths together this morning?" I looked up at him. "Surely it is not a coincidence."

"I wanted to see you."

"And?"

"Nothing more."

I shook my head at him. We arrived in front of the blacksmith. The large barn doors in front of the shop were only slightly ajar to keep out most of the windchill. The sound of metal chimes became clearer the closer we got.

"John?" I called out.

Inside, the shop was just as rustic as the outside. A roaring furnace stood proud in the industrial space, governing over its dominion. Next to the furnace, there was a brawny figure swinging a mallet down on a red-hot rod of metal. Pieces of cherry-colored metal flaked off to expose bright yellow on the rod underneath before calming down to the same red. The flakes turned ashen as they settled.

"John!" I raised my voice over the ring of the hammer.

The tanned man turned to see me and flashed a smile as bright as the furnace itself.

"I didn't see you there! I would have held on to your tools until tomorrow—it is far too cold to be walking about today." He submerged the hot metal with a hiss in the water barrel next to his anvil and approached as he discarded his leather gloves.

He gave me a friendly hug before holding me by my shoulders at arm's length.

"I think you are the only customer I can greet with a hug since your attire is usually as black as the soot on my hands," he laughed, wrinkles at the outer corner of his eyes appearing along with his smile. "Who is this young gentleman?" He glanced over my shoulder before he passed me.

"Silas Forbes—" He held a hand out for John.

"There is no need for formalities; come here." John laughed merrily before wrapping his arms around him, slapping the back of Silas's shoulder before pulling back. "Any friend of Alina is a friend of mine."

I physically recoiled at the mention of friends, but it only amused Silas.

"It is such a relief to meet someone genial in this town; it has been quite a task making acquaintances," Silas joked. "I would be completely lost without my hospitable *friend*."

"I figured I would take my tools now. I understand you will be closing the shop for a few days to prepare for incoming weather." I removed my hat so I could shake the moisture from the melted snow.

"Of course! Though if you did not pick them up, I would have dropped them at the house," he reached under his work bench and pulled out a leather bag that was rolled neatly in a log shape aside from the handle and strap that held it together.

"I wouldn't ask that of you."

"You never ask anything of anyone." John raised his brow and handed the bag to Silas. When John let go of the bag, I could see Silas jolt due to the weight of it, but he recovered smoothly and pretended it didn't happen. I suppose he didn't expect the weight.

"Will you be coming for Christmas?" I did not want to sound too hopeful in case he had other plans this year, but it was nice having him visit.

"If you want me to, I will come," he replied, his eyes somber.

John had lost his wife three years before Phoebe and I arrived, and he spent his Christmases alone, he had said. We invited him to our own Christmas celebration, since we were all people with no one else to spend the happier days with, aside from our untraditional family. I remember the first time he came, he brought molasses cookies that he used to make for his wife. The next year, we made them together as a Nest with him.

"Come by, the girls would love to see you, as always. Phoebe has been playing with some recipes that I am sure she would love to trade with you." I squeezed his shoulder.

"Of course." He smiled, then snapped himself into his usual chipper mood. "Ah! Hit the road before it storms later. I will not hold you pigeons up any longer!"

"I will see you next week, Pops." We retreated through the opening between the tall door shutters, the wind biting my cheeks as it leached the heat from them as if it were merely borrowed.

"Pops?"

"Yes."

Silas raised a brow in confusion.

"If you thought that you were safe knowing my father was dead and there was no one to bless your horrid idea of an engagement, you thought wrong. John is the man who would beat you with an iron if he knew our history."

"So he is the one who would bless it?" he teased. "Shall I run back and ask his permission?"

"You should be seeking *my* permission, but it seems that is not good enough for you."

"God, woman, *what* is in this bag?" He adjusted the weight of the strap on his shoulder.

"A hatchet, carving knives, some butcher's saws, and the like." I shrugged. "Bone really wears them down. I like to keep them maintained."

"Where to now?"

"Mortuary," I answered simply as we rounded a corner.

The block we turned onto was more exposed to the sun. I could almost feel a slight prickling on my face as it itched for warmth.

"Who died?"

"I do not know yet."

Upon approaching the morgue, I opened the door to quickly duck inside.

Bodies were already on tables, and the sink was full from the morning's work. Bags of rubbish were sitting in the corner, ready to be taken out.

"Henry!" I called, heading directly down the hallway and into the last room on the right.

The small overhead window allowed some light since there were no windows along the typical spots on the wall for privacy reasons.

Henry was already preparing the morning's cadaver. He must have been so engrossed that he did not hear me call. When he caught me out of the corner of his eye, his stern expression softened, then it hardened once more when he saw Silas.

"You didn't tell me you would be bringing a visitor," Henry moped.

"I didn't know I was going to have one either. He joined me on my errands," I offered the explanation, though Henry waved dismissively at me. Now that they were both in the same room, Henry was like a shorter, skinnier version of Silas in terms of looks, apart from those dark eyes. They were polar opposites in personality.

"Apologies for intruding. Silas Forbes, nice to meet your acquaintance." Silas held out a gloved hand.

Henry glanced at Silas's hand, as his own were elbow deep in the cadaver. In a thinly veiled attempt to not be rude, he raised a brow at Silas.

"Right," Silas mumbled, his hand retreating, seemingly annoyed that he had made an effort to be cordial at all.

Henry always made himself look busy when he was flustered. I suppose he was threatened since I suspect Henry had a small favorability for me.

"What came in this morning?" I stepped beside the shorter blond man. "I heard there were two bodies."

"Animal attack is my best hypothesis." He shrugged.

Henry was less talkative than usual; that was all the confirmation I needed to know he was upset. I shot Silas a look and jerked my head toward the door.

He furrowed his brows; then raised one before looking toward the door and then to me.

My eyes narrowed at him expectantly.

A rumble of protest in his throat before he silently agreed to stand in the hallway.

"Who is he?" Henry didn't pull his attention from his task.

"Silas—"

"To you, I mean."

"Hardly a friend."

He nodded as if that answer revealed something that I wasn't saying. I know he was hurt seeing someone else chaperoning me.

"Are you ready?" I put on a set of leather gloves as we inspected from either side of the corpse, covered by the modesty of a sheet.

He nodded, carefully peeling away the edge of the sheet to reveal the face, then the neck, then the chest. When the sheet reached the abdomen, there was nothing else to see.

It was only a torso.

There were large wounds on the abdomen, neck, and face. The skin around the wounds looked like they had been gnawed on by the likes of a dog, but the pattern of the bite marks were distinctly human, making messy horseshoe-shaped marks along the flesh.

Henry did not seem fazed, but he did not say anything. He was processing it calmly, rationalizing the sights before him.

The corrupted were who I suspected caused it, though there could have been others wreaking havoc. As destructive as the corrupted were, I did feel pity for them. Empathy, even. They did not choose to be turned into those repugnant shells of people. I cannot imagine being turned and having all the impulsive desires of a starved Vipera with no biological hardware to feed easily. While Hosts have dormant organs and teeth that develop after turning, typical humans had to make do with the standard. The frustration of the messy feeding process made them irate, causing them to tear at the flesh and ultimately kill those they fed on. Luckily for us, the corrupted did not have the ability to turn. Which means it was Vipera being careless and leaving it for us to clean up later.

"Coyotes? Wolves?" I asked Henry.

"It is hard to tell; a lot of the flesh is torn, and the bite marks are atypical of wild animals, but the pickiness is unusual." He used forceps to lift the skin, then used a glass rod to poke around and count the organs left over.

"How so?"

"Animals usually aren't picky about which organs they eat, especially if they are starved or rabid enough to try for a human."

"Where was this body found?"

"In the wooded area north of the city."

"Anywhere else?"

"Both bodies were in the same spot."

I reached into the abdominal cavity to peel the skin away. I stuck my hand further upward into the ribs, feeling around.

"I feel a partial lung, and I have yet to feel the heart," I mentioned.

"Whatever it was must have stuck its muzzle up into the cavity to try to pull out organs," he mumbled, mainly to himself.

"What condition is the other body in?"

"More or less the same . . . no liver and is just as much of a mess as this one."

"Ah, good to know. Which reminds me, I have to set more traps soon," I removed my hands, the sound of moisture squishing as I removed my arms from the cavity.

"Discard those in the sink," Henry instructed.

I pulled the gloves off over the basin and then turned the water on over them, watching the blood flood the drain before dissipating until the water ran mostly clear.

I nearly forgot that I had a golden-haired guest waiting ever so patiently at the door until I looked over and saw him leaning on the frame, watching. His pale eyes watched steadily, I do not know for how long.

It was a grim reminder of a different kind of predator in our midst.

AFTER DEPARTING, I COULD not hear anything Silas said; I was deep in thought as we passed through the park on the way back, since the sun was fighting through the overcast clouds before the storm ahead. I watched my skirt as it dusted the fresh white powder on the path. With each step I avoided cracks and rocks to distract from the bitter cold.

I was stopped in my tracks by Silas hooking his fingers into the back of my collar, stopping me as I nearly choked.

"What is it?" I clicked my tongue.

"Could we talk?"

"What is there to talk about?"

"It would be harder to choose what *not* to talk about."

"Spit it out then." I crossed my arms.

"Why do you use venom?"

"How else do I test a drug?"

"No, why do *you* use it? You know it works; you do not need tests."

"I quit drinking."

"In exchange for something more dangerous?"

"You did not mind it when it was *you* envenomating me."

He was stunned, shocked as if he didn't know how to respond. I would not let go of my pride, not so he could lecture me. What did he know about coping? He was the one responsible for the phantom pains that lived within my body; he had no right to judge me. I did not need a coat anymore, for I could feel the heat rising in tandem with my anger.

"I will never understand you." He swatted some of the snow from his hair as it steadily fell from the sky.

"You never will, that would require empathy."

He laughed and shook his head. "I do not need empathy to figure you out. You refer to me as a simple creature; you are not much different. You are a feral, disagreeable villain—"

"Then leave me be if you think so low of me."

"No, my dearest shadow." He stepped forward to cup my face in his hands. "It is what I like most about you. Every time you look at me with those unforgiving eyes, I feel you could do anything to me. You could squeeze my heart, and it would still beat proudly for you, swelling until it bursts in your fist."

"Always the poet, never the lover," I scoffed, but I did not dare move away from his touch.

"I will always be your lover, even if that love is unrequited." He glanced at my lips through lowered lashes, our foreheads resting against each other. I found myself shaking, his touch reminding me how chilled it really was. "You won't admit that I am the only one to make an unfeeling thing like you feel alive. *Truly* alive," he whispered.

"Do you make me feel alive, or wish for death?"

"I would give you both, if you let me."

Our breath mingled in the air. How jealous I was of the mist that could escape. Even then, just us being close enough to let each breath disguise itself together was too scandalous of an insinuation for me.

"Use me." The corner of his lip curved upward into a smirk. "Let me keep you warm for a while." His whisper nearly registered as a hiss when the wind whistled through the small gap between us.

"Will you not grant me any sort of peace?" I mumbled, pushing at his chest.

"We could only be each other's peace; we are too chaotic to find it elsewhere."

"What do you *really* want from me?"

Silas's eyes narrowed, his pupils constricting as he stared. He smirked after a contemplative pause and tucked a loose piece of hair behind my ear. The leather of his gloves were cold and impersonal despite the soft touch. "I want *everything*."

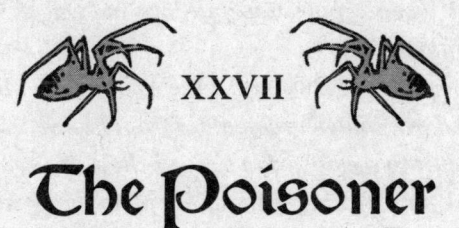

XXVII

The Poisoner

AS I WALKED THROUGH to the market square, the build-ings seemed much taller than usual. They were misshapen, stretching high and distorted like a caricature. It was like how you imagine a childhood home, or at least an attempt to remember it. The more steps I took, the taller they became. Or, perchance, it was I who was changing in size, becoming smaller and smaller until I could sit on a flake of frost.

No, a simple illusion, nothing more.

The wind howled as it whipped around the corners of the stone and brick buildings. An animalistic yet artificial sound as the buildings groaned, calling, begging me to not continue the path I had chosen.

A chittering rose around me, echoing and knocking against the walls of the alley.

As the small street opened up to the square, a gathering swelled with interest. One or two voyeurs added to the mass, a shuffling of dark figures. Like buzzards collecting a crowd. Their croaks and squawks congealed into one audible mass.

I passed one, then two, then many, the crowd becoming denser the further I traveled, the harder I tried to peer through the crowd *at the spectacle. My body was squeezed between the others, unable to move any closer before I saw.*

An erected wooden pole atop yule logs, old wagon wheels, anything they could find.

Tied to the pole was a woman. One whom I don't think I could forget if I tried. An image I remember from two years ago in that Den, resurfacing to me at such a time as these. A tired, exhausted woman, black hair sticking to the sweat of her brow, and her chest pulled open, her ribs spread like wings for the crowd to see. Her chest cavity bare, only trails of blood from what was taken, her heart discarded at her feet. Used while she was useful for what she could provide.

I rubbed the spot on my shoulder, remembering two different pairs of teeth that pierced the spot, both memorable in their own ways.

The voices around me began to change. This was not the noise of chatter, of conversation—not even of outrage. This was squishing, ripping, and chewing.

"Look," a voice said.

The woman's blank eye straightened from its dead gaze, slowly sliding across the white of the eye to land on me. She mouthed something.

"What do you need?" My voice was ragged, shoving through the chewing noises, even making it past the mass of bodies, like something was trying to pull me away. "Tell me; I want to help!" Even when shouting to her, the volume was dampened.

I climbed the piles of rubbish; it cracked and snapped under my feet, splintering under the pressure.

"I want to help!" I shouted again, finally seeing her eye to eye.

"You want to help?" she mouthed.

A crackling sound snapped and hissed in my ear. Shaking as I begged, "Let me."

"Help yourself."

Her arms shot out, heat searing into my skin as she grabbed my face, yanking me close. Her pale eyes steadied on mine, her brow taut. Her hold on my face was motherly, painful, but out of love, of fear.

"Forevermore, even in death."

The crackling was louder; it was right under my feet. I winced and tried to pull away, but her grip was tough like ragweed. Red burst from the corner of my eyes, the head no longer just under her fingertips, but the bottoms of my feet, my back, the air in my lungs.

"Wake up."

My own voice split through my eardrum in a howl I would expect from a madwoman, or a cry marking a death. The fire around seared our flesh.

"Wake up!"

Fingertips squeezed my head and face on either side, shaking my head rapidly as if it would clear the fog.

Everything ached, from my head to my fingernails to the toes of my numb feet. When I opened my eyes, I was met by another pair. Fleeting vulnerability lit them, a haunted intensity that evaporated faster than eighty proof.

The pounding in my head was either coming from a raging headache or Luka's grip on the sides of my head.

A drip of black slid down his cheek, three lines hatching over the old scar, exposing the demon that was just below the skin.

I lifted my trembling hand, black crust under my nails.

He didn't say my name; he did not comfort me. The only thing grounding me was his grip, as if to scruff a feral animal.

"If you can't keep your head on straight, someone may *cut it off.*" He jerked my head once he realized I was awake.

I stumbled back, looking around. I was in the square, maybe a block or two from the shop.

"Where is Silas?" I staggered back, my body desperate to create distance.

"He's busy," Luka said coolly, stepping toward me again.

"Stay away!" I swung my hand at him.

He caught my wrist. "You'll break all on your own if you keep refusing help."

"I do not need your help."

"You can't afford to be so picky much longer. Whether you deny my help or that from someone you believe to be more well-meaning—you will crumble all the same. You hide your wounds better than most." It almost seemed like a compliment. "Your Nest may not even notice until it is too late."

"It's been late since before they were here. It's *always* been too late for me."

"Only if you let it."

I spat in his face, and he threw me over his shoulder.

"Leave me!" I pounded my fists on his back, my voice cracking as the noise slapped against the bricks in the empty square. I screamed at him until my voice croaked, exhausted from being unheard.

ALCOHOL STUNG AGAINST MY foot, a low hiss as the cotton ball touched the scratch.

"Bite your tongue," John muttered. "You're lucky it was only a few cuts."

I squirmed in my seat at the kitchen table, directly next to John and a bag of home medical supplies courtesy of Edith. He held my leg, inspecting the cuts and bruises from my nightly excursion. While I had hoped it was just a dream, the evidence of Luka tucked under my fingernails told me it was very real.

"It was not luck," I corrected. John raised a brow, and it made me slouch in defeat.

He checked my shoulder, then my hands. He pushed up my sleeve to reveal an irritated collection of marks in the pit of my elbow. John's face lifted quickly, and I snapped my sleeve down.

"Are you not worried?" John squeezed my hand, not letting me take it away.

"No, why would I be?" I pushed his hand away and stood.

"Between sleepwalking and that Nest you angered, you don't think they will plan to retaliate?"

"Not with them knowing a single cut will turn them into ash to feed my springtime garden," I muttered, grabbing my coat from the back of the chair as I slipped away.

I told everyone to keep their rings on, but not because I was paranoid. I was just being cautious. In the living room, there were more girls gathered than usual. My presence made the group disperse when they caught me in the corner of their eyes.

Rebecca relaxed in her chair instead of fleeing, giving Adeline a reassuring squeeze before she fluttered off as well.

"Rough night?" Rebecca raised a brow, sipping the black coffee from her handmade mug.

"Something like that." I pulled the blanket closer over my shoulders and sat on the couch across from her. My hair was still a bit damp from the night outing. I hadn't even bothered to change into house clothes before falling asleep in the kitchen.

"What kept you up most of the night, then?" she asked. Her deep brown eyes were always so stoic, like she knew the answers before she asked questions.

"Too much to think about." My breath slowed, heavy from exhaustion, like I was floating through the conversation.

"I guess that does come with being a Dam in your own right, even if you are only a human," she laughed.

"Was there another reason for everyone gathering before? The dispersal wasn't very subtle."

Rebecca was in no rush to answer. She took a slow sip of her coffee, the rich aroma reaching my nose as she savored her morning brew.

"When we were dumping parts in the woods, we encountered a corrupted."

My eyes widened. "Is everyone all right?"

"Of course." She raised her hand in a calming gesture before reaching forward to place her cup on the table. "We took care of it, but it has some girls a bit worried. They were trading gossip, asking which way you might lean on Mr. Forbes's proposal."

My jaw tightened as my teeth ground together. My fingers aimlessly plucked the wool pilling on the blanket. "What did you tell them?"

"I answered honestly. I said you were not in favor of it. It did not calm them."

My only reply was a nod. My thoughts raced, thinking of how I could possibly ease the crowd without giving in to a monster. It would be like making a deal with the devil, completely undermining our cause.

"There are only a few more days left," Rebecca mentioned.

"I do not need a reminder."

"I'm just speaking plainly." She paused to choose her words carefully. "The needs of the few do not trump the needs of the many."

"Are you *and* Phoebe going to lecture me this week?" I left my spot on the couch so I could get ready for the day ahead.

"Where are you going?" Rebecca stepped into my path.

"I need air."

"We all need some air, but maybe you should wait." She spoke lowly, throwing a glance at the girls. "For their own mental well-being, they need you here."

"For their own physical well-being, I'm going for a walk. I have to think. Unless you want to do that for me. Unless you have a quick and easy solution to all our problems, Rebecca?" I looked down at her, cocking my head.

She pressed her lips together, looking away again.

"That's what I thought," I mumbled, pushing past her shoulder and out the front door.

They may be comfortable hiding, but they wouldn't get far if they barricaded themselves like startled hens. Someone had to keep it business as usual, no matter the interruptions along the way.

There was something I had to do, and my window of opportunity was closing fast.

TO SOLVE MY CREATURE problem, I had to stop hesitating. There was no use stalling it any longer. It was time for him to go.

Since I was already acquainted with the reception, it was easy to get in. All I had to do was tell them his last name and flash a pretty smile.

How gullible.

I stepped down the luxurious hallways, covered in ambient light, the hallways were decorated like a small palace. It wasn't long before I was in front of his door.

I clutched the small key in my hand, fiddling with it as I took a deep breath. I may only be holding a key, but I had not come unarmed. Tucked away in the dark tendrils of my hair was a hairstick; within it, a needle doused in poison. It was my single greatest weapon against these fiends, and this time it would not fail. I knew better now.

I turned the key in the lock as quietly as possible. Slipping into the room, I latched the door subtly behind me.

The room was dark, quiet even. As my eyes adjusted, I gathered the surroundings. The curtains covered the windows, not even the streetlight snuck between the fabric. The shapes of furniture formed in my vision, and my eyes landed on the bed.

I approached, noticing the bed was untouched, no creature in sight. The sheets were still neatly pressed and tucked into the frame.

I had come too early.

I bit my lip, ready to turn back and abandon the mission altogether, but then there was a rustling outside the door, a key fitting into a lock.

The blood rushed down to the floor, draining me in my mortification.

Without thinking, I opened the closet doors and stepped inside, in time to watch the light from the hallway blaze a trail through the darkness of the room. I watched through the vertical seam of the doors as a silhouette appeared, entering the room as he tossed his jacket on the chair.

Silas's dark figure wandered over to the small bar in the corner, pouring something for himself. He combed his fingers through his hair. He relaxed, quiet in the almost mundane scenery. It was easy to forget he was a creature at times like these. He seemed . . . dare I say, *lonely*.

I half expected him to keep the company of strumpets or other easily acquired entertainment, to be throwing parties and accompanying the bar until the early hours of the morning.

Instead, he was alone.

He threw his head back as he swallowed the rest of his drink, clicking his tongue against the roof of his mouth before placing the glass down. He stared a minute, possibly lost in thought, before he returned toward the door out of my view. I only knew he left because of the light of the door opening and closing.

When the door clicked shut, I opened the closet.

What was I thinking?

When I turned to exit, there he was, staring down at his time-piece as he leaned against the door, only glancing up after a few beats. Those dead eyes glared my way, subtly reflecting the light like a cat.

"Thought I smelled a rat." Silas crossed his arms as he awaited a reply.

I stiffened, unsure what my options were or what his next move would be.

"What? Didn't you come to play?" He laughed, but he sounded tired rather than amused. "I thought it was rare for a spider to leave its web?"

"*Is it so hard to believe I wanted to see you?*" I threw his own words at him.

"Touché," he said, shaking his head, "but that's not why you're here."

"Perhaps not."

"Your hair is done up," he commented, his eyes a bit sad, but it was too dark to tell. "For me?"

"That is up to you."

"Tell me"—he pushed himself off the door to approach, and I stepped back—"do you think killing me will solve your problems?"

"Yes."

"Do you think there will be another as kind as me?"

"You threatened me—"

"Someone else would simply kill you, not bother with threats." He stepped closer.

"It would at least be fair."

"Fair? You want me to be fair? If you prefer I act like any other with no regard to who you are, then fine! I can do that," he growled, grabbing me by my coat collar. "Do you want to know what they would do to you?"

I swallowed hard, shoving his chest to create distance.

"You come in here to stab me in my sleep, and *I'm* the one you expect the worst of?" He seized me by the neck.

"Silas!" I yelped, but was swiftly cut off by the wind being knocked out of me from the force of him slamming my back into the wall.

"Don't." His words came out in a hiss, as he lifted me slightly in his grip.

I had to stand on the very tips of my toes to breathe. I reached up for my needle, and he leaned in to bite my wrist, making me retract quickly.

"What did you expect?" I gulped for air. "Did you think I would leap into your arms at the sight of you?"

"You were going to be in my arms either way."

"Delusional," I spat.

He squeezed again, and my head began growing light from the lack of air and the uncomfortable position. A wicked glint flashed in his eye as he watched.

I gasped when I went up on my toes, sinking back down into his grip when I couldn't keep the posture.

"Is this how I must calm you every time? I feel it won't be good for that pretty head of yours."

"I guess . . . My head is no stranger to your . . . concussions," I panted, squirming in discomfort.

His free hand brushed against my cheek, a soft touch that made my skin crawl, knowing who it was coming from. Before I could get too comfortable, his hand trailed from my cheek, down the front of my blouse, between my breasts, then pulled up my skirt.

I pushed out a huff of air through my nose, barely able to make any other remark.

"Alina," he chuckled, "is this really the type of thing to get you hot and bothered? Was I too modest in the past with you? You filthy thing." He pressed his palm flush against my pussy, supporting me only there as he was firm on my neck.

I shook my head, stretching my neck out to gasp for air before my knees buckled, and he gripped between my legs even tighter.

He rubbed gently, his fingers slicking between my labia, collecting the wetness quickly forming between.

"I'm simply torn," he removed his hand from between my legs, forcing me back on my toes. "You've made such a mess I don't know whether to fuck you or eat you." He let out a wicked laugh. "What say you?" he asked in mock curiosity, squeezing the sides of my throat a little tighter.

"N-n . . ."

"N-no? N-next time make sure to shove a rag in that haughty mouth of yours?" He unbuckled his trousers. He pressed his hips between my legs, loosening his grip enough for me to breathe.

I gasped for air, mouth agape, desperately trying to take in as much as I could.

Then his hand pressed against the sides of my throat. "Don't get ahead of yourself."

I glared at him, held against the wall by his hips, slightly above eye level. "You lied."

He raised his brow, patience visibly thinning.

"You said you don't know whether to eat me or fuck me." I glanced down before meeting his again. "It seems your mind was always made up."

"You think you're clever." He shifted his hips. I could feel the tip of his cock slick between my legs.

"I've never been in any danger, have I?"

He squinted at me, almost a sneer.

"You've never killed anything powerful. You're a dog who picks off the rats to make himself feel better about the pack leaving him beh—"

He squeezed my throat, shoving the tip inside. I yelped and dug my nails into his wrist.

"How good you are, it's like your body remembers," he leaned down to whisper in my ear, slowly rolling his hips. "You feel like a dream. I can feel each pump of blood your heart forces through you, calling me like a dinner bell."

"*Sick*," I managed.

"Yes, you make me violently ill, crazed and feral at just the sight of you," he groaned, lifting my leg up on his hip, thrusting forward with an audible thud against the wall every time. "Every godforsaken day, you are chronic. Incessant, ever present, and vicious, the way you leave me with phantom pains."

I don't know if it was the high or his words, but something inside me was growing hot. I hooked my leg on his hip tightly, using the support to lift myself higher, to gasp for breath. Once I did, he thrust again. I flinched when my hips hit the wall again. I sank back down, his grip a little lighter, and I lifted myself again, only to be met with another rough thrust that prompted a yelp.

I sank back down, and he was still. Was he . . . only fucking me when I breathed?

I held my breath, and he held me against the wall unmoving. I could feel his chest rise and fall against mine, my heart beating faster, and my head slowly beginning to throb. Finally, I pushed myself up to breathe, and he shoved his cock so deep inside it hit the back.

"Silas!" I yelled; it almost came out as a sob.

"Say it again," he said breathlessly, "say my name."

"No!" I shouted at him, but he thrust again. As he pounded, my head sloped to the side. I didn't have the energy to hold it up. He leaned down, nipping gently at my earlobe before sucking gently on my neck.

"Please," he whispered, almost tenderly, "say it again." He

begged, his hand still on my throat, but gently squeezing the sides on and off. He didn't want me to go just yet.

"*Silas,*" his name came out as a pitiful sob, and he pulled both my legs around his waist.

We stopped moving, a stalemate met by only each other's breath, by our pulses as we were caught in each other's grasp. Each exhale, the ghost of words we wished to say, but knew might haunt us forever.

"Don't make me do something I'll regret," he whispered breathlessly.

A drunken smile played on my lips, the image of him blurring in and out. "Do you regret me, Silas Forbes?"

"Never." He spoke low, lifting me away from the wall.

The world was spinning until I landed in the soft expanse of the bed. He flipped me on my stomach, and the world just kept spinning. I barely had time to gather myself.

He climbed over me, kissing and leaving soft bites at the back of my neck as he reached around to unbutton my blouse.

"Wait," I mumbled, glancing back at him.

He kissed me over my shoulder. He held his palm against my front, my back flush against his chest as he prodded between my legs again, but didn't go in.

Against my better judgment, I kissed him back. The room stopped spinning, and I was in a delightful high, willing to indulge.

"Alina." He swallowed, like it physically pained him to wait, poised.

I pulled away, his hands smoothing over the fabric, as if it was making him impatient with the lack of skin contact, shaking feverishly.

"You are the same creature you've always been." I swallowed. "Will I ever be rid of you?"

"In death, plausibly." His lips lingered by my ear. "Mine or yours."

I peered at him over my shoulder; his eyes were black, only the silver halos present, watching me with that starved intensity. I nodded, gripping the sheets to brace myself.

He pushed in, jolting me forward in tandem with his grip on my hip. The low groan from him, coupled with the dangerous frequency of clicking, reminded me how exciting it was, how *dangerous* it was.

He began to roll his hips, working with my movements until my body relaxed entirely.

His pace picked up until he bottomed out every time, pushing my body forward. It was beginning to get sore.

"Slow down," I whined. "Please."

"*Shh*," he hushed me, gathering me in his arms to turn me over.

I was on my back, staring up at him, though this view was more terrifying. He loomed over me, an ever-present threat. I would have been embarrassed to be caught like this, but his eyes were focused on something else.

He moved his hips slower, pushing in and out and watching himself do so.

I covered my mouth when a moan escaped; I wanted to melt into the sheets. I didn't know what was more mortifying; him seeing me or him knowing I might be enjoying it.

"Look at you," he practically purred. "Does it feel good to finally give in?"

He thrust hard into me when I opened my mouth to answer, an incoherent sound manifesting.

"Music to my ears." His eyes raked over my exposed chest. He gripped the waistband of my skirt, using it to pull me into his thrusts. He began to get more forceful, his hips slapping against my thighs.

I arched my back, my elbows rubbing into the fabric and forming an inevitable burn.

"S—" I gave up on words, but it just made him thrust harder.

"Let . . . it out," he panted, staring at me with such intensity I wanted to shrivel away and hide.

I shook my head in protest.

He grabbed my face as he thrust harder. "Say it," he breathed against my lips, and I embarrassingly held mine open for him, wanting a taste, craving it. "Your blood, your screams, your pleasure. They belong to me."

"Silas," I whined.

"What do you want, Alina?"

"I want," I began, staring at him through my lashes, my cheeks sore from the grip of his hand. "Harder" is all I managed.

While my demand wasn't complicated, it was all he needed to keep going.

He turned me on my side, my leg thrown over his shoulder.

He placed one hand on my leg, the other on the bed as he fucked me so hard the only thing I could manage was a cry of pleasure. There were no words I could utter that would capture an appropriate response.

I bit down on my lip to muffle the moans.

Then he slowed to a stop.

He looked like he wanted to say something, but he gripped my hips, shoving his cock hard inside. I expected the pierce of those venomous spines, but they didn't come.

I looked up in confusion.

He stood on his knees, only the tip inside me as he finished. Between my legs I could see the spines on the underside of his cock flex, disappointed they weren't latched into something. His cock twitched with every release, making a shiver shoot up my spine.

He leaned over with his hands grasping the sheets on either side of me, out of breath.

I swallowed hard, as if our breath mingling was more scandalous than what we had just done together. More intimate in the post-lust sobriety.

He leaned closer, and I thought he was going to kiss me. His forehead touched mine, and to my disappointment, he didn't open his eyes.

There was a change in the air, a switch, then finally, a retreat.

He shoved my leg off his shoulder and stepped away. The sudden change was tinged with an air of disgust. Regret, perhaps? Whatever it was, his posture changed, something that could have possibly been *shame*.

He fixed his trousers and sat down in the chair in the corner of the room.

Each limb shook, and every inch of my skin crawled. I hadn't realized how much until my arms covered my chest. My skin rose in bumps as the chill settled in.

"Why do you look at me like that?" he spoke. "Why do you cry for me just to push me away? Like this isn't a gamble on your life every time? Why must you dare me with the look in your eyes as if I'm not capable of consuming you whole?"

I blinked, barely registering his question.

"What? Now you have nothing to say?" He scoffed, sinking farther into the chair and plucking a cigarette out of his pocket. He flicked his lighter a few times unsuccessfully before he got a flame, the light striking his face every time, but it revealed something more. His brows were creased, his jaw tense. He *hated* this.

We sat in silence. Not because I didn't have things to say, but I was in shock. I was embarrassed, consumed with loathing for the man.

"You are no different from them. There is no use pretending like your heart doesn't beat faster when you say such things to me," I whispered finally.

"Oh, no," he laughed cruelly. "The things that make my dead heart sing are much worse than anything I've dared to say to you."

"Then say it, you coward."

"I will say them over your grave someday, you have my word on that."

"You will undoubtedly be the first to perish, and I will *revel* in it."

His expression softened, shaking his head knowingly at me.

"There it is," he praised, "even your words of malice are sweet like honey."

"You betray me again and again. Your loyalties lie with nobody except yourself."

"*Betray* you? You *left* me!"

"You abandoned me when I needed you most and then joined in on the fun."

His brow furrowed as he breathed in, the tip of his cigarette growing brighter from the anxious drag. "I did not feed."

"Liar," I bit out, "you didn't fight for me."

"It isn't so simple."

"You killed many around me for a simple raise of the tongue, yet you couldn't kill Luka."

"He has years on me and was surrounded by people with whom I am not in good graces with."

"You *joined* him."

"What was I to do? Watch him tear into you? Listen to your screams? Watch as he drained you within an inch of your life?"

"You should have found it within your cold, dead heart to kill me," I snapped.

He was quiet, shaking his head, a smile of amusement on his face. "Then what? You turn? You told me to be less impulsive and to think about how my actions might affect you—and that's what I did."

"How?"

"Well, you're alive, are you not?"

I swallowed, watching as he ashed the cigarette, seemingly losing interest in it and me, as he stared off somewhere.

"You can hate me all you like, if it makes you feel better, but I did not *join*," he spat the word like it was rotten in taste, rubbing his thumb over his brow as if the conversation was wearing him. "It killed me to know that the only kindness I could give to you in your moment of need was sedation. It hurts more knowing that you saw it as a betrayal. I was *helping you*."

"You're selfish."

"I *am*. I'm selfish, I'm greedy, and I wanted you to *live*. I knew you would hate me, but I know you well enough to know you would have hated yourself if you became . . ."

"Like you?" I finished for him.

"Like me," he repeated quietly.

That is where his comments ended. Something about his words was tired, longing to say something more, but deciding against it.

XXVIII

The Poisoner

THE MORNING LIGHT SHIMMERED as it passed through the specks of dust lazily floating through the bedroom.

Something had changed since yesterday, and I wasn't sure if I liked it. I could not say that I didn't miss him, but it scared me. Something about his vulnerability was uncanny and ill-fitted him. It made me fear something far worse than the creature itself . . . It made me fear being *wrong* about him.

Two years ago, I had nothing to lose—maybe Phoebe—but as I found out, she was never in any danger at all. Now, I have family, property, and a public-facing reputation.

Everything was on the line. It made me all the more hesitant to let anyone have any part of me. I was married to my work, and I would not be taking mistresses.

"Are you awake?" Phoebe crawled over to my side of the bed.

"I think so," I whispered back to her, glancing over my shoulder.

"Are you busy today?" she hummed.

"Not terribly, only tending to the animals." I rolled over to my side to face her. "I'd rather stay in bed. It's gotten so cold. I feel it in every joint now."

"You need someone to cuddle with," she teased, wrapping her arms around me.

I rested my chin on her head and closed my eyes.

"I wish we could just lie here all day."

"We have chores to do."

"I know. That won't stop me from wishing." She shrugged.

After we reluctantly left the comfort of the bed, we tidied up the sheets and got ready for our day.

We made breakfast for the house—blueberry porridge and eggs. I was not much of a cook, but I could cook eggs. Phoebe took care of the porridge. I still do not know how she could cook without tasting it herself. She would make me taste it occasionally to check during her process, but naturally, she seemed to understand how to balance flavors without tasting them.

After breakfast we cleaned, splitting up to sweep the entire house. While Phoebe dusted, I cleaned out the fireplace and brought most of the charcoal outside.

All weekend chores were typically done by sundown. We spent time in the barn to tend to Duchess and Horse. They were both a bit dusty since we let their coats grow out so they would not be as cold. The only downside was that the longer fur and hair would catch every speck of dirt, hay, and dust possible.

"I don't understand how he gets so dirty, even with the blanket on," I complained as I scrubbed the curry comb over his coat, each flick of the bristles kicking up debris.

"I can't say I've suffered that same affliction. Duchess is a perfect princess who does not get dirty," Phoebe laughed.

The stalls were separated by a piece of wood and metal bars starting halfway so that the horses could see each other. Phoebe was in Duchess's stall, braiding and sewing the hair into little neat knots along the crest of her neck.

"I am tempted to roach his mane, cut it all off so he cannot turn it into a nest for the birds." I pulled the brush through his tangled hair.

"He would look handsome either way," Phoebe hummed. "Right, Duchess? Would Horse look handsome if he were bald?"

"I give up. I think I need to go back inside and get my comb for his hair." I tossed my brush into the wooden box with the rest of the grooming supplies. "You are a *mess*." I patted him on the side of his neck, giving him a good scratch high on his shoulder.

The horses were startled by a high-pitched screech, rearing slightly in the stalls.

"Whoa! Whoa!" I tried to calm Horse as he yanked on the cross ties. Phoebe had already left the stall, grabbing the shotgun propped against the side of the barn.

I shoved the stall door to the side to follow, running toward the wood-splitting stump to yank the axe out of it.

Someone was on the ground, the white snow already stained red. A jittering pale thing slouched over the small form.

"You!" I screamed at it.

Its neck rolled, vertebrae by vertebrae, to crane in our direction. Its eyes were undoubtedly human, corrupted, filled with dead blood. Fresh crimson from beneath it drooled in thick streams of saliva as it chattered its teeth at us, its dried lips curling back.

I ran toward it, and it mirrored my actions, lunging at me as I swung, my blade swiping the side of their face. I wasn't close enough; the blade cut through both cheeks and passed between the upper and lower jaw. The loose flesh flapped to the side, and steam rose from the fresh blood.

It screeched and lunged again, grabbing my axe and tumbling us to the ground. It snapped its jaws at me, blood dripping onto my face as I shoved the axe handle up into its jaws to keep it from gnawing on me.

While the corrupted were human, something about the feral transitory stage gave them something like farmers' strength—not to be judged by how they appeared.

The firing of a shotgun made my eyes snap shut. Hot blood sprayed over my face, stinging along with pieces of shell that landed in my shoulder and cheek. The creature slumped against me, and I opened my eyes, tracking Phoebe as she ran in the other direction.

I shoved the creature off to chase after her.

My boots slipped and crunched the ice below, the shouts and clamor bouncing off the side of the house and around our open field, only to smack my eardrums again. I had no time for mental checklists, no head counts, hell, I couldn't even see, everything was moving so fast.

By the time we got to the front of the house, Rebecca and Mary had already taken care of another.

"Are you all right?" I dropped my axe, rushing over to the girls, checking each face. No wounds other than shock.

"Relatively." Mary ignored me, glancing past and looking more troubled when she saw that only Phoebe was with me.

We were still, the morning quiet again as we caught our breath, gathering our bearings.

Despite the blood covering us, there was no sign of what had just occurred. Birds chirped, the breeze clipped through the leaves of the fir trees, whistling faintly in the distance as the wind zipped over the smooth surface of the snow. Whether it be white or red, it was all the same.

"Where is Addie?" Rebecca panted, clutching her gun as she caught her breath.

Mary paled at the question.

"She is not with you?" Phoebe spoke.

Rebecca elbowed past us and off the porch.

"Rebecca!" Phoebe shouted after her in frustration, but a certain strain in her tone was unnerving.

I jogged after, nearly slipping again as I turned the corner of the house, facing the wide-open field where Phoebe had shot the first one.

Rebecca was headed straight for the red stain in the middle. *No.*

I wish my heart would be still.

"Rebecca, wait—" I chased after her.

Rebecca's legs moved faster, desperately, when she saw the small body surrounded by a red puddle in the distance.

"Rebecca, stop!" I screamed.

My lip quivered as I watched her fall on top of the body, shaking and gripping it desperately. She cupped Addie's cheeks, checking both sides and then over her torso, as if she were trying to find an injury she could come back from, despite the neck being chewed down to the spine.

The others gathered beside the house, watching the two forms in the distance, highlighted in the white expanse like they were the only things to exist. Sunlight cut through the clouds and shifted over the two.

I was an intruder, a voyeur, afraid of breaking the illusion of one last tender memory.

There was something haunting about the silence before the wail that came next.

The sound that came from our strong Rebecca . . . I would not blame poets for thinking it came from some malevolent being. A sound the forest would remember and tell tales of when the wind carried its sound as far as people were willing to listen.

When I finally took a breath, it only emerged as a sob.

Rebecca sat there for hours, and if we had not forced her inside, she would probably have stayed like that for days. She was practically fused to Adeline by the time we finally peeled her away, the frost beginning to make their clothing stick.

THE HOUSE THAT NIGHT was the darkest it had ever been. No matter how many candles we lit or fires we started, a grim shadow remained over the household.

We gathered in the living room; no one wanted to separate from the group. We all settled on sleeping by the fire, but I suspected no one would be sleeping at all that night. There were somber conversations, though it was hard to take joy in speaking of anything. I was sure they were all words of anxiety and fear. Many glances were traded and stolen as I paced the kitchen alone.

All I could focus on was picking off the dried blood from my skin. Where were all these corrupted coming from? I needed to gather bear traps, possibly purchase another gun. I could leave my tools at the farmhouse for the girls. What if Phoebe and I hadn't stepped in? What if it had been the middle of the night? What if they had gotten inside?

Hands firmly gripped my shoulders, interrupting my pacing.

"Deep breath, Alina." Phoebe stood before me, squeezing my shoulders tightly to pull me from my manic state.

"We need more traps, more guns, more defenses," I rambled. "We can all stay in the house for a while. No one needs to leave. Tell Edith to come home. She shouldn't be out . . . Wait . . . what if she is h-hurt, too?" I stumbled over my words as my throat strained, refraining from working myself up.

"Breathe, please, calm down for me, all right?" Phoebe gulped, glancing at something over my shoulder.

When I craned my neck, the girls were huddled at the entrance of the kitchen, Mary at the forefront.

"We need to go get Edith—" I began.

"We telephoned the hospital already, it is taken care of," Mary said.

"That's good," I exhaled. "We need to get the knives from the lab and see if John can spare a gun . . . maybe we buy more. I think we need one for every—"

"Alina," Mary spoke, a sorrowful expression on her face. She looked as if what she was about to say was going to hurt both of us. "As a Nest, we have all been talking." She took a deep breath and glanced at some of the other girls. She picked at her nail beds and took a minute to build up the courage to look me in the eye again.

I furrowed my brows and glanced at Phoebe, who refused to look at me as well, seemingly aware of what would happen next.

"What is it?" My voice cracked as I stared at Mary.

"We think it is best you take the deal," Mary said firmly.

"I cannot—"

"While autonomy is one of the three tenets of the Nest," she spoke over me, standing taller, "we cannot ignore how rejecting this deal would be a great disservice to what we've built, our cause, and our survival."

I opened my mouth to speak, but I could not think of a single word that I wanted to say. All I wanted to do was scream. After all I had done for the Nest, they would throw me to the ground like this?

"I'm not ready." The pain in my chest was unbearable. "Phoebe, tell them."

Phoebe said nothing.

"We did not decide this lightly, or out of malice." Mary adopted an almost pleading tone. "He is promising stability, funding, and safety. Imagine how much good we could do with those kinds of resources. It would put us thousands of miles ahead of where we thought we could ever reach alone—"

"You do not *know* him."

"Consider this a sacrifice for the betterment of the Nest."

I had nothing to argue. Every word that came to my mind was unhelpful.

All I had left was rage.

"Before you accept his deal," Mary continued, "we want to add our own terms."

"What would that be?" My eyes narrowed, my nails digging into my palms.

"We want the men on the property moved in for our own protection."

That was the end of my wick.

I shoved past the crowd and went upstairs, Phoebe chasing after me.

How could they do this? How was it that I was the only one suggesting solutions while everyone looked to me as a last resort?

When we got in the room, I slammed the door so hard into its frame that it shook the house.

"After all I've done for this Nest, *this* is what I get?" I screamed.

"Calm down—"

"Calm? You want me to be *calm*? Tell me—do you want Luka around the girls? Do you want Silas watching our every move? Luka doesn't even use venom. It is cruel to ask anyone to feed him."

"Alina! Quiet down!" Phoebe shouted and rubbed her head. "Let us think about this."

"I have done nothing *but* think about this!"

"We won't let anything happen to you. I won't allow it," she said sternly, gripping my shoulders tightly. "At this point, it's two against many. They are outnumbered, outpowered. Just think about it. We have everything."

I shook my head, but she jolted me in her grip.

Even in the dark, I could see her glassy eyes. "This is the only way. I don't know what else we can do."

"You could have told them."

"It is not for me to tell." She raised her voice before choking out, "It is the only option we have yet to exhaust. It will be fine as long as we watch each other's backs. You have our loyalty; we won't let anything happen to you. Those men would sooner have bullets in them before they even think of insisting on moving a single hair out of place."

I nodded and took a deep breath, wiping my clammy hands on my skirt before sitting down on the edge of the bed.

"Next issue—Luka." Phoebe sat next to me. "Just starve him. There is no faster way to get a rowdy Vipera to cooperate. Father used to do it—"

"Right." I cut her off.

"As for your marriage to Silas . . ." Phoebe continued, grimacing at the thought. "If his accounts are as good as he says, he is a wallet at best. At worst, we can remove his knees and keep him as a pet."

I laughed, but my heart was heavy.

"Besides," Phoebe tried to make light with a joke, "we will be sisters-in-law for real this time." She laughed, but it was laced with some sense of loss.

I rubbed my face with my hands. I had never been so defeated; nothing was going like I wanted it to.

Where I thought I had a choice before, it was now a demand.

I rose from my seat and collected my coat from the chair.

"Do you want me to telephone him?" She threw me a concerned look.

"No, I have terms to negotiate."

The Creature

SOMETHING DISTURBED MY SLUMBER, some low vibration I could feel deep in my bones. The instinctual crawl of the skin . . . I was not alone.

I sat up, peering at the figure sitting in the chair against the wall, directly in front of my bed.

Tilting my head, I smirked at the delightful surprise. This brought back such fond memories of watching my sweet Alina sleep, and now she was doing the same for me. She really knew how to melt my cold, dead heart.

"Have you come for some witching-hour fun? Here to cast a spell on me, you vile thing?" I bantered. Her figure was still covered in the dark.

A sharp click sounded from where she sat.

My smile faltered slightly. "Is that a gun?"

"Just insurance." There was a sweetness to Alina's tone.

"For what? I thought we had moved past this." I reached over to grab a half-finished cigarette from the nightstand, then rested against the headboard as I lit it. "I would have dressed for you if I knew we had a date. I don't usually see guests in only my underclothes."

"I come only to strike our deal, nothing more."

My eyes flicked up to stare at her, a slow grin crawling across my face as I took a drag of the cigarette. "Based on the weapon, I take it you mean to accept?"

"I want to renegotiate first."

I gestured around me to an invisible crowd. "I am but a willing audience."

"No marriage, you agree to keep the tenets and cause of my Nest, and you and Luka live with us," she mumbled the last one, but I heard her.

"Counter—all of the terms mentioned, *and* you are my wife."

"Is that really your dealbreaker?"

"Yes."

"Why?"

"Because it is fun to anger you, my dearest."

She was silent, the pistol on her knee shaking as her restless leg bounced.

"I will not share a room with you."

I groaned in irritation. "Fine."

"You have to take on all financial responsibilities of the *entire* Nest, not just me."

"I assumed as much." I lifted a brow at her, waiting for her next inevitable demand.

There was another pause of silence.

"I want an allowance."

"How much?"

"Three thousand a month."

"That is all?" I scoffed. "I thought it would be more. You can have access to all my money if that is what you want."

More silence.

"Alina?"

"Yes?"

"Are you making these terms up as you go?"

Yet another silence from the shadow.

"I want thirteen oranges in my room at all times."

Now she was just being difficult.

"If you want oranges, I will get you oranges." I tapped the cigarette in the ashtray. "Come here; do not treat me like a stranger. Negotiations don't have to be so cold."

"I have to go back." Her voice wavered.

"Alina," I warned, "come here, or I will drag you by your hair. You choose."

She took a moment for herself, releasing an exasperated sigh. She rose from the chair and slipped through the shadows.

The streetlamps cast faint light through the window, illuminating the omen before me.

Remnants of dried blood, Vipera and human, interrupted the elegant lines of her features. The skin around her eyes was red, and she had fresh cuts on her face.

Tears filled her eyes, her lip quivered, and her lips moved to form my name, but she didn't have to. Her knees crumpled beneath her, her grief too heavy to carry any longer. It didn't matter. I was already there, my arms enveloping her, my palm at the back of her head.

Her arms flung around me. Her quivering grip just made me want to squeeze tighter; I wanted so badly to steady her.

"What happened?" I whispered into her hair, the metallic scent of blood and tears burning my senses.

She shook her head and swallowed, her lip quivering once the question left my mouth. "I'm tired of this. I'm tired of bearing the cost of being decent, of being honorable, and only rewarded with hardship."

Her sorrow was familiar. The rage, the anger, all made from

the same kind she threw at me before she left for good. This was it. This was her limit.

"Come here." I slipped the gun from her trembling hand and pulled her into the bed. I gathered her long legs over my lap and held her head against my chest. "You're shaking."

She did not answer me, and I hated it. Silence from Alina was never a good sign.

I smoothed her hair, the crust of dried blood clumping the strands together. I lifted her chin, inspecting the cuts across her face. She couldn't look at me. There was no spark tonight, an utterly defeated demeanor, no fire in her.

She lifted her eyes to me, waiting for me to say something.

"Could you at least find it in you to be angry with me?"

Her fine brow arched. "If you return my pistol, I could *show* you."

I placed it in her hand, guiding her finger to the trigger, and pointed it under my chin, her armed hand between my own, clasped like a prayer.

Every second passed was another I could hear our hearts beat, one of hers was three of mine, and she owned every single one.

She squeezed the trigger, the hollow click of an empty chamber following.

"You *did* miss me."

"How could my heart forget a betrayal like yours?"

"I wasn't aware you had one," I whispered in her ear, "but it's good to know it can be stolen once more."

She suppressed her laugh in vain. It was like music to my ears.

I wrapped my arms around her, burying my head in her shoulder.

"How about we celebrate?" I suggested.

"I am not in the mood."

"Not with that attitude," I laughed.

Even with a lighter mood, she was too tired to react. I stroked her hair, then cheek. The sensation of dry clotted blood was an uncomfortable texture to touch. I couldn't imagine how it felt.

This wouldn't do, not like this.

"I HAVE ANOTHER TERM," she mumbled between bites.

"Will you be asking for zebras next?" I joked, tilting her chin up so I could carefully remove the shards of shotgun shell from her cheek and shoulder.

I ordered food to be brought to the room, but she didn't eat anything except the pastries and the wine. We both sat comfortably facing each other in the middle of the bed so she could eat, and I could work.

"I want us to pick a word. One word that if we even so much as whisper it, we both stop what we are doing. No matter what we are doing."

I squinted at her in confusion. "Interesting. Why would you need that?"

"I don't trust you," she explained. "With that being said, if I am going to be with you for this arrangement, it would make me feel better knowing I have one word that will save me from you."

Hearing her say it hurt a bit, thinking she needed to be saved from me, but I had no room to judge a fair request.

"Which word would you like it to be?"

"*Pest.*"

"No need for insults, I am trying to be nice."

"No, *pest* is the word."

"It sounds like you thought this through," I chuckled. "I think you need a different one. You use that one too earnestly."

She did not speak for a while after that.

The collar of her blouse stuck to her skin. I opened it slowly, unsure of how dry the blood would be. Her shoulder was mainly dry, but the pieces of shotgun shell were still wedged in the skin, cutting more with each movement. I picked at the pieces as best I could to remove them, running my tongue over the wounds after to close each one.

She flinched, but then her shoulders slumped when she realized I wouldn't bite.

I smirked at her reaction, grabbing her face gently and licking the wound on her cheek.

She glared at me.

"You don't want it to scar, do you?" I winked.

Her bloodshot eyes made the blue of her irises look so beautiful. Her eyebrow twitched as she knit them together. Her fingertips feathered against the side of my face, and I flinched.

"Is this treatment temporary?"

"I do not know what you mean."

"Will it go away once you have everything you want?"

"I have always had what I want, no matter the expense," I scoffed. "You're worth much more than that."

To me, I wanted to say. *You are worth more than that to me.*

She thought about my answer, playing with a misplaced piece of my hair before brushing it back. A subtle clicking chittered in my throat at the feeling of her nails against my skin.

"Can I stay with you tonight?" she whispered

"You need not ask."

"I don't think I can handle seeing that crowded house right now." Her eyes darted away, though the tension in her jaw couldn't be good for her mood.

"That reminds me." I tugged my shirt on, copping my trousers as I tossed her coat at her, then her shoes.

Her eyes followed me with a cocked brow as she caught each boot thrown at her.

"Get dressed," I said. "I have something for you."

The Poisoner

"**WHAT IS THIS?**" I had to strain my neck to witness the grand tenement building in front of me, five stories at least. He had made me walk all the way down near the park for this.

It was a tall, stable brick building. Sturdy and more utilitarian than aesthetic. Even if it were unsightly, though, it seemed solid . . . safe.

The town around us was dark and overwhelmingly uneasy. Towns were not meant to be seen so still. It was a place people should be, that *life* should be. It was an evolutionary trait to dread such a place, so out of character and time. Like a silent forest at the sun's peak.

"Come." He nudged me with a gesture, unlocking the front door at the top of the steps, though he had to jolt it with his shoulder to unstick the stubborn door.

The building was a bit run-down and in need of cleaning. A long, skinny hallway led from the front door to the large foyer, with rooms lining the first floor. A grand staircase was poised in the middle, leading up to the other floors. The wood of the stairs in the middle were scratched and worn from use. There was a deeper color in the middle, as if a carpet runner had protected it for many years. Along the sides were doors to flats, some missing their numbers. It smelled like mildew and dust, though I am sure the nippy air was hiding other scents that had yet to be discovered.

Even though it lacked beauty, you could trust the floorboards were thick and sturdy, the walls decently insulated and dry, the bricks tight, and the roof reliable.

"What did you want to show me?" I turned to Silas, who stood in the entryway of the hall, inspecting the disrepair.

"You asked what I wanted from you." He returned his eyes to mine. "I know you think I want to ruin you, but I think we could be . . . What was it you said all those years ago? We could be *mutually beneficial*?"

"How does this benefit me?"

He glanced around us, holding his arms out and gesturing in the air. "Have you not outgrown the rooms you share with over a dozen women?"

"I asked you what you wanted from me."

"I am telling you." He closed the gap between us. "Did you not ask me to take care of your Nest as one of your terms?"

"I only just added the term." I blinked at him, looking to my side to stare at the building before glancing up at him.

"I don't need a fortune teller to anticipate what you would ask of me," he laughed. "I acquired it as soon as I learned you kept . . . company."

"Are you telling me you bought me property?"

"Do you like it?"

"I might."

"Then yes, I did." He grinned.

"Why would you do that?"

"Well, you can't do your work in that shack anymore."

"You are not making a joke out of me when you say that?"

"No, I mean it." He nodded. "I told you I would support your endeavors."

I turned from him, following the dirty tile pattern on the floor until I got to the stairs, touching the banister. "It is mine?" I glanced back at him as if to check to be sure.

"Yours." He chuckled, approaching and taking my hand to lead me up the stairs. "I can buy another if you hate it, but I thought of you when I saw this."

"Now that *must* be a joke."

"Not intended! You'll see why." He gestured for me to follow.

We ascended the staircases, one after the other, until we got to the top-floor flat. Upon entry, it was no more than an empty room. The woodwork was nice and the windows were large, but what caught my eye was on the other side of the large main room.

Light poured into the space, more than the others. The room opened up to a glass observatory, a simple square of glass with a curved top. The front corner held a semicircular glass pattern that reminded me of a rising sun. One of the window panels was left open, and some crusted leaves were left in the corner with a broom.

No matter how dirty it was, I could imagine setting up a couch and rug, plants littering the space. I imagine the morning light would be beautiful from up here, and in the afternoon, unobstructed views of the sunset from above the park.

Silas was already staring by the time I looked back at him. He lurked in the shadows, only approaching when I acknowledged him, as if he was giving room for my imagination to breathe.

While his eyes always represented something dangerous, they always managed to be so gentle when they dared to look my way.

"You did this for me?"

They drew me in like a crow to something shiny, abandoning my resolve for the overwhelming need to possess. His leather-clad hand cupped my face. "Who else would I do it for?"

I searched his face for anything, any reason to run from him, but he was not lying. He was a simple creature to read; there was nothing in his tone or words indicating he was not entirely serious.

"Every day I spent without you those years ago was a day wasted. But the days that came after realizing that you were not coming back were the loneliest in my lifetime."

"Silas." His name came out like a plea before he silenced me with his lips, embracing me tighter than he had ever before, enough to leave bruises with his fingertips in his desperate grip.

"Do not leave me again, please."

"I need to think." I swallowed.

"You do enough of that." He rested his forehead against mine. "Do what *feels* right, not what you *think* is right."

"That sounds like a dangerous path."

"What is life if you cannot find something you love, and let it kill you?"

I shuddered at his words, tempted to pull away, but for some reason, I didn't. "I'm cold."

"Let me keep you warm," he whispered, holding me tight in our embrace.

"You are the coldest man I know. How will you manage that?"

His eyes darted past me.

I glanced behind us, and propped against the wall was an obviously new bottle of champagne. I suppose the room was cold enough to store a bottle.

"I don't drink anymore." My gaze returned to him.

"Yes, you do," he laughed. "You just don't drink in *public* anymore."

I rolled my eyes, but the gesture was enough to fluster me. The entire situation was enough to throw me off.

There we were. No furniture, no decor, not even proper champagne glasses. Just him and me.

We sipped the bottle empty on the floor, by the company of a single used candle left behind from the previous owner. It was one of those instances where you forgot who you were, or who you were posturing to be in the outside world. The only version of yourself that existed was in the room, developing along with the night hours. We talked for so long that the flame ran out of wax to melt, but we didn't need it anyway since the sun was beginning to peek through the frosted windows, and our time was marked by an empty bottle.

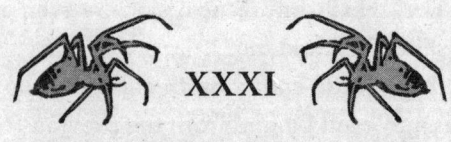

XXXI

The Poisoner

THE SHEETS WERE SMOOTH against my skin, a simple pleasure considering the soreness of my limbs and cuts on my skin from the day before.

The sheets smelled clean. I wasn't entirely sure of the perfume, but it was an intimate touch. I was so deep in sleep, I barely remembered crawling into bed. Late nights were always blurry, especially paired with champagne.

Champagne.

I nearly forgot. We were up until early morning, just talking. The time completely escaped us, and I'm sure Phoebe was worried sick.

My cheeks grew hot; I covered my face with the pillow. Even though my memories were only of us speaking, they made my stomach flutter. I was either smitten or severely ill. Possibly both.

Then the inevitable guilt settled in along with my memory.

One of my own was dead, and I was wrapped in hotel sheets worth more than a week's wage while the girls of my Nest probably slept on the floor, huddled in fear of another occurrence, praying I reached a deal with Silas.

My arms stretched out under the pillow, burying my face as I lay on my stomach. A clink of a cup beside the bed sounded.

I peeked at the disturbance. Silas placed a cup of tea on the nightstand. He was fully dressed already, freshly ironed and starched. He looked like he had been up for hours, the scent of fresh cologne invading my morning senses.

I hid my face back into the pillow and groaned.

"Good morning to you as well." His voice was a low rumble, a sensitive sound to my ears. The bed dipped beside me as he sat down, his fingers brushing my ear.

"It's *a* morning." My words were muffled by the pillow.

The door to the room slapped against the wall as it flung open. "Phoebe telephoned this morning—" Luka stopped. "Who is that?"

"You should learn to knock," Silas scolded, getting up to shove him out the door, the door closing behind them. Even then, I could still hear their bickering.

"She asked if I had seen Alina; apparently she phoned a few times," Luka spoke lower. "I suppose I'm a bit late to the news."

"I told reception no messages."

"Right, then can I assure her everything is all right? You wouldn't believe the threats that come from that pretty mouth of hers."

"Tell her to get the girls packed; we are going to move to the building downtown."

"So Alina—" Luka whispered.

"Yes, pack your bag, as well."

"Mine? Are we moving with them?"

"Yes, the girls felt better having extra bodies there." Silas paused. "Behave yourself, or I will personally make sure you starve."

"Why do you always think I will do something?" Luka tutted. "Always assuming the worst."

"That is because you *are* the worst," Silas nearly hissed. "I will speak with you later."

There was no reply, and the door clicked when it shut again.

The bed dipped again; his palm smoothed down my back. I peeked at him again before turning to my side.

"I had the hotel wash your clothes, they are on the chair when you are ready."

"Are you not staying?"

"I have errands to run."

"What errands? You do not run errands."

"We have an entire tenement to furnish, remember?" He smoothed stray strands away from my face. "I would say you can come with me, but I assumed there were some things at home you needed to tie up. I can call you a coach."

My heart squeezed tightly in my chest, remembering. I was quite literally avoiding the skeletons piling up in the closet. I dreaded looking them in the eye after losing the girls.

"Call it now. I will only be a minute." I exhaled before slipping out of the bed and sheepishly approaching the chair with my garments.

Silas approached me from behind, smoothing his hands over my shoulders before pushing down gently. The tension thawed slightly. I stretched my neck to either side before I propped my leg up on the chair to pull up my stockings.

Though last night was calm, this morning was especially sober, painfully so. There was an itch, a settling discomfort.

"I will meet you at the downtown property. Do you have any special requests before I go?"

"No."

His hands lingered on my thigh before they slipped away. The sounds of his footsteps retreated for the door before it clicked again, marking the solitude of my morning.

The dress was clean, but I could see a slight shift in hue hidden in the dark wool garments. No one could possibly notice it, but I would. *I* would notice, and it would torment me until I finally burned them in the furnace.

I dug through the pockets, feeling around the wool until I reached the leather casing. A breath of relief as it surfaced from the fabric in my hand.

I pried it open with shaking fingers, my syringe and vial of medicine intact, unharmed, and unused.

THE COACH RIDE WAS only thirty minutes, but every minute was torture the closer I got to the place I called home, now only a solemn reminder of who we'd lost. Not even a healthy dose of venom could calm the impending confrontation.

I practiced looking sad, rather than anxious. I did, genuinely, care. I just couldn't bear the thought of them thinking I didn't care *enough*. To appear apathetic was to endanger your standing in a very delicate social balance. Appearances mattered more than anything in the matter of mourning.

The first thing I noticed was a gathering in the field behind the house. I often joked that I wore black in case of a funeral, but I had never planned for that to be the case.

The girls were gathered over a mound of freshly turned dirt, no stone to mark it.

Seeing them all cloaked in black with draping veils over their heads made them look like priestesses of long ago, a bonding of trauma and reverence.

As I approached the gathering, the crowd parted solemnly until all I saw was Rebecca positioned like an altar before the unmarked graves. Her eyes were not angry or sad, but empty.

She read from a small Bible fitted in the palm of her hand, the page marked by a baby blue ribbon. Sending the soul away with the words of its own book, the first time it left Addie's nightstand was to be read aloud to honor her.

A terror rose deep inside me; there was nothing more dangerous than a woman's rage, especially when it is presented calmly like the stale air before a hurricane.

One by one, the girls climbed into several coaches that awaited nearby to take them away. Rebecca was last to move, closing the small Bible and holding it close, as Adeline had done. Her eyes lifted, and I could see the reflection of my dark figure isolated by the snow in her dark eyes.

After a solemn departure, I went to say goodbye to the structure that had kept us safe these past few years, the first one I had called home in a long time. The place had turned gray without the teeming women within the household. We hadn't been there long, but there were outlines on the walls where picture frames had hung, or the pale ghosts of rugs lining the floors. All signs of a house well-loved.

"Are you ready?" Phoebe spoke from the door, the wind whistling against the frame as it raced in to greet me. Her question held a certain gravity, not only asking about our departure, but what came next.

My finger traced over a spot on the wall where an oval frame once hung.

This house was full of ghosts, and they would follow me to no end.

"Yes." I clasped my fingers together, breathing against them for warmth as I approached her.

Those green eyes searched for something before she placed both hands on the sides of my face. "You are so brave, Alina."

"Do you say that out of admiration, or fear?"

She didn't answer, which was an answer in itself.

I EXPECTED THE GIRLS to be angry with me, but I suppose it was an impractical fear since I had done what they asked.

I watched the buzzing of activity from the stairs, making myself comfortable against the banister. I held a book and a pen, but I could not focus on any annotation while I watched my new environment, like a relocated zoo animal.

All the doors were open, including the front door, so we could sweep any dirt or leaves out of the building. The windows were wide open to prevent any stuffiness as we tidied.

There were enough rooms where the girls could have one to themselves, though many chose rooms close to their friends and feeding partners. There was a high frequency to the air; it made me feel a little better as I basked in it. It was enough to be in the presence of a lighter mood, even if I was not taking part.

I could see Rebecca and Mary in the first room to the left of the stairs; they were covering the bed in linens and dragging around chairs to see where they would fit.

Two girls clumsily coordinated as they decided on the best way to carry the couch to the second floor.

In the foyer area, three girls were hovering around Luka. He had one of the girls sitting on his shoulder so she could reach the stained glass above the doorway to the hall entrance. The other two were holding tools as the one on his shoulder scraped away paint that covered the beautiful stained glass.

A group had already worked on scoring the crust of old wallpaper, scraping as they scrubbed vinegar water to loosen it. The hinges on the doors needed oiling, window clasps were missing in a few rooms, and the carpets were hiding suspicious stains until we could survey the total damage to the floors.

John even came to help carry in the furniture that was delivered in the afternoon.

This place was so alive, it eased my worries about the displacement. It was a long way from clean, or even beautiful, but it would in time become what it was meant to be.

I rested my head against the wooden railing as I turned the pages of the book cradled on my lap. No notes were scribbled, as I was utterly uninspired. Usually books were an excellent distraction, but not today.

"Have you gone up yet?" Silas descended from the stairs, knowing the answer but using the question as a reason to speak to me. He sat next to me on the step, his shoulder nudging mine.

I shook my head and flipped another page.

He plucked the book from my hand, using his thumb to save the page I was on as he flipped the cover.

"*The Devoted Friend*," he read. "Did you get tired of medical journals?"

"Yes." I snatched it back. "I haven't had the time to build a collection. This one was a gift. I only have time for short stories."

"If you are receptive to poetry, I could bring some for you."

"No more gifts."

"That I cannot promise, unfortunately." He clicked his tongue against his teeth and shook his head regretfully. "It is impossible to look at you and *not* shower you in the finest of material things."

I blew air through my nose in a scoff, standing to ascend the stairs.

"You don't believe me?" He followed.

"I believe you." I kept my eyes on my book, but I couldn't help but smile. "The wording reminded me of when you filled my tub with blood in my inebriated state."

"Blood is liquid gold! I couldn't think of something more

perfect than the only two things that could satiate a terrible thing like me," he joked.

"Amusing."

"I live to please. I am sure I would have been a jester in another time."

"So we both agree that you are a fool?"

"It is good to know that your tongue didn't get dull while I was away."

"I sharpened it just for you."

"I expected nothing less," he laughed, watching ahead as girls fluttered in and out of the rooms, organizing their things and making our new dwelling as much of a home as it could be. "They look happy."

"Not everyone."

"Your mood is always glum."

"I am the reason they're in danger."

"You cannot control where the corrupted wander; there is nothing you could have done."

"I could have taken the deal earlier."

"You were considering your options, like a good leader."

"I was being selfish," I muttered, underlining a string of words on the paper as I climbed the third flight of stairs.

"You were acting on self-preservation."

"Why are you defending me?" I snapped at him, peeling my eyes from the ink on the page.

"Because I know you," he said plainly. "An immediate acceptance was not what I expected from you. I know better than to expect you to roll over so easily."

"How curious. You are the only man I know who would chase this hard after being rejected in every way possible." I laughed, but I was angry. "You are even self-aware that you are not wanted."

"You are stubborn; you're punishing yourself."

"Punishing myself by staying away from *you*? Do not flatter yourself." I scoffed as I opened the door to the flat on the top floor.

The brass doorknob was so new it was gold to the touch as I turned it, the hinges of the door producing a low moan as it opened.

"You deny yourself pleasure and happiness because you feel there are others who are more deserving," he chimed from behind me, and I looked back at him. Just the action itself made him keep going. "You think of yourself as an exception. Women should be treasured, but not you—you don't deserve it. Women are weak and need protection, but not you—you are strong and capable, of course. God forbid Alina is caught soft like cotton before she is spun taut enough to tether ships." He appeared almost bored despite the violence of his words.

"You are just trying to be hurtful."

Silas leaned against the doorframe, effortless as he continued his badgering. "You are a misogynist, no different than any man, and you are robbing yourself of life's most beautiful pleasures because you cannot but keep punishing yourself for being born a woman, and nothing being made for you in this world. You burden yourself with the world's problems, only to mirror them in your frustration."

I threw the book at him, but it hit the wall instead when he moved, consequently shattering something.

He looked at me, victorious at the ruse. He nodded as if in understanding and retreated down the hall.

My attention was drawn to the glass on the floor. What a mess.

I hastily knelt beside it, plucking the shards from the floor on top of the photograph like a tray. The figures of the girls and I were bent and warped under the pile of glass.

Quickly, I salvaged what I could and set it on the table.

Wait . . . table?

I expected an empty floor plan, a blank canvas. I realized there was a reason that Silas asked if I had come upstairs recently.

The once-desolate open floor plan of the main room was decorated similarly to my shop. Dark wood furniture was spread around the room, creating many smaller collections of furniture as if to make as many nooks as possible.

In the kitchen, there was a circular table next to a window, with a couple of chairs around it. In a crystal bowl in the middle, there were oranges. I did not have to count them to know there would be thirteen.

On the other side of the room, a bench had been placed in front of a window, a bookshelf on either side of the bench to create a nook. A tea table was placed in front of the bench with a vase on top.

Along the walls were collections of things to fill the space. There were dried flowers, framed illustrations of poisonous plants of North America, and other little curios he must have found at a market.

Several collections of furniture littered the space, neatly separated by the rugs they were positioned upon. He had chosen sage green, dark wood, and brass for most of the furnishings. I suppose it was to match the best part of the room.

Directly opposite the front door was the observatory that protruded out of the wall like an oversized bay window. He had filled it with monstera, Dracaena, anthurium, and assorted fig shrubs. It reminded me of the botanical gardens. There was a couch or chair on each of the three walls of the glass room, a table in the middle with an ashtray and a lighter. Plants hung in the corners and were placed on the floor or side tables, depending on their size. The greenery was what I craved the most every winter.

I was the last person who deserved this. It felt like I had sold something valuable for material nothings.

I plopped down on the couch and buried my face in a decorative pillow, lying down with my knees pulled to my chest. I screamed into the suede before it turned into a sob. My body shook, but it was not from the cold.

My mind screamed at me to keep him far away, but my heart wanted him to comfort me, to hold me, to hide away from the world with me in the home he had made to cage me.

Before I knew it, I had soothed myself to sleep where I lay.

I CAME BACK TO consciousness at the click of the door. Phoebe approached with a bowl.

"Apologies, I didn't know you were asleep." She was a bit distracted by the details of my room. "I brought soup."

"I didn't realize how long I slept; I would have joined you." I sat up and wiped a bit of dried drool from my face.

"It was a long day," Phoebe commented and sat on the floor in front of the tea table, opposite me. She slid the bowl toward me along with a spoon. "How are you feeling?"

"Fine."

"Truly?"

"No," I grumbled.

"What did he do this time?"

"He bombards me with shiny things in hopes of distracting me from his foul play," I huffed. "He is insufferable."

"Right," she said slowly.

"Then—*then*—he has the audacity to judge me for not trusting his intentions. Can you believe it?"

"I cannot." She pressed her lips into a fine line, as if she were biting her tongue.

"Say it," I demanded. "I know there is something you wish to say."

"I think . . ." She paused to choose her words carefully. "You know well that I am no fan of my brother, but with my knowledge of his distasteful spirit, in my own judgment, he may actually be concerned for you. No matter how questionable his methods, he rarely does much for anyone other than himself."

I stirred the pieces of vegetables and potatoes in the broth, watching the oil swirl at the top.

"You are angry," she huffed. "You told me to say what was on my mind."

"I am not angry."

"Then why are you not saying anything?"

"Forget it," I conceded.

"You must understand me clearly. I do not believe you to be broken. You are *traumatized* by him, and in turn, also myself. It makes sense that your mind is trying to adjust, just like it did, knowing my nature. You need time. You are not obligated to accept change quickly, especially from *him*."

"Then why does it feel like I am holding everyone back?"

"You are moving us *forward*, not backward." She put her hand on my leg and squeezed. "We wouldn't have what we have now without you. No one is angry with you for things out of your control. We are all grateful, the girls only speak about you in admiration and awe."

"That is a lie."

"It is not! I swear on it!"

"You are just trying to make me feel better."

"You missed the most amusing banter at dinner." She grinned, but her throat bobbed in a thick swallow, as if to make the question brewing disappear.

"What is it?"

"Luka," she sighed. "The girls are asking. They can't get a good read on him or you. Do we tell them if he is a friend or foe?"

"Tell them they're not to let him feed," I said carefully. "He can scavenge in the town, not that any local Guilds will take a stranger."

Phoebe nodded and took in the new surroundings, watching the snow flutter by the panes of foggy glass. She moved from the floor to my side on the couch.

"Anything else?"

She bit her lip and shook her head.

"Phoebe," I winced, "what is it?"

"Nothing!"

"Phoebe!"

"It's nothing to worry about!" she laughed. "Just . . . the wedding is a high point of discussion."

My only response was to grimace, taking another mouthful of soup. It burned my tongue in an attempt to delay a response.

"I know it's not going to be your favorite topic, but they're excited to have something good happen. Something to celebrate." The last part seemed to hesitate as it passed over the tongue, her hand touching my thigh along with a reassuring squeeze.

I glanced at her hand, and then the long red lashes shading her eyes, not sure if it was some sort of sadness, but it was somber. An expression of loss.

I swallowed and cleared my throat. "It does sound like I missed an eventful dinner."

"Eventful indeed, but in good spirits. That is what matters."

ONCE AGAIN, I WAS left alone with my thoughts.

Looking up through the observatory glass, I could see the faint speckle of stars scattered in the expanse. A stray cloud passed by every now and then as I watched. I found myself entranced. Many hours could be wasted in the glass chamber within my flat. I was thankful I was allowed to room alone, for I would need a place to escape if I couldn't physically run from this place. The urge to flee weighed heavily on me, the guilt curling around my chest and squeezing tight. I was privileged to be in this situation, and my sacrifice would mean safety and security for my girls. So why did it feel like this barter would eat away at me?

Retreating to my bedroom, I carried a candle with me to the bedside. The bed had a wooden canopy with heavy curtains gathered neatly together by rope, exposing the dark green sheets below.

Every new thing I found in my room caused a deep stain of dread.

Miscellaneous dried assortments decorated the walls next to old pictures in more expensive frames than previously. There were French doors leading to a small balcony, adequate lighting for the artisan desk, larger than the one we had in the old house. Of course, like everything else, it was brand new. Not one scuff to mark its short lifetime. Everything was more expensive, yet still personal. Familiarity without history, making it just decor, not belongings.

I should be happy to have such material things. To not have to worry about choosing between food and finer living. The idea of being taken care of did not sit right with my soul, though; it utterly refused it.

"I can't stand this," I groaned, blowing out my candle before leaving my room.

Down on the second floor, I approached one of the wooden doors. I had to step over a few bags and boxes as I approached. I wanted to knock, but my body was screaming at me not to. Many breaths were taken, and several scenarios crossed my mind, but I chose to ignore them. I lifted my hand to knock but opted for the doorknob instead.

"I was wondering how long you were going to huff and puff out there." Luka's eyes never left his sketch pad.

"I would imagine you'd understand the need for a breather before interacting with you."

"I don't know why everyone keeps saying that." He glanced up from his pad. "I think I am absolutely charming."

He flashed a quick smirk.

He had taken a comfortable position against the headboard as he placed his bound paper down. His blood-filled eyes studied me from afar.

"Why are your eyes . . ."

"To see the colors." He gestured to the array of different-colored oil pencils scattered on the bed.

"I thought that was an involuntary function." I frowned.

"It is involuntary." He started to grin, like some hungry dog. "Occurring at states of high stimulus, particularly arousal—"

"Enough! I do not need to be subjected to those images," I huffed.

"You are the one who asked," he laughed. "Something must be troubling you if you are coming to me for comfort."

"It will be you seeking comfort when I'm finished."

"Pardon?" He let out an exasperated laugh.

"I don't like that you're here."

"I don't imagine you do. But we do what's best for *our* Nest, isn't that right?" His eyes narrowed; his tone was playful, like a dare.

"You're not allowed to feed on them. Touch them. Nothing."

"And who decides that?"

"I do. And they will listen."

He leaned back and nodded, as if to jumble the options around in his head.

"You are not allowed to feed here. Do I make myself clear?"

"Doesn't seem fair, if you ask me."

"The last thing you deserve is *fair*."

"Fine, I'll find my own food. Only because your mangy pack may upset my stomach," he huffed, but the twitch of his mouth was like a sneer. "If you hate me so much," he started, his eyes gliding over to land on me, "why am I not as dead as I was promised?"

"Because Viktor isn't dead to me, and I haven't decided whether or not your skills are worth keeping."

"Oh?" he smirked.

"But," I continued, "I don't know if I can trust that we have similar goals in all of this."

"My goal is survival. I don't care much as to how. So if that means helping you, then it's as simple as that. Do not confuse self-preservation with charity."

"The only reason you are still alive is because you were requested to be here."

"It must hurt to know they disregard your safety for their own, letting something so hated by you sleep in their beds and steal warmth from your hospitality."

I straightened, glancing away.

"They don't know, do they?"

"No. And they will never know."

"What happened to not keeping secr—"

"Tell them, and I will make both sides of your face match."

He was silent.

"If they want me to use you, I will. But as you made it *painfully* clear last time, you don't take your job seriously. You take too many liberties. You are a liability more than you are an asset."

Luka tipped his head back in annoyance. "I'm sorry."

"For what?"

"You know what."

"I want to hear you say it."

"I am truly, deeply sorry that you fell for a mirage."

"What you did to me was despicable."

"That's why I did it."

"How do I know I can trust you?"

"You shouldn't." His expression did not change. "But you can trust that my motivations are the same as yours."

"That's not good enough. You've betrayed me once; you can do it again."

"Alina, don't be so childish." He rolled his eyes. "Think of it as if we are both diplomats. We both have people depending on us, and both parties need this deal to work in order to survive. As much as killing you would be fun, it would be terrible for business, and my head would surely be on a spit in return."

"Then let's hope you've learned that nippy dogs get put down."

Luka spared me a look, which was painful without any words to break the intensity. Those auburn eyes were so deep, I remembered the fear of falling for them. I couldn't tell how my words made him feel, but I hoped they made him feel something. "Well, at least when you don't dwell on the past, you can look to the future. You may be wise after all."

Heat rose in my neck, a sickening rage steadily overflowing.

"Now you may spend more time planning on how to expand with the new resources that you have."

"New resources?"

"Yes. I have ideas," he started, "though I would like to let you hear them sometime if you will stop being so grim. I could help you with certain things."

"Like what?"

"Well, I could poke around and see if we can sort out this *corrupted* issue."

"Why?"

"Because your problems are my problems now."

I turned my head to look at him, considering his words carefully. "What is it you want in return?"

"The return is that I get to be part of something new, and I get to be at the top of the chain."

"I don't know if I trust you to be anywhere near the top."

"Get used to it, because it will come naturally with my close proximity to you," he practically purred.

"You are foolish to think I would let that happen again."

"A lot of talk from the girl who has barely made it through her first life—"

My foot was crossing the threshold before he could finish, the door slamming snug into its frame before I tucked myself against the wall. I didn't have to let him get to me, but lord knows he could. The stress of alternating threats persisted around me, and I had no way of stopping it. A proper conundrum. My chest would cave in if I kept it all bottled up, yet the glass of my body was heating fast, threatening to blow with every throttle. The headaches of the past few weeks were enough to make my eyes feel like they were popping from my skull.

Even so, it must be kept tucked away as an interior struggle. It would only be for a bit longer; the dust had to settle soon. I just had to breathe, because being alive was enough resistance, and I had to find a way to tie all the fraying strings together.

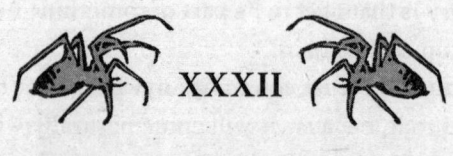

XXXII

The Poisoner

"LADIES! PICK A PAPER before you run off!" Phoebe held a chatelaine purse open as we gathered around.

One by one, hands dipped into the purse and pulled out small strips of paper.

Phoebe insisted that we choose our secret gift exchange recipients while we were at the market, so we could potentially pick some small gifts for each other.

The sun was bright today, reflecting harshly off the ground and nearly blinding me as I wandered past the maze of tents. Unfolding my paper, I read the name.

Silas.

Of course I had picked his name. Fate taunts me every day; today it had a sense of humor. I wouldn't know what to get for someone like him, if not my boot up his—

"Who did you get?" Edith chirped by my side.

"No one." I crumpled the paper and stuck it in the pocket of my coat.

"Oh." Her face held some sort of dejection, like I had shot down an advance.

"Have you seen anything you like at the vendors?" I asked her. "Did you want to bring anything to work for your coworkers?"

Her face lit up again. "If you wouldn't mind, I would love to bring them some saltwater candies. Something small!"

"You don't have to convince me; it is on Silas's dime," I laughed.

"Do you think he will lend me some extra for it?"

"He will do what I tell him. Just tell him I said yes." I drew a cigarette from my purse. "Go on! I saw him by the fountain next to the fruit vendor."

She nodded excitedly and disappeared into the flowing crowd.

I pulled out a match, striking it several times before it lit, and dragged a breath through the smoky taste. Not much chased the stiffness from my bones nowadays; I took what I could get.

I passed by Phoebe and John, who were both hunched over a list of ingredients they would need as they traded recipes. As I passed, John spotted me from the corner of his eye.

"Alina!" he called, bidding Phoebe a quick pardon before I approached. He tucked his hands in his pockets, his pipe leisurely hanging off the corner of his mouth. "What has you looking so stoic today—does the market not excite you?"

"It is . . . loud." I breathed in before plucking the cigarette from my mouth, blowing outward.

"I think the problem is that you haven't seen the good vendors yet," he laughed, looping his arm through mine as we walked. "Cheer up."

"It is hard to be cheerful right now, you know that." I relaxed my head against his shoulder.

"That is why you must try. Even pretending helps once in a while."

"I am tired of pretending. It feels like I am pretending so much that I am never myself."

"You know that I understand you." He led me through the many tables, leaning over so I could hear him through the crowd.

"When Elisabeth passed, it was useless to pretend. I thought there was no one to pretend for. Nothing I did would matter. But then I realized the one that needed that facade most of all was myself. To convince myself it was fine, that I was fine. You will too."

"I feel guilty that I haven't visited my father," I spoke into the shoulder of his jacket. "I don't think he'd appreciate his grave being ill-kept."

"Look here." He brought me aside, placing his gloved hands on my face.

I shouldn't cry; the tears would freeze on my skin, but my lip was already trembling.

"He would be proud of you, Crow," John assured me. "Now, no more tears, you'll catch a cold." He wiped the tears with his thumbs. "Did you see the oranges? Let's go look at them."

I managed a simple smile and nodded, looping our arms again as we continued to stroll. I blinked the last of my tears away, swallowing them as if to will the emotions away.

Holidays were not my favorite; there was too much noise, too many expectations, so many things to manage at once. I was lucky I had Phoebe and John to help, or else I fear I would have drowned from social expectation.

As we approached the fruit stands, I spotted Luka with the girls, swapping papers and laughing with one another. He was holding someone's basket, complete with small ribbons. He hung off the side of the group like some tall, awkward lamprey; reluctantly participating, hardly present.

Phoebe and Silas were standing stiffly by the fruits, not speaking in typical sibling fashion. The two side by side were comical, a bright fluttery butterfly like Phoebe next to the intruding shadow that was Silas. They silently passed a cigarette, maybe the stress was getting to Phoebe too, if she resorted to stealing a huff or two.

When we walked up, Phoebe hurriedly gave the cigarette back to Silas, making him look at what caused such haste.

His eyes narrowed when they landed on me. The nagging in the back of my head told me he could smell the tears, or at least see that my eyes were red. However the case, I did not want it acknowledged.

"Phoebe, walk with me?" I took her hand, and she posed no protest.

"A treat for us." Phoebe smirked, producing an orange from her pocket.

"Ah, it makes the whole trip worth it," I laughed.

"Who did you get for gifts?" She picked at the skin of the orange, holding a slice of the plump fruit.

"I thought it was supposed to be a secret." I raised my brow and plucked the slice from her fingers, popping it into my mouth. "Who do you think I got?"

She laughed it off, a little annoyed at the lack of an answer, or the fact that I didn't want to tell her. She seemed to be carefully reading my expression in the same way I was reading hers.

"You know already, don't you?" I laughed, nudging her.

"Doesn't matter," she sniped. "The girls have already told each other. Now it's a process of elimination."

"How clever you must think you are," I teased. "Will you tell me who you have?"

"No." She pressed her lips in a thin line.

"Fine, keep your secrets." I laughed and took another slice of orange from her palm.

When we finished looping around the market, I spotted Silas again. He and Luka were with the rest of the girls. Luka passed him a small, rectangular piece of paper. They spoke with their heads close, Silas looking toward the ground, stone-faced, while Luka carefully emphasized his words. Silas was creasing the paper in his blank-stared grip, the snowfall already blotching the eggshell paper.

Luka left him to follow the girls, leaving Silas in their wake alone. The sable-haired man seemed to hover close to Edith, despite my warning for her to keep her distance from the likes of him. Of course she decided to wander closer, like a sheep in need of instant direction.

"Do you have any reservations about them?" I didn't look at her as I spoke. "Do you ever worry about the implications of him having the financial power?"

"I do, but he wouldn't be here if not for you." Phoebe sighed. "Plus, everyone knows it to be fact. No one would question your position, especially since if you left, he would, as well."

"How do you know?"

"He is a wallet to them, a means of survival. You are the power that orchestrated it all."

In the distance, Silas's eyes met mine. Everything became quiet once we spotted one another again. It was enough to ignore even the elements, tunneling with only one way out.

"That could be so." I broke my trance to look down at samples of fudge on one of the tables in front of us. Under my shoe was a small bunch of mistletoe wrapped in a crumbled, soiled ribbon. I leaned down to pick it up, inspecting the damaged good. "Let us hope he is as obedient as you assume he is."

XXXIII

The Fixer

A LINA REQUESTED THAT WE come to the lab after hours. It took both Silas and me by surprise that she would willingly want to spend time around us. I guess a perk of this business arrangement meant that she wasn't going to kill us, at least.

The apothecary was creepy and off-putting after hours, just like its owner. I would never get used to seeing it.

We were let in through the side door by Edith, who was quieter tonight than usual.

It was like she had been told specifically not to talk to us. We were to be let in and nothing more.

The staircase seemed narrower and longer, but maybe that was because it was like we were being led to an execution. The ambiance was less than hospitable.

When we entered the flat, we were graced with quite an image. It was almost hard even for me to swallow.

Dangling from the ceiling was a cocooned silhouette, a body hung by a hook in the ceiling. I imagined the most abominable moth would emerge from such a casing. As wonderful as that would be, though, it was merely a man. At the bottom of the form, slow drips seeped from it and landed in a bucket of dark liquid. Only then did I realize it was a Vipera, bound and being drained of his blood like a pig in a butcher shop.

My stomach lurched from both disgust and the reminder of my hunger. She was a cruel thing, planning on starving me out. With the deal in place, I could only hope she meant to let me eat soon enough. So far, none of the other Hosts had budged.

A few members of the Nest stood off to the side, with the exception of Rebecca and Alina. They were standing in front of five men, who were propped up against the wall. Rebecca had a fist full of one man's hair to keep his head up.

Alina stood, tall and dark like some phantom. As always, she was dressed in black, but she wore men's clothes for this endeavor. I suspect it was for practical reasons.

When Edith closed the door behind us, it caught Alina's attention. She was like a raptor bird, dialed in to everything in her domain. Her eyes traveled from Edith to the two of us, lingering on Silas.

Silas held an impersonal demeanor, but I could tell there was a silent standoff between the two of them. It dawned on me why we were here. She was sending a message. She was making a point.

"Edith." Alina's voice was sweet but dangerous. "Take Rebecca's place today."

Edith flinched at the call of her name.

Oh Edith, Alina will eat you alive if you cower like that.

She was no better than any natural predator; it was like she had grown a hunger. An instinctual need to dominate.

The Catholic sheepishly approached; even Rebecca shot Alina a look as if to ask her reasoning.

"Grip by the hair, make sure the chin is tilted up," Alina instructed, picking up a wooden wedge and shoving it into the man's mouth.

His eyes were wide, frantic, and his muffled babbling increased in tempo.

"I don't . . . I don't think I can do this," Edith whimpered.

"You need to grow thicker skin." Alina stepped aside and picked up a long axe that was resting against the wall. "I do not know how you survived on your own before this."

The victim's muffled words became shrieks when he eyed the axe.

"I don't know—"

"Edith," Alina warned. "I am making you do this because I care about you. I want you to go off and do great things, but you are holding yourself back. You need to go from doing what you are told to anticipating what needs to be done." She spoke slowly, stepping a few paces forward.

"I think I will be sick—"

"Don't." Alina stopped and raised the axe with the blunt side forward. "You need to see this."

Before she brought it down, she flipped the axe to be blade-forward, then brought it down on the wooden block between the man's jaws. The wicked blade split effortlessly through the wood and through the man's skull in turn. It was quick, but hardly clean. You could have blinked and missed it, though the thin splatter of blood across Edith's face was a clear indication that the horror was real.

Though it registered to everyone involved when the top half of his head slid off and landed on the floor with a harrowingly blunt *flop*.

"Ah." Alina straightened, stretching her neck from side to side, "How foolish of me. I meant to just crack the jaw. I guess we have two subjects donating blood today." She laughed as if she had simply mixed up the sugar with the salt. "It is a good thing that you followed instructions, that could have been your finger if it had been a hair *out of place*."

Edith's eyes slowly tracked up to Alina, something like shock and alarm in her eyes.

"Rebecca, I think you can handle the venom for tonight." Alina handed her the hilt of the axe, stepping past us spectators as she left the way we came.

Silas and Alina came face-to-face. She paused, and so did everyone else. There was no room for a stray insult, not even a spare breath.

Silas was cold, his pupils nearly black and fixated on her.

Obsidian blood adorned her face, marked by her ambition alone.

Then she left.

The girls did not even exchange glances before they went on to business as usual, prepping the next subject.

It became clear to me that Alina was not at the head of her Nest because people loved her. She was their elected head because she was their best chance of survival, as long as they went along with her madness. They feared her; that much was clear.

From what it looked like, they had all convinced themselves they worked toward a noble cause. She was weaving an intricate web that could only get larger from here. Now that she had been made to accept our arrangement, they needed her more than ever.

Silas's expression hadn't changed from the last time I checked.

"You created that nightmare," I told him. "Are you not pleased?"

"I think that was a love letter." The corner of his lip tugged into a grin, and his eyes shone with what could only be described as deep reverence. It only made sense that he was just as disillusioned as her. He was hopeless. They were the most chaotic pair this world would know, and unfortunately, that would serve them well.

I feared for those who found themselves under their boots.

XXXIV

The Poisoner

THE PAIN IN THE back of my skull was like a needle, undoubtedly from falling asleep on the sofa of the flat.

I wiped the side of my face, scratching the deep impressions left by the embroidery of the pillow slip.

Smoothing my hair back, I picked at the crust of leftover blood. Rolling the filth between my fingers, I groaned in defeat and wiped it on my clothes from last night.

Speaking of which—they were soaked.

I had sweated through them from the night before; that was apparent as the wool collected in a pile on the washroom floor. I had to peel off my undergarments and petticoat. Even with all the sweat, I was as cold as a brass knob.

I used a sponge to clean myself in the small hip bath in the corner. For some reason, the mere activity was a labor of endurance. I was nowhere near lame; there was no reason for me to be hard of breathing from holding a *wet sponge*.

I breathed in hard, but my nose barely let anything through. I pressed the hot sponge into my face, reveling in the melting sensation of my sinuses.

'Tis the season.

I was starting to think I had overdone it the night before. Everything had to be perfect, to reset the expectations.

But I didn't think that was the cause of my dreary health today.

I dressed and wrapped myself in a wool shawl draped on the end of my bed. The light from the windows throughout the tenement was warm and delightful—if only it wasn't making the pain in my skull drum like a hare's foot.

I could hear the morning chatter of breakfast, lighthearted humming, a bickering or two about some irrelevant gossip. It was like a birdsong to my ears. My recurring nightmares were of waking up and the house being silent. I had spent enough time alone that my outlook changed the minute I allowed myself to be surrounded by company.

I stepped down to the bottom floor. I don't really remember how I got there, but I saw Phoebe's silhouette sweeping the dust from the carpets out the front door, a cool breeze licking my face, my breath hitching at the sudden bite of fresh air.

Her voice was a bit muffled, and she slowly grew nearer, until I could make out a concerned face in the blinding backlight.

"Are you well?" she asked gently, the back of her hand tapping my cheek, then forehead, only to cup the side of my head. "You look like death."

All I could manage was a sigh and a slight head shake.

"Go back to bed, I can bring you something. You need water at the very least."

"No, I'm already behind on chores."

"I've got them," she insisted.

"Where are they?"

Phoebe raised a brow. "The boys are out." She started to sweep at my feet, herding me back toward the steps.

"I haven't much to do for you to take on my chores," I complained.

"I'll help," Rebecca chirped from around the corner.

"We did most of it the other day, anyway," Mary muttered, taking a break from a journal to chime in.

"See? We've got it." Phoebe slapped my back end with the broom. "Back upstairs you go. Take a day, we don't need you on the decline."

Reluctantly, I went back up the stairs, but I wasn't ready to return to my room.

Along the hallways, I realized I hadn't really gotten familiar with this new home. The photograph of the small group hung proudly at the end of the hall. Phoebe, Rebecca, Adeline, Mary, Edith, and finally myself, sitting on the very end with my grim attire, noticeably stark against the white tea gowns around me. John had taken the photograph, and I remember how excited he was to receive it as a gift. Having one around was important, or maybe an indulgence. But it made them all happy, that's all that mattered.

Other mementos lined the wall: dried flowers, embroidered squares of cloth, and whatever else we wanted to save from the last home. It looked every bit familiar, yet strange at the same time. Maybe it was the rushed move, or the unfamiliarity of the space itself. It was hard to settle into place.

I stopped at one door, this one bearing no decor like the rest of them. Just a plain wooden door and a brass patinaed knob.

The door hinges wailed, unprepared for the sudden use.

Silas's room was mainly storage. There was not much evidence he even used the room, aside from some clothing half unpacked off to the side. The bedsheets were crisp and tucked into place, collecting a thin layer of dust on the linen. I inspected the bag thrown on the cloth-covered chair. Just small, unimportant things. Some cash, some shirts, half a pack of cigarettes, to which I helped myself to. I dug for a lighter, just to find some old matches at the bottom.

The small note desk was uncovered, papers scattered like a map. I sat in the small chair, the dry wood creaking and settling much like I did. I pulled the cigarette, my nail burning on the dry match before pushing the smoke through my nose, though it didn't do much to help the stuffiness.

The collection of papers on his desk looked something like a mix of invoices, transcriptions, things of a business nature. All addressed to NEW YORK, NEW YORK. I propped my elbow up and shifted through the papers with my free hand, picking up a small square of paper.

Fifth Avenue—*Chimera*. Scrawled across the bottom, presumably in Silas's handwriting.

It was a small, muddied photograph of a tall corner building. It looked like it could be some sort of expensive hotel.

His handwriting scrawled across most of the documents, small notes in the corners, sometimes some mathematics in the margins. His spellings were odd, with an excessive number of vowels or strange variations of the consonants. He wasn't illiterate, but his writing habits aged him.

I allowed myself a quiet laugh and leaned back in the chair, remembering the sharp pain in my head.

"Something funny?"

I nearly dropped my cigarette, hitting my knee under the desk when I flinched.

Silas leaned on the doorway, head tipped against the frame as he watched.

"Just looking." I relaxed into the chair again, a bit dizzy from the fright. "You're under my roof after all."

"The devil loves holding idle hands." He stalked over to the desk, glancing at the papers and then to me. "Hopefully it wasn't my number work making you laugh."

I shook my head and smirked. "Two hundred."

"Pardon?" His brow creased, and he leaned over the desk to glance at the papers again for the correction.

"Two hundred years old."

A small smirk teased as he looked over to me. "I beg again, *pardon*?"

"When we spoke those years ago, you spoke of a plague." I shook my head laughing. "I assumed the first Black Death of 1300, not the Great Plague of 1665, since you never specified."

"What of it?"

"Nothing." I shrugged, putting out the cigarette on the ashtray. "I just thought you were older."

"Older?" He laughed. "How old did you assume I was?"

"I don't know, but your spelling tells me about two hundred. I was a couple hundred off."

"You have an odd compulsion to be *right*. I don't know how this information serves you." He rolled his eyes.

"Entertainment. That is all."

"Are you?" He tilted his head at me. "Entertained, that is?"

I shrugged, thinly veiling a laugh.

"Is this how you tell me I'm too young for you?" he joked, sitting on the edge of the desk.

"Practically a boy." I shook my head, picking up the small square photograph. I pinched it between my fingers and held it up to him. "Is this it? Your Nest?"

He squinted and plucked it from between my fingers, "It looks less impressive on this tiny piece of paper, but yes."

"This won't work you know," I exhaled, nearly a mumble. "Not if you can't learn to roll over."

"Roll over?" He raised a brow, tossing the photo gently onto the pile of papers. "I thought that's what this was." He gestured around to the abode we resided in.

"I still have a hard time believing that when this is all over, we will be equals," I began, standing from my seat slowly to prevent vertigo. "The more I think about it, equality is not what we need. It's equity."

"Elaborate." He crossed his arms.

"While we could maybe kill each other almost as easily, there are things you can do that I cannot. Which is why I need to know what is protecting me and my girls from the likes of you." I stopped in front of him. "How do I know I won't be locked in a dull gray room again with nothing but a collar and clean sheets?" I traced a finger over the edge of the desk and down to his leg, leaning close as if to tell a secret. "How do I know I won't be like every other Host promised a good life?"

He didn't answer, didn't lift his eyes to meet mine, nothing.

"Something to think about." I left him there to let my words marinate.

JUST THE INTERACTION HAD me drained, needing to recover from nothing at all.

I could smell food cooking in the kitchen; it was well into lunchtime, though I'm sure some of the dinner prep was starting while the fire was hot.

Even the venture up the stairs was a chore, having to stop at the last flight before reaching the top. As I entered my own room, I knew my day was about to get longer and longer.

Phoebe and Edith were in the living area. Edith was clutching her skirts with white knuckles; Phoebe was stiff-browed with arms crossed. Both of them let go of their tension when I walked in, the two of them immediately standing.

"I didn't want to bother you today—" Phoebe started.

"Phoebe thinks it's her night to feed, but I'm pretty sure it's mine this time," Edith talked over her.

"No, you missed your feeding night, so you don't get one. Tough luck when you can't keep a schedule," she snapped.

All I could hear was the jaw snaps of hungry dogs. The throbbing in my head made me falter against the sofa, sitting down on the cushions and clenching my eyes shut.

"You don't have to if you don't want to."

"We can just do one today, one tomorrow?"

"Just do it now." I took a deep breath. "Both of you. No need to fight."

"You probably shouldn't while sick." Edith sat next to me on one side.

"It really is fine if you want to delay." Phoebe quickly sat down on the other side, like it was a race for my neck the minute I assured them that all was fine and they weren't being selfish in the smallest sense.

False concern from both parties, no matter what they lead on with their words.

I leaned back against the couch, brushing my hair out of the way. "Just do it."

Edith and Phoebe exchanged looks, a competitive sort of glare as they neared. Phoebe rested a hand on my upper chest, grazing my collarbone, her fingers fluttering over the square neckline of my nightgown.

Edith preened some hair sticking to my skin away, breathing shallowly against my neck.

Phoebe didn't hesitate to go first, sinking her teeth into one side, more sure of her bite than usual. Like an animal exhibiting resource guarding tendencies that had yet to be trained out.

Edith went next, her bite clean, practiced, relatively painless.

The two of them feeding wasn't bad if you ignore the blood loss. Two hits of venom numbed my head and my nerves, except there was nothing to stop the intrusive thoughts. I could feel my skin heating up, delicate fingers holding me, touching like they wanted a better grip, leaving no room as if someone would steal their piece of meat.

The stars and colors behind my eyelids were so pretty, especially when they changed when someone spoke.

"*Edith, enough,*" Phoebe's muffled voice scolded.

"*I didn't take any more than you did,*" Edith's voice echoed.

"*Alina!*" Phoebe's voice knocked against the inside of my head, asking me to come to the door to answer, but I did not want to.

The darkness from the corner of my eyes bled over like tightly woven wool. Suddenly, the weight lifted from me, and I was floating, as if submerged. One nice moment of peace. No one wanted anything from me, and neither did I from them. Free of responsibility, such a fantasy to indulge in.

"Alina!" My body shook, snapping me awake. Edith and Phoebe hovered over me.

"Why are you staring?"

"You were having a seizure."

"No, I wasn't." I shoved them both aside to sit up, the scene around me trailing in colors. "I just closed my eyes."

Phoebe grabbed my wrist, and I snapped it out of her grasp.

"I'm hungry," I muttered, pressing my palm to my tired eyes.

The two of them threw looks at each other before Phoebe got up to leave the room, jerking her head at Edith. Edith hurried to my side, grabbing my waist and my elbow to lead me.

"I'm not one of your patients." I yanked my arm from her and departed the room.

"Alina stop—" Phoebe tugged my forearm back.

"Stop *touching* me!" I raised my voice, but Phoebe didn't flinch. Her lack of reaction boiled my blood. "You need to get a hold of your jealousy. Biting and gnawing at me to prove some sort of sick point to Edith. To *anyone* you have to share me with!" I seethed.

Phoebe's lip twitched, her eyes filling with blood, the green irises stark against the dangerous glare. Unrecognizable to the sweet image of my oldest friend. "I shouldn't have to share you with dirty little things like her."

"What is wrong with you?" I snapped.

Edith stood in the doorway, an awkward shuffle as she pushed past us, a quick wipe of her sleeve over her eyes.

"Look what you've done now." I gestured toward where Edith disappeared. "You're creating a hostile living environment."

"I did?" Phoebe spoke, slow and venomous. "*I* am the one who created a hostile environment?" she repeated, stepping close. She studied my face, as if my reaction would answer her question. There were no more replies, no more words of distaste. Just a smile full of animosity, and a headshake of disbelief as she shoved past me.

I WAS AT THE dining room table, unsure when I arrived, and didn't have the energy to worry about the lost time. I swallowed thickly; my head was pounding like a funeral procession. Every flicker of the candles made me want to pull my own eyes out to stop it from mocking my senses.

Everyone was eating happily, sitting nicely and chatting. When I looked up, though, I nearly caught a stray glare or two; no one would look at me, everyone pretending everything was normal. Nothing about this was normal. What were we doing, pretending like our lives hadn't just been completely uprooted?

Perhaps it wasn't that they were pretending, and the real reason for their averted gazes was a sinister second option. Plastered smiles, forced chatter . . . can't bear to even look at me.

I reached for my spoon, and Mary flinched beside me. With a frown, I looked across at Edith, who dug at her bowl, a tremor in her wrist, making an awful chiming noise every time it scraped the bowl. Rebecca steadily watched me out of the corner of her eye.

Fear. They're afraid.

On the other end of the table, Phoebe didn't regard me whatsoever, but she was next to Silas, whispering something in his ear as she glanced my way. His unwavering eyes reflected back at me, watching carefully.

"Alina, are you going to finish that or are you going to waste a meal?" Luka joked a few seats down.

I glanced down at my bowl.

Rice.

I shoved my seat back, a horrid screech across the wood floor silencing the table. Not one person moved at the sudden disruption until I whipped the bowl at Luka, and the girls scrambled up.

The bowl hit him in the head, spilling rice across the table.

"Eat well, you fucking pig," I spit my words like hot embers on the tongue, shoving past a body or two in the crowded dining room to depart. Only when I left the heat of the crowded room did I realize my cheeks were wet, and my throat was sore with an anxious rage.

NO MATTER WHERE I turned, it was hot. I kicked the blanket in discomfort, swamped with air too heavy to get a proper breath, and the unmistakable feeling of being watched. I couldn't open my eyes, every movement granting me a sinking dread heavy on my chest.

An image made itself known to me. A dark expanse, a sticky, red wetness pooling on the floor. A bottomless echo that vibrated deep within my chest cavity, a growing sense of despair. My limbs were paralyzed.

Around me was darkness, slowly revealing it was more than just a void. There was something there, waiting for me.

The bed dipped beside me, a smoky scent offering some clarity to my sinuses.

Fingertips at the front of my throat. My hair smoothed to the side, the fingers falling to my chest and tracing down my sternum. Then the heat of a body in close proximity to mine, sharing the air around us.

I gasped for air, all I could see behind my eyelids was a dim red light, colored with my blood.

"Shh . . . you're awake. It's all right," a deep voice whispered.

"What's going on?"

"You were having a nightmare." The words came out like a rattle, accompanied by a predatory chittering.

"Is it you? My nightmare?"

"What dares to haunt you but me?" Silas whispered, the words floating around in the dark, trapped with me inside my head. I could feel him close. His hands were warm; he wasn't wearing his gloves. The smell of his cologne and tobacco clung to his clothes.

Every quickening breath was accompanied by small stammers. A cold sweat was heavy on my skin. I closed my fists and opened them. I could choke.

"Relax yourself. Listen to me . . ." His voice trailed off, hands on me, hot trails over my cold body. "Feel me . . ."

My breathing picked up, and it was hard to focus. I couldn't move. I could twitch my hand, nothing else.

Warmth on my lips, his lips on mine. A gasp was captured by his kiss, like he wanted every last thing from me, even if it was my last breath.

"Silas." I swallowed, and he kissed me again, harder at the utterance of his name.

"Will you tell me to stop or keep going after such a sweet call of my name, Alina?"

"You call for me so often," I panted. I could move my arms now, my head feeling like it was finally resurfacing from the dream. "I'm beginning to think you just like the sound of my name on your lips."

"Maybe I just like the taste." His words manifested like a snake wrapping around my limbs, ready to devour me whole.

"Careful, cyanide tastes remarkably like almonds." I reached up without opening my eyes. "It only takes a little bit of sweetener to pass an unremarkable death."

"Then so be it, my sweetest demise." His words were almost a purr before he wrapped his arms around my waist, lifting me up to kiss me and touch along the back of my neck and down my back.

I kissed him back. As far as I was concerned, this was a dream, and I wasn't going to open my eyes to make sure.

His hands smoothed down to my hips. "Will you let us be each other's ruin?"

I silenced him with a long, steady kiss before resting my cheek against his, hugging him tightly. "May it be in another nightmare, my creature."

I let go, sinking into the softness of my bed.

I didn't know when he left, or when I went to sleep. I hadn't the slightest clue of how many hours could have passed.

On my bedside table, he left me a small truce.

A small, simple bowl of sliced peaches, a glass of wine, and a cigarette. His mechanical lighter was placed neatly beside for lighting ease.

I rolled over, the scent of his cologne lingering on the pillow, the sheets, my skin. Or maybe it was just a sensitive nose from being ill.

Figures my one place of ease in a time of need is with the man who makes it his life mission to torture me.

XXXV

The Fixer

"DO YOU ALWAYS SMELL like hickory and thyme?" I purred, brushing the dark strands of hair away from the Host's neck.

"I . . . I suppose. I-I'm usually cooking—"

I pressed my palm against her back, smoothing down each vertebrae of the spine before giving the lobe of her ear a gentle bite. Our bodies were hidden away in the dark, abandoned hallway while the others communed.

So supple, so delectable.

I could feel the heat radiate from her skin; it made it all the more stimulating. My stomach twitched, forcing me to close my eyes and hold it together just a bit longer.

Patience. Patience is a virtue.

"That tickles." She let out a breathy laugh, her hands pressing on my chest.

"Does it?" I left kisses over her shoulder, pulling at the loose nightgown. I leaned closer, my other hand at the back of her head as she leaned against the wall of the hallway. "Are you this sensitive elsewhere? Or will you let me find out?"

"Luka!" she scolded, glancing to either side as if someone would walk in.

"Are you shy?" I whispered against her skin, lingering closer to her neck.

"Someone might see!"

"Is that a problem?" I hummed, my eyes glancing from her face and back to her neck.

I lied, she didn't smell like hickory or thyme. She smelled like sweat. The nervous kind that agitated my appetite. Her skin was so warm. Her neck pulsed steadily, each bulge of the artery giving me a beautiful image of the blood pushing through, pump by pump. Soon, the pulsing of her neck and my own heart synced. My fangs scraped against my tongue as they pushed forward. Writhing. Wanting. *Starving.*

"No!" A sharp shove to my chest.

A trickle of wetness dripped down my cheek. I wiped away the blood from my eye, staring at the feeble thing. *No?*

"You know you're not allowed." She glared, a small furrow in her brow as she pretended to keep her composure.

I raised a brow, looming over her. "Here I was thinking we were really hitting it off."

"We have strict rules here, Mr. Novikov."

"And who are these rules for? Hm?" I leaned down slowly to meet her at eye level, leaning my elbow on the wall just above her head.

"A-Alina said you are not to be fed."

"And what do you get from this rule? You are harming no one except yourself by letting me feed from you. Is autonomy not part of your silly rules?"

Her throat bobbed, swallowing thickly as her eyes darted around, anywhere but at me.

"Fine," I snarled, standing straight.

She slipped from between myself and the wall faster than a wet fish. Slippery, skittish.

I leaned back, resting my head back and gently tapping my head against the wall.

I was far from starving, but *damn*, it was frustrating. The people in this town, Vipera or human, seem to be skeptical of new faces. They remembered them, too.

At least here, there are also fewer people to hide from, and a fast-moving river to dump the body.

THE BETTER HALF OF the evening was spent in the communal space. The first floor consisted of all shared rooms and shared spaces used by the entire Nest. Today we were in one of the living room lounge areas by a fire. We called this one the green room due to the wallpaper. The dark setting made a perfect place to destress, something cozy.

The setup was similar to the farmhouse, except three couches boxed in the mantel with a table in the middle. I sat on one of them in the middle with a girl on either side. Phoebe was in a similar position across from me. We all had things to do, whether it was reading, writing, embroidering—I was reading, but it was interesting seeing what the others did in their free time, especially at quiet times like this.

"Are you going to the market tomorrow? I wanted to get a few things," Phoebe whispered to the woman next to her, handing her a small list.

"I thought your group didn't like to overspend," I commented, glancing up from my book.

"It has been a rough few days. I feel like we could all use a hearty feast to raise morale."

"You mean to raise Alina's morale."

"No, I mean for *everyone*," she gritted.

"If you say so." I shrugged, glancing at my book, but the huff that came from her made a smile tug at my lip.

"What is your problem anyway, hmm?" Phoebe glared. "Always questioning things. You've not been here for more than a week and suddenly you know better?"

"I know a devoted friend when I see one." I smiled.

"What is that supposed to mean?"

"You fuss over the wrong things."

"It is my job to do so. How else do we manage a Nest?"

"You know that isn't what I'm speaking of."

"Now you are just talking to talk." She brushed me off with a gesture and returned to her embroidery.

"Do you ever do anything for yourself, Phoebe?" I snapped my book shut and rested it on my lap, reclining back against the couch. The other girls glanced up from their things before averting their gazes. "You give her everything."

"I do not!" she raised her voice.

"Not yet."

"You say that like it's a sure thing."

"Unrequited love does terrible things. I've seen it all before." I tilted my head at her, watching her reaction. "Like letting their friends take everything, letting it consume them until they are thanking the other for cleaning the meat from their bones."

There was a fire in Phoebe's eyes, but she said nothing. Surely she must know there was some truth to what I said.

"Ah! What do I know," I chuckled. "I'm just a simple old man who has lived too many lives."

A creaking came from the doorway.

Both of our heads snapped in the direction of Edith, who startled at the movement.

Phoebe's expression soured when she saw the little blonde.

"Apologies if I am interrupting." Edith stepped into the room, looking over at Phoebe. "Would I be able to borrow some of your cannabis?"

"Why?" Phoebe continued with her embroidery, not giving her the decency to look at her while she spoke.

"I have a toothache."

"You're a nurse; why didn't you grab some from the hospital?"

"Because I didn't have a toothache while I was there," Edith huffed, frustrated with the line of questioning. "Please?"

"No."

Edith's hands balled up into fists, unable to sort through her frustration and not sure how to counter Phoebe. The other girls held inconspicuous smirks as they pretended not to listen.

"Edith, come here." I patted my leg to ask her to sit. "I'll look at it for you. I might have something stashed somewhere."

The others glanced up when I made my gesture, glancing between me and the timid blonde. Edith seemed just as, if not more, surprised than the others. Phoebe glared at me, her fine fingers pinching her needle extra hard.

Am I disrupting your power trip? Amusing.

Edith timidly approached and sat on my knee.

I reached up. "Open." I cupped her face, tilting it back.

When she opened, her fangs flicked forward, but one quivered as if it was taking significant effort to bear it out. Around the gumline was a bit of inflammation, the part responsible for flexing it in the first place.

"It looks like you overextended these." I used my thumb to lift her lip up on that side. "Is it sore?"

She nodded.

"In my room, into the washroom, I have laudanum," I instructed. When my gaze returned to Phoebe, she had stopped what she was doing.

Edith nodded, stumbling up and brushing her skirt awkwardly. She abandoned the room like a canary set free from her cage.

I smirked at Phoebe. "What? Just being helpful."

"Don't undermine me."

"You're a soft-horn, and you know it."

Phoebe scoffed, shaking her head in disbelief.

"Like I said before, unrequited love does terrible things. It makes the prettiest of us repulsive." I collected my book. "Time for me to turn in. You ladies have a good night."

I don't know why, but it was amusing poking at Phoebe. Such a proud woman, but she was as prickly as a porcupine. Jealousy was quite the color on her; I swore if she kept this up any longer, she would turn green.

As I exited the room, my stomach pinched, and the room began to waver. A wave of vertigo hit me faster than if I had consumed an entire jug of moonshine, like trying to navigate in a dream. I sluggishly made my way up the stairs, down the hall, and all the way to my room at the end. It was isolated from any of the occupied rooms. I don't blame them, but it had some ironic sort of nostalgia to hear the laughter and chatter from far off, softly taunting me.

In the corner of the room, Edith sat in the chair, fiddling with the bottle of dark liquid.

"Did it help?" I mumbled, tossing my book onto the small table.

"I know your heart is in the right place . . ." Edith began.

An impulsive sneer was my only response.

"But you can't insult her like that. In front of everyone," she finished, lifting her eyes to me.

"She was being unpleasant." I walked up to her. "How will they know that they can't just say anything without recourse?"

"It makes my situation worse, tenfold." She looked up at me, her brow creasing slightly.

"It can only get worse before it gets better—"

"Luka!" she snapped.

Whatever I was going to say after was caught in my throat from her abruptness. Edith and I suffered from the same sort of isolation, though I think she had it a bit better than I did currently. Only because she was free to feed, even if she wasn't on friendly terms with the others. I suspect that's why Alina was her feeding partner.

She was standing now, haughty of posture, with a firm scowl. Even with her confident facade, I could see the vein in her temple pulse, her breathing shallow. Fear was not as shy when it waved its flag.

She was nervous. The sweat smells different when it's from anxiety. From fear? No, from anger. Her eyes stayed on me, but my focus was more on the pulsing on her little neck, peeking from under her head covering.

The drumming of my head was louder, the pinch in my stomach nauseating. I approached her, only to be met with a hard shove.

My hand enwrapped her curly blond hair, the head covering pooling around her neck. The thrashing made my vision narrow. My own saliva collected fast enough in my mouth to choke me. Another hot drip of blood from my eye scored down my cheek.

I pried her neck to the side.

"Stop!" she shouted. "Luka!"

The sound of my name hit me, a shaky semblance of whatever was left of my civilized self. It was not enough.

I bit her. I bit her right through her scarf, my fangs long enough to pierce straight through.

She yelped and pushed and shoved.

I drank, but it just came back up. I couldn't swallow it; it tasted purely acidic.

I shoved her away quickly as I turned toward the wall, hunching over and coughing, expelling the black blood onto the floor. It was like my body didn't want it to go past the esophagus in the first place. It was worth a try. Even if it was to trick my body into thinking it wasn't as hungry as it really was.

"Why," she cried, yanking the scarf from her head and inspecting the black stain on it.

"I'm starving."

"Blood sharing is—"

"I know," I groaned, turning around to lean on the wall. "I don't know what else to do, Edith. She's starving me out."

"I don't care what you have to do," Edith nearly hissed, something I hadn't seen from her before. "Make amends with Alina. Barter, beg, subjugate yourself—I don't care. If you think she will forgive you if you wait it out, don't bother. She is not a woman of mercy."

"I will not beg—"

"Then you can die."

Her lip quivered, staring at the floor paces away, fidgeting with the stained scarf.

For the first time, I was able to see the fine, jagged line across her throat. A faint white that was easily missed. The mark of creation, her greatest shame.

Her bleakness took me back, like this was a prediction rather than a suggestion. I wasn't sure if this was just from my fever or if she was being serious. The look in her eyes told me she was sincere. In my own disbelief, she shook her head at me and left.

Except when she left, I barely recognized the creature Edith had become. I was frankly unsure of whether to be proud or concerned.

Something in me twisted.

In hunger or shame, I didn't know.

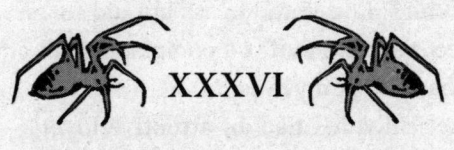

XXXVI

The Poisoner

M Y NOSE TICKLED. A slight tingle, just barely felt, brushing over my nose, then my cheek. Something *furry*.

I peeled open an eye to a tail in my face. Though when I snatched it, it was utterly limp.

We do not have pets.

"Twenty." Silas's voice came from the corner of my room.

My view was blocked by a brown pelt. Leaning up, I could see him laughing at me just over the fur.

"Excuse me?" I cleared my throat, pushing the pelt down only to reveal another.

Around me was an assortment of such clutter. Rich browns and tans, spots and stripes, silken and coiled. He had built the most expensive nest around me, and I was surprised I hadn't suffocated in my sleep. *Smothered* with gifts would be an appropriate term.

"I was able to cover you in twenty coats before you began to wake," he laughed. "You sleep like a corpse."

Another one hit me in the side of my face when he tossed it at me, only to be caught in his hand after I failed to notice he moved closer.

His cold eyes drifted, and I found myself grasping what appeared to be a mink cloak to make myself decent.

"What is this?" I hesitated to ask but did so anyway.

"I was becoming tired of you complaining about being cold." He glanced back up at my eyes.

"Hypothetically, if I had an attentive lover"—I leaned up toward him—"my bones wouldn't chill so easily."

"Is that so?" His tone was nearly a sneer. Even in anger, he couldn't help a glance at my lips while I spoke.

I expected to offend him, but he took it as a challenge.

"I've known warmer flasks," I mocked, my final word sharp.

"Have you now?" He withdrew from me, studying the floor he walked on as he approached the window.

He opened the window, the fresh, cool breeze puffing some snow powder from the windowsill into the room.

He came to the side of the bed, cocking his head. "How is the temperature?"

"Fine." I swallowed, clutching the fur over my body.

He snared the end of the cloak I was holding, yanking it down and exposing me. My hands flew to my chest, legs crossed. "Are you sure?"

"Yes," I said firmly, unable to help a tremor when the wind whistled through the window again.

I was surrounded by fur, either too stubborn or too scared to grab one for cover. He was waiting for it, waiting for me to give in. This was his game—to make me depend on him.

I straightened my back, chin held high. My body shook from the cold or from a small dose of exhilaration.

"Now you don't have a reason to complain; you have something in every color." He tossed the rest of the pile onto the bed. "Not that you have much diversity in your attire."

"I don't need them."

He yanked my ankle, dragging me toward him through the fur. His knee dipped into the lush mattress.

There was something scandalous despite the tameness of the scene around us. This man had chased me, hunted me, and used me as food. Now he wore everything but the coat, starched and pressed like he had some important business to attend to, yet he was here, looming over me while I was rather indisposed. Sometimes the lines between what I would entertain and what I enjoyed were becoming a singular line in the dirt.

I did not give him the pleasure of squirming, kicking, or yelling. I relaxed back into the scene, arching my back as I became comfortable.

"For someone who refuses to be spoiled," Silas began, reaching down and tracing his finger across my hip bone, slowly across to the other side, "you sure seem to be enjoying yourself this morning."

"You won't get a rouse out of me any longer. You are harmless, we've established this."

"To your body, reasonably." He flattened his hand on my abdomen, smoothing it up between my breasts. "Your ego is never safe, though."

I glanced at his hand, then back up at him. The light from behind him made him look like some gloomy premonition. "Neither is yours, as we have learned."

His hand slid further, resting on my neck, the tips of his fingers pulsing with anticipation, a reminder of our positions.

His other hand moved on my thigh.

The wind from the window blew infrequently. As his fingers trailed over my skin, I could feel goose bumps rise just with the slightest touch, even in anticipation, like being touched by a ghost.

The hand on my neck did not frighten me. No, it was the softer touches that posed a far more intense terror, one of accepting that I might want such tenderness from the monster that haunted me.

He was gentle, his hand hovering between my legs. I could practically imagine the warmth the touch would hold, only to be deprived of it. Sharp shivers rippled through me.

I finally looked up; his eyes weren't even looking where his hands were acting; his eyes were on only me.

"I am not scared of you." Another shiver.

"I know," he replied calmly. There came a whisper of a touch on my inner thigh, venturing higher.

"I'm not!"

"I believe you." He leaned down, his bottom lip brushing my nipple, already taut from the chill.

I bit down on my lip, my hip bucking subtly, but I didn't want to give him the impression of enjoyment either.

His lip dragged over my nipple, then across the skin of my collarbone.

I tilted my neck and turned my face from him.

He placed a kiss on my neck, his grip on the sides of my neck a little tighter to pull me closer.

"Get yourself dressed," he whispered, before withdrawing completely.

The sunlight from the window was in my eyes now. Any warmth that had come from him was gone in a second.

"Don't make demands of me." I sat up.

"Wear one today." He tossed one of the rabbit fur cloaks at me.

I held the coat close, raking my fingers through the fine texture. The hairs of the rabbit were so fine, fluid as I dragged my fingers through them. "Why today?"

"Because we are going out." Silas picked up a pelt to inspect it. "I asked Mary to take over your chores."

"I can't just avoid duties because you are in need of something to kill your boredom."

"No one else contested. I bought them a new wardrobe, as well."

"That isn't how we do things here."

"You can run your Nest however you like, but I won't let anyone in drab wear represent us." He grimaced. "Appearances matter."

Silas picked up one of the capes, of a gray and black color. The fine hairs tickled my neck as he wrapped it around, engulfing me.

"A fox wearing a fox; how fitting." Silas smirked. "I found something that reminded me of you." He handed me an oddly colored hand muff. It had black fur with streaks of white, making me assume it was from a piebald animal.

"You must think of yourself as quite funny." I held it in my hands, tracing over the white streaks.

He lifted my chin, tracing along the white of my eyebrow, then my lashes. I turned away from him, but he only smirked. "While I enjoy comedy, I thought it would match perfectly. Rarities are expensive for a reason."

"It sounds like you plan to sell me."

"You aren't for sale." He laughed. "Meet me downstairs when you are finished."

He left me alone in my pile of pelts. I placed my hands in the fur, spreading my fingers wide as I touched them. I slumped forward, lying in them for a minute. Everything was so warm, so soft. They reminded me of our first time, though I am not sure if that was his intention.

The ghost of his touch toyed with my mind, threatening to replace the memories of violence. But it is those memories that aided in my survival, to remind me who, exactly, I was dealing with.

AFTER A BIT OF deliberation, I chose a black cloak with matching fur. I put my hair half up, deciding a bit of effort on my part was the least I could do if I was going to wear something so expensive. I wore Phoebe's emerald earrings that she often lent to me. Finally, I decided on wearing the piebald muff.

Passing some of the rooms was like peeking into windows uninvited, despite the doors being wide open. Hosts and Vipera fluttered from room to room in girlish excitement, like pollinators in spring, trading new and old garments to try between each other.

My posture became awkward as I descended the stairs. It had been a while since I wore anything this eye-catching, but I had missed it.

With all the enthusiasm for the material things above, not many were on the bottom floor. It was warm down here, even with the fire neglected to embers. Mud and sand littered the floors from being dragged in without someone to sweep. I had to remind myself that they deserved a break, to ignore the mess, that it was a problem for a later date.

I hesitated in the middle of the empty floor.

What am I doing? This was obscene.

As I turned to go back, though, Silas was blocking my way to the stairs.

"Having second thoughts?" he teased.

"Would it matter if I were?"

"No." He stepped down the last few stairs before standing before me and extending his hand. It was almost like he was going to touch my face, but he just brushed some dust from the fur lining of the cloak. "You sure took your time."

"I did. So make this worthwhile." I shoved his hand from my shoulder.

Instead of letting his hand fall away, he turned it to latch my palm in his.

When I turned to look, he had already pulled me into his side, his arm looping with mine.

There I was, trapped on an outing with my personal nightmare, at his request.

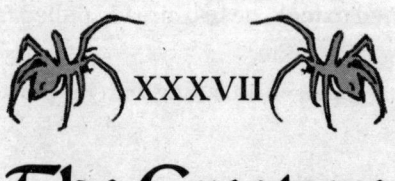

XXXVII

The Creature

IT WAS HARD TO believe that Alina was here, with her arm looped in mine without resistance or complaint—well, *minimal* complaints. I half expected her to ignore me and go back to sleep. I wouldn't have blamed her. The pile of pelts looked comfortable.

After the other night, I figured out what I needed to do for her to relax. Clearly, she was establishing her place in the Nest. She wanted me to know that. The fastest way for her to accept me is if I accepted her flirtatious threats. The absence of resistance to her message was all she needed.

Today I wanted to try something different. We had always tangled in the dark, and she resisted bringing our *relationship* to see the light of day. Now I had the opportunity to show her I am not here to fight.

There was a street market this weekend. The tents lined the snowy streets, closed down to carriages so patrons could stroll.

She inspected the sweets, then some of the dried herbs. She appeared the most at ease that I had seen her since arriving. It was like a state of wandering, with no goal in mind. It was best to keep her occupied.

I noticed she wore one thing I bought her, which gave me an odd warm feeling in my gut. Her neatly gloved hands with the fur trim danced over the goods of the market, inspecting the broad display of goods closely as if each thing she purchased must be to her impossible standards. She had even done her hair; it was braided and twisted and gathered neatly with a ribbon, the thin silken bow dangling at the nape of her neck.

She picked out a bundle of eucalyptus for the tenement flats while we were there, though I did see her eyeing the crates of oranges. Her eyes caught my attention; I recognized that look. She was begging me.

"Pick what you like," I encouraged, "we have all day."

"You're sure about that? I can have quite expensive tastes."

"I can afford it. I wouldn't expect any less from you."

She eyed the sweets, then looked at me expectantly. Then she started to gravitate toward them so quickly, I had to pick up my pace to catch up with her.

"What about this?" She picked up a fruit.

"Do you think I can't afford fruit?"

That only made her smirk. She moved one booth down, pointing to some wreaths and decor fashioned with ribbons. "This, as well?"

"If that is what you like."

She moved again, this time across the path to a booth it seemed she knew well—baked goods.

Before I knew it, she had to buy a wicker basket to hold all the sweets and fruits she bought. She was quite the spendthrift when she wanted to be, but I suppose that was the point. It didn't matter to me; I had more money than I knew what to do with. Every penny spent on her was worth it.

"What are those?" I pointed to a candy in her basket.

"Sherbert Lemons; Rebecca likes them." She plucked one from the bag in the basket, holding it up for me.

I shook my head. "Taste it for me."

She raised a brow before popping it in her mouth. "It tastes like lemon, sour in the middle."

"Well, is there anything else bitter or sour? Aside from yourself."

"Cough candy." She dug through the basket again and held up a tan piece of hard candy.

"What does it taste like?"

"Clove. You won't taste anything except the spice and bitterness, but it is supposed to be sweet, as well." She held it up to my lips.

I hovered over her, locking our lips together. She nearly jumped at the action. It was quick, breaking as soon as it happened. Her eyes were wide, the snow around us making them seem all the brighter. Her face was turning red, her poliosis looking whiter than ever, not even the snow compared. She wanted to look away—I could see it in the way her eyes shifted—but she refused to, anyway. Somewhere in my observation, I forgot what I was going to say.

I pulled away, licking my lips. "I like it."

"Why didn't you just eat one—"

"I don't know," I admitted breathlessly. "I suppose it was just an impulse."

She huffed, her cheeks becoming rosy. It wasn't from the cold.

We strolled leisurely until we were past the street and at the entrance to the park. The day was perfect for being outside, though I'm sure she was comfortable under the fur.

Experiences as menial as a market and tasting candy may seem a bit childish to take pleasure in, but when you have spent as many years on this earth as I have, there is rarely an original experience. The only thing I could do is relish in the pleasure of reliving them all again with her. Every old experience becomes new through her eyes, and I simply have the pleasure of being present. I have seen everything from every view, except *hers*. It was like experiencing everything for the first time again; she made all the things I took for granted seem new and exciting.

Sometime along our walk, Alina began to stiffen. That could only mean she had disappeared inside that head of hers.

Her brows furrowed, deep in thought. Occasionally, I could see the muscle in her jaw twitch from clenching her teeth together for so long. So much tension for such a cruel thing like her.

"I almost forgot. I have something." I broke her from her thoughts. I pulled a round object from my pocket, placing it in her hands.

It was an orange.

"We just bought oranges." She scrutinized it.

"No, peel it." I smirked.

She picked at the skin, peeling away the orange to expose the blood-red pulp inside. She blinked, and then her eyes trailed back to me.

"It is a blood orange." I grinned. "I thought maybe you would like it."

"I do." She placed the orange in her basket as she stopped walking.

"What is wrong?"

"I see what you are doing."

Not this again.

"What do you think I am doing?" I raised a brow.

"Parading me around like I'm some prize," she scoffed. "Buying me things, bringing the girls new fancy clothes—you're showing off."

"Well, you are a prize," I said matter-of-factly. "And it would be a waste not to parade you around."

"See? There it is. You think this is funny. You mock me."

"I assure you, this is not a mockery. You would know if it was."

"You are *undermining* me."

"You think too highly of yourself," I laughed, stepping toward her. "I am investing in you."

"You are trying to make it seem like I am some object to you now." She took a step away from me, but I stepped closer.

She backed into a tree along the pathway, but my pursuit didn't stop until I hovered over her.

"Has it ever occurred to you," I lowered my face to hers, making sure she was looking at me, "that I show you off because I am proud of you?"

I could see her pulse jump by the throbbing of her jugular. I could smell the change in her blood sugar just from those simple words. I had a feeling she didn't hear those words often.

"I *am* proud of you," I repeated. "You could be made of stars the way you outshine everyone around you, including myself. I am simply happy to be bathed in the light." I cupped her face with both of my hands. "Do you understand me, now?"

"You don't *really* believe that."

"You deserve all of the attention this world can afford."

"I don't believe you—"

"If I could change true north to wherever you stood, I would do it."

"How do I know I am not just food to you?" she snapped, placing her palms on my chest, but it wouldn't stop me from holding her.

"If you were food, I would treat you like food," I breathed. "I clothe you, feed you, adorn you, fawn over you, and you think that I only see you as food?"

"You have a need to control."

"We both know there is no controlling you; I gave up on that long ago." I laughed. "I don't want you under my boot, Alina, I want you in my arms."

"I'm going home." She nearly slipped from my grasp, my fingers clasping with hers in one last attempt to keep her.

The shock on her face at seeing our entwined fingers was more severe than when I had nearly killed her in that alleyway.

"Wait," I begged. I didn't understand why she still thought the worst of me. That could be my own fault. I hadn't been fair to her. I didn't know how else to prove to her that I was not trying to trick her. "We have one more place to go."

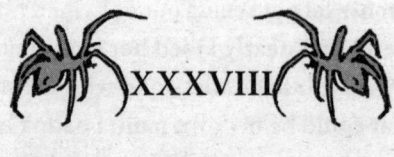

XXXVIII

The Creature

THE DELICATE SCRAPING OF porcelain among small chimes of cutlery greeted us upon arrival. I trusted the recommendation of Edith, who had given me an address and nothing more. It was a gamble, but I'm thankful I trusted her.

The grand, open room was full of fine dining and even finer guests. Pristine velvet, imported patterns, high thread counts—and that was only speaking of the furnishings. The people were dripping in pearls, emeralds, plated gold, and galvanizing colors.

None compared to the piece on my arm, just her hand could command the attention of a crowd without added finery.

I watched as Alina's pupils dilated and constricted, flicking from detail to detail, ever calculating. As if this were some sort of trick, a playful illusion I had concocted to spite her. Her eyes were so bright, even in such dim lighting. She wore something nicer for our date underneath her cloak, a good sign, though it was still mourning attire. That meant there was at least some possibility she would be killing me tonight. I would try my luck anyway.

An attendant swept her cloak and muff away, as if they had just dusted something off.

I took her hand politely before leading her off to a table along the edge of the room, nestled beside a wall with a small lamp placed in the middle.

Above us, most of the ceiling was made of glass, a dome proudly protruding in the middle, like a conservatory.

She looked less impressed than I expected. The twitch of her brow, the unchanging expression, the hesitancy to touch anything other than her own skirts. Something was on her mind.

"Have you abandoned your typical courting routine of breaking into my rooms or a light attempt at stalking?" she said plainly, and just the inflection made me laugh.

I pulled out her chair behind her, speaking beside her ear. "I'm adaptable."

She sat without a retort.

I took my seat across from her, though her energy was quite trite. The tension in the air was like solid tallow.

She took her time adjusting, smoothing down her skirts. Her dress was slimming, a double-textured black vertical stripe, alternating deep velvet and satin. She plucked gently at each fingertip of her gloves. She caught my stare, and she removed them slower.

Cheeky.

"Are you hungry?" I asked her.

"Are you?"

I took a deep breath, laughing off the riposte.

The waiting staff brought the drinks I had ordered ahead. A sweet orange blossom tea and a whiskey neat were placed before us.

"Why are we here?" She rested the gloves across her lap, eyeing the drinks.

I picked up the glass of whiskey, taking a leisurely sip and shrugging as if I hadn't meticulously planned the evening. "You wanted me to treat you like an equal."

"So you take me for dinner to entertain you?"

"No, so *I* may entertain *you.*" I leaned back in my seat, watching her closely.

She wasn't fidgeting, wasn't chewing her lip, or picking at her nails. She was at her sharpest. Though it saddened me to see that she needed to be this sober. At the very least, it would at least make our conversation easier.

"You told me you wanted to be equals." I gestured loosely to the scene around us. "I wanted to show you that the reason you are here isn't because I wish to have the upper hand." I paused, but she didn't look around; she was here for answers. Possibly sick of the pleasantries. "I want us to be partners," I said.

"In what way?"

"Our Nests will eventually join."

"No."

"It's already happening; it's what they want."

"What they want and what is good for them are entirely different things."

"I'm coming to you as a business partner. We both have something the other needs." I pulled out a cigarette and let it hang loose on my lips as I dug for the lighter. "Even if we are both unwilling to admit that, we are at a loss if we remain separate."

"Does that mean you are willing to devote yourself to my cause? To *me*?"

"Depends on your definition."

She didn't answer immediately; she just stared at her tea. She pulled the saucer close with her delicate fingers, smoothing over the gold glaze detailing. "I learned a thing or two about devotion in these past two years," her voice was steady, like the gentle plucking of an alto piano scale.

I pulled the first fresh breath of smoke through my lungs, reluctant to release it, letting it sear in my throat.

"You have to rob yourself of things you want for a bigger purpose. Temporary pleasures are cheap wicks." She picked up the silver steak knife. "They won't keep you warm through the night." Her eyes snapped up at me, piercing me as the knife slipped across her palm.

I flinched and sat up straighter, watching the blood pool into her tea, a gentle stream that slowly came to a drip. With her bloodied hand, she pushed the tea across the table, swapping it with my whiskey.

I looked to her for an explanation but was met with a smirk as she sipped my drink. "Aren't you thirsty, Mr. Forbes?"

I reached forward and snatched her bloodied hand. She flinched at the movement, everything down to each finger of hers tensing. The blood of her palm dripped down my wrist and arm under my suit jacket.

"Absolutely parched." I squeezed her hand gently, but even the slight pressure must have stung on her palm. I lowered my lips to her hand, kissing her knuckle before wrapping it in a handkerchief, refusing to acknowledge the pulsing veins of her hand in mine, the sweet scent of her mixed with the herbal remedy in fine porcelain, even the smears on my hand, I did not dare taste. "I've had some time to practice many things you'll find, if you care to get to know me."

"Who is this stranger?" she replied with a smile, seemingly pleased with the interaction.

I pushed the tea back toward her, blood on my hands but not a lick of it on my lips, "My name is Silas Forbes." I held out my red-stained hand. "A pleasure to meet you."

Her eyes skated across the table, her posture straightening, proud and tall. "Alina Lis," she replied, grasping my hand in a firm shake. "I look forward to doing business with you, Mr. Forbes."

XXXIX

The Poisoner

MY NEW FLAT WAS full of the scent of pine and apple. Phoebe and John were in the kitchen sorting out the goose and pies, Rebecca and Mary were tending the fire, and everyone else had found a seat on couches, chairs, or cushions on the floor. The glass observatory was the most popular seating area, as the girls enjoyed looking at the busy streets below or the sky above.

We had to use nearly every full kitchen for the geese since they had the largest ovens. The breads were done in the ground-floor communal kitchen since it would be closest to our pantry with the flour. Others made their own small dishes in their own kitchens to fill out the plates.

We managed to find a decent tree to display this year. It was tall and proud in the middle of the room, the centerpiece of the evening, with the couches rearranged around it. Last year, we completely forgot and ended up sticking a broom in a corner to mark where the presents would go.

The tree was covered in strings of cranberries and popped corn while fruits were nestled in between the branches, waiting for when they would be plucked off later as a late-night treat. Candles balanced on the branches, flames dancing like timid ghosts.

The mantel on the far side of the room had a long pine garland draped over it, adding a pleasant scent to the smell of burning hickory. Decorating the garland were dried circular slices of orange to add a bit of color to the green.

The girls were dressed as festively as their surroundings. Velvet textures, knitted blankets, and borrowed ribbons as accessories. They made perfumes from spare orange peels, juniper, or concentrated vanilla.

With all the ruction, I never knew what to do with myself. Much like typical parties, I found myself becoming a mute in a far-off corner, the silent observer most comfortable in the shadows.

Not only was I out of my typical environment, but I was barely in my own clothes. A deep green gown with black ribbon details. One of those ribbons was tied around my throat with the bow to the side. The stones in my ears were almost as heavy as my hair. I styled my locks half up, yet I could feel the soreness starting at the back of my neck. Borrowed clothing, borrowed jewelry, borrowed time; all to myself.

The entire morning was dedicated to cooking, starting as early as four o'clock. I helped make apple cider, the only thing I knew how to do. The trick was to add an orange and an equal amount of red and green apples to the simmer pot, then add bourbon or rum to taste.

The geese had been cooking most of the morning. They were huge, and justifiably so due to the number of mouths we were feeding. Some girls made other small dishes to pick at with fresh bread.

Phoebe interrupted the chatter by ringing the dinner bell. "The geese need to rest, so let us trade gifts while we wait!" she announced.

The dampened muttering returned to life as people got up to grab their presents to distribute. One by one, people plucked the wrapped boxes and scurried to find their gifts' intended.

I planted myself in the corner, out of the way, in no rush to participate.

Luka was sitting off to the side, watching the mayhem as well. It seems that I wasn't the only one with the same line of thought. I almost expected him to harbor some sort of animosity in that proud posture of his. Instead, he looked disjointed, longing, awkward above all else. He sent unsure glances at his cup, in embarrassment of wherever his mind wandered to. He reminded me of a terrible child knowing that coal awaited him under the Christmas tree, not bothering to get his hopes up for anything more.

Then, Edith approached him, sitting next to him as she clutched a small, parchment-wrapped box with twine string. Luka gave her a puzzled look as she spoke. I couldn't hear what she was saying, but I watched her lips move quickly; then she stopped and bit her lip.

She handed him the box, and he froze, unsure of what to do. In clear shock that he had received anything at all. As he tugged the strings and unwrapped the box, he gently lifted the cover from it. His face went through what looked like the seven stages of grief. He glanced back at her before looking down again. He lifted a proper inking pen from the box.

I didn't think it was possible, but I swore I saw tears in that man's eyes.

He raised his hands, my heart leapt, only to settle when he slowly hugged her. Though in the embrace, his chin buried in her shoulder, and his eyes clenched shut, like he was holding any sort of human resemblance back.

The gesture made me flinch; it was wholly unexpected from a thing like him.

Everyone formed groups after trading gifts, gathering around to spectate as they shared their gifts with one another.

Mary made another member a skirt with embroidered flowers along the trim. Rebecca bought Mary a few porcelain thimbles with little blue details painted on them. Others traded ribbons, hats, shoes, sweets, and whatever else they had collected or made for one another. The whole thing was very heartwarming.

The unfortunate part of all this merrymaking was that, even with the beautifully touching atmosphere, I ached inside. I itched for something stronger than the liquor in the cider. The way I couldn't find a place to put my hands unless they were crossed, shifting on my heels as I leaned against the doorway to my room, the urge to retreat quietly and close the door behind me.

I was able to break away from my post to refill my cider, moving to the kitchen where a pot of cider rested next to the turkey, potatoes, vegetables, and pie. As delicious as it looked, I couldn't bring my appetite to allow it.

"Alina?" Phoebe spoke from the archway of the kitchen.

"Oh, merry Christmas, Phoebe." I smiled tiredly, eyeing the pot before reluctantly turning away from it. "I'm beginning to doubt we can finish all of this food, for once."

She stepped forward, eyeing the cider pot. She was wearing a red dress, bolder than her usual girlish colors. The sturdy fabric extended high on her neck, framing her pale face between the fire of her dress and hair. It made her seem older, mature. For once, there was something more vibrant than her locks.

"Merry Christmas." Her eyes fluttered to mine, her hands behind her back.

"No," I caviled. "I told you I do not need anything this year."

"Don't worry; I didn't spend a dime," she laughed. She took my left hand. "Close your eyes."

I sighed but gave in to her request. She pinched around my

fourth finger. When I opened my eyes, a ring lay there. It was a gold band with small diamonds and a ruby stamped within small, engraved designs. The circular ruby was placed in the middle with a smaller diamond on either side. The gold gave it an expensive glow. I already knew it was too much.

"Before you scold me about money"—Phoebe held my hand tightly—"it was my mother's. I came across it recently when going through some of my things. I am not a fan of rubies, but I didn't have the heart to sell it. I thought it would look best on you."

"You didn't have to."

"I wanted to. I don't trust anyone but you to do it justice."

"You are a sap." I smiled, hugging her tightly. "It is lovely. Now I have a total of two pieces of jewelry," I laughed.

"I wanted to give it to you before I started carving the geese," she giggled. "Go relax. Rest. Enjoy the holiday for once."

"You say that like I have become elderly."

"Twenty-five is quite a rickety number."

"We are the same age."

"I'm about ten months younger, if we are going to nitpick!" She pulled away to begin prepping.

I played with the ring, spinning it on my finger with my thumb to watch it shine, abandoning my original reason for going to the kitchen.

As I turned to enter the archway to the living room area, I bumped into a hard chest.

"Did the raven find something shiny?" Silas purred.

"Gifted, not found," I corrected.

That is when I remembered.

I was supposed to get Silas a gift.

I gulped, fidgeting with the ring, hoping he wasn't bold enough to expect anything more from me. I didn't have to look at him to know he was staring expectantly.

He placed his hands on my waist and stepped forward, making me take a few steps back to meticulously place me in one specific spot on the floor.

"What are you doing?" I mumbled, glancing at his hands on my hips, keeping me firmly in place.

He smirked, then he tipped his head, staring directly above us.

Hanging from the wooden beam on the ceiling was a piece of mistletoe, neatly wrapped in a black ribbon.

"If I give you this, will you leave me alone?"

"If you don't, does that mean I get to bother you for the rest of the night?" His voice was just above a whisper, lingering above me. "Well, that seems more fun, if you ask me."

He tensed under my palms as I smoothed them over his shoulders.

I stood on my toes, whispering close to his ear. "Must everything be a game to you?"

"It seems to be the only way to keep you interested."

"You're lucky I entertain it at all." My voice was so quiet, the words almost didn't manifest as my lips hovered over his.

Then, like some irresistible force, I kissed him.

His lips moved against mine, like they were waiting for an excuse to meet, waiting to be invited with steady patience.

As I relaxed against him, his tension melted like sugar turned to caramel. I could taste the cider on his tongue, or was it from my own? The mix of pine from the room and the familiar scent of tobacco teased my senses, the thread of good memories at the tip of our tongues.

His hands found their place around my waist, and my rigid posture thawed under his palm. One hand cupped the side of my neck, gently this time, his thumb brushing against my ear. A small gasp came from him in an attempt to breathe, to gather himself before deepening, tipping me back slightly as if desperate to keep me, in fear I would run.

For a minute, I forgot that itch to be elsewhere. My arms slipped around his neck to keep from falling back. I was, for once, feeling like I belonged right where I was. There was no deal, no Vipera, no death, no qualms.

I broke our kiss to breathe, and I caught him looking at me. He raised his hand to touch my cheek, then my lips, then to raise my chin again so he could taste me some more.

"Silas," my voice shook, "we can't."

"Why not?" he whispered, straining.

I didn't have a good answer.

"Will you visit me tonight?" he teased, his thumb running over my cheek.

"We are in the same place."

"No, later." He smirked.

"I think you have to earn visits like that."

"Shall I buy another building? I can do that, too."

"Silas," I scolded, but I admit it was a cheeky comment.

"Will you really be so cruel? After not getting me a gift?" His head sloped to the side, refusing to look away.

"My presence is your gift, that is what you have been begging me for, is it not?" I pried myself from his arms, almost instantly regretting the absence of him.

I did not have to regret it for long, as my hand was snatched back. He pulled me along the wall, past the excitement of the evening.

"It's almost time for dinner—"

"I'm not hungry," he interrupted, slipping me past the crowd and closing the door to my room behind us.

Compared to the parlor, my room was dark and muffled, like waking suddenly from a vibrant dream. The only proof of color was peeking from under the door, a warm light closed off from the lonely confines.

I stepped back, the sudden muffled sound of Christmas music

and people merely a thrumming in the background, dampened by the walls between us.

He approached, his hand reaching out, but I avoided the touch.

"Don't be like that." He pinched the tail of the ribbon around my neck. "My present wrapped up all pretty for me? You shouldn't have."

My breath hitched, feeling the ribbon tighten on my throat before it loosened, slipping away across my skin.

He played with it between his fingers, brushing the silk against his cheek. "There is nowhere to run, nowhere to slip away to," he reminded me, taking a step forward.

I stepped back in tandem, my back hitting the French doors of the balcony.

He hung over me, his eyes reflecting the last bit of light that was quickly disappearing over the buildings. If I looked too long, they would burn into my retinas, and I would never be rid of them again.

"It's a bit warm in here," he mumbled, slipping his hand behind me to unlatch the doors, sending me stumbling backward.

He tugged me forward by the waist.

My nails dug into his shoulders, squeezing tight.

He leaned down, his lips skating across mine. "Do you want me to let go this time?"

I let out a quick, nervous huff of laughter, side-eyeing the semi-circular balcony edge.

He hooked his free hand around my waist, the other one removed from my neck, and took my hand in his. The neck ribbon from his hand fluttered into the air when a small breeze blew forward, sending it out into the air and getting smaller as it descended toward the street below.

"You wouldn't let me go, even if I asked you to," I finally replied, my breath hitching when the cold air hit my face.

His slow smirk grew at my words. "Escaping me would never be as easy as a request, my dearest fixation."

"Then where do we go from here?" I hummed.

The music from the main parlor room traveled lightly with the wind. It was quieter being at the top floor of a building, so all we had was the music traveling from the cracked window, and the smell of crisp winter to wake the spirits.

He held me close, and then a small sway along with the music, my hand in his, his hand on my waist. "We will go wherever you please."

I laughed again, leaning against him. "And if I say I'd like to go beyond the clouds?"

"I will find a way."

"Even if it is impossible?"

"I think we have shown each other enough of the impossible already." He lifted my hand, giving me a slow spin before dipping me. "Everything worth something has a place."

"And where is yours?" I asked. "Your place?"

"Wrapped around the fourth finger of your left hand."

I rolled my eyes as he pulled me up straight, and a bell chimed sharply in the distance, within the main rooms.

We stood, nearly nose to nose. Every breath was impossible to hide when the frozen posture gave away how much or how little we did so in each other's presence. I leaned up on my toes again, my lips against his cheek and then his ear. "Merry Christmas, Mr. Forbes."

With that, I left him for the warmth of the festivities. He did not join us for the feast that night.

XL

The Fixer

THE COMMUNION SHOULD FEEL good. Gathering with loved ones, the celebration of thoughtfulness, or even just to get drunk on someone else's dime. For me, it was invasive. Like a mirage from long ago, tempting desires never acted upon. As if I touched anything in the scene before me, the illusion would crumble before my eyes.

A real tree, with real gifts under it. Real people who may actually, truly care for one another. All strangers to me, almost as strange as the concept to me.

Holidays were never my favorite, no matter the tradition. For those privileged enough, it was a time of joy. For others, it is a reminder of what was absent, or what god didn't bother to give them.

Celebrations in the orphanage were sterile, bleak. Once upon a few centuries, this was all I dreamed about. And it was only dreams that would feel real.

Here I was, a trespasser in yet another unfamiliar home, with someone else's family.

Yet, in my lap, a firm grip on a gift. For *me*, which was a more surprising detail than the former. My knuckles were white, a pulsing grip of disbelief.

I sat alone for a while, I do not know how long I contemplated for.

Edith had gotten up to give something to another. Which made it dawn on me that I wasn't part of their little white elephant swap to begin with. She did that on her own.

How pitiful.

It wasn't hard to slip away from the celebration. It was exciting and shiny, enough to where I could leave without the party missing a beat.

The vibrance of the party made the hallway and, subsequently, any other room in the building dark and cold. That could also be due to the worn floors, wallpaper peeling in some places with suspicious stains, or the fact that only half the gas lamps worked on a good day.

With even Silas distracted, I was sure I'd enjoy a moment of peace.

His room was undone and unused. I didn't see how he deserved an entire room while I was forced to take a couch. I wasn't even offered blankets.

The corner of the room, the one with the desk, was the only proof that the room wasn't completely abandoned. The papers and reports I had seen before—hell, I helped him with his numbers.

I sat tiredly in the old creaky chair, picking up the small photograph clipped to one of the folders. It amazed me that at the drop of a dime, so much wealth could be spent on the runaway idea of a woman. He didn't hide his ambitions or motivations. He was honest in action if not in declaration.

Among the papers were a small stack of telegrams, telegrams that I bound myself to keep organized. Then, a single telegram beside it. New.

I sat up and placed my finger on the corner, dragging it across the papers.

I didn't remember this one.

You have until midsummer. See you very soon.

—*Leviathan*

I checked the back of the note, as if there would be more. As if hoping it was a cruel joke. Why hadn't he told me?

I placed the note carefully back where I found it before my hand went as numb as my mind. If I moved with any less caution, I might become sick.

Midsummer. It was too soon.

I loosened my tie, releasing a few buttons of my shirt. Everything was too hot, uncomfortable. Yet the moisture on the back of my neck was cold, clammy.

My stomach roiled; I nearly doubled over. I gripped the edge of the desk, placing my forehead on the surface, eyes clenched.

A wretched noise in my gut, then my throat. My head was on fire; I swore the pain sloshed around inside like liquid, the steam steadily increasing in pressure the more it stewed.

No, this was no good, and I couldn't blame the stress for it at all.

I needed to make her see the reason. I needed to feed again. I couldn't live on rats forever; they barely lasted an hour.

I would apologize. Yes, that was the first solution. Would she accept? I had no way of knowing. Alina was unpredictable, much like her lover. If I put my ego aside, put myself in debt, it could be tempting enough.

Now I only needed the energy; something I didn't have. I was running on booze and less than positive thoughts.

"Luka?" Edith's voice.

"Leave."

"I came to see—"

"Go. *Please.*" I retched, the last word almost coming out as a gag.

I was pulled up by my hair, my back smacking against the back of the chair.

"Edith—"

Her dainty fingers clutched my face, her nails digging into my cheeks to open my mouth. I grabbed her by her bodice, shoving her. She didn't let up, she planted herself in my lap, her other hand held a flask.

Something hot and thick washed over my tongue, and her hand released my face, only to slap it over my mouth, trapping the liquid there.

I was about to bite her hand before I recognized the metallic taste tingling in the back of my throat, my teeth aching in relief.

She raised a finger as she held the flask, bringing her bloodied finger to her mouth in a silencing gesture.

I nabbed the flask, practically pouring it down my throat, there was no need to swallow. When it ran out, I found myself grasping with both hands as if I could squeeze just a few more drops. At this point, sustenance was sustenance. I couldn't afford to be picky, even if the blood tasted a bit acidic.

Edith pulled the empty canister from me.

"Why," I demanded between recovery breaths.

"You're starving. You can't do this much longer." She twisted the cap of the flask securely.

"If she finds out—"

"You didn't break any rules."

I stared at her, my grip on the arms of the chair tight. Not that I couldn't move them, but as the pain in my head dulled, I was becoming more aware of what was happening.

"I got it from the hospital, from a patient," she said quickly, filling in the questions in the air.

"It doesn't matter where you got it, she will assume it's from—"

"You are my only friend," she interrupted, settling in my lap and sighing, unable to look me in the eye yet. "I'll be damned if you starve."

I nodded hesitantly, glancing over her shoulder to check the door.

The way she looked at me was with a different kind of hunger. A craving, no less, but for something deeper. It wasn't something I could give her. Edith leaned in, and my hand snatched her arm firmly.

She nearly startled. The pause was succinct, as if to contemplate her actions before she ultimately decided to ignore it.

That is when she kissed me.

Her soft hand touched the side of my face, the one numb from the scar. I barely felt it. Her lips trembled, vulnerable, asking me to open for her. Her eyes fluttered closed, holding me so tight despite my resistance.

I stared, wide-eyed, lips unopened.

She looked up at me, her eyes shifted from my good eye to my blind one, searching for even a dim flicker of interest. Surely, she would have given up on trying to read me by now.

Edith's lip trembled, her fingers traced my scar from my cheek down to my lip, her last plea.

I took her hand, removing it from my face.

"You should go back." I swallowed. "Please."

"Don't you feel it?" She was breathless, manic. "The pull?"

"You need to leave," I said, slower this time, no longer a suggestion.

Her nose flared, her lips pressing into a thin line. I could smell the tears before they started. She stood from my lap, pulling her arm from me as she backed away.

I couldn't decide if it was worse for her or myself.

She wiped her face with her sleeve before leaving, slamming the door behind her.

I sat, petrified, at the desk. I finally let go of the arm of the chair, having to flex my hand to recover from the tension.

I needed to fix this. I couldn't let it get that bad again, and I certainly couldn't rely on Edith.

I needed to talk to Alina.

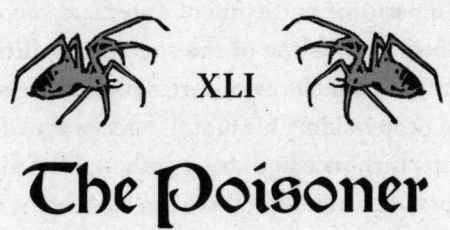

XLI

The Poisoner

FOUR MEN WERE BOUND on the floor of my lab, tied and naked. The men were on their knees, bent over until their noses nearly touched the floor. Their arms were straight by their side, tied to their ankles. At the same time, their legs were in a bent position to negate the possibility of getting up, with an extra knot securing their legs to their torso. The knots and position allowed for easier blood flow, as I did not want to harm them yet. I needed them alive to collect. Phoebe had figured out after some experimentation with ropes that this was the easiest position to collect saliva.

While the image was no longer shocking to me, I was familiar enough to appreciate them properly now. Their tired bodies were bathed in the purity of dawn, unworthy of such beautiful lighting.

Their mouths were held open by a mouth prop, typically used for holding a patient's mouth open during surgery or dentistry. Today they were used for a similar purpose, but the procedure was less complicated.

On the floor in front of their faces was a metal bowl to collect their saliva. All I had to do was spray their mouths every once in a while with a perfume bottle full of water and keep a close eye.

I knelt down before one of the specimens, lifting his head by my grip on his hair. His eyes were dark and sagged from discomfort. The prop holding his mouth open was making the skin around his lips turn pale and dry. I gathered the glass perfume bottle and sprayed water directly to the back of his throat.

"Swallow," I demanded.

The subject flinched and tried his very best to let the water go down without inhaling it. The same was repeated for the others.

A steady throbbing in my temple had begun, a slight thrum. My eyelids were heavy and puffy. Each breath felt like some extra labor. My day of rest was anything but. Nevertheless, work needed to be done.

"You have always been so *creative*."

I spun quickly to face the dark and elusive man leaning against the doorframe.

"Would you like me to give you a personal demonstration? Don't slither around like that," I warned.

"If it means that I will end up like them—" Luka tilted his head toward the men on the floor, a slow smile making a dimple appear on his cheek, "actually, I would not mind it."

"That is because you are a *freak*."

"Says the woman who left thousands of teeth as a gift."

"It was not a gift; it was a warning."

"Is this how you get it? The teeth? The venom?"

I neglected to answer and turned to my workbench, beginning to gather the glasses and filing them on the cabinet beside the table. Not once did I turn my back to him in the time I pretended to look busy.

"I didn't come to visit to be pleasant."

"When are you ever?" I sneered.

"Alina." His voice wavered. "Can we put aside our differences?"

"What differences? I'm fine with the arrangement as it is."

"I want to eat."

"You have one rule."

"It's unfair!" he snapped, slapping his hand on the edge of the table.

I paused, slowly looking up at him. "*You* are worried about *fair?*"

"I have bent over *backward* for you and your insufferable behavior. I've let myself become the sack you kick when you're frustrated."

"Is that not what you deserve?"

"It may be, but it is unproductive. When will you just admit that you need my help since Silas is entirely delusional with no knack for leadership? He doesn't know what it's like out there. We do."

"*We?*"

"You've seen what it's like out there. How these jokes of Nests function, how they act. Without any sort of order, a free-for-all is the last thing we need. You and all your girls are in danger if they suddenly decide they don't want their food dictating the rules."

"Hold your tongue before I let my shears do that for you," I snapped.

Luka stepped forward, his shadow casting over me.

I refused to look his way, his shadow cast over the glasses as I handled them.

Then, a thud, and a hand on my calf.

I glanced down at Luka.

The view of him on his knees painted an intimate picture of his silent suffering, only now beginning to surface like ink bleeding through a page. He looked unwell. The waterlines of his eyes were pale, making the skin around his eyes red and tired. His skin was ashen and missing the tanned warmth he was undeservedly known for. His hand on my thigh had a slight tremor, an anxious tick. Not that I cared for his well-being, but he didn't look like he was in any sort of shape to fight about anything. The image of him looking this pathetic did brighten my mood, though.

"Alina . . ." He swallowed thickly, his voice a dry rasp. "You need my help."

"Are you trying to convince me or yourself?"

"*Proshu*," he pleaded, looking as if keeping eye contact visibly pained him. "I need to eat. I'll . . . do anything. Name it and it's done. I don't want to be your enemy."

"I don't want anything from you. Not your apologies, not your pleas, certainly not your performance."

"Alina, you will only get this once." His hand gripped my leg, his nails digging into my skin, almost enough to make a mark on my skin through my skirt and stocking. "I am begging you. Take out my tongue, break my knees, rip out my fangs monthly if it means we can move on."

I tapped my foot, crossing my arms.

He moved his hands up my leg, bunching the skirt in his grip, clasping his hands above my knee. "Please, let me eat." The words whispered against my leg, his eyes staring up at me through his lashes, a starved sort of depravity to them.

I stepped away without warning, and he stumbled forward.

I opened a drawer of the workbench. "You want to make it up to me?" A gleeful hum warmed in the back of my throat, a jump of excitement in the pit of my stomach.

He slowly rose to his feet, wary of the excitement laced in my words.

I plucked a small paper box from the desk, slapping the drawer shut. I stepped to the middle of the room, one slow step at a time.

I opened my palm to look at the small box, sliding it open like a matchbox. Dozens of small nails were neatly stacked. I looked over to Luka. "Strip."

"Pardon?"

"Clothes off."

"I'm not—"

"Luka." I shook my head slowly. "*You don't want me to be your trainer.*"

His Adam's apple bobbed, and he glanced awkwardly at the other subjects before undoing his shirt, then his trousers, just the under layer, and then there was nothing left. At least he would have the comfort of not being the only unclothed thing in the room.

Fleetingly, I saw Viktor. Awkward, unsure, modest—but this time it was *real.* He shrugged his shirt off those broad shoulders, taking extra time with the buttons before folding it modestly over the chair. His torso appeared incredibly lean, the fibers of muscle rippling subtly under the skin. A lethal build is of no use when malnourished and dehydrated, I suppose.

He turned his body away from me.

Isn't fun being on the receiving end, is it?

I tipped my palm and let the small nails chime as they reached the floor, in a small, scattered pile.

The noise made him look over his shoulder, delaying his putting his trousers and undergarments neatly with his shirt.

"Come," I said, no inflection, void of any emotion.

Luka knew what it meant, but he didn't fight it. He knew why this was happening. It was only fair.

He took each step carefully, meeting me at the center of the room, awkwardly covering himself. He raised his chin in the air, with one last puff of dignity, of defiance.

When our eyes met, it was like a fire was alight within me, burning deep in my core, enough where I swore the smoke would cloud my vision. The rage, the excitement, my heart beating so fast. Restitution; something very few women gain.

My entire reason for poisoning in the first place.

My natural purpose.

I couldn't help a sarcastic smile. "Kneel, Luka."

Without so much as even a huff of disapproval, he lowered himself steadily to his knees, only wincing once he put his full weight on the nails digging into his skin. He never once broke eye contact with me. The determination was almost admirable. Unwilling to contribute to my pleasure, but willing to do what needed to be done.

The view could be better. I stepped back, reaching for my broom.

"I trust you still remember the rules." I smoothed my hand over the wood, stepping to the side of him and leaning by his ear. "For your sake, I hope you do."

He didn't answer; he was determined to see it through. His eyes barely regarded me. He was positioned straight on his knees, the skin around the edges dark from the blood. He was fixated on the small window, I assume the one with the small crack in the ninth panel, the one with an old web collecting dust beside it. A couple of dead flies rested on the sill.

I stepped back to grab my chair, letting it shriek against the floor as I dragged it to sit leisurely beside him, facing his profile. He was nice like this, still and *quiet*.

With the broom against my lap, I waited.

Soon, he leaned back.

Thwap!

The wood end of the broken broom came down on the back of his thighs.

He flinched, but not as much as I had hoped.

Thwap!

"*I wasn't leaning,*" he growled through clenched teeth.

"Oh, you weren't? Apologies." I hit his front this time, and he nearly keeled over.

I stood, clutching the wood tightly in my hands. I wanted him to give me a reason. Just one reason to beat him until I couldn't lift my limbs for the final strike. But I refrained. I wanted to know how long he would entertain me. How long I could play with my prey.

I slowly stepped behind him, glowering over him. My knuckles were white from just the grip on the handle.

As I looked closer, I saw a slight tremor in his legs, a small twitch of his head. If he could take any more, it wouldn't be for long.

I tapped the right trapezius, then the left, then hovered the blunt end just a hair above his spine, all the way down. I know he could feel it, all too aware of where it was, the possibilities, the déjà vu.

I moved finally, circling to the front.

One would think that having a traitor in such a position would bring nothing but elation. It is a natural instinct to want those who have subjugated you to suffer, to feel the pain you once harbored deep within your bones. I looked at him now, and the power in my grasp was strong enough to make my very soul clamor. Yet a puny mustard seed of sorrow was implanted deep within.

I used to see this man as a friend. I *believed* it with all my heart. Despite my age, those years ago, a girlish wonder was alight the minute someone paid attention, truly took inventory of my person, acknowledged my mind over matter, and did not expect anything from me in return. He was my laboratory partner, a peer, a friend. It was my own stubbornness that kept me from letting him in again, I know that, but among his faults—he was right. If I want to reach my aspirations, I need someone who knows the belly of the beast as well as his own appetites. I can't make it in their world without a professional.

The only question remaining was—*will he yield?*

"How do you test a dog's obedience?" I hummed. "As a trainer, you have to be absolutely certain that they know they'll never bend the rules again."

Luka was silent.

"Look at me."

He glanced up, glaring with a tense brow.

"Open your mouth."

A spark in his eyes told me the request threw him, but he hesitantly opened.

"I've learned a lot about Vipera in my time here." I pinched his jaw, tilting it up. "I never expected vermin like you to be useful." I laughed, feeling the roof of his mouth and pulling a fang forward, putting pressure on it once it was fully extended, watching the muscles of the gum stretch to accommodate. "I could be rid of you now. According to legend, you are unattached. Now you have no Nest, no family, no kin. You see, you may think you are clever for figuring out the bit about my father, but I did some research on you, as well, in recent years." I paused, pulling harshly on the large fang. "Did you use venom on those orphans, or did you withhold that kindness from them, too?"

He flinched and tore his face away. "They don't love you," he spat.

A slow smirk rose across my lips. "Oh? Have you reached your limit, Luka?"

"They only follow you out of fear," he spat, venom lacing his words. "You spin webs around them and pull the strings; eventually, you'll pull too hard, and they'll suffocate under you."

I lowered myself forward, pinching my skirts neatly so I could see him eye to eye, "Did you know that a certain species of spider will eat her own kind, her kin, even her mates, to make sure she survives?"

Luka's jaw ticked, staring with exhausted and strained eyes, the whites turning black, and a single drip of blood tearing down his cheek.

I cupped his cheek, smearing the blood across it, touching along the jagged scar. A gentle smile settled to accompany my words. "The arachnid doesn't have to suffocate her prey for them to know she is dangerous; they need only believe she is venomous."

I pulled a long hairpin from my hair and dragged it across my palm.

His eyes widened when I flicked my hand, splattering red across his face like throwing pennies for a beggar. "That is the last of my blood that you will taste. The next drop may be accompanied by your own."

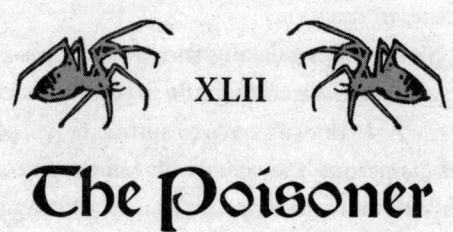

XLII

The Poisoner

HE FOOTPATH OF THE forest was already beaten many times before, though I admit I couldn't tell if it was others before me or my own trail I'd forgotten I'd taken.

The snow made it so the moonlight was enough for the lorn trail, shining through my damp nightgown. The coolness of the fabric threatened to slow my joints, freeze my bones, to rust me to a halt.

There was a shallow pond just beyond the trees, creating a glass clearing.

In the center was a stag, recently passed as a result of a leg through the ice, broken. He was still warm, judging by the steam that steadily rose, lending his warmth to the sky until he would have no more.

I stepped onto the ice; it was solid. A murky reflection of myself shined in the surface, water weeds and bubbles of air shifting beneath, frozen in their hibernation.

Kneeling beside the stag, I ran my fingers through its hide, petting apologetically as if I could comfort the dead. I could feel its heat radiate through my palms. I could even feel a pumping, a pulsing.

With a sudden surge of force, one hand plunged through the skin, then the other.

Hot. So hot. I'm burning.

The joints in my wrist and elbows thawed, feeling returning to my fingertips, the warmth heating something inside me, a different sensation.

My stomach growled, the smell of tannins and blood overwhelming me like a wet sheet pulled taut around my face.

Inside, I could feel a thrumming. I tore, the wetness making it hard to catch a grip. Finally, I grabbed it, nails dug into it as I pulled.

In my hands was a heart. It was small for a beast of its size, the aorta pushing and pulling as it pumped. The twitches of the organ were slow at first. I brought it closer to my lips; the blood dripping down my elbow was hot, viscous, and thick. As it neared my teeth, it beat faster, faster, two hundred beats in a single moment.

My mouth watered, salivating before finally having a taste. It was a timid bite at first, then a mouthful. It was a flavor like no other, the taste of life. So sweet was the flesh, I couldn't put it down.

The repast warmed me to my core, the chill fleeing from my body. I smeared it from my mouth to my neck, then over my chest. It was like wearing a blanket, a warm bath, healing in a way I couldn't ignore.

I plunged my hands back into the chest cavity, feeling for the ribs and cracking one in frustration as I scratched and dug. I bit down on the hide, the skin, the tendons, the organs.

The honeyed flesh was fragrant, but not in the way you would imagine. A complex taste, like wine, the scent of peonies . . . the skin soft, touchable.

I licked over the skin, not daring to waste a drop, but not wanting to waste the warmth either. I cupped a breast, kissing the skin of the sternum up to the neck.

I opened my eyes: a woman, not a beast.

My body threw itself back. Staggering, scrambling, the warmth leeching the further the distance. I could be sick, but my body wasn't willing to give up the meal.

Her identity was possibly horribly distorted, yet I had the over-whelming feeling that I was forgetting. Her recognition at the tip of my tongue, my mind, but it escaped me when I got too close. I couldn't tell if this was a way of protecting my psyche or a bad case of déjà vu.

Her chest cavity was broken open.

Could that have been my doing? No, an animal must have done that.

THE WIND CALLED ME awake, my body heat fading as fast as the memory of the dream itself.

The body melted into the landscape, the blood bleaching until it matched the pure midnight snow.

I looked down at my feet, the edges of the skin red from the freeze.

I knew this field.

I turned around; the old farmhouse stood before me. Within the home was a family, a new one. They were in the living room. I could see their vague shadows puppeteering in front of the fire.

Somehow, a deep loneliness took root. The loneliness extended past physicality, a certain yearning for something familiar. As quiet as a shadow, I returned to the Nest.

XLIII

The Fixer

"How do you shoot anything like that?" I scoffed. "You'll dislocate your shoulder."

Alina frowned and brought her shoulder forward into the butt of the rifle, staring down the barrel. Her eyes were a bit sullen. It was more than just ill-rest.

"Better." I puffed the cigar. "Now shoot. Any animal would have run, found a mate, and had several spawn by now. You can't be this slow."

"Enough commentary." She squeezed one eye shut before she pulled the trigger, leaving a puff of dust in a far-off tree. We had drawn some targets for practice, but she wasn't hitting many. For her sake, I hoped she was better with a blade.

"You should consider dressing warmer; you'll get sick. Can't have our very own Annie Oakley dying on us."

"What did I say about commentary?"

"Did you expect me to listen? Adorable," I laughed, taking off my ushanka hat and plopping it on her head. The brown fur fell over her eyes slightly.

"You almost look like a real American frontiersman, *Doro-gusha*."

"Do you forget I am the one with the gun?"

"I would be worried if you could aim."

She clicked her tongue in disapproval before returning her attention to the target.

"Do you have any news about this corrupted mess?" She shot another bullet, this time grazing the tree.

"There is something." I squinted at the far-off target. "From the sources I've spoken to, they don't seem to be coming from the Nests or Guilds around here. They're clean."

"Then where are they coming from in such big numbers?"

"They are saying there is a colony. Small town roughly four hours from here."

"Why do you think it is them?"

"It is an entirely Vipera population, and they seem to be a bit brutish." He took in a sharp breath of cold air. "They said speak to a man named Cormac."

"Just . . . Cormac?"

"They said that's all we will need to know. He's the founder of some sort."

"It is a start, I suppose."

"What is your plan?"

"I mean to pay them a visit. I hope it can be solved in a civil manner."

I laughed at her, coughing slightly as smoke caught in my lungs. "That is quite hopeful, no? What if they aren't the friendly type?"

"I will take you or Silas with me." She shrugged. "These brutes can't keep discarding their mistakes for the rest of us to deal with."

"From your description of the corrupted, it sounds like they are freshly turned, too."

"How do you know?"

"Usually, the corrupted can mostly get a hold of themselves after their first feeding, but if they go more than a day without feeding, the body begins to eat itself in desperation. The strain on the body makes for a quick decline. The brain is the first to go due to the deprivation. You can't come back from brain damage, unfortunately."

There was a pause, and a serious expression on her face. A question was brewing.

"Do the Hosts go crazy like that after turning?" she spoke slowly.

"It is worse."

"How?"

"Growing pains. Hosts have to sprout their fangs, and their bodies go through a lot. Half do not survive the turn. Then half of those who successfully turned beg for death before they can adjust. Some do not have kind friends, and they must end it themselves. The pain was more intense than anything you could ever know."

She was quiet upon hearing the new information. I did not wish to shock her or tell her these things because I thought it would scare her; I told her because it was important. If she was going to be involved in this world, I would hope she had a proper perspective.

"Do you know this from experience?"

"I was a Host, yes."

"Do you remember what it was like? The pain?"

"Clear as day. Like my flesh wanted to rip itself from my bones. We are abominations." I clipped the cigar and stuck it in the pocket of my coat.

She contemplated the answers. I almost wondered where the curiosity came from—until I remembered it was Alina and her thirst for information would always be insatiable.

"I have to go soon," she said after some time.

"Heading to town?" I glanced up at the sun, watching a few flurries of snow shine as they passed through the trees.

"The mortuary," she mumbled.

"I'll follow." I looked back down at her. "Get a pulse on any rumors in town."

She eyed me carefully with some residual hesitance to cooperate.

"If you don't mind giving me a ride, that is," I added.

She nodded, looking back at the targets, a pause to carefully consider the words she was about to utter, "That's a good plan."

The Poisoner

"YOU READ OSCAR WILDE?" Henry flipped through a small booklet. "I'm surprised. I would have thought you'd read nonfiction."

"I believe I was gifted a short story by a patron." I stuck my gloved hands farther into the corpse, organs squished as I went at least elbow deep.

"How are you doing with your exploration?"

"Just fine."

Henry had called me in for another corrupted that was brought in.

It had black blood and was completely dead. It was like it had spoiled inside the body. Their insides were always in rough shape, like they had worked five times as hard to keep them running, most notably their livers being the worst out of all of them. While a healthy liver would have been vibrant in color, a deep red, the corrupted had such bad scarring that it had turned the color of charred beef. Lastly, their heart was enlarged, utterly overworked from the rapid pace just to keep them conscious.

Then there were the physical traits. They were skinny and lean enough to where I could see their veins clearly, their skin becoming transparent enough to reveal the blackened structure.

"I should have known you would be elbow-deep in a body by now," Luka chimed from the doorway.

"Who is this?" Henry frowned.

"A friend." I took a deep breath. "I told you to wait outside if you were going to insist on coming."

"Ah yes, the best of friends, very close." Luka sauntered in, poking some of the embalming instruments curiously.

"You should keep your dogs on shorter leashes." Henry glared at Luka. "They should learn not to touch things."

"*Ya tebe pokazhu gde raki zimuyut.*" Luka grinned over his shoulder at Henry.

"Luka!" I scolded, removing my hands from the corpse and heading toward the sink. "Apologies, Henry, I couldn't shake his company."

Luka stepped over to the sink and turned on the water for me. "I can't eat that one?" he whispered.

"No," I snapped, washing the fluids off and discarding the gloves.

"You must be popular, first the blond and now a brunette? Your taste is all over the place," Henry joked, kicking his feet up on the table as he read his book.

Luka left my side and sat on the desk next to Henry's ankles, shoving his shoes off the surface. "Unsterile," Luka said with a smile. "What do you do anyway, errand boy?"

"I'm an undertaker." He glared up at Luka, getting flustered now that Luka was so close. The sable-haired Russian made Henry look puny next to him.

"It looks like Alina is more of an undertaker than you right now."

"Luka," I warned from the other side of the room.

"Is he your chaperone or something?" Henry joked nervously, glancing from Luka to me.

"A friend," I repeated.

Luka loomed over him where he sat, and Henry swallowed hard. "Let me help you." Henry scurried from his seat.

"Just the brass tools need to be cleaned; I already did the glassware." I collected my coat.

"Right," he grumbled, eyeing Luka as he took his place beside me.

"Have a wonderful weekend, Henry!" I waved and flashed a sweet smile before leaving the building.

The sun was already setting, and the air was turning chill. The ground was hardening due to the changing temperature.

"Why do you tolerate a little mange like that?" Luka caught up beside me.

"I need his workspace, and he also helps me keep a pulse on this corrupted situation." I looked up at him. "Speaking of—any luck?"

Luka shook his head. "I have a few places to visit tonight to see if I can pick up a word or two, so far not much chatter in the public. I checked the town bulletin in the square while you were occupied and asked around. They think it's rabies."

I nodded and shoved my hands in my pockets, watching my frozen breath dance before my face.

"What are you studying, anyway?"

"I tell Henry I want to be an undertaker. I'm already quite good at chemistry and dealing with bodies." I shrugged. "I figured it can be something to keep me occupied and grant me inconspicuous access to a crematorium."

"You have more *hobbies* than I have had jobs in my lifetime," Luka frowned. "Do you ever get tired?"

"No, my work is never finished, and I prefer a job well done. So if it means a little extra effort and curriculars, then so be it."

"Fair enough," he said as we stopped in front of the shop. "Stopping here or going home?"

"I have some things to clean up before I head back. You can tell Phoebe I'll be home not too late."

He nodded but threw me a knowing glance. "You're sure?"

I nodded.

Something about the chaperoning was familiar, in a sickening, bittersweet way.

It was like a vision of the past, walking the courtyard of King's College or the late-night escorts back home. Even now, I'm not entirely sure it was an act—not *all* of it at least. The simplicity of ignorance would have been better if it lasted longer, unknowing of the danger that now walks beside me. Now I know it was a performance by a master scavenger, not a shot-caller by any means. Possibly the start of learning which habits were real and which were for show, another thing to put to the test some other time.

With that he left, quickly fading into the darkening town.

I unlocked the side door to the shop, taking the stairs directly to my lab.

I missed the old lab in London. There were so many instruments I had left behind. They were all probably collecting an absurd amount of dust by now. I couldn't bring myself to sell it, so I still paid the taxes on it. Or rather, Phoebe did.

I sat down on the stool, staring at my workbench. I didn't even bother to take off my coat. I needed solitude to recover from a day of socializing.

Under my bench, covered in dust, there was an old trunk. It was black with brass hardware, the initials *JL* inscribed on the metal latch.

When we fled, it was quick. I packed vital instruments, light and simple clothing, and a few mementos, one of which was my father's trunk. I hadn't opened it, afraid of what I'd find or what

I would feel. I knew he kept some journals and trinkets inside; he used to bring them with him to expositions. I threw the most important items in it, along with some scraps left behind. It wasn't until we unpacked in Buffalo that I realized some of his journals were hidden away inside some pockets of the inside.

I knelt down on the floor, sliding it forward. I polished the dust on the latch with my thumb, rubbing the fallout away from my hands.

I popped it open, the dust rustling like a ghost fleeing the sudden movement.

The hinges creaked as it was pried open.

There were lots of papers, some miscellaneous tools, and assorted photographs.

One photograph was of my father at the lab. He was sitting, turned sideways at the camera, like he was in the middle of papers, and everyone else was just set up around him at the desk. Dr. Hayes sat next to him.

It was hard to tell with the lack of color, but his hair was a light, singular color, a light dusty blond missing the grays that he would later gain on the sides, and eyes bright like my own.

Secured to the inside was a picture of myself. I was so small, a little rounder in the face before I outgrew the fat cheeks. I must have been about six in the photograph; the dress I wore was borrowed from Phoebe for the occasion. We'd had our photographs done the same day; her father had offered to include us since my father had never had his portrait taken. The white of my brow and lashes jumped out, more than usual, since it was a tintype photograph.

Among the papers, I lifted an unbound stack that I had read too many times before, when we first arrived. I remember being so scared to look at his work, his *unfinished* work. Perhaps I was afraid it would humanize him.

The cover page read:

The Poisoned People:
The Effect of Blood Disease and Adaptations
on the Human Body

It was fifty pages, yet it was all things I already knew. All things I found out on my own. He had a simpler hypothesis, and the workings of a meticulous technical experiment to test the bounds of Vipera basic ability and the components of their blood that made it special. It felt good to be more knowledgeable than my father about something, though it was never fair. He may have known more if it weren't for me. I had a head start in a way.

It turned out my father suspected the Vipera's existence, but he did not see them as creatures, but as an affliction. People who could be helped.

How ironic it was that he was the optimist, and I was the pessimist in this particular instance. My father was not perfect after all.

I had not thought of my father in some time. I suppose when you are surrounded by those who were family adjacent, there is less pressure to mourn the ones who are no longer here.

I wiped the wetness on my face that went unnoticed until it pooled at my chin, dripping onto my hands.

How silly were feelings like these? I would never understand them.

THE SOUND OF RINGING metal was clear as day, echoing against the street of brick facades.

I went where I usually did when I found myself looking for assurance, John's shop.

As I stepped into view past the double barn doors, John stopped to wipe his face on a dirty rag. His demeanor lit as bright as the furnace when he saw me, his smile easily melting all who saw it.

"Alina! I wasn't expecting you today."

"That makes two of us." I smiled, moving over to sit on one of the stools by a small wooden table. "Horse's shoe fell off."

"I did his shoes a few days ago." John raised his brow. "Are you ever going to name that poor thing?"

"Afraid not; he knows it as his name now," I laughed.

"What troubles you, Crow?" John frowned, dragging another stool forward and sitting, brushing off the dirt from the table with his cloth. "You don't have to make up a reason to stop by."

"Feeling more lonely today than usual." I rubbed the back of my neck.

"Those lads aren't giving you trouble, are they?" His voice was stern.

"No—well, yes, but I'm just feeling a bit foolish. I read my father's papers again. I don't know why I keep reminding myself."

"Because you miss him." John took one of my hands and clasped it between his. My hand was so small between them, so fragile. It was scary to be vulnerable, to talk to someone. I think I had spoken more to John in these past two years than I ever did while my father was alive. It wasn't until I met him that I realized the extent of my neglect. I think if I asked my father's ghost what my favorite fruit was, he would say apples. Or if I asked him what mother looked like, he would hesitate before saying her hair was black.

"I don't know if those are the right words for it, and it kills me inside."

"It always helps to focus on what is present. No use debating to have or to have not."

"I suppose." I glanced at the blazing fire, heating the room as if it were a summer's afternoon.

"Those boys, the new ones. Are they . . . the viper kind?"

"Vipera," I corrected. "Yes."

"And the blond one," he started.

"Silas."

"Is there something there?" he teased. "You got quite flustered when you brought him here."

"He asked me to marry him," I replied sheepishly, not including the fact that he demanded it.

"That is wonderful news!" John squeezed my hands, his face lighting up. "Where is the ring?"

I shook my head. "I wouldn't accept anything he suggested. I don't want people suspecting anything about where the money is coming from."

"Sounds like he has expensive taste," John laughed. "When I proposed to Elisabeth, I bent two pieces of copper wire into a knot until I could get her something nicer."

I smiled and nodded. I didn't want to get too deep into the nuance of it all, but simply pretending to be happy was working. It was better than chasing an adrenaline high, having someone beam with pride and happiness for how your life is going.

"Is he good to you?"

I lowered my face to hide my blush, not really wanting to answer. "He knows me well."

"But are you happy?"

"Yes," I said, though I didn't think I could answer that entirely honestly either, without feeling some sort of guilt.

It was just nice to share news that normal people rejoiced over, and pretend it was all normal and fine, that someone was happy for me. Someone who wasn't aware of how entirely complicated it had made my life.

XLV

The Poisoner

T HE DELIGHTFUL SOUNDS OF morning chatter buzzed from outside my door. Every morning, we would all meet for breakfast. Today, everyone was up later than usual due to the raw weather and poor insulation in the building.

I left the serenity of the sheets and wandered into my main dwelling. The overcast sky made the room seem duller. The fireplace still had ash from the night before, as I was too lazy to clean it. I would take care of that later. The tree still smelled lovely, proudly standing in the middle of the room with a few fruits left on it. The last remaining orange was my breakfast.

Another aroma teased my senses as I peeled my fruit.

I couldn't help a small smile. "How nostalgic. Reminds me of old times. Though typically your tell is the cigarette smoke."

Silas stepped out from the kitchen area with a cup of freshly brewed espresso in his hand. "Is that your way of asking me for a light?"

"What are you doing in my flat?"

"I wanted to see you."

"So you let yourself in?"

"What if I never left?" He sipped, pausing to decide how he felt about the taste. "Besides, if this were old times, I wouldn't hesitate to watch you sleep."

"Do not lie, you still watch."

He smirked and lifted a shoulder.

I sat comfortably on the sofa, pulling my silk robe tighter to hide the thin nightgown.

He placed his cup on the coffee table as he sat next to me.

"Why are you here?"

"Is it so hard to believe that I wanted to say good morning?" He laughed and draped his arm along the back of the couch. His fingers lightly traced along my shoulder. It made me shrink.

"It is hard to swallow the idea of you being any sort of cordial or kind."

"Is it really? I think your memory must be rotten if you cannot think of a single nice thing I've done for you."

I shook my head and finished eating my orange, leaving the pile of peels on the table so I could use them later as fire starters.

Silas took my hands in his. He slipped the ring Phoebe gave me off my left hand and placed it onto the fourth finger on my right hand.

"What are you doing?"

"Making room."

"For what?"

"Did you think that I wasn't going to get you a ring after all that trouble?" He shook his head. "You really *do* think low of me."

"I think the worst of you."

"Likewise," he replied, but something in his tone made it sound like a remark of endearment.

I rolled my eyes at him and stood. "I need to change; leave me."

He rose as well, placing his hands on my hips from behind. "I could be of assistance." He bunched the fabric as he slid it upward.

I gripped his hands on my waist, his chest pressing against my back as he refused to leave.

A terrible pain bloomed suddenly in my abdomen, nearly making me keel over. He must have noticed the change in my posture because he wrapped his arms around me.

"What is it?" he whispered against the back of my neck.

"Nothing." I swallowed, waiting for the pinch to subside. I struggled against him, but then a trickle of blood ran down my leg.

His eyes narrowed at me, and I heard the clicking.

I swallowed thickly. "Silas," I warned, "don't."

He tightened his grip around my waist. "Were you going to hide from me all week if I hadn't found out just now?"

"Hiding doesn't seem to work," I said through a tense jaw.

"Don't you want me to help?" He spoke against the nape of my neck, his fingers scraping up the back of my neck before forming a fist in my hair.

I bit my lip, focusing on the pain pricking my scalp.

"You do, don't you?" He licked his lips, flashing that split tongue.

"What if I told you I did?"

He raised his brows in surprise.

"On one condition."

"Which is?"

I wrestled his hands off me, peeling myself from his grip and spinning on my heel to face him. I stepped back, and I held my hand palm outward to signal him to *stay*.

His brow twitched, confused at what I was doing.

I retreated, one step at a time, toward the light of the conservatory.

Drip. Drip. Drip.

The blood from between my legs left small droplets on the tile, following me until my back rested against the cold window.

Silas took a step.

"No!" I shouted.

He flinched, an air of annoyance in his glare.

"Well, aren't you the one who enjoys savoring things? I am sure you can handle a bit of edging," I teased. I reached down, lifting my nightgown to expose an ankle, then just above the knee, a slow line of red trailing down my inner thigh.

"Please." He swallowed. "It's unwise to keep me hungry for too long." His voice was low in warning.

"I don't think you want it bad enough." I tilted my head. "You're not even on your knees."

His jaw ticked, clenching as he processed my request.

Slowly, he lowered himself to one knee, then the other, his neatly starched trousers and shiny dress shoes looking extra nice, scuffing the floor. He sat back on his heels, slowly rolling his shirtsleeves to his elbows, already anticipating my next request.

"You're a bit far for a taste, Silas." I pointed to the floor before me. "Come," I demanded.

He inched toward me, leaning on one hand touching the ground, then the other, forced to ignore each drop of blood as he crawled forward, though his eyes didn't leave mine as I watched his fill with inky blackness.

When he nearly reached me, I lifted my leg up, resting it on his shoulder. The stream of blood trickled down my calf. He watched it get closer. Before it could even grace his tongue, I pushed down on his shoulder, forcing his chest to the floor.

"If you are so desperate for a taste, you should accept it however it comes," I hummed, letting the blood drip onto the floor next to his face.

At first, he didn't move, just processing the position he was in.

"Will you waste it?" I prompted, pressing my heel harder into his shoulder. He shot me a look from the corner of his eye, then he slowly dragged his tongue over the tile, blood smearing in its wake. His eyes closed, accompanied by a groan . . . a whimper, if you will.

"Good boy," I whispered, and that is when he grabbed my ankle. "Let go!"

"That's enough. My turn," he bit out, standing on his knees and throwing my leg over his shoulder. His hands smoothed up my thigh as he placed his chin on my pelvis and looked up at me. A wicked gleam lit his eyes. "Lift your gown for me, dear."

With shaky hands, I gripped the gown, pulling it up and bunching it at my sternum. He held my hip as he supported my leg, kissing over my pelvic bone before going lower, leaving a warm trail of his lips over my stomach, then a kiss on my thigh. He placed my clitoris between his teeth and sucked gently, flicking his tongue over it as he savored me.

I moaned gently, slanting my hips forward, a plea for more.

His tongue flattened over the skin between my thighs. There was no doubt I was wet on my own without the help of his tongue.

Why was he pausing?

"You made quite a mess," he said, as if scolding me, and glanced up at me through his lashes, "and you've made me quite impatient. We have to fix that."

"What happened to—" I jolted when his tongue laved between my legs, small, wet sounds making my face unbearably hot.

One of his hands smoothed up my thigh, and his tongue pressed past the slick opening of my vagina, dipping in and out. The smudges of blood were just within reach now, his breath tickling as he exhaled. A clicking followed.

I leaned more of my weight on the window, the frost from outside countering how hot my body was. I tipped my head back, resting against the cold glass. I was hot despite the weather, but the cool air coming from the window helped the heat subside.

His nails dug into my hips as he licked and sucked at the fresh morning blood. I could feel his eyes on me, his hyper awareness of everything I did, every sound I made, every time my body twitched under his touch.

His tongue dipped in and out, taking time to give attention to my clit, the entire area becoming wet from blood and spit, his split tongue twisting and playing in the ways he remembered would get a reaction out of me.

I couldn't make myself look. I clenched my eyes shut, my grip white-knuckled on my gown, but it did little to distract me from what he was doing.

"S-stop . . . stop it," I breathed, but it only made his mouth press firmer against the warm source.

He slicked his tongue inside. The feeling made me jump, as I had forgotten he had a tongue like some snake. He used the two split ends of his tongue to press against the inner walls as he moved in and out, going deeper every time.

"Deeper," I begged, throwing my head back, my hips pushing needily against his mouth.

He responded with a sort of growl, reaching deeper inside me and pushing his tongue up, then he would make it move in a gentle rhythm, faster and rougher as he worked up to it. His hand on my thigh slid up to my abdomen, pressing down, the pressure more intense than before.

"*Ah—!*" I yelped, blood rushing to my cheeks. I wanted to say something, but I could not find the will or the words, and I settled on closing my eyes as I was absorbed in the quickly approaching tension, the slow throbbing becoming quicker and quicker until I had my release. My abdomen tensed, and my insides throbbed like they were trying to spell something in Morse code.

Silas removed his tongue and flattened it along the outside, relishing in the afterglow. Little did he know, I was not finished yet.

My leg slipped off his shoulder, and I forced him back, lowering myself onto his lap and hastily grabbing at his trousers.

"I need it inside me, now," I panted.

He did not argue, but my demand made him move quicker to open his pants.

I positioned myself above his cock, but I found myself hesitating in a terse moment of clarity. Then I realized, I didn't want clarity. I didn't want to be sharp or have my wits about me. I wanted to be drunk, I wanted to indulge, to do what felt good.

I sank down until his hot tip slipped inside of me. I sat down fully, possibly moving too quickly to adjust properly, and I flinched. I held him close, wrapping my arms around his neck as I sat down on his length, desperate to get it as deep as my body would allow. I had not forgotten how thick he was, and I loved the feeling every time. It added an extra sensation that I could no longer distinguish, pain and pleasure feeding each other like a mated pair of songbirds.

Silas's proximity allowed me to hear every gasp, every moan that came from him as he buried his length inside of me.

"More . . . please . . ." I begged, riding his lap.

"You can have it all . . . I want to give you everything," he growled, biting at my shoulder as one of his hands held me by the back of my neck.

My knees were scraping against the tiles below us as I rolled my hips. He stopped going deeper, cautiously limiting himself so that the spines could not reach me, which meant he was close.

"Do it," I whispered to him, licking his ear playfully. "Make me yours," I begged, becoming rougher with my movements.

He let out a strained moan before he let himself go, forcing my hips down and holding them there.

Pain shot between my legs as his spines hooked into the wall of my vagina, holding me in place as he pulsed, emptying with every throb.

I laid my head on his shoulder, holding on to him as I focused on the pulsing rather than the pain, though that faded as the venom from his spines did their job. Even with the concentrated dosage that I made for myself, nothing compared to Silas. No bliss could compare to my angel-haired woe.

His arms wrapped around my waist, holding my hips firmly as he caught his breath. "I like when you're selfish," he whispered in my ear.

"You were just here at the right place, right time. Do not fool yourself."

"That's not what it sounded like when you were begging me to—"

"Quiet." I pinched him.

"So this *isn't* a good time to tell you that you smell extra fertile today?" he teased.

I shot him a panicked look before pinching him again. "That isn't funny; you said we're biologically incompatible."

Swiftly, he switched our positions, my back hitting the floor a bit rougher than anticipated, his hand gripping my jaw.

He let out a subtle laugh, his fingers digging into my cheeks to kiss me, rolling his hips slowly with his cock still spined inside. "That doesn't stop me from fantasizing."

"You are a sick man."

"Does that make you an illness, infecting every part of my brain until I know nothing else?"

I pushed his face away, my head bumping against the tile as I refused to look at him. I don't know what came over me, but I was too exhausted to care. The floor was cold, and my cramping was gone, and I had an *insane* urge for a bath.

THE ENERGY OF THE ground floor contrasted starkly from the one within my room, because it seemed brighter. In the main foyer area, there were many seated around in the scattered chairs and couches as the girls enjoyed each other's company.

We collectively decided that the Nest needed a communal area, so we designated the first floor to be shared spaces. One of the flats served as a library now, the room with the most up-to-date kitchen was the dining room, a lounging room for the one with the largest fireplace, and so on. The general foyer area had many collections of furniture for people to lounge and converse, with a long rug leading from the stairs to the skinny hallway that led to the front door.

"Someone woke up late." Phoebe greeted me at the bottom of the stairs. "Heading out finally?"

"I have to feed Edith after I get some work done at the lab. I shouldn't be too long," I assured her, wincing when my abdomen pinched again.

"Do you need something for the pain?" Phoebe offered, glancing from my abdomen to my face again.

"No, no. First day is always the worst. If it gets unbearable, I have tinctures in the lab."

"If you insist." She shrugged. "No need to go to the market today; we have enough from yesterday to make something new. Thinking of a hunter's stew tonight."

"Noted." I gathered my coat.

Phoebe threw me an odd look, something lingering under the impression of politeness. Something awkward, like she wanted to wrinkle her nose at something she wanted to say but chose not to in the name of being proper. The moment was short-lived before she returned to a group enjoying their morning tea.

I don't know what it was about our group, but we were different. In a way, we were all closer. A trauma bond from everything we had built together, all that we had survived.

Though some of them, Rebecca namely, had reverted to cold shells, as if she had not known us all these years. I could just be intellectualizing her trauma. I couldn't imagine it, but even her interactions with her friends were reserved. She could barely look at Mary.

I looped my scarf around my neck before reaching for the door. A hand yanked my wrist.

"Are you sure you should go out like that?" Silas eyed me critically.

"I am wearing nothing unusual—"

"That is not what I meant."

My cheeks grew hot. The way he lowered his voice made me feel entirely dirty.

Phoebe threw a glare at him as she whispered something to Mary nearby.

"I'll be out for not even an hour. I don't see the problem."

"Can't someone else do it?" He argued. "It's a petty task; get someone else to go. Someone not as . . . noticeable."

"I'm beginning to think you're insulting me." I tore my wrist from his hand.

"Let me help."

"With what? Holding my wicker basket?" I laughed.

He let go of my hand and furrowed his brows. His posture was rigid, clearly uncomfortable. I wasn't sure if it was from our encounter upstairs or because he was worried. Either way, I didn't need a chaperone.

"Promise me you will not follow," I warned him.

"Tell me where you're going, and I'll stay put."

I clenched my jaw, feeling a twitch in my brow. "Just the shop, then straight to the hospital. I may pick up things for this week's dinners."

He studied me, as if trying to detect a lie, a plan. While we were on lukewarm terms, it didn't take any particular attention to feel the residual anxiety in Silas that I was quickly coming to know.

I WALKED INTO TOWN rather than by saddle.

Nothing much could be told about the lab. I would have liked to say that I was productive, but I spent most of my time getting distracted or daydreaming. The most I could do was wash the glassware before I did a fresh blood draw for Edith.

The blood transfusion apparatus was propped tall and proud on the workbench next to some gauze in preparation for the extraction. When I opened the drawers to grab the tourniquet, I caught sight of the bottle with my special venom solution in it. There was hardly any left, but I wasn't able to spare any for myself from recent extractions.

I ignored that insufferable itch at the back of my neck for now; I had to focus on the task at hand.

I set the apparatus up on the table, one tube resting in a glass bottle, and the other tube was intended for my arm—functioning similarly to a standard transfusion.

Tying the tourniquet around my arm, I inserted the needle into the vein in the crook of my arm. When the needle was set, I could use the apparatus to control the flow, sluggishly filling the cylinder. When it reached about a liter, I turned a dial to allow it to flow out and into the glass bottle.

I pinched the needle from my arm and wiped it with gauze, but before I took off the tourniquet, I grabbed the bottle of venom at the bottom of the drawer and a brass syringe.

I might as well use the rest.

I drew the last of the golden solution up into the glass of the syringe, studying it as I held it up to the light.

One more.

I placed the needle in the nape of my arm, and the solution shot through my veins, invading my nerves and instantly numbing me into a state of tranquility. Any pain from before dissolved along with its memory.

I placed the needle on the table, rubbing my face with my hands. It was like the air was cleaner when I breathed, cooling me from the inside out. I felt like a passenger in my own life, so I might as well do something that I could control.

I barely remembered putting my coat on. I was floating through the scenes like a picture book. First, I was at the lab, then downstairs, then watching my skirt collect snowflakes as it dusted along the sidewalk. I had my basket in hand, needing to check three times to see if the bottle for Edith was still inside.

Memory loss aside, I was lighter. Maybe the memory loss was a part of that.

Along with my memory, time must have also escaped me, as the sun had already disappeared mostly, leaving a purple dusk across the sky. The streetlamps would likely be turned on soon.

I stopped for a minute, looking up at the stars that appeared. I couldn't help but smile as they winked at me, fading in and out as I viewed them from glassy eyes.

My thoughts were interrupted by the only thing that could jolt my heart enough to panic me. A muttered gargling from a strained throat sounded from across the street.

There were no carriages passing at this time; most had gone home, and shops were closed for the day after Christmas.

On the other side of the street was a hunched man covering his face with a hat. He was nicely dressed, with a finely tailored coat, though his resolve was anything but as put-together as his outfit. His shoulder slumped to one side, and he limped as he approached the street.

My gut curdled, and a wave of skittish energy overcame me. He froze.

He lifted his head, shaking as if it took significant effort to do so.

Slowly, I could see his face appear from under the rim of his hat, a pale, sickly face that made even the snow look off-white. He started to hobble forward, limping faster as he set his sights on me.

I quickly backed up, a spell of vertigo making it hard to stay coordinated from the sudden spike of adrenaline.

The man approached faster than I anticipated before he wrestled me into the snow of the alleyway.

His hoarse throat strained as he hissed and clawed at me. I held my hand out, and he bit down on my palm. I screamed and couldn't pull it from between his teeth.

I reached for my basket and my shaky free hand grabbed the bottle, swinging it across his face and making some of my blood spray into his mouth.

As I scrambled to my knees, he dug his fingers into my leg and clamped down on it with his jaws, growling like some wild animal as he shook his head, tearing at my calf.

The howl that escaped me was muffled quickly by a breathless sob.

There was no time to think. I couldn't afford to go into shock now.

I shattered the bottle against the brick alley wall, plunging the shards into his neck, his shoulder, wherever I could hit him.

He didn't let go of my leg until I plunged the broken bottle into his face, then kicked the bottle with my free leg to bury it further. I assume a shard must have gone through his eye and into his brain, because the slump of his body was so sudden.

I. V. OPHELIA

As I dragged myself across the ground, the searing pain in my leg was too great to be fully disguised by the venom in my system, but it certainly helped me stay calm. I held myself against the wall, my bloody hand pressing against the wound on my leg.

I was seeing specks of color in my vision one by one until it fully clouded my eyes.

The sounds and colors blended in a symphony of unconsciousness, until all I could see was the red blood behind my eyelids.

XLVI

The Creature

I DID NOT PAY ATTENTION to the nurse at the front desk as I flung the front doors open.

"Sir!" she shouted, but I was already halfway up the stairs.

I shoved open the doors one by one, letting them slap on their hinges and wail on the returning swing.

Phoebe and Edith were huddled by a bed, quietly bickering with each other. I did not bother to listen, as this was no time for chatter.

As I got closer, the image before me truly sickened me. A trembling returned to my hands, similar to the time I witnessed her seizure—except this time it was true horror. An uncontrollable, knee-jerk reaction. It shook me, and I wouldn't pretend it didn't.

Alina was too pale, almost ashen in complexion. There was barely any pink left in her lips and cheeks, and a subtle redness around her eyes. Her hand was wrapped up in gauze, but blood was already peeking through. Similarly, her calf was wrapped in fabric, and small bits of red were staining the flimsy patient cottons.

"Are you both going to be so useless? These bandages need changing. She will get an infection if you keep being so neglectful!" I snapped at them.

Edith and Phoebe both looked horrified when they saw me. It may have been because I yelled at them or because they told Luka not to tell me that they found her. What did they think would happen? That I wouldn't notice that she wasn't home? She told me she would return and neglected to do so. I had hunted her for two years; another day was light work.

"Alina?" I slid a stool over to her bedside.

"She has been sleeping for the past five hours." Edith gulped, picking at her nails in distraction.

"What happened?"

"A corrupted attack. She fended him off with half a glass bottle," Phoebe said. "Edith found her."

"You didn't think to tell me?"

"You would overreact, as you are now. We already risked enough attention bringing her in. It was closer than the tenement."

"Grab fresh bandages." I snapped my fingers at Edith and pointed toward the cabinets.

"You need to calm down."

"Did you check for frostbite? Concussion?"

"Silas."

"When was the last time she had water? She looks dehydrated."

"*Silas!*" Phoebe shouted. "Stop *nagging* me, you useless *fool!* Your carelessness will nearly kill her a second time!"

She reached over the hospital bed to crack a hard slap across my face, nearly giving my neck a good lash.

I clenched my jaw and slowly looked back at her.

"Calm. Down." Phoebe spoke in warning.

"How can I be calm? How are *you* calm?" I scoffed.

"She is going to be fine." Phoebe pulled a seat up to sit next to Alina on the opposite side. "You are angry at the wrong thing."

I glared at her before picking up Alina's hand. The coldness of her fingertips was one of my favorite sensations, but not like this. It was like I was holding plain ice. The blood was turning the gauze red with a halo of pink staining at the edges as it crawled through the fibers.

Phoebe was right; I was angry at the wrong thing. I needed to focus on cutting down every hand that touched her. I didn't care if Alina hated me for intervening on her behalf, but I couldn't allow things like this to continue happening.

"Luka thinks there is a colony of Vipera outside Buffalo causing this," Phoebe said. "Alina was planning to pay a visit."

"She's not going."

"She will find a way to go if you don't let her."

"Fine, then I will go with her."

She opened her mouth to say something else, but for her sake, I was glad she didn't. The muscle in my jaw twitched from how hard I was clenching my teeth together. The hospital was making my skin crawl. Everything was so white and sterile. The windows barely kept out any of the chill.

"This is no place for her. Where are her clothes?" I huffed, standing and looking under the bed and around the vicinity, slapping the curtain away.

Edith returned finally with the gauze and extra linens. "It isn't a good idea to move her—"

"I do not care; she is coming home. She needs more blankets and rest, and food that doesn't look like rations." I gave up on finding her clothes and took off my trench coat, wrapping it around her and buttoning the front over the hospital gown.

"Silas, you are acting irrationally," Phoebe started.

I didn't care to hear the rest. I scooped Alina carefully into my arms, cradling her against my chest as I made for the door.

It appeared no one was competent enough to at least check on her. It was about time I took over anyway. She wasn't leaving my sight. Ever.

XLVII

The Poisoner

THE SHEETS STUCK TO my clammy skin as I returned to consciousness. Not often was I anything less than freezing.

I flexed my toes, the motion causing a sharp pain in my leg that squeezed a groan from my heavy chest. My fingers still worked, but one stung more than usual. I couldn't move it.

I cracked open my eyes, the light glassy as I adjusted. I was in my room again, the balcony doors letting in a soft light, bright as it reflected off the snow on the rooftops and into my flat. My eyes narrowed at my hand, though I was surprised to find that not only was it wrapped in a bandage, but there was someone else's hand as well.

Silas was on his knees, his head resting in his crossed arms with my hand in one of them, pressed against his cheek. Silas was beautiful when he was asleep, more so because he was silent.

Had he been like this all night? He was still in his day clothes. I realized I was cocooned in his trench coat. No wonder I was sweating.

The sharp pain in my leg shot up my limb as I sat up. The blurry memories seeped to the front of my mind as I emerged from the brain fog. I dug through the sheets to pull my leg out carefully, inspecting the bandages around my calf, then the bandage on my hand.

What a mess.

I slipped out of bed, careful not to wake the sleeping lion as I reclaimed my hand.

I limped out of the room and headed downstairs. My hands gripped the railings tightly as I carefully took one step at a time, cautious of the weight I was putting on my leg.

The girls were gathered in the parlor areas. Some swapped journal subscriptions, others practiced handheld hobbies or were still waking up along with their morning brews. It seemed as if nothing even happened, or they didn't care.

My foot landed on the creaky step, alerting everyone to my descent.

I expected greetings, but all I got were gasps before silence.

Judging them for not caring may have been harsh; I was starting to suspect they didn't know.

"Alina! What are you doing up?" Phoebe tore herself from the group she was conversing with to fuss over me with a nervous laugh that didn't lighten her furrowed brow.

"I was claustrophobic." I looked around at the girls, who shot cautious glances toward me. "Is something the matter?"

"No! No, they hadn't heard what happened quite yet."

I glanced down at myself. The hospital gown was stained red from my leg, and the palm of my hand was in need of a new bandage.

"They don't need to know; it was a freak incident. It was just one."

"Do you really think omitting information is the best thing for the group?"

I glared in response to the insinuation. She wasn't entirely wrong, but I didn't appreciate her tone. "Fine. I need help packing for Buffalo. I would like to gather my things before Silas wakes."

"You are not going alone."

"I am."

"I will wake Silas myself if you don't agree to take at least one person. You are injured and not in your right mind."

"I'm perfectly within my average mind, now come and help me dress." Before she could respond, I was already limping up the steps, which was a greater task than going downward.

Now that I was past my waking daze, the pain was settling in. Like roots burying deep in my legs, a pulse gripping down to the bone.

Phoebe was close behind, though her expression looked more reluctant to help, with shifting eyes and uncertain steps as she followed.

When we reached the top floor again, Silas was already awake, lounging in the chair with his coffee.

"Going somewhere?" He cocked his head at me.

"Brief excursion." I glared at Phoebe as if she were conspiring against me, though he could easily do that on his own.

"My bag is packed already. Would you like to go horseback or wagon?" Silas replied.

"Horseback for myself, and you stay here with the Nest."

"I will meet you in the middle and say wagon. I don't think you can ride with that leg. I will bring my bag to the first floor." He straightened up from his seat and rolled his sleeves.

"Neither of you listens," I grumbled.

"You would be dead if we did listen to you." Phoebe followed me to the bedroom.

"I will meet you downstairs," Silas chirped. He was more awake than I expected him to be after how tired he had looked. "We should leave as soon as we can. There is an inn halfway to the town."

I chose a small bag. I had low expectations for packing.

"Can you grab four blouses and skirts? I will change into one now and pack the other. Oh, and wool stockings, four of them. I'll layer." I talked through my packing list as I removed my clothing.

"You don't want to wait? Or send Luka and Silas on their own?" Phoebe handed me my corset and wool stockings.

"What kind of diplomat would I be if I can't attend myself?" I sat down on the edge of the bed, putting on layers of wool socks over my legs, taking special care with the injured one. "Besides, I wouldn't trust those fools to empty water from a bucket with a hole in it on their own."

"Part of being an affluent figurehead is sending other people to do things as small as investigate disturbances." She sat behind me, clasping the corset in front and then tightening the laces in the back.

"I think that would make me look weak. I do not wish to hide from conflict." I stood, putting on my petticoat and corset cover.

"You need to choose what battles are worth it. There may be worse to come." She handed me the blouse and skirt.

"I'm picking this one." I dressed myself, finishing before closing the small traveling case with only essentials in it. "Help me downstairs, please."

Even with the pressure on my leg, the wool stockings held a steady compression, warm and secure. My boots were mid-calf, supporting my ankle a bit more. The only thing that would make this better would be some numbing.

When we reached the bottom floor again, Silas and Luka were already by the front door talking. Their conversation stopped abruptly as we approached.

"I'm ready." I placed my bag down.

"No, you aren't." Luka frowned. "Where is your coat?" He threw his hands up as if I should have thought of that as he retreated to the coat closet. The truth was that I was already feverish in what I was wearing. "Here." He made me put on a fur-lined jacket.

"It is like my mother never died, and she is here to pester me through you all," I grumbled, gesturing to the lot of them.

"Save your complaints for the long journey; the talking will keep you warm," Luka laughed, resting his elbow on Phoebe's shoulder, though she shot him an unsavory look.

"Let us go, we can get to the inn with plenty of daylight if we leave now." Silas glanced at his timepiece impatiently. He picked up my bag and took it outside.

I glanced at Phoebe. "You will be fine for a few days?"

"We can handle it, right?" Luka wrapped his arm around Phoebe playfully. "A few days is nothing."

I shot him a glare, hesitating before pushing open the front door.

It was a clear day, perfect weather for travel. The only issue regarding travel was that it would have to be with Silas attached to my side like a leech. He was already fastening the wagon to my horse.

A sharp breath pushed through my nose as I tilted my head back to stare upward.

Keep it together. We only have to do two hours at a time. It will be fine. Get it done.

I approached. Silas offered a hand, which was promptly ignored as I organized the reins in my taut fingers.

He stepped up and took his seat next to me. I flinched when he disturbed my leg again.

Some of the girls crowded in the shadow of the door, Phoebe in full light, waving gingerly.

It was not often I left my girls alone, and it admittedly filled me with dread, enough to make me feel lightheaded. It gave me some solace knowing Phoebe was there, but not as much as I would like.

The draft lunged forward, unsticking the wheels from the rigid snow.

I was really doing this, leaving them.

I wouldn't make it fifteen minutes without becoming nauseous if I let the thought settle.

Over my shoulder, I saw Phoebe. The small, receding image of a pink figure standing on the doorstep, watching wistfully like a widow on her peak.

They will be fine, I preached inside my head, *they all will be fine*.

As we made our way out of town, the buildings and houses became fewer and fewer before they were replaced by trees and an endless path. While the journey started off silent, I didn't find it as awkward—I would rather he not talk, anyway.

The morning air was fresh and clean. The cold worked some magic that numbed the throbbing in my leg and hand, though the reins rubbing between my fingers would be unpleasant after a while.

"Will you ignore me for the next hour and a half or will you grace me with conversation?" Silas spoke in my ear, his words hot as he spoke against my neck.

"I am not in the mood."

"What about a quid pro quo?"

"Ah, yes. Your favorite."

"*Our* favorite."

"Fine, shoot."

"Why did you poison your father?" Silas's words rang in my ears like tinnitus.

"Don't say it like that."

"Is it not true?"

"It was an accident."

"I thought poisoning his assistant *was* the accident."

"It was the *same* accident." My voice wavered; I was grateful he couldn't fully see my face. "I didn't know they would drink together. I should have poured the wine myself, offered it while he was separated from my father. Lured him somewhere . . ."

Based on Silas's lack of a retort, I sensed he almost regretted his question.

"What about your parents?" I cleared my throat. "Last time I saw your father, I must have been but sixteen," I changed the subject.

Silas became rigid at the mention, adjusting in his seat beside me. "You have to be more specific."

"What was your mother like?"

"I wouldn't know." His voice was stoic, entirely too steady to shield himself from any emotional labor. "She was a blonde."

"Very insightful," I muttered. "What about your father?"

"Also blond," he said flatly.

"All right," I sighed. "What *can* you tell me about your family?"

He paused. "I have twelve sisters, including Phoebe."

"That's a start." I looked over to him, but he was focused on the path ahead, arms crossed. "Do you remember any of them?"

"I remember the first five; the rest are a mystery to me. I wasn't there." He dug in his pockets for cigarettes. "I have visited Phoebe almost every year since she was born. I will never forget that carrot top when I first saw her." He paused for a minute. "Phoebe and I spent a normal amount of time together, more than I did with any other siblings. They had been married off in what seemed like the blink of an eye, so I learned to never get attached. I just happened to visit London when Phoebe's arrival was announced."

"And then you became attached?"

"How can you not? When something so small, so innocent and washed of any blame is thrust into this world like that, and for it to be in the palm of your hand, something changes in you when you realize she will end up like all the others."

"All the others?"

He waved his hand, "I didn't want to see her disappear like the rest of them, that is all." He offered out his cigarettes to me, but I declined. "I had a rather nasty fallout with my father when she turned sixteen, and I didn't visit for a while. We disagreed on certain practices that my father treated as tradition."

"What were those?"

"It wasn't important. I wish I had continued to see her, then maybe she wouldn't have been as angry when I showed up those years ago."

"Why did you come back?"

"I told her I returned for the city life and crashing her parties," he laughed, "she was so cross with me. She says it was because I eat her guests, but I know some of that anger is from my time away." I could see the leather of his gloves tauten as he clenched his fists. "I came back because I got word that my father planned on shipping her away. Marrying her off to wash his hands of her."

"She was betrothed?" I shot him a look over my shoulder.

"Not yet," he said with a shrug, "but you solved that issue for me, taking her here."

"Oh." I frowned, turning to face forward again. "It seems I really knew nothing about her."

"Nobody really knows anyone," he said solemnly. "People are too complex to be understood in a single lifetime."

Somehow his words made me feel better, but only a little.

"What is your real name? You and Phoebe have different last names."

"We take our mother's last names. Silas is my birth name. It is all real." He gave a tired smile.

"So what is your father's real name? I called him Mr. Astor."

"Astor is the last surname he took."

I nodded in understanding, not wanting to push it any further.

"What about your mother?" he asked, draping his arm over the back of the seat bench to play with a piece of untucked hair. The gesture was so simple, yet it still made me blush.

"Passed in childbirth," I explained, leaning back against his arm.

"I suppose you don't have much to tell me about your family either."

"I like to pretend that I knew her. That she had my eyes and my black hair. I at least knew those two things were true. I imagine she was kind and decorated the house with dried flowers. Sometimes I try to imagine her voice. As a child, I desperately wished I could know her voice, to know the comfort of a mother."

"We have more in common than you would like to admit." His arm tightened slightly around me as I spoke, a small, comforting gesture.

"I don't think I want to know how much we share." I rolled my eyes, but it accompanied a laugh, and he couldn't help a suppressed smile.

XLVIII
The Fixer

THE HOTEL WAS LIVELY tonight, the bar in particular.

This was the same place where we had first met Edith. I always did wonder why she came here, of all places.

She was fidgeting, her palms clammy. I could smell the sweat starting to form on her neck and forehead.

"What bothers you, Edith?"

"Just a bit warm in here. I haven't stopped moving since I got here."

"The temperature is fine."

"Says the man who has been sitting for five hours and arrived three hours late to work."

"Are you nervous about something?" I stood, blocking her path to the bar.

"No! My mind is just busy. Very busy," she stumbled on her words, her eyes averted.

Her pulse picked up.

She was *lying* to me.

"Then calm yourself. Let's enjoy some time away from that spider, yeah?"

She steadied herself and took a deep breath, nodding once she was ready.

We placed ourselves at the bar, glancing about at the fluttering meals. Today, I insisted on hunting with her. With Alina absent and not many friends in the Nest, I could empathize with wanting a bite without trouble. Besides, it was easier to share food when at least one of us had potent enough venom.

"Do you ever wonder why God would create something like us?" Edith spoke suddenly, picking at the patterns of the crystal glass with her nail.

I groaned and craned my neck at her. "Why do you ask such things?"

She shrugged sheepishly. "I think about it a lot. And it has made me wonder."

"About?" I ebbed her on.

"What if we were created to save them? The humans."

"We eat them, Edith. I am afraid to hear what you think saving is in that context."

"We hold venom that numbs their pain, and when they turn, they lose every ailment they've ever known."

"And it cuts their lifetime in half, if they are not Hosts," I reminded her.

"But is a life of pain really a life? A half-life of bliss is a good deal."

"Edith," I warned, "I do not know what makes you say things like this, but you should be careful."

"Why? Because I am correct?" She glared, clutching her glass with a stiff hand.

"Because you take care of those who are ill. I don't think people would be very comfortable knowing their nurse thinks it is better they are turned into cannibals—or dead, rather than in pain."

"What if it is better?"

"Do you think the corrupted prowling around are good? Are those things we should strive for?" I narrowed my eyes at her. "If a horse breaks its leg, you put it down. Prolonging a life not meant to be had is dangerous."

"They are not animals; they are people." Her lips pressed into a fine line. Her eyes were glassy, overwhelmingly frustrated. "They need help; *we* can help them."

"No." I slid the stool back, ready to leave.

"There was something my convent used to say," she began.

I sighed at the sound of what seemed like an anecdote and settled back into my seat, turning to her.

"They used to say that in order to achieve immortal life, you had to strive to help as many people as you could, never turning away someone in need, to prevent the least amount of suffering to the most amount of people." She swirled her glass, watching the liquid swish around the crystal. "Now that I seemingly have a life with no end, I wonder if, when I finally die, if I will be allowed in if I just make up for it. The longer the life, the more people you can help—but I died, already. So how do you go to heaven when you're stuck?"

"There is no after, only *now*." I shrugged. "You are doing fine. No need to worry yourself with hypotheticals."

"I idolized Alina because of her rules. I was at a dark point when she found me, but once I heard their mission, I knew it was in *His* plan for me." She smiled. "She wanted to ease the suffering, do what is best for the masses. I was just happy her plan included Vipera. For once, I saw us differently, not as abominations, but as instruments of something larger. Wouldn't focusing on turning suffering people not take away the most amount of pain?"

"Not everyone wants to turn, Edith."

"That is because they do not know what is good for them."

"Is autonomy not one of the tenets?"

Her hands clenched her glass a little tighter. "Does autonomy matter if it is what is best for everyone involved?"

Edith's pupils were wide open, more so than if it were just for poor lighting. I wouldn't insult her by saying she appeared hysterical. The spark in her eyes was hopeful, an exhilaration only known by a new idea. I've seen it in many people throughout my life, for better or for worse. Mania is one of the most powerful drugs, taking hold when all seems dim. Even so, she was only on the cusp of understanding what she was saying.

No amount of back and forth would change her mind. Such foolish words from a foolish child. The dangers of first thoughts managed by ill experience.

XLIX

The Creature

P AHEAD WAS AN elevated trail of smoke extending out into the overcast sky above. I assumed that it would be our inn. By the time we handed off our horse to the stable boy, my legs were stiff from the long ride. I helped Alina down and offered my arm for support.

The inn was attached to a local tavern. There was a cluster of buildings around the wooded area, but it was the densest town before we would reach the colony. All the buildings were the same shade of wet brown wood, topped with mildewed shingles on the roof.

The inside was much more welcoming than the outside. Despite the low light, there was a fire crackling away to keep the guests comfortable. The flickering of the flames reflected on the rows of bottles behind the bar counter.

I needed a drink.

The room wasn't dissimilar to the tavern. A rugged wooden room with a small carpet and bed. A feature I didn't expect was the small burning stove in the corner for extra heat, with a small basket of wood placed beside it. I assumed any extra would be costly.

"Go rest, get comfortable." I gestured to the bed as I set our bags down.

I tossed some wood in the fire, lighting it with some matches left on top of the burner. The smell of pine crackled and snapped within the chamber, steadily glowing behind the sooty glass window.

Within the closet, there were a few stray hangers and some shelving below. I spotted two extra wool blankets that I gathered and brought over to the bed.

Alina was undoing her coat, gingerly removing it as she stiffened from soreness.

As she removed her top, the corset cover peeked through. The thin fabric was light, comfortable on skin flushed in fever. Something so small, yet I couldn't help but be one of the lucky few who got to see even a glimpse underneath her staunch exterior in tailoring and personality.

I sat down next to her, wrapping her in one of the blankets. This time was most certainly delicate. A wrong move could mean she distanced herself from me again.

"Let me change your bandages." I knelt in front of her.

I lifted her skirt and took her leg, slipping off her boots and sliding the wool stockings off her limb carefully. Slowly, I unwrapped the bandages. Her leg was tender, her skin pink around the wound. The bite was mostly healed. I assumed Edith had used one of their many tinctures made from their victims to speed up the process. As cruel as their crusade was, it was kind of brilliant.

"I think we can let it breathe tonight." I smoothed my hands over her skin, checking each of the scarring marks.

"Quid pro quo," she said, staring down at me.

"Oh? You still have the energy for games?"

She shrugged, picking at the lint on the bedding. "I thought you wanted to start over. There are things I don't know, and it bothers me."

I nodded, taking a seat next to her. "Sometimes you have to be comfortable with the idea of never being able to know it all."

"Don't get philosophical." She pinched my arm. "I meant about you."

"I'm an enigma; what can I say?"

"Silas."

I tipped my head to look at her. She didn't look well, if I were being honest, but I wouldn't tell her that. The loss of color in her skin made her eyes look a bit pink around the edges, feverish. It reminded me of how she used to look: frail and unwell.

"Why do you avoid talking about your father?"

"I don't know what you mean; I already told you about him."

"Yes, you've given me a surname and not a detail more." She waved her hand dismissively. "You couldn't help me back then because there was something you weren't telling me. Even with your excuses, I feel like I was missing something about why it had to be *me* specifically that had to suffer."

"I didn't think it was important." I took a deep breath, glaring ahead at the fire as if I could will it to burn brighter.

"My father," she began, clasping her hands in her lap, "my father was not a bad man nor good, but he was respectable and true, which is all you can really ask for. An indifferent parent creates strong-willed children with an iron-clad sense of self." She shook her head and laughed. "That's what he used to say, at least. He wasn't much different with his students, though I argue he spent more time with them than me."

"He was a professor, you said."

"A great mentor, just not to a daughter." She shrugged.

"Then why did you cry for him when you killed him?"

"Because there was still hope that he would look at me the way he looked at Isaac." She picked at the skin around her nails, and I reached out to hold them, to comfort, but she pulled away.

"No amount of wit and institutional accomplishment would have outshone the fact that I killed my mother at birth, and how cruel it was that I am her spitting image."

There was a long pause, though I assumed it was because she was about to cry. I could smell the scent of tears building.

I stretched my legs out as I leaned back on my hands, "I'm the only son of a man who thinks the world dances in his palm," I chuckled, "and as a child, I believed it too. I thought it would dance in mine next."

She gave me a look, like I was humoring her. "Don't we all think what's theirs will be ours?"

I shook my head. "The difference is realizing that not all things inherited belong to us."

"What do you mean?"

"You asked why I couldn't help you before." I tilted my head at her. "I was stuck in a sort of stalemate with my father for a long time. Everything he built has a foundation of bones. He wanted me to continue, but I couldn't do it. And I was outnumbered. If he allowed them, they would tear me apart."

"And then my poison—"

"I don't think you realize that what you did was historically thought to be impossible," I told her sternly. "We are virtually made of poison. The fact that you could permanently maim one of us with no ability to heal was something we never saw before."

"It was an accident—"

"Don't lie," I laughed. "It evened the playing field. About time someone did something about us."

"What did you disagree with your father on?"

"I'm tired of losing people when the only explanation is 'it's just the way things are.' I've been taught it's selfish to have everything, that there must be sacrifices. To pursue exactly what you want in life or to change what they tell you your purpose is, is to betray yourself and your duty to your family."

"Is that what this is?" she asked quietly, our hands next to one another on the bed. She reached her pinky out, brushing it against mine. "Are you betraying yourself now, Silas?"

"I don't . . ." The tingle of her finger skating across my hand sent such electricity through me. "I don't want to hurt people anymore."

"What epiphany brought you to that conclusion?" she teased.

"My father called it a necessary evil." I glanced down at our hands cautiously. "But if necessary evil is what it takes to protect a birthright, maybe it should not be in the first place."

"And what is this birthright?"

"The Nest." I paused, unwilling to elaborate.

"It sounds like the Creature has finally developed empathy," she whispered, placing her head on my shoulder as she played with the hem of my sleeve.

"Too much for my own good, I fear."

"Empathy is a strength, a necessity to *know thy enemy*."

"I don't know how much longer I can empathize with my father."

"Are you telling me you abandoned them for me?"

"I abandoned them at least a decade ago, and it was a long time coming. But it should have been sooner."

"How much sooner?"

"Early enough where, just maybe, I would have been good for you when we met."

She stared absently. She stopped playing with my sleeve, and her jaw tensed against my shoulder as she rested there, though she did not pull away.

Was it something I said? Did I do something wrong?

If only she were as easy to read as one of those books she fixated on.

"Why aren't you speaking?"

"I am tired. It has been a long few days," she whispered.

"Well, rest, we have more traveling tomorrow." I stood, beginning to untuck the quilt, and gathered the extra blanket.

A wave of vertigo hit me, and my stomach pinched. I leaned against the frame of the bed to steady myself.

Her scent was strong, and it wasn't from the blood on the bandages. The temperature outside made it easy to hide a scent like that, but now that we were inside, it was hard to ignore the hunger.

"Silas." Her voice pulled me from my haze.

"Yes?"

"You look pale."

"That is my complexion, much like yours."

"No, you're hungry."

I raised a brow. "You can tell?"

"Of course," she replied, like it was common knowledge. "You are an easy read, like a grammar school pamphlet."

"You say that like it is an insult."

The bickering brought a smile to her face before she shielded it from me.

I lifted her chin. "Don't hide from me, you fox." I smirked. "Let me see."

"Don't make this weird." She stumbled over her words, unsure where to look, struggling to hide her emotions.

"Are you getting shy on me?"

She shook her head and grinned. "Why? Do you like it?"

"Not at all; I like it when you bite." I leaned forward and placed a knee on the bed, and she pitched backward. She laid down on the bed, and I hovered over her. Visions of her in the garden paid my mind a visit, a delightful memory to make this taste even sweeter.

I leaned closer, nearly nose to nose with her. I touched over her corset cover, though she was using it now as nightwear. The lacy hem and thin material were a tease as to what was underneath.

"I don't think you'd want me to bite you; just ask Luka," she teased, biting at my bottom lip softly.

There was a fluttering inside me, like an animal was skittering around. I would say she gave me butterflies, but it was likely a different kind of hunger.

Her eyes fluttered up, concerned with my hesitance.

Don't look at me like that.

I snaked my hands around her and placed my hand firmly on the back of her neck, lifting her slightly to me. It was taking everything in me not to tangle my fingers in her hair and ravish her here.

My heart was beating a thousand times faster than I knew it could, and I knew she could feel it too. My eyes trailed from her eyes to her neck. I could see every pulse, feel every pump of her heart send that crimson gold through her veins every second.

She reached up and circled her arms around my neck, pulling me closer. Her head reclined to the side, inviting me with her extended neck.

I lifted her toward me and traced my lips along the spot on her neck, feeling the pulse vibrate.

The low clicking bloomed in my throat like a cicada in late July.

With vigilant attention and care, my fangs flicked forward, flexing far as if to reach her sooner. I grazed them over her skin, scraping lightly. The anticipation was making me salivate. It was like a dream, the way I could be here with her, her attention dedicated only to me.

"Why do you hesitate?" she whispered, resurfacing me from my thoughts.

Alina seemed calm, but she couldn't hide the twitch of her brow, then the tension in her jaw. This was fear, not like the trepidation from hunting her.

No, it was the fear of rejection.

Her heart skipped, her breath shallowing. Was she afraid I would refuse her? Or the thought of all this emotional labor being just a means to feed from her?

"You know I like to take my time." I chuckled, my other hand stroking her cheek. She leaned into my touch, closing her eyes. The sight made me want to melt into a puddle, intoxicated from every reaction she would spare me.

She relaxed in my arms, and her hands smoothed up my shoulders and up the back of my neck, her fingers making a home tangled in my hair. With that, she pulled my head close.

A satisfied hum escaped me when she did that. Who knew the feeling of being desired could feel like this?

Without much delay, I gently kissed her neck, sucking at the skin tenderly. She tasted so sweet; I wanted to taste every inch of her. My fangs ached as they reached forward, poised above the milky flesh.

I sank my canines into her, biting down quickly so there wasn't much time to feel the pain.

She held on to me, trembling after the initial bite. The reaction only made me bite down harder, hoping that soon the venom would calm her nerves.

The hot, decadent blood washed over my tongue and made my senses swim in its flavor. It was like tasting fine wine, the most unique and expensive notes hidden under the metallic surface, wrapped in an ivory casing that was my lovely Alina.

Her slender form eased into mine, either from blood loss or from the venom.

I took one long swallow before I removed my teeth from her, flattening my tongue over the wound. It pained me to stop. My body wanted to throw itself at her just from the lingering taste of her on my tongue. She was provocative enough that I would want to beg her to use me in any way she could, just so I could get another taste.

When I peered down, her eyes fluttered open like she was pretending her eyes were not closed just before.

"Are you well?" I whispered.

She nodded and stared sleepily at me.

Once again, I found myself wanting to disappear inside her head so I could see what was making her look at me like that. Such softness and endearment, I didn't understand. How come she can look at me like this, like she had before in my garden, then flee from me?

"Rest; I will return with something to eat." I collected her in my arms so I could position her comfortably in the bed. The wool blankets wrapped around her as she lulled off.

It physically pained me to separate from her. There was a screaming in the back of my head, an undeniable need to protect her and shield her. To curl around her until she safely woke.

Sometimes I feared that would never be a reality with me by her side.

L

The fixer

THE GATHERING AREA ON the ground floor was fluttering with bodies. There was an odd protective urge now that I was tasked with watching Alina's Nest. The gas lamps were turned on and flickered dimly tonight. Vipera and Hosts paired for the evening for feeding, and I was left alone in my chair, a simple voyeur today.

There was an old feeling clawing inside me, like an instinct long forgotten. These girls were, unfortunately, no longer bodies in my mind, as much as I tried to keep them that way, unattached and unfamiliar.

I knew their names now, their hobbies; I counted heads out of curiosity, and now out of concern. One or two were missing moments ago; it sent a shock through my organs in the most terrible of ways before I remembered one retired to her room from an ill stomach, and the other went to check that the other fireplaces were clear.

I leaned over, dragging my nails over my scalp. I didn't enjoy being a keeper, but I worried I was the only one keeping track. If, God forbid, anything happened to any of them, no one would fight it if Alina deemed me responsible. I couldn't afford any liability, for my sake and theirs.

I was allegedly allowed to feed, but I didn't trust that Alina wouldn't detach my head from my torso, regardless. My stomach pinched as I watched the others taking their fill. I had to admit, the environment was calmer than the Dens I used to know. I imagine it was the absence of men that made it this way.

The weather was predicted to be bad the next few days, and snow was already starting to come down consistently outside.

Despite the formidable weather, the heart of the congregation remained cheerful. The building still needed a bit of work, and the decor was quite eclectic, but it was admittedly growing on me.

I sipped my coffee, hoping it would take the edge off the faint hunger that grew, just until I could go out to find a meal tomorrow. Rebecca and Mary were with a group of girls who played cards. Some women scattered in quieter corners to read. Phoebe was standing against the wall and watching the game of cards, more reserved than usual.

The cheerful chatter dampened when a loud thud sounded at the front door.

The parlor settled down to murmurs, all eyes on the door.

A scritching, skittering teemed against the wood, dragging across the door before it settled into a quieter scratch.

A burst of bangs, like a drunkard locked out of the bar. The wood door heaved, a splintering sound that made even my own heart leap. Then nothing.

We were truly lucky that the corrupted were almost entirely brain-damaged, or it would have realized it had nearly gotten in. A couple more heaves and the door may have failed. The strength of a feral beast also comes with the attention span of one.

I shot a glance across the room at Phoebe, but her eyes were already on me.

We waited. Not a noise was made. I doubt anyone knew what we were waiting for, but the girls sat still and quiet. This seemed like a familiar occurrence.

I glanced over at Rebecca; her eyes were frozen in a wide position, her lip trembling as she held herself together by threads. Mary was whispering something to her, an attempt at avoiding a breakdown.

Then, a horrific screech echoed from outside, mixing with the whistles of the bitter wind.

"Rooms," Phoebe demanded quietly, and they scattered like mice, quietly gathering their things and all moving to the second story.

I approached the door before noticing Phoebe doing the same.

"No," I said plainly.

"I'm going."

"You're not. You're going to stay here. I'll deal with it before it comes back."

"I won't let you push me—"

"Phoebe," my voice was stern, but pleading, "please don't make me have to explain to Alina what will happen next."

She swallowed hard, backing down.

"Just make sure everyone is calm. This is nothing; everything will be handled."

With that, Phoebe hesitantly retreated up the stairs to join the others.

When I opened the door, the cold bit at my face and my nose with such force that you wouldn't have remembered what it was like to be warm if you hadn't just been inside.

The street was dark, almost murky. A subtle fog from steadfast snow, a warm light here and there in a lone window or two. Small, timid candles danced in the windowsills, shyly winking for no one at all. The pathway was decorated for festivity, which made it all the more harrowing to see it so devoid of life.

I closed the door tightly behind me, fighting against the steadily growing winds. At first glance, the streets were empty. There were no coaches, no people, no discernible creatures. One way was just as empty as the other, the alleyways retreating into darkness. That is when I caught a glimpse of slight lumps in the snow that were already being smoothed over by the weathering, trailing beside our building.

I turned the corner into the alleyway, the footsteps becoming clearer in places shielded from the wind. There was no streetlamp, not much aside from the moon and its shadows to dance among the path. The snowdrift piled against the sides, large from having to dig the path daily, making a convenient track directly to the small livery stable behind the buildings.

The small, wooden leftover of the past was overwhelmed by the progression of brick around it in the present. A single glimpse of a leftover by necessity withstanding the trial of time.

Inside was dry, the smell of barley, straw, and the stink of animal hitting thick like a wall of humidity, despite the scent-dampening cold. Even with the smell, it was peaceful, still. It was relatively empty, to my knowledge used only for Phoebe and Alina's horses, relatively abandoned since the last owners of the tenement.

As I ventured farther into the swelling, a gushing, squelching sound cut through the noise of the night. I thought it had been from stepping through the slush.

I stopped, listened.

Now that I was pulled from my thoughts, I did not see Phoebe's horse, who was impossible to miss considering the size. I didn't think the mare had left the stable on her own.

I stepped forward, avoiding any hay or gravel on the floor, one step at a time as I went down the line of stalls.

There was the first one, I peeked over.

Empty. Some undisturbed shavings, anticipating a tenant that had yet to come.

The next one beside it.

Empty.

The noise augmented, the details of the disturbed sound becoming clearer.

The next stable door was open.

I stepped slowly, looking away as if I could anticipate the image.

There in the stall was a jittering mess of a woman that I maybe would have mistaken for an addict escaped fresh off the pipe.

She was gnawing at the horse's neck like it was the first time she was eating at all. If she opened her jaw any wider, it might dislocate. In all honesty, that was the likely case.

Despite my interruption of her feast, she paid me no mind. She was dressed in white, despite the blood quickly dying the fabric of the thin cotton, and the blue bandana in her hair did little to keep the matte of hair from becoming unruly.

She bit down on the hide, jerking herself backward to pull at it, to tear it off since her flat teeth would do little to make her feeding efficient.

The woman paused after she tore a piece, distracted from her meal. Her posture straightened, vertebrae by vertebrae. Her eyes twitched to me, her irises shaking among the black expanse of her eyes, jittering almost as much as her jaw.

Then, a shotgun fired.

The woman let out a harrowing squeal, like a mountain lion. She turned, half her face dappled with fresh pellets patterning her face in inky blood. Her blackened eyes darted, looking for the source of the disruption as if it were just a stone cast in her direction. When her gaze landed on me, her trembling mouth opened wide.

Then, another shot. The woman lurched, the back of her head smacking against the wood of the stall. Lifeless this time, she slumped over next to the horse.

I slowly checked over my shoulder.

Phoebe held a sawed-off shotgun, holding it up still. Her gaze never left the woman or the horse, frozen in her place. The look she held was grim, too much so for a graceful thing like her.

I stepped to her side, following her line of sight.

Snow fell in from the stall window, where it turned red upon contact with the quickly growing puddle of red and black. The only sound was the wind now.

I reached up, carefully grabbing the shotgun, my hands overlapping hers.

She flinched upon contact, beginning to shake.

"Phoebe," I whispered, "let go of the gun."

Her eyes snapped to her hands, and she quickly unhanded it, though it was like she wasn't sure what to do with them after.

"There we go." I took off my coat, draping it over her shoulders. "Let us go inside now. There is nothing left for us to do."

LI

The Creature

THE NEXT TOWN BUSTLED with the same liveliness as any other working-class town. Wagons full of goods passed us in every direction as we rode. There was cheery chatter as we passed, particularly when we went by several taverns. The ground crunched under the hooves of our draft as we approached the middle of a town, where a stately, simple steeple watched over the domain.

To think that all of these people were Vipera made me more comfortable than I was in the last town. It was nice to be around familiar species until I remembered who I was traveling with.

She was sitting beside me in the wagon, her head sloped against my shoulder as my arm wrapped around her. She must be exhausted. Injured, traveling, and Eve's curse was visiting her this week. It admittedly drove me nuts, her scent making my teeth ache. I wanted to tear into something, preferably not her.

We stopped in front of the inn. It wasn't very fancy, but it was the fanciest one this town could afford. I was told the nicest bar was here, which often hosted the man we were looking for.

"Alina." I nudged her, gently touching her cheek to wake her.

"Hm?" She didn't open her eyes.

"We are here; let me help you dismount." I slid off the wagon and held my arms out to her. She gingerly lifted her leg, and I helped her down by her waist. She was a bit pale for my liking; I needed to make sure she ate some meat at least.

"Go on inside, I'll bring the horse to the stable. Take the bags in," I instructed, handing them to her before she trudged up to the front door.

Out here, everyone did everything themselves, no need for any sense of hospitality. I didn't expect much from a place like this, but I didn't mind the work either. The horse let out a huff of breath as I led him, jolting his head up and nearly yanking the reins from my hand.

"*Whoa*, calm." The beast strained out of the corner of his eye before letting me lead him forward.

What a fussy thing.

I brought the horse to the stable, leading him to an empty stall. The tack was dismounted, and I hung it outside his door. The big, burly horse was happy to be idle, even happier when I threw a few flakes of hay into the small box. Though I think it only seemed small because of his sheer size.

I brushed him off and covered him with a blanket for the night. While I didn't prefer drafts, I could appreciate a hearty beast. My own horse was quite flighty, not quite built for travel like this.

"Goodnight, beastly thing." I gave him a firm pat on his neck before heading inside.

I stepped in through the back entrance, stamping my boots off on the carpet before trudging in. I saw many faces huddled around tables on the first floor. There were two small fireplaces on either side of the common area, cabin-like with exposed beams and taxidermy decor. The bar was by the back door to the left with a barman busy cleaning glasses—he doubled as the innkeeper. On one of the many couches, there was a crowd, and in the middle, Alina.

Couldn't you have negated attention for a few more minutes?

As I approached, they all listened to the damsel intensely.

"And then when they can put it on the nightstand, no one would ever know it was poison, as it just looks like perfume," she explained.

"Do you only make one kind? Was your clientele via word of mouth?" asked one of the men.

"Yes, and it was easy since *all* the wives do is talk and spend money, so it was rather good for business," she laughed tiredly.

"What profession are you in now?"

She paused and grinned. "Pharmaceuticals, naturally. Traded poison for poison in some ways. Which has created a demand for my second profession that I am training for."

"What would that be?"

"An undertaker."

The men had a round of laughter. I suppose she knew how to work a room. I cleared my throat, and they quieted.

Alina smiled sheepishly. "This is my . . . travel partner I was speaking of earlier." She introduced me.

"Ah, this is the man we were waiting for," one spoke from the chair next to her. "How kind of you to join us."

The man next to her had the complexion of finished wood from a walnut tree and hair blacker than the coals that rested in the pit of the fire. His eyes were dark as well, reflecting the amber light. Most of the men around us shared a similar complexion, except for a few here and there. I was happy Alina showed up first, because I had a feeling my presence was not the most appreciated in a small town like this.

"Silas," Alina started, looking at me before turning to the man, "this is Cormac McCallister. This is his town."

I stepped forward and held my hand out to him. "Silas Forbes, pleasant to meet your acquaintance."

He stood to grasp my hand, shaking it firmly. "It is always a pleasure having fresh meat in my town." His hands were rough, calloused despite his young appearance. "As lovely as your missus is, I have to ask respectfully what your business is here," he stated, giving a cautious survey of my appearance.

I sat down in one of the chairs, and he returned to his seat next to Alina. The air became a bit thicker, tense. Most of the men stayed put.

"Our visit is purely out of curiosity. We have had disturbances—" I began.

"So it must have come from a town of mangy, brutish, forest dwellers. Correct?"

"No, that's not—"

"What Silas meant to say," Alina cut me off, "is that we come seeking advice."

Cormac paused, and he turned his attention to Alina. "What kind?"

"We keep getting more and more feral corrupted showing up down in Buffalo—we can't figure out where they are coming from. We thought it would be wise to ask an established Vipera colony."

Cormac stared at her for a moment longer than I was comfortable with.

I was itching to move over to her, but I had to remind myself that she could hold her own. She was much better at diplomacy than I; the only one better than her would be Phoebe.

"How many?" Cormac leaned forward in his chair.

"In the past few months, possibly twenty—three of whom killed one of my girls."

"My deepest condolences." He frowned, bowing his head

slightly out of respect. A couple removed their hats. "I take it you have a congregation."

"A community of Hosts and Vipera. It is my job to keep them safe, and I've failed. Forgive us for coming on such short notice, there is nothing else we know to do."

"Well, if you were wondering if they came from us, we haven't had any new humans in some time. Most just pass straight through. We have our own community of Hosts, so we have no need to hunt passing travelers." Cormac reclined in his chair and picked up his whiskey glass. "We actually had one instance of a corrupted, but it came from your direction."

"From Buffalo? Do you think it's possible it came from elsewhere?" She knit her brows together, chewing her lip anxiously.

"I am afraid so, or at least they aren't coming from us." He shrugged.

"I see." An unmistakable weight of defeat hung in her words.

"I wish I had a better answer for you. I do wish you luck in finding the source of your disturbances." He rose from his chair. "It is about time to return to my own home, though you two should stop by the bonfire later tonight. It is the perfect night for stargazing." He turned to Alina and took her hand. "Goodnight, if I do not see you this evening." He kissed her knuckle before turning to me, nodding. "And goodnight to you, as well. Thank you for letting your missus entertain us with her stories."

I nodded in return, figuring it was more modest not to speak in this instance.

With that, he left, sliding his glass to the bartender before gathering his coat, leaving with most of the men who had surrounded us before.

I watched Alina from across the seating area.

She watched the fire. The hospitable expression she held before vanished without proof it was ever there at all. As upsetting as the new information was, I understood the frustration. I suppose it was good to do something other than sulk tonight.

"ARE YOU SURE YOU want to go?" I asked her as we approached a field, an almighty, blazing fire lighting the way.

"I'm not tired; I want to see." She gripped my hand as we approached the giant flames.

The heat stretched across the snow, melting it as we got closer to expose the dried grass. Many people put down blankets as they drank cider and beer. Food was brought in carts for sale. Women and children danced around the fire joyously as a small group played odd, haphazard instruments that were full of playful folk tunes.

Alina's face was so bright, so curious about the entire endeavor. There were a few bales of hay stacked in random spots on the ground for sitting.

"I didn't think a fire could get this big; it's blinding."

I glanced over at her. She was doe-eyed, taking in the scene and the warmth of it all. Some color had returned to her face, or perhaps it was simply from the heat of the fire.

A group of children ran past us, giggling. One of them stopped and stared at Alina, seeming surprised at the unfamiliar face. He shouted something at his friends in a language I didn't know, but then he took her hand.

She looked unsure before the little boy dragged her away.

They wanted her to dance for them. The children led her closer to the fire, jumping excitedly and twirling, trying to show her what to do.

She was painfully awkward, unsure of what they were say-ing, but with a few gestures from the children showing her how to dance, she followed along. It seemed to be some sort of folk dance consisting of simple steps and twirls that went along with the high-energy music.

I sat down on a bale of hay, admiring her from afar. I could see her form, backlit by the raging fire, though nothing could compare to the one that burned inside of her. The passion, loyalty, and strength—she was terrifying. But right now, she was like some goddess, in the presence of fire as fierce as herself.

It was like I could see her as time slowed. Her hair whipping around her as she spun, her smile brighter than ever, like no one was watching. Her cheeks were red from the excitement and joy of just being free. There was no one here to see her, no mask to wear, not a soul to judge. I was blessed to even witness her in a rare time such as this. It pained me terribly that she couldn't always be this free.

Her frozen breath came out like smoke as she stumbled away, panting from the excitement of the dance. She walked over to the edge, far away from the heat, until she reached snow, flopping down on her back, cradled in the white powder.

I walked over to her slowly, as if I were approaching some wild animal that might flee at the sight of me. "You look feverish."

"I feel happy." She watched the endless sky, flakes of snow dappling her hair and making her cheeks look bright red.

I lay back, staring up at the stars next to her.

"Do you ever think about how we got here?" she whispered.

Her eyes never left the stars, and mine never left her. The reflection of them in her eyes was fitting, as they were wide with wonder, large enough to hold entire constellations in them.

"Why would you think on the past?"

"Because the future is infinite, and it is easier to wonder about things before us. Don't you ever wonder?" Her eyes met mine finally, her chest rising and falling as she was regaining her breath.

Her smile was so bright, so genuine and alive. It was so beautiful I could weep at the sight of her.

"I don't think I care much for anything that came before you." The words fell from my mouth; I hardly believed they were mine.

Her smile faded, but I quickly learned it wasn't from displeasure. She rolled over on top of me, cupping my face as our lips locked.

My eyes were wide, and I couldn't bring myself to close them immediately. I hardly believed she was real most days. I thought the scene would disappear if I blinked and woke up for it to have just been a hallucination. The moment was something I didn't expect, but it made me think maybe I was the feverish one, in the midst of a dream.

I snaked my arms around her, a hand resting on the back of her head as I deepened the kiss.

She was perfect. My beloved tempest of storms and rage, of the quiet calm before a rumbling thunder, a force strong enough to move the stone that sat in place of a heart. Her lips were so cold it made me want to devour her entirely, to make sure she was never leeched of warmth again, to be the only one who touched her flesh until the day she died, and even then, I would sit at her grave until she returned to me in her next life. I didn't care how long it took; what good was being immortal if you didn't have something worth living for?

She broke our kiss, her lips just above mine, a teasing distance. "Do you love me?"

"No," my reply was nearly instant, and my heart squeezed tighter. "Love is too weak a word to describe what I feel for you, but simultaneously the only word I have to describe it."

She was staring at me, the stars behind her shimmering like a halo around her.

"I feel that if you left this earth, the stars would die, and the flame within me would smother along with them. I would stay by your side, even in death, until I, too, started to decay where I stood. I would gladly feed the birds, the bugs, and become foliage as nature intended, right beside you."

"Silas . . ."

"I know where our deal stands, but I wanted to ask you the right way."

I slowly reached for the lapel pocket of my coat, producing a small, shimmering item.

"Please, Alina." I held her face close with one hand, our foreheads touching, my thumb brushing over her cheek. She was so warm, so alive. I closed my eyes because I was afraid to look at her. I held the item between us. "Be mine."

I waited, my mother's ring pinched between my fingers, my heart on display like a flayed man.

"Will you ask me to do it?"

"Do what?" I opened my eyes, our heads still touching, but her eyes were on the ring before they held my gaze.

"To turn."

I didn't want to offend, but I laughed. "I could never make you do anything."

"Why haven't you asked me to turn?"

I let out a long breath and leaned my head back, resting it in the snow. "I know you well enough to know that if you wanted to turn, you would have asked me already."

There was a pause, then she moved.

When I looked again, she had slipped her finger through the ring, her face hovering so close to mine. "Then yes, you have me."

Something overcame me, and I wrapped my arms around her tightly, holding her head against me. I feared I would suffocate her within my grip, but I didn't care. I thought it would never come, where I could hold the only thing that mattered to me.

I kissed her, softly at first, then harder again, and again, unable to contain my excitement. I was only elated that she kissed me back, that I was met with laughs, and her hugging me tighter instead of pushing me away.

May we never be rid of each other for as long as we live.

LII

The Fixer

"**WHAT HAPPENED?**"

"There's nothing to worry about."

"Was that a gunshot?" another asked.

"We have to call for Alina!"

"With what telephone in her possession?" I snapped at the girl.

"Watch it," Phoebe snapped at me, smacking her coat to rid it of snow.

"You answer the questions, then," I nearly snarled, pushing past the crowd steadily forming at the door. My body was heavy as it finally sank into one of the parlor chairs. All I could do was rub my temples, to imagine this was the last problem I'd have to deal with tonight.

"Do you think there will be more tonight?"

I glanced up at the new voice.

Mary stood next to my chair, staring at the hearth, at the crackling fire. This wasn't a question of panic, but a tone of pro-activeness I had only seen in a few, aside from Alina so far. She seemed stoic, focused.

"Yes," I said honestly. "I think tonight will be long."

A few more filed into the parlor area. Some filled in the seats of the couch, some sat on cushions on the floor by the fire.

"We should stay together tonight," Rebecca, standing by the arm of the sofa, suggested.

"Should we sleep in shifts?" one seated on the sofa asked.

"I'll stay awake," I said.

"So will I," Mary decided, looking at the others. "Anyone else?"

Rebecca raised her hand, and a couple more hands as well.

I glanced over my shoulder. Phoebe was leaning against the wall, looming in the shadows. A red flickering of her eyes gave her away. Not that she was hiding, but she seemed to have retreated in thought.

"We can trade off sleeping," I said.

Phoebe's eyes flicked to me in the dark.

IT ISN'T EASY TO distract yourself during a crisis. Most aren't very good at it. It's a tricky thing to master. But there is one thing that is nearly foolproof.

Food.

To my surprise, Phoebe said my suggestion would be wasteful. Though Phoebe never had to learn how to make simple pleasures out of nothing.

Two pots on the stove, one with foraged berries for the Hosts, and the other for the Vipera. It wouldn't be easy to mix up.

I hadn't had Kissel in a long time. A *very* long time. It was like a jelly, a cheap treat of berries and potato flour. Two ingredients that were plentiful for Alina's Nest. Though I was curious about the berries used for the Vipera.

"What are you using?" Mary spoke from beside me.

She was staring into the pot as I steadily cooked down the berries.

"Blackberry for the Hosts, rosehip for Vipera."

"May I help?"

"Of course, just stir them both steadily," I instructed, stepping aside to hand it over.

She took the spoons, a bit stiff and awkward as she stirred.

I mixed some warmed water and the potato flour. "Just keep stirring," I said, slowly pouring the mixture into the pots.

"Do you think Alina found where they're coming from?" she asked, scraping the sides of the pots as she stirred.

"She could have," I said truthfully.

"Would you lie to us even if you knew she wasn't going to?"

The question made me pause, and I thought on it for a minute. "Would you blame me if I did?"

She shook her head solemnly, "If we go to New York City with you and . . . Mr. Forbes," she began, shifting the pots off the hot burners, "don't lie to us."

"I understand."

"No, I don't think you do." She looked up at me. There was a stark tension in her brow, a determined spark. "My sister is dead because we were left in the dark about how real this threat was. I don't blame them entirely. I understand keeping calm. But promise me that you won't lie. That you will let us know if we can prepare better, be stronger."

"Where is this coming from?"

"They're too distracted with their own workings to realize that the Nest is a tool. I overheard Mr. Forbes talking about the Nests out there being as fierce as chicken coops, to be protected and helpless."

I nodded slowly.

She took in a frustrated breath. "Promise that you will help us make sure we are never waiting docilely for slaughter."

"Well, I think that would be up to each of you."

"If we never know how to help ourselves, we may never get the choice." She held up her hand, pinky out. "I want your word."

"Why mine?"

"Because despite being starved out, tortured, berated, and despised, you are still here." Her dark brows furrowed, grabbing my hand and forcing it in hers, pinkies locking. "You believe in this just as much as we do. Help us make it work."

I was hesitant to accept, but I did, anyway. The eagerness is all I needed to see to make me believe that maybe this would work. Maybe this mess was temporary.

"You have my word then." My pinky squeezed hers.

"I DIDN'T TAKE YOU as a baker," Phoebe muttered as her spoon scratched against the bottom of her cup.

"Not all of us grew up with a full support staff," I teased.

"I feel bad for Edith; she's missing out." Rebecca nudged Phoebe.

"I can make more. I'll be awake when her shift ends." I checked my timepiece. "She's usually off at about two in the morning, right?"

"Yes," Phoebe confirmed, an irritated chime of her spoon in her cup before getting up and collecting a couple empty dishes from the coffee table.

Many sat around, temporarily pleased by the small treat.

"At least we got to enjoy it before she tells us it's unhealthy," one joked.

"Or perhaps rambling about medical anomalies while we are attempting to keep our appetites," another said.

"My appetite is as good as gone just looking at her," Phoebe mumbled, followed by a chorus of laughter.

"Phoebe," Mary warned, her jaw clenching as she poked at her dessert.

"What?" The way Phoebe's eyes snapped to her reminded me all too well how much she resembled her brother. "Is something the matter?" The question was a challenge.

"I don't know, *is* there an issue, Phoebe?"

"It's just a bit of fun, take a moment to gather your emotions," Phoebe laughed, surveying the others for approval.

"It is fun when it is a harmless poke here and there, diluted across all members of the group." Mary placed her cup on the table. "But you seem to use Edith as the wick for every burn. Butter upon bacon. Excessive."

"I apologize for not being as sensitive as your nature, sweet Mary."

"My sensibilities are perfectly fine; yours have lost their polish."

"It is not too late to take those words back." Phoebe placed the tray of cups down, her jaw tense. "Before you choke on them."

"Is that all you do?" I spoke up.

The girls quieted, dread in their stares. The conversation was already like cold water on tallow.

Phoebe straightened her back, her chin in the air. "And what is it that I do?"

"I feel like I've heard this before. Stories about a young, fire-haired socialite who threw fits when she didn't get what she wanted." I laughed. "Your father didn't mind a brat, but unfortunately, they get on my nerves after a while."

She scoffed, a slight snort of pure amusement. "Don't pretend to know me."

"But I do." I leaned forward, elbows on my knees. "When you meet enough people, you've met them all. And I've had my fair share of the likes of you, dear Phoebe."

"You *think* you do, which is your mistake," she snapped. "You thought you knew Alina too."

"I was wrong," I said steadily. "We aren't perfect."

"And it cost you an eye." Her hands clenched. "Watch yourself before you lose the other."

"What kind of leader bullies one of the most useful members of their Nest?" I rose from my chair, and some of the girls seated on the floor made room in case I stepped forward. "She's a nurse, she earns more than any singular job any of you have, and has real, useful knowledge that benefits *everyone*."

"I have no room for incompetence. None of us do."

"Do you really believe that? Or do you just crave Alina's approval?"

She laughed, glancing down. "Is that really a question?"

"Is her friendship not enough for you that you must sabotage any of her other relationships?" I stepped forward, and the girls moved away, like our presence was lined with needles, quick to move so as not to be pricked.

Phoebe stepped back. "Nothing comes close to our bond."

"Does it hurt?"

"Excuse me?"

"Being the only one who hasn't had her heart?"

She stepped back again, and I matched in pace.

"Does it hurt knowing that you will always be the last choice?"

Her back hit the wall, her foot knocking against the umbrella holder.

"How does it feel to know she fell for my mirage before she ever thought of you as more than a rug?"

A prominent click, then a long, hard barrel shoved at my chest, the sawed-off shotgun retrieved from the umbrella holder.

"Keep going; I've been itching for a reason to kill you," Phoebe spoke low, her eyes filling with blood, though in the dark her eyes were nearly a void.

"Phoebe!" Rebecca shouted from behind me.

Shuffling from the girls behind us as they scrambled, not wanting to be in the line of fire.

"Who is this?" A smirk pulled at my lip, and a drop of blood from my eye landed on the barrel. "I don't believe I've met the woman before me."

If it weren't for her breathing, I'd easily mistake this stillness for a statue. Even with quick breaths, her weapon and eyes were steady. I fully believed that if it weren't for the others in the room, I would have had a hole in me.

I put my hands up, taking a few steps back. "I recognize you now." I chose my words carefully. "That's your father in you. You look like him more and more every day."

"You confuse me with my brother, old man."

"Am I, though?"

She pulled the trigger pointed at my foot, and I jumped back. "You missed."

"I don't miss," she said sternly, "that was a warning." She shoved past me, smelling of gunpowder and peonies, and headed for the stairs with her smoking gun in hand.

I followed her with my eyes, noticing Mary and Rebecca standing by, unsure of what had happened. Rebecca gave Mary a look before following Phoebe up the stairs. Mary looked back at me and gave what I swore was a small flick of the corner of her lip, before she followed suit.

"Girls," I muttered, settling down into the parlor seat again, now alone to watch the fire and wait.

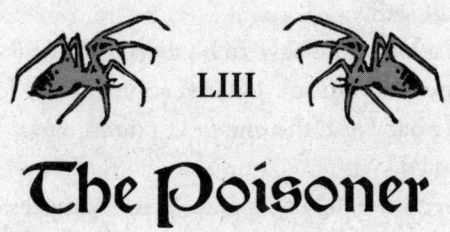

LIII

The Poisoner

MY BODY QUAKED FROM the dampness of my clothes, despite sitting in front of the small fireplace in our room.

I inspected the ring. It was an outdated kind of soul, by a few hundred years at least, one with an entire life of experience.

Inside, there was the smallest of inscriptions.

Ad infinitum—etiam post mortem

Silas poked at the fire, adding more wood. When he finished, he sat down on the floor by my side. There was a certain nostalgia overwhelming me. He and I in front of a fire, sitting on a pelt rug.

"What do you think?" Silas spoke.

"About what?"

"The corrupted. Do you suspect any other places?"

"I don't want to think about it. All I know is we are back where we started. No answers." I rested my chest against my knees as humble fire danced before me, not nearly as warm as the bonfire.

He pinched at my coat, peeling it off my shoulders. "We don't need to think about it, then."

"I'm sorry, you know," I whispered.

He studied me, unsure if he heard correctly. "For what?"

"For what I said."

"You talk a lot; you'll have to be more specific."

"You know what I mean." I glared at him before looking at the fire. "Back at your Nest, the one in London."

"I deserved it."

"You didn't, though," I snapped. "It was unnecessarily cruel. I didn't want you to look for me after."

"Come here." He pulled me into his chest and squeezed tightly. "There is not a single thing you could say that would make me abandon you."

"I wish I could say you were on my mind, but I didn't expect you to come," I whispered, pinching the fabric of his shirt and studying the threads. "It seems that I forgot. Out of sight, out of mind."

"Then maybe it is time we jog your memory." Silas raised my chin, our noses nearly touching. He froze, watching me through lowered lashes as if to get one last look before kissing me.

"Tell me you would never betray me." I smoothed my hands up his chest and over his shoulders, my fingers tangling in his hair.

"Why would I—"

"Say it." I balled my fist in his hair. "I need to hear it from you."

"I would never in my wildest dreams think to turn my back on something as deadly as you." He ran his thumb over my bottom lip. "To betray you would mean a life without you, which would be no life at all."

I clung to his damp shirt, and he cupped my face in his hands. The gentle touch nearly made me whimper.

He brought one of his hands over mine, guiding it up around his neck. My only problem was that my hands couldn't stay still, following the hems of his finely tailored clothes, and his exploring mine. Our hands played an elusive game of chase as they swept around our bodies, further tangling us in our pursuit of comfort, of pleasure.

"Silas—"

"Kiss me, Alina," he breathed. "Kiss me, hit me, curse my name until you forget what I've done to you."

His hands grabbed my hips roughly, and I bit down on his lip playfully, though I tasted a familiar tinge of blood. He deepened our kiss, running his tongue over mine as if afraid I would poison myself again.

I loved how desperate it was, the eagerness. His grip was possessive, as if afraid I would slip away as I've done many times before, but this time he wouldn't allow it. He was determined to mark me, claim me for himself.

He forced me backward, pinning me to the fur of the rug as he kissed my neck, trembling as he pinned my arms above my head.

"Let go," I breathed.

"Why? So you can slip away from me?" he teased.

"I want to hold you."

He admittedly looked a bit thrown off. He let go of my hands, sliding his hands down my arms and to my waist as he lowered his head between my breasts, kissing lightly down my sternum, his eyes focused on me.

The fire reflected from the back of his eyes, a gentle red glow.

He removed my blouse, then my skirt.

I raked my fingers through the golden strands as he teased my skin, venturing lower. My thighs clenched when he reached them, and he left delicate kisses along the hem of my stockings.

I propped myself up on my elbows, slowly undoing the front of my corset.

Silas tugged his shirt over his head and tossed it away, not wanting to miss a single thing I did.

I popped each latch of my corset slowly, even slower as it opened up.

He yanked my legs forward, making me fall onto my back, and he opened the corset fully, exposing myself to him.

"Impatient," I huffed, lifting my foot to poke him in the chest.

He caught my ankle, stretching my leg up so he could kiss down the side of my calf, then to my thigh, then lowered himself between my legs.

He slid his tongue out and teased gently at my clitoris before sucking gently, continuing to push on it with his tongue.

I moaned and covered my face with my arms to hide my embarrassment.

Then, he stopped.

I frowned and glared down at him.

"If you hide your face, I won't continue."

"Why," I huffed.

"Because I want to see you, is that so terrible?" He smirked.

I rolled my eyes as I leaned up on my elbows.

"I love that your face reserves a very specific shade of blush, just for me," he teased, returning his face down between my thighs.

He teased and licked between my legs, probing my vulva with his tongue, begging to slip inside.

I bit my lip, unsure where to look.

He slipped his tongue in, watching my reaction closely.

I held back a moan, but his response was to stretch his tongue deeper, curling it inside and putting pressure against the walls.

"Silas," I moaned, moving my hips in time to his rhythm.

He groaned against my skin, his hand gripping my thigh a little tighter as he worked harder to get the same sounds out of me.

My breath hitched, and my hand combed through his hair, pressing my hips up against his mouth.

He suddenly pulled away from between my legs, sitting up. He jerked me up by my arms, so I was straddling his lap as he sat back on his heels.

I smirked and dragged my nails over his chest. I reached lower to his trousers. I unbuttoned them and pulled out his already stiff cock. I rolled my hips in his lap, stroking up and down his length as I kissed his neck.

"I want you, Silas," I whispered to him. "I want to make up for lost time."

He sloped his head back as my lips left hot trails across his skin, his hands firm on my waist as I worked.

"I can't wait anymore," he breathed, lifting my hips above the tip of his member.

I cupped his face, making him look at me as I lowered myself steadily onto his length. It was hard not to let my eyes roll back at the feeling, and I ended up closing my eyes.

One of his hands snared my face, enticing me with a rough, hungry kiss.

I sat fully in his lap, his cock hitting my cervix as I attempted to adjust.

"*Please . . .* " I whimpered in between our kisses, moving my hips on his lap.

"I can't hear you," he whispered, biting my bottom lip, "you have to speak up."

"*Silas.*" His name was shaky, hesitant to leave my tongue.

He forced my hips down on him roughly, making our pace slightly quicker with more vigor.

"*Silas!*" I cried, wrapping my arms around his neck and digging my nails into his back, dragging them along the hot skin.

"That's right. You're only allowed to cry *my* name like that." He chuckled, wrapping his arms around my waist as he buried himself so deep that I was starting to believe I would bruise.

He suddenly took his cock out and turned me onto my hands and knees.

"What—"

He grabbed my biceps and helped me up on my knees, then used my arms to pull me onto his length, jolting me forward with each thrust.

I cried out and clenched my fists, throwing my head back as he forced his length deep, his muscular thighs slapping against mine as he buried deeper.

"Ah, look at you. You really are quite a spectacle," he chuckled, his rhythm rough, possessive.

When I looked over, I saw what he meant.

The mirror in the corner showed both of our bodies bathed in the firelight, our skin glistening as we moved.

I could see the red in my face rising, and I could no longer hold my doppelgänger's gaze.

"Ah-ah! What did I say about hiding your face?" He laughed, letting go of my arms to grab a fistful of hair, pinning my face to the ground as he towered over me.

I had no choice but to look, and it made that knot in my abdomen tighten, practically vibrating with excitement.

He thrust slower, making every move purposeful.

In the mirror, I watched the veins in his arm pulse as he gripped my hair, the muscles in his hips and thighs twitching every time he shoved himself inside. His free hand smoothed along my waist.

"What a beautiful animal, trapped between my claws." He leaned forward to my ear, jolting every time he buried his length to the hilt inside me. Now my insides, as well as my outsides, were shivering.

"Look how divine you look under me," he whispered, our reflection staring back at us, like they were watching the show.

"You would look even better with my teeth in your neck and my seed dripping down your thigh."

The words edged a whimper from me, my hands clenched in the fur of the rug.

He nipped at my ear before kissing down my neck, sucking tenderly at the skin before his fangs brushed against it. He bit down, then lapped at the wound. He bit my shoulder, then lapped at the wound again. He repeated this a few times in the places he could reach.

"Why aren't you feeding?" I breathed.

"Because I'm marking what is mine." His voice held a harmonic clicking that was almost eerie, barely holding back. "It is long overdue."

He then held me up so that we were kneeling, my back flush against his chest. I could see my full reflection in the mirror, the way he placed his hand on my womb and one on my chest to hold me against him as he thrust up into me.

I moaned and rested my head on his shoulder, looking up at him with glassy eyes. That was the last straw.

Silas kissed me roughly over my shoulder, pressing firmly inside as he finished, the fine piercing of the spines hooked into me and the euphoria blooming within. His grip on me was so tight as he kissed me, I could feel everything. Every throb of his girth, the heat of his skin, his seed dripping down my thighs as they trembled. Nothing could compare to the way he held me. I feared he would never let go.

A pathetic noise eased from my throat, and I clenched my eyes shut and waited for the pain to subside.

He buried his face in my hair, his hands softening and smoothing down the hot skin. "You're doing so well, my dearest demise," he chuckled. "It'll be over soon." He left kisses along every inch of skin he could.

We never slept that night, not even a wink, if it meant we lost sight of one another.

LIV

The Fixer

PHOEBE DECIDED IT WAS best to have a sleepover. On the ground-level lobby. On the *floor*. She might be able to throw a party, but managing a crisis was not within her skill set. They all gathered around the fireplace. Their chatter thinly masked the anxiety and horror of it all. Never had any Vipera seen this amount of disarray caused by their very own community. Though I don't think we can count corrupted as part of either species.

"Who uses Duchess the most?"

"She's *mine*." Phoebe pulled her face from her hands, Rebecca and Mary on either side of her.

"Let's be realistic," I warned, "who uses her the most?"

There was a pause. "Edith rides her to work most times."

I placed an empty glass bottle on the table. The bottle had remnants of dried blood at the bottom, Alina's blood.

"Where did you find that?" Phoebe glared.

"In one of the saddle bags. She must have forgotten to bring it in after one of her shifts," I explained, "the fact that it was Alina's was probably the only reason that thing didn't come through the window. You're lucky it was only a corrupted."

"Lucky?" Phoebe scoffed. "If it were a turned Host, I would still have a horse."

"How selfish." I sat down across from her. Most of the girls were gathering outside the kitchen, pretending not to listen to us. That was fine. They all should know. "You have a house full of Hosts. Do you know what really happens when Hosts turn, Phoebe? Have you asked? Has anyone here been turned as a Host?" I raised my voice, swiveling my head over my shoulder at the gathering crowd.

The girls were silent.

I returned my attention to Phoebe. Her brow twitched, but she did not interject.

"If you thought the corrupted were bad, you haven't seen a hungry Host after turning." I lowered my voice. "The process is painful. Your insides start to shift, and your bones grind together. The changes that should take years quake through your body in a matter of months. Many painful months. There is a reason Hosts aren't turned and would rather beg to taste hot lead from a barrel."

"We wouldn't do that to a Host."

"But you feed on them often enough to have to worry about someone else *killing* them."

"Why are you telling me this?"

"Because you have a house full of Hosts, and you should be worried. You're lucky it was your horse. Someone is turning people en masse, and I don't think they are being picky. Do you really want that fate for your girls?"

Phoebe was silent, picking at her nails.

"Where's Edith?" I glanced up, first at the three in front of me, then at the crowd. "Has anyone seen Edith? Is she home yet?"

"She hasn't returned from her shift," one of the girls from the parlor piped up timidly.

I clicked my tongue against my teeth and retreated toward the parlor, stepping past the crowd before stopping at the telephone placed neatly on a small table. I wanted to be wrong, but my gut was telling me otherwise.

I picked up the receiver and called for the hospital. My foot tapped anxiously as I waited for a reply. A receptionist piped up at the other end.

"Put Edith on the phone, it's an emergency," I said quickly, glancing over my shoulder.

The phone crackled and rustled before her voice spoke. "Hello—"

"You need to come home."

"I'm working—"

"Edith," I warned. "Your shift ended two hours ago; why are you at the hospital?"

"I am just taking your advice."

"What are you talking about?"

"You said, *don't let other people get in the way of the greatness you want to achieve.*"

"Why are you at the hospital, Edith?" I repeated.

"Living is suffering, Mr. Novikov."

"Edith, what did you do?"

"They'll wake soon; I have to go."

"Who?" I shouted into the phone.

The phone line blurred. She hung up.

"Phoebe!" I shouted. Already whipping my coat off the hanger by the front door. "We have to get to the hospital. Immediately."

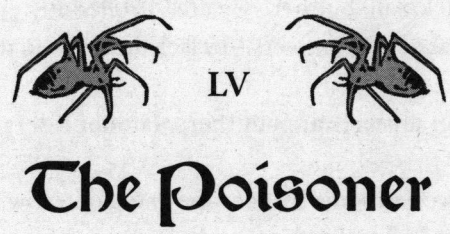

LV

The Poisoner

WE LEFT BY EARLY morning, headed back for town, attempting to make the trip in a day. The sun was beginning to set earlier, painting the snow from hues of purple and blue all the way to the warm shades of mandarin.

Much of the noise of nature was muted by the snowy insolation. You would think it made the journey feel long, isolated. Luckily, there was no time lost in decent company.

I flinched at the teeth in my wrist. "No more, you greedy thing."

Silas furrowed his brows and removed his teeth from the skin, licking over the wound. "Greed would be telling you I plan on being drunk on you every day."

"A waxing poetic," I mumbled, the other hand holding the reins.

Silas flashed a grin before lifting my hand, kissing each finger before slipping my glove back on, the warmth invading the appendages aching from the bitter air.

"You're quiet," he said, lacing his gloved hand with mine. The air froze around his words before dissipating into the air.

"Tired, is all."

"It is bad luck to start a marriage with lies," he teased, squeezing my hand playfully.

"So is blackmail, but here we are." I rolled my eyes. "I'm not feeling good about the answers—or lack thereof—to the corrupted problem."

"Whatever answers are out there, I doubt it was back at that town."

"At least we had some sort of rope to tug on. Now I don't know where to start," I admitted.

"Well, consider it a new puzzle. Start from the first piece." He shrugged.

My expression must have turned him off from jokes. His arm wrapped around my shoulder, holding me close as we approached downtown.

It was a single comfort. Warm, quiet, content.

We arrived in town by mid-morning, but it looked to be deserted.

The shops were closed, the streets were empty, and there was nothing left but the clinking of a flag against the pole in the square.

We rode through the street, the entire width to ourselves. We passed by a stack of newspapers scattered across the street. As we rode past it, there were pink stains of blood in the snow surrounding the papers.

We stopped at the apothecary, empty like every other place in town.

"What in the hell . . ." I rubbed my sore neck, Silas's bite marks from early morning starting to ache. The venom was making me a bit spacy, but I knew I wasn't imagining how off the town appeared.

I peeked through the glass door, the sign flipped to "Open" and the door unlocked. There was an inescapable itch in the back of my neck, the heat rising around my cheeks, and the gut-curdling feeling that something had gone wrong. It was more than a feeling; it was grossly apparent.

With a quick wind at my heels, I ran across the street.

"Alina!" Silas shouted after me. "Where in God's name are you going?"

I ran for the mortuary door. It wasn't just unlocked; it was shattered, the glass crunching beneath my heel as I stepped through. The hallway loomed, long and dark. Even through the ringing in my ears, the only sound was the dripping of water.

Silas grabbed my wrist, and I glared back at him. He shook his head slowly, a nervous glance toward the hallway before returning to me.

I ignored his silent plea and went anyway, listening for any sign of life lingering past the walls.

The door to the embalming room was ajar, only a slight glow of light coming from within. I reached out, my fingers grazing the wood. Before pushing, I could see inside, just the slightest crack.

The smell was horrid. I could see the hand of a long-dead corpse, a limb here or there. Ripped apart in frustration for the lack of blood. Frustration manifested into one singularity, a red smudge across the floor, a blond head cut off from my view.

I grasped the doorknob and pulled it gently shut.

The hallway got longer, my hand smoothing against the wall to remind me it was not really moving, it was all in my head. It was all in my head, and these past few months were merely dreams.

Silas wrapped his arm around my waist to pull me out. I didn't even have to move my feet. He swept me outside. The cold air burned in my lungs as I struggled to breathe. My daze was disrupted when my back hit the brick wall.

"Look at me," Silas demanded.

He was going in and out of my vision; the adrenaline was too much. He lifted my own hand, placing it on my neck.

"Breathe." His other hand steadied my head. "We have to go home."

"Edith!" I gasped. "She's at the hospital, we have to go—"

"We don't know if it's safe. If this was a horde of corrupted, the hospital is a buffet of sitting ducks, roasted and seasoned. You're in no state to go."

"I can't let another drop be spilled for my negligence!" I argued; he just held me tighter.

"Fine." He rested his forehead against mine. "Let me go with you if you insist."

I STUMBLED OFF THE wagon before it had even stopped. There were nurses splayed across the ground outside, the last sign of a desperate escape, slowly disappearing under the steadily gathering snowfall, the ground turning red like a carpet to the entrance.

I burst through the front door. Up the stairs, I hastily flung through the rooms.

Empty.

Empty.

Empty.

Bodies.

Bodies.

Bodies.

There was blood everywhere. An endless loop of similar scenes through each door, forcing myself to be subjected to scene after scene of carnage until I found one with something *living*.

Nurses' bodies were displayed in unnatural fashion across the floor, some limbs were missing, while others were unrecognizable.

There was not one white linen in the hospital room that wasn't stained.

The hallway was quiet, only the sound of the howling wind outside. The tiles of the floor were smeared, blood tracking in and out of the rooms, across walls, and staining the viewing windows of the doors.

Yells and shuffles stirred through the hallway.

"What is wrong with you?" Phoebe screamed, the inflected echo bounding down the hallway. "You ruin everything! Why couldn't you just be happy with what we all had?"

I rounded the corner and shoved the door from where the voices were coming from.

"I saved them! They are free! We are their salvation!" Edith screamed back, shakily holding a knife in her hand.

The heads of the three turned to me when my boot crushed some glass from the door.

Luka was behind Edith, unfeeling and cool in demeanor.

I stepped forward. "What did you do?"

"I-I didn't *do* anything! I helped them!" she cried, holding out the jittery knife. If her eyes strained any harder, I thought they would burst from her head. They darted skittishly, bouncing from person to person, exactly how I would imagine a cornered fox, bared fangs and all.

"Edith, calm down. Whatever you did—"

Phoebe turned to look at me, just for a moment, before Edith hooked her arm around her neck from behind, pointing the blade under her chin. "Don't get any closer!" Edith shouted.

I froze in place, my eyes only seeing rage as I saw the blade pointed at Phoebe.

My dear friend gaped at me with horror, unable to contain her panic. Nothing pulled at my gut like seeing her eyes glazed over in fear.

I held my hands up slowly. "Edith," I warned, "let her go, we can talk through this." I glanced at Luka behind her, giving him a pleading look, but he just stood there, unable to look at me.

Bastard.

"I know you can see it. It's the whole reason you decided to use us to make medicine in the first place. Everyone deserves a chance," Edith croaked.

"All right, all right. Tell me about it." I lowered my hands calmly.

"The corrupted are not monsters; they are people. They can be used for good; I know they can be good. They remember me after they turn. We could tame them, build an army of them. I've been working on this for months, for you! You told me to take initiative." Edith smiled wildly, loose curls of blond hair sticking out from her head covering, blood smudged across her cheek. "If we all worked together like we do on collection days—"

"Did these people want to be turned?"

"Yes! They were in pain!"

"You asked them?"

"N-no, but they were suffering. They asked me to make the pain stop, and I did! I did . . ." She was becoming frustrated at the back and forth, pressing the knife a little harder against Phoebe, drawing a thin dripping of blood.

"Wait! Wait, Edith, tell me more." I took a slow step forward. "How do you want me to help?"

"We could get a group together! I wouldn't need many—a few to help tame them, feed them, and show them the way things work. I already have Luka to help; I just need a few more." She turned to look at Luka, but he couldn't look at her, either; he was stoic, frozen, *useless*.

He glanced at me, and something in those dark eyes told me something was terribly wrong.

"Edith." I took another step while she wasn't looking, hoping the more I said her name, the more likely she was to wake from this manic frenzy. "We can't just take people's autonomy away, remember? Autonomy is one of our tenets."

"So is utilitarianism. What are we if we don't have manpower? What if someone else gets the same idea, and we lose more than we did the last time? If you aren't willing to take risks, maybe you shouldn't be the head of our Nest."

"Maybe I shouldn't." Another step. "Who would you suggest?"

Her expression went from feral to something softer, something youthful and full of hope. "Myself and Luka." She beamed, turning her head to look at him over her shoulder.

That is when I chose to move. I slapped Edith's hand away from Phoebe's neck and shoved her roughly out of the way.

"Alina!" Silas shouted from behind me along with the slap of the door as he entered, but it was all clouded to me. Too quick.

Edith and I were nose to nose, my hands on either of her shoulders.

Edith's wicked stare met mine, flashing some deep rage within her that I could not place before her eyes immediately widened. I even caught a tremble in her lip.

Why is she looking at me like that?

All I could do was stare into her eyes. I swallowed and tilted my head at her, unable to comprehend the scene before me.

My blurring vision trailed down until I stared at the knife pointed at me, but I couldn't locate a blade, just a hilt and a white knuckled hand holding it there. My vision filled with red—no, the red was on my clothing. I was bleeding. My brain connected where the blade was, and I grimaced at Luka, his eyes wide when he realized.

Everything was moving so slowly. Luka's eyes darted behind me toward Silas, fear and trepidation twisting his features before he looked at Edith again. His eyes held something tender in that last expression.

His hand reached out and caressed her chin, turning her head toward him. The look in his eyes was nothing I could ever expect from a monster like him. Then his other hand rested at the back of her head.

Edith smiled so brightly that she may have been mistaken for some lovesick child, a complete shift of her energy when he touched her. Such hope and joy in that last breath.

He pulled back, snapping her neck where she stood.

The old scar opened across her neck, black as tar. A martyr twice over.

Now more than ever, I understood what that look was before. That tenderness he held when he looked at her, I realized, was *mercy*. He wanted to be the one to do it. One last kindness.

"Alina!"

Silas called my name again.

It was unusual when it hit me. I was certain that at a time like this, I would be alone. A near-zero chance, I was sure. A thing like me must be all right with loneliness. It was expected. But today, I was not alone after all. My fate sealed by one of my own, surrounded by the only ones who knew me, truly knew me. It must be intentional, a cosmic joke.

My knees hit the floor with a muffled thud, the impact quaking through my body, movements like cold molasses.

Behind my eyes was a red-hot moon. Like the glow of an ember, the red illuminated the backs of my eyelids, the outside light desperately wanting to burn through. The red vessels pulsed steadily until they slowed, and the blood ran black.

READ ON FOR AN EXCERPT OF

The Cannibal

I

THE ONLY WAY TO battle the redolence of a dead body is with the merciless spice of fresh-cut lilies in your lungs, burning away any remaining twilight visions.

First the breaths were shallow, then deeper, crackling as they filled with air, then deflating in defeat.

Light veiled over the dark, a glow of the outside. The sound of a gentle wind came next; I could breathe as it did, mimicking life until my body believed it, then soon my mind came to it.

A mobile horn bellowed so sharp it made my stagnant head dizzy.

Too loud.

When my eyes opened, it was a softer light than expected. A blur of cream, some flashes bouncing from the window glass, refractions scattering as quick as they came, like fleeing sprites. Everything was beige or white, the lighting made it hard to tell.

Above me, a canopy, then posts of a bed. Fabric of the frame curtains thick, buttery, and double-faced. The light caught on some of the threads, a silky sheen the color of buttercream.

The walls were blank, unused. No dresser, no other furnishings, not even a side table. Just a chair placed to my left.

No.

The moment I shot upright was the second I regretted it. Pain in my abdomen, my head too. Some great claw had grasped me and wouldn't unlatch its talons. A wave of nausea made me turn my head in case I had to expel, not that I felt I had anything to do so with.

As my hand propped me on my side, something crisp crunched beneath it.

A browned rose under my palm. Not just there, everywhere. The bed was almost completely covered in bundles of rosemary, forget-me-nots, roses, helichrysum, and red carnations—a grand portrait of a garden in all stages of its cycle. The freshest addition: white lilies. All of which surrounded a silhouette of where I lay.

If my only company was decaying, what did that make me?

There were better questions, but the perpetual fog had yet to lift from my mind. The room was disorienting.

It took a couple of swallows to properly salivate, my lungs rattling with every gulp of breath, struggling to expand like a new wine skin.

The bunches of flora rustled to the ground as I moved my legs off the bed, slower this time so as not to invite another fit of my apparent migraine.

The window, so tall it nearly touched the ceiling, was open, and the drapes just as lush and long. The light hazed as the thin fabric of the drapes beckoned, dancing between the inviting breezes.

My toes touched the floor, but they were just coming out of their numbness. Only a slight coolness on the skin.

I pushed myself up, the sheer night dress hanging off my shoulder, brushing against my legs as I approached the window.

I collapsed in front of it, taking hold of the windowsill as my knees knocked against the parquet hardwood.

The breeze hit my face, forcing air into my lungs, which stopped my breathing as I tried to register. I brushed the hair from my face, but it stuck to my skin in tendrils. The humidity made the breeze feel a bit cooler.

I was staring at more windows, another building. The road below was teeming with people, carriages, mobiles. The sooty smell of smoke and gasoline stinging more than the lilies did.

Am I back in London?

I looked to my left.

No, not London.

At the end of the street, a vast green space. Trees and grass, a pond, people walking among little sheep grazing; you could barely tell them apart from so far away. Then, on the other side, more buildings. My window was nearly on the corner of the street.

This is Manhattan.

I sat down on my knees, away from the edge of the window to take a proper look at the room behind me.

The ceilings were tall like a palace's, expert molding along the top and bottom of the walls. It almost didn't need decor for it to look luxurious.

One foot, then the other, using my grip on the wainscoting of the wall to lift myself up. My knees cracked and whined with every step like unoiled hinges.

I was able to swallow now, battling the dryness that consumed my mouth. If I opened my mouth any wider, my lips might split and bleed.

I coughed finally, my body catching up with its irritated state.

The thirst began to register along with the aches that introduced themselves as I found them. A sterile smell on my skin, not unlike the patients back at the hospital because of the rag washing.

Before me were double French doors with ornate brass handles. Perfectly intact, clean, polished. *If I grab them, will they open? Am I prepared if they are locked? If I am trapped once more?* I was almost unwilling to find out, but there was nothing else to do but try.

My fingers wrapped around the handles, adjusting my grip. The numbness now worn off, I could feel everything. The doors, the temperature, the pain in my abdomen, my head, the deep-rooted ache that burrowed everywhere it could.

The doors opened with ease, not even a creak.

Scratchy, arid arrangements were swept out of the way on the other side of the doors, little cracked leaves trailing in their path. It settled on me, then.

The flowers covering the bed, outside of the doors. These were funeral flowers, and when the flowers were fresh, there would have been a postmortem photograph taken before they were allowed to wither.

Blooms well past their prime crumbled between my toes and the stone transition of the floor.

The hallway was empty, quiet.

Rosalia marble stretched the length of the hallway, many tall windows not unlike the one in the room creating bay overwatch areas, decorated with small tables within the nooks to hold fresh manicured arrangements. Along the wall were small displays and antique decor.

There was no reason for my hesitance other than my disorientation. Nothing seemed amiss. I was still in New York, just not where I last remembered. Yet, there was very little trust that I was in good hands.

I stared down at my hands. Pale, but I was no specter. I was as real as the crumbled foliage piled in the bed.

I touched a potted fern along the wall. It was lush and green, waxy to the touch. The light was filtered now, orange. It was after-noon, not morning. Which meant it would likely be dark soon.

Move, I urged myself.

Voices echoed from somewhere, vibrating in my ears and tick-ling my jaw in the process.

I could only limp down the hall, I soon found. *What happens if I'm seen? Will they throw me back in the room?* I wasn't willing to find out.

On the wall, a mounted display of pristine sixteenth-century rifles with bayonets under a painting of hunting dogs on a fox chase. I pulled one from the hooks; the gun was heavier than expected, but that could easily be my fatigue.

A curdling of my stomach pinched me along with a wave of lightheadedness. My vision blared with vivid colors in between the pulses of pain in my skull.

I tucked myself behind a curtain beside a bay window.

The voices were closer, laughing, merry chatter.

Below me on the outside, people walked along the pavement. If I shouted, would they hear? Would they see?

A cold sweat made the solid piece of wood and brass between my fingers hard to grip, the weight not as manageable, but there weren't many other options. I couldn't steady my heart, I felt each beat make me tremble, there was no satiating it. There was no point counting the beats; they were all too fast. They were loud, so incredibly furious in my ear.

Two women passed, a blonde and a brunette I could see only the backsides of as their voices chimed, their words jumbled as if my brain couldn't work fast enough to decipher them. Dressed in fine silks, daywear ready to be paraded.

The scent of something in my nose burned again, different this time. It was like a rich perfume oil, except I couldn't place any notes.

When the voices dampened, I moved. The farther I ventured down to the end of the hallway, the more voices I heard. A small crowd, I guessed. Mumbling, chattering, some laughter.

I leaned against the wall, clutching the gun to my chest.

There was no doubt now that I was in a Nest. There may be too many to take on myself. There was no gunpowder in the rifle. No, it was too clean. For display only. But the bayonet was sharp and solid and would have to do.

My toes curled against the marble before stretching again.

Don't fail me now, throw me out the window if you have to, I thought as if my own legs would respond back.

On the other side of the wall, a melodic voice. It tickled my ears, my mind swam, searching for the familiarity. It was just on the tip of my tongue, a hazy image in my mind as I searched.

"No!" A shout.

Phoebe.

As promised, my legs carried me in what could have been my last twenty seconds of being brave, of being strong. A shot of adrenaline so fierce I forgot that my stomach was ready to shrivel and expel. Enough to where the colors around me burst into vividness, enough to make my eyes tingle. I felt they were on fire. If it weren't for the adrenaline, I'd be sick.

The rifle pressed into my shoulder, pointed straight with my last thread of strength.

A grand, red room. The chandelier so dazzling, I had to squint. A giant parlor palm in an ornate vase, so large, in fact, there was bench seating around it. The mirrored walls made the room seem larger; it frankly didn't need it. A parlor room gilded like a palace.

Screams cracked in my ear, a mass of movement around the room as people stood. They clutched one another, staring.

They were staring at me, abject horror.

"Alina . . ."

I swung, the rifle pointing to the voice. The crowd ducked the barrel like they were some sort of tidal wave.

At the end of the bayonet, wide green eyes.

She was like I remembered her, like I was watching a memory of her before, a return of what was once familiar. She was swathed in a lustrous pink day dress that matched her cheeks. Her hair was so vibrant, red and curled in a perfect silhouette. Except her face was different, taut with an unpleasant kind of surprise, a deep sadness ready to unwind in front of me.

My eyes hurt, the sickness was beginning to tingle at the back of my throat, the pulsing of my temples almost too much to bear. It was hard to swallow, or perhaps the words were just getting stuck.

So many words could have come. An apology was my first impulse. The only thing that came was a recoiled weep.

With one shaky step forward, I dropped the gun and my legs gave out.

Phoebe hooked her arms under mine and held me up. Her silk-covered fingers grasped at my nightgown, my hair, whatever she could to hold me up.

I couldn't control it any longer. The pain came all at once and released all the same, in a cry into her bluebell-scented hair.

In the mirrored wall, uncertain shuffling and hysterical faces shifted between the bleary view. When I looked at us, though— Phoebe and I—I saw her back; it was her. I saw my own fingers grasping the fabric as I embraced her. What looked back at me, though, was not me. There was a horrifying creature, pale with black-filled eyes.

My reflection was no longer recognizable.

A creature had replaced me.

About the Author

I.V. OPHELIA is the author of the *Poisoner* series. Born in small-town New England, she now haunts the streets of New York City, writing the most unhinged tales she can conjure. When not crafting gothic romance, she works as a full-time artist, hoards nineteenth-century gowns and antique furniture, dotes on her menagerie of pets, and plots her next literary transgression. Learn more at ivophelia.com.